Advance Praise for *Wedding of the Season*

"Elin Hilderbrand meets Edith Wharton meets *Brideshead Revisited* in this delightfully juicy tale of a Newport family's fading fortunes on the eve of a society wedding. I loved every minute."

—**Meg Mitchell Moore,** *USA TODAY* bestselling author of *Vacationland*

"Like a modern-day Jane Austen, Edmondson examines love and family against the particular mores of our time, reflecting our desires, fears, and foibles back at us with a fictional family that lingers long after the last page."

—**Jamie Brenner, bestselling author of** *The Forever Summer*

"Set amongst the sumptuous Gilded Age mansions of Newport, Rhode Island, *Wedding of the Season* explores themes of love and money with brilliance and heart. I loved meeting Cassie and her wild family."

—**Amanda Eyre Ward,** *New York Times* bestselling author of *The Jetsetters*

"*Wedding of the Season* brings Newport society alive in one summer leading up to a much-anticipated wedding. Filled with sharp, witty dialogue and a gorgeous sense of place, this novel is as delightful as a perfect summer day."

—**Jillian Cantor,** *USA TODAY* bestselling author of *Beautiful Little Fools*

"Atmospheric and clever, with captivating, evocative characters, *Wedding of the Season* is perennial—like the best sort of party where the memory echoes long after the final toast. A must read for every book club!"

—**Joy Callaway, international bestselling author of** *The Grand Design*

"RSVP Yes to *Wedding of the Season*! With wit and charm, this delightful novel plunges the reader into a world of high society, faded glory, and the weight of legacy to uncover what really makes a family."

—**Gina Sorell, author of the** *New York Times Book Review* **Editor's Choice** *The Wise Women*

Also by Lauren Edmondson

Ladies of the House

WEDDING
of the
SEASON

A NOVEL

LAUREN EDMONDSON

GRAYDON
HOUSE

GRAYDON
HOUSE®

ISBN-13: 978-1-525-89999-7

Wedding of the Season

Illustration of house by Letterfest.com

Graydon House
22 Adelaide St. West, 41st Floor
Toronto, Ontario M5H 4E3, Canada
www.GraydonHouseBooks.com
www.BookClubbish.com

Printed in U.S.A.

To Christopher, Bellamy, and Shepard

WEDDING

of the

SEASON

Summer afternoon—summer afternoon; to me those have always been the two most beautiful words in the English language.

—Henry James

This level reach of blue is not my sea;
Here are sweet waters, pretty in the sun,
Whose quiet ripples meet obediently
A marked and measured line, one after one.
This is no sea of mine that humbly laves
Untroubled sands, spread glittering and warm.
I have a need of wilder, crueler waves;
They sicken of the calm, who knew the storm.

—Dorothy Parker

May

1

A single weekend, I assured myself as I turned onto the Avenue and slowed beneath the canopy of mature trees—oaks, willows, maples. Pink flowers and vines cascaded from black streetlamps, styled to look old-fashioned, and ruler-straight hedges teased glimpses of the staggering, lavish mansions beyond. Old. Exclusive. Private. There was the hulking Romanesque revival, its tan sandstone tower making it more castle than house. To its east, the exaggerated Italianate villa and its second-story loggias that allowed residents to look down their noses from every direction. And, too soon, the wrought-iron gate of The Land.

Driving from this direction, it always felt as though my world was narrowing.

I unbuckled my seat belt, leaning halfway out my window to punch in the code: 1899, the year construction finished. The gate creaked open and I inched my greige rental sedan through to the pea-graveled allée that over the centuries had welcomed everything from livery and horses to Model Ts to Aston Martins. Maybe I should've had a heavier foot on the gas but despite the circumstances—I was running late—two miles per hour seemed plenty.

Straight ahead, in all its conspicuous excess, loomed my destination, tall above the rustling tulip trees. The Gilded Age titans and their heiress wives referred to it as a *cottage*. On their website, the Historical Society describes it as *a beaux-arts masterpiece*. Some locals might still call it *the Coventry mansion*. For me, it had been home.

For so many years, I believed we, my siblings and I, were The Land's heartbeat. What oak tree on the property hadn't we climbed? Which one of the Cottage's thirty rooms hadn't been explored, turned into pirate ships or volcanoes, floors bubbling with lava? Which of the property's outbuildings hadn't been ruthlessly annexed as a clubhouse, no adults allowed? But I hadn't been back in almost a decade, and it had managed to go on without me.

I bent forward to look through the windshield as the quartet of massive Corinthian columns appeared, the stucco garlands hovering above each window, some rectangular, some square, most bracketed by dramatic black shutters. Iron Juliet balconies edged the windows of the imposing east and west wings, which jutted out symmetrically on either side of the main hall. The roof was a varied landscape of peaked gables, flat cornices, brick chimneys, and—on the conservatory off the east wing—standing-seam metal the color of a polished copper pot. The first place I got felt up was in that conservatory.

Garrett with the great hair. Tall. Sweet. Decent kisser. And no longer in my life because—well, because of everything.

At the end of the allée, delivery vans and catering trucks packed the roundabout, the flag staked in the grassy center snapping in the breeze of the sound. Staff in black uniforms hurried into and out of the Cottage—we'd adopted the Gilded Age nickname—with trays of glassware, round tables, flower arrangements bigger than bar stools. I tapped my brakes for a guy with a stack of boxes, then again for a young woman hauling a crate of liquor bottles. All this commotion for my sister's engagement to her childhood sweetheart. Make no mistake, Maggie and Jack deserved to be celebrated. I just wished I didn't have to face half of Newport in doing it.

I heard a mechanical, grinding hum, followed by the twin clanks of the gate slamming behind me.

Maybe it was the five hours on a fabric seat, or being back on the island, that had fatigue suddenly tapping at the backs of my eyeballs and raking its fingers down my neck. I came to a full stop at the spot where the driveway branched—one direction looping toward the Cottage, the other toward the rear dependencies. I rolled down the windows, took a deep breath, and closed my eyes.

When I opened them again, a goat was staring at me, its fur a flat gray, its horns wrapped in what appeared to be white packing foam. The animal ambled past my front bumper, sniffing at the license plate, nosing around the lights, then simply wandered off, nibbling at weeds between the gravel as it went.

Sending upward some half-muttered prayers that the winds would be favorable, that the memories of Newporters would be short, I released my foot from the brake and coasted down the drive.

2

The mammoth bronze front doors to the Cottage were open, gas lamps on either side flickering in welcome. Valets in red jackets assisted guests out of their cars. Servers arranged themselves on the stairs, silver trays of champagne in hand. However entitled, I'd loved this place in my youth, thinking The Land majestic and mysterious and mine. But technically, nothing on this property had been *ours* for going on fifteen years.

I made for the service drive, lined with delicate purple flowers, and snuck in through the basement. The Cottage had no shortage of trap doors, secret passages, hidden call boxes, discreet pulley systems for dumbwaiters and—what would come in handy for me today—back staircases. Inside was a frenzy. The massive coal-fired stove Maggie and I had used to play restaurant was a staging area for chafing dishes, and the original butcher-block island, ten yards long, was piled with aprons and towels and enough punch bowls for a year of cotillions. A group of caterers charged down the tiled service staircase, a whirlwind of endless demands and barked instructions. The Cottage was built, above all else, to impress. To dazzle. This meant hiding the work that enabled its survival, keeping the madness and the sweat tucked away.

I let the caterers by, then skipped up two flights, where a swinging door dumped me out in the part of the house reserved for the lords and ladies. "That credenza can't be moved!" I flinched at the commanding voice of The Land's grande dame, and my sister's future mother-in-law, Susie Utterback, echoing from below. "It's heavier than a damn whale, just leave it be!"

As kids, my siblings and grandmother had put soap and water onto these parquet floors and turned this hallway into a barefoot ice-skating rink. Now it was so plushily carpeted I couldn't hear my own quick footsteps.

Keep it moving.

I recited these words—this prayer—in my head past my old bedroom. Though I hadn't seen inside since we'd moved, I knew Susie had torn out the small reach-in closet of drawers for pressed undergarments, as well as the high-tank pull-chain toilet and the cloudy onyx sink that I'd stained pink with an ill-conceived adventure with hair dye.

In Susie's orange-sherbet sitting room, Maggie could not turn her head—a young woman with a holster of makeup was applying her lip liner—but still she beckoned for me. "Cassie!" She was perched on a tall director's chair, wrapped in a plush bathrobe, bare feet, long clips in her hair. Around her, a team of three swirled—the makeup artist, the makeup artist's assistant, the hair person with the spray and the iron. "You made it!"

I toed off my sneakers by the door; God help me if I tracked dirt into Susie's boudoir. "Hello, my Buggie Bug Bug," I said, squeezing between the group to give her a tight, wiggly hug.

I wasn't thrilled to be back in Newport, but I was very glad to see her. My sister: those defined calves! The graceful, swan neck! That glowing skin, touched now by the flattering bronze of early summer! I'd hate her if I didn't love her so much.

"I missed you," she murmured into my ear. She smelled of oranges and summertime.

"I missed you, too." I pulled back and took her in. "Oh, my God, you haven't been engaged three months and already you look like a bride." I pointed at her, unable to contain my excitement: "The *bride*, you guys!"

"We know," laughed the makeup artist, who'd introduced herself as Jules. "You can see the ring from space." Not a terrible exaggeration; I didn't know much about diamonds, but even I could tell Jack didn't skimp. It sat beautifully on Maggie's finger, square cut but soft edges, the size, I estimated conservatively, of a manhole cover.

"You want your hair and makeup done?" Maggie asked. "Might as well." Jules stepped in front of Maggie and directed her to gaze up to prepare for the Applying of the Mascara. "What are you wearing?"

I spared a glance at my outfit—the oversize camo jacket, the black jeans, the beaten-up canvas sneakers. "Not this, I promise. I have some other pants," I said, hunching over my bag and riffling around for my outfit. Long ago I'd discarded all my Lilly Pulitzer. I no longer owned anything with an embroidered anchor or trimmed in ribbon. And I'd never, not once, slipped my feet into Hermès flats or clutched a Chanel quilted purse. I much preferred to be behind the camera's flash, not seeking it out. "And a—" my hands fluttered around my stomach "—a simple shirt thing with, like, a belt."

Maggie narrowed her eyes. "Pants?"

The room grew silent. The assistant looked up from the dresser, where she had been sorting lipsticks in a giant plastic bin. The hairdresser, hands full with brushes, blinked slowly. Jules's head turned from my sister to me, peering, curious, mascara wand frozen in the air.

"Uh-oh." I stood, gestured between the four of them. "Now, see, the way you're looking at me has me alarmed."

"Cassie," Maggie sighed. "There's a theme. Didn't you read the invitation?"

"A theme?" I felt a plummeting in my chest. Already Susie's parties were like running a marathon barefoot on Legos. Now I had to deal with costumes? "Please tell me the theme is 'everybody drink wine and be pleasant.'"

"Roaring twenties," said Jules, somber.

"You have to *read* things, Cass." Maggie pursed her lips. "Texts, invites… We were discussing this over email, like, last week."

"We are expected to read *everything* that comes into our inboxes now?" I protested. "Productivity culture has gone too far!"

"Oh, so when your editor emails you, you just let it go to junk?"

She had me there. Never keeping up with the family email chain, only checking it periodically, like a credit card bill, was probably the worst of my vices, along with buying too many pairs of expensive socks and camera straps. I considered my options. Not that there were many of them. I had no time for another errand. Borrowing clothes wouldn't work; I was taller than my mother and broader than Maggie. But what could I do? The Veuve was ordered. The linens laid out. "It's okay," I told my sister. "I'll wear a trash bag and walk around with my mouth open and people can just toss their shrimp tails and toothpicks at me."

Maggie rolled her eyes. "God, Cassie, you're too much."

Jules shifted, so I was able to grab my sister's hand, playfully swing it back and forth. "Oh, don't be mad at me, Buggie. Look! I even got you a little present." I placed on her lap an unwrapped box.

Maggie looked between me and the gift, until I persuaded her to *just open it already*. Earlier, I'd braved the gridlock on Lower Thames to pop into the little shop that had been there forever—you know, the one where you could buy whatever you wanted, provided it was a silver picture frame, a lobster Christmas ornament, or sign that said It's Wine O'clock Somewhere—and gotten a framed a photo I'd fished out from an old album in my New York apartment.

My sister smiled when she saw the photo. A grinning Gerber-baby-faced Maggie, probably aged two and a half, holding a one-year-old me, cheeks covered in something, jam or raspberries, in one of those old-fashioned playpens with the wooden bars. Maggie was cheesing, but I was wailing, tiny, dimpled hands clinging to the top rim, midstruggle to escape what I surely considered infant jail. Our mother crouched in the foreground, clutching the ends of her short bob, eyes crossed, exaggerating a look of *my God, these kids!*

"I love this," Maggie said, softening. "It captures us so perfectly."

I was glad to have done this right, at least.

Jules returned with a brush that seemed like it could dust a ceiling fan, and a palette of pink shimmer. Maggie handed me the frame. "Put it over there for now." She pointed to the Chippendale secretary desk with the ornate brass drawer pulls and tasseled keys.

The polished top of the desk was already filled with photographs of Susie and various people of renown. Her and Iris Apfel, Jay Leno, the late, great André Leon Talley, and—oh, I would need the story behind this one—Kris Jenner. Susie, to her credit, did not do anyone the disservice of hiding her social ambitions. I found room for us Coventry-Gilfords near the edge. "Maybe you should leave this for Susie. I'm sure she'd enjoy having a picture of Hope in her bedroom," I said dryly.

"How many years have your and Jack's mother been feuding?" asked Jules, applying a final layer of shimmer onto Maggie's cheekbones.

"It's basically a pastime."

Fifteen years ago, when our mother, Hope Coventry-Gilford, learned that our father had made a handshake deal to sell the estate that had been with her family for over a century, she'd predictably exploded. Despite The Land's impossible upkeep, she'd never expected it to be lost. She'd called Susie Utterback and relayed the story of the pending sale tragically, playing up my grandmother's recent death, my brother's diagnosis, and the Coventrys' history on The Land. Though Susie was not about to renege on the deal, she offered to rent us the property's carriage house, which my granny had converted into an apartment and artist's studio in the '70s, for five thousand bucks a year.

I'm pretty sure Susie Utterback has regretted that decision ever since.

Jules withdrew, and the hairdresser, who told me to call her Miss Fawn, took over, standing behind Maggie's chair and attending with quick fingers to all those clips. "Wasn't there also a thing with an old tree on the property?" asked Miss Fawn. "I remember my parents talking about it years ago."

"Hope fastened herself to a bulldozer, or something," said Maggie. "Right, Cass?" Though Maggie fit into Newport like Cinderella's foot in the glass slipper, even she could not deny that our family, Hope its de facto head, was—as Susie might say with delicacy—*different*.

"It was just a few saplings Susie wanted to take out." I shook my head in amusement at the memory. "But Hope continually scared off the gardening crew with a shovel. Christ, I'd forgotten about that. And to think, you're now going to be related to *both* of them."

"Are you a kind of offering, Maggie?" Miss Fawn said as she put the finishing touches on my sister's finger waves with the curling iron.

"Like in the olden days, when they would make the daughter marry into a family so they could join property, or whatever," Jules chimed in, passing her brushes to her assistant for sorting and cleaning.

Maggie and I both found the idea of such a long con hilarious. "That's exactly what you are, Buggie!" I declared. "You and Jack—a strategic alliance."

"Well, maybe now there will be peace," said Maggie. With permission from Miss Fawn—after she'd been sprayed just so—she rose from the director's chair, her hair set, and appraised herself in the floor-length mirror leaning against the wall. She turned right, left, then right again. Hairline, neck, décolletage—it was all rigorously inspected. She flicked something invisible off her cheek. One wayward hair was tucked into place behind her ear. Finally, satisfied, she faced me with a wide smile. "Maybe now everyone will just get along."

"You know what?" I decided to let myself be cheered by present company. "I should get my makeup done, if Jules wouldn't mind." No, Jules assured me, she didn't mind at all. I took Maggie's former seat on the director's chair. "At least my mug will be decent now, and distract people from the fact that my outfit is wrong."

"You'll look amazing in whatever you wear," Maggie said in a way that suggested she wanted to convince me as well as herself. "And you're the famous photographer. People expect you to be *avant garde*."

"Give me some small-talk prep," I said as Jules slathered

primer on my cheeks. "What are Susie's guests chatting about these days? Farrow and Ball paint? Boat shoes?"

"Dolly Parton is playing the Folk Festival this year," said Miss Fawn. "People are losing their minds."

"Big debate in town council about short-term rentals," added Jules.

"An oil guy wants to buy the old Henry place on Ocean Avenue," said Maggie.

"I can imagine that's going over Newport like a cash bar," I said, laughing. "But it actually doesn't matter. No one is going to talk to me, anyway."

3

My outfit was decidedly *not* flapper-esque—black wide-leg pants and a cream tank that clung to my stomach. I'd brought my camera, which was hanging from its strap on my shoulder. Perhaps people wouldn't recognize me, or would think I was the staff. Perhaps I could slip by largely unnoticed.

"Newport's prodigal daughter!" Archer called immediately, striding up the drive. "She's single! She's sexy! She's promised to transfer some of her frequent-flier miles to me, and still hasn't done it!" My brother's hug, when he arrived, lifted me off my feet.

"I will, I will," I told him. Once he set me down, I gave him a once-over. He looked well, I was grateful to see, still with his skinny legs and torso like a minifridge, still holding himself with the type of confidence reserved for favorite children. He was shaggy-haired, baby-faced, and under his blue sport jacket, he was wearing a T-shirt of *Chicago* starring—who else?—Lisa Rinna as Roxie Hart.

"What are those, Archer? Board shorts?" asked Maggie, frowning at his legs.

"I know Susie doesn't like synthetic fabrics lurking around her property, but this isn't a *ball*. Hey—Cass—why can't we ever be evicted?" He flipped up the edges of his swim trunks. "Because I be *squattin'*!" We moved aside in the drive, letting an SUV pull forward and dump out a car of chattering Daisy Buchanans. Maggie waved to them, elegant flicks of the wrist, the aristocratic practices of a ballerina infused in every gesture.

"I think you look dapper," I said to my brother as he distributed air kisses to the group. "As you probably guessed, I didn't get the memo about the costume."

"You're skipping emails again," he observed, linking one arm with mine. In a flash, Maggie was on my other side, and they began encouraging me toward the Cottage's doors with enough force that I didn't have time to even grab a glass of proffered champagne.

As I hunched forward and powered through into the two-storied central hall, I noted new details, things Susie had replaced or repaired. Yet my eyes stubbornly sought out what remained from the time we'd lived here. The floor was still marble, black-and-white checkered, the walls dappled limestone. The plaster bust of Teddy Roosevelt—a onetime guest of The Land and, overall, representative of the other problematic individuals who slept here—still kept lookout from its fluted marble base in the alcove under the grand, curving stone staircase. On one side of us, wide arched doorways still led to the mirrored dining room. On the other, one could glimpse the library with its carved oak bookcases and massive fireplace.

"Don't tell Susie," Archer whispered to me, tracking my gaze, "but I snuck in some books she'd definitely call *socialist propaganda*." This was followed by a chuckle and Cheshire cat grin. "I just want her to be giving a tour, showing off, and see Bernie Sanders staring at her from a spine."

I glanced at my brother, fastidiously avoiding everyone we passed. "When do you even do this? In the dark of night?"

"I'm always in and out of the Cottage, especially when I need a Hope and J.P. detox," he explained. "Besides, Susie has better snacks."

In the back of the house was the expansive living room, once the ballroom, with ceiling fresco, angels and cherubs. More waiters with trays of canapés held open sets of French doors to the veranda. As we got closer to the green-and-white-striped canopy that extended from the back of the Cottage, the unmistakable sounds of a Newport party reached us. The clinking glass, the twinkling music, the inflated laughter.

One of Susie's guests, then another, noticed our approach in a little cascade. All well-heeled, in Jazz Age regalia. Some Al Capones. Many Gatsbys. There were fur stoles. Expensive wigs. There was someone wearing a very short, beaded dress and a long train made entirely of feathers. A few raised their glasses, others tossed me wan smiles. A few ignored me completely.

But guests fell around Maggie in a happy, sloppy embrace, exclaiming, marveling, congratulating. She clutched my hand for as long as she was able before, with one final look and entreaty to *have fun, Cassie, okay?*, she was pried away from my side.

"There she is!" My mother's voice landed with a thud. Hope Coventry-Gilford, all hundred pounds of her, had gone full Party City: elbow-length gloves, beads, sequins, a feather in her hair—and stoplight red, no less. "Cassie, why do you look so tired? And where is your costume?"

Our Lady of Everlasting Deodorant, I prayed, *please watch over me.*

"I was in Moldova thirty-six hours ago," I said as she gave me a dry kiss on the cheek. "And I'm waiting for some of these women in feathers to shed. Then I'll put something in my hair."

My father flung open his arms. "Look who the cat dragged in!" This was a familiar greeting—half surprised pleasure, half *where have you been, young lady?* J.P.'s interpretation of the theme included a newsboy cap and suspenders, both of which I suspected were from his own closet.

"You were supposed to get here Wednesday!" Hope scolded. "I had a whole thing planned! Archer and I were going to throw ticker tape from the top windows of the house as you pulled up. Weren't we, Archer?"

I turned to my brother. "Ticker tape? That would've been an ordeal."

"I told HCG that you'd hate it. Complain about it blinding the sea turtles, or whatever. But we know better than to plan around you." There was a quick humorous glance between everyone who wasn't named Cass; it made me feel like an outsider. But I'd long ago come to peace with the sacrifices of my profession and promised myself never to apologize for it, for what was required of me. I would not be an *I'm the worst* woman, even though, kind of, I was.

Kent, Susie's longtime house manager and The Land's chief of staff, appeared with four sunset-colored drinks on a silver tray. "Who needs a spritz?" he asked, peering over his glasses. His expression was perpetually professional, his white polo starched, always, to paperlike crispness.

"Does a goose go barefoot?" said J.P., helping himself.

"Is the Pope Catholic?" Archer took the one that was the fullest.

"Does a bear shit in the woods?" I asked, which made Hope snort into her drink.

Kent handed Hope a napkin. "Welcome home, Cass," he said, tucking the tray under his arm. "You've been missed."

Home, he'd said. The Land wasn't my home. Not anymore.
Home was in New York City, on Avenue A, in the apartment
I barely used more than a week at a time. I had grand plans
for it, like maybe I'd do some decorating, hang some of my
pictures, dig out from storage the sculpture Granny Fi had bequeathed to me, get a throw pillow. Eliminate the flophouse
vibe. Maybe soon I'd invest in a real bedframe. Eventually,
I'd use the stove. But what point was there in correcting him?
I'd just hurt my parents' feelings. So I said, "Thank you,"
and began to inquire about Kent's family, but he winked and
slipped back into the crowd.

The orange on my glass's rim glistened, and I nibbled, sa-
voring the bubbles and the bitter. Say what you will about
Susie, but she delivers impeccable drinks. Hope treated herself
to a few deep gulps. We were in for a performance tonight, if
she kept up that pace. I wondered what worn tale she might
fall back on: the story about sharing a cigarette with Diana
Vreeland in a ladies' room at the Met? The one about sneaking into the von Bülow's last Victorian croquet party before
the hostess was killed—supposedly—by her enigmatic husband? Or would she instead bless the crowd with the recent
results of my father's mole removal? Could be all of the above!

Hope, though, lowered her glass and stuck out her tongue.
"Cass, go and grab me a tequila?"

"I don't think the caterers brought shot glasses, dear," J.P.
said.

"Oh, all right," said Hope, "put it in a wineglass."

"It's time to mingle," Archer announced, spotting a familiar young man across the party. "I need to bring myself to the
people." As I watched his retreating back, I realized that the
crowd around our small group had thinned. People peeled
away, aiming for the outside bar set up between the veranda's columns, the antique furniture arranged in conversation

sets on the great lawn, or wandering across the mosaic-tiled floor to literally any other place that didn't have Hope and J. P. Gilford.

Or me.

Instinctively, I touched the wound at the back of my head, healing but still tender, hidden by my hair. Only last week I'd been running on adrenaline and no sleep, navigating a dense crowd of people red-faced and chanting, trying to evade the overeager bodyguards of a particular strongman who—let's just say—didn't treat my Nikon with the respect and care it deserved when they got hold of me. But I couldn't help feel that the muscle in Moldova was more hospitable than folks in this town.

In the distance, a low privet hedge, trimmed now with military precision, was the only impediment to the sea, which today had a soft chop crumpling the surface, turning it into a panoramic expanse of Santorini-blue linen. The sailboats and motor craft were out enjoying the start of their weekend, headed north toward the bay or south to the sound. The early white blooms of the hydrangeas encircling the perimeter of the lawn nodded and quivered in the breeze. If you listened closely, you could hear the waves breaking against the crags and rocks below the Cliff Walk, rumbling their retreat over the stones.

"For a minute earlier this week, they were calling for storms," Hope was saying. "I just would've *loved* to say I told you so to Susie. Who holds an outdoor gathering in Rhode Island in May without a tent?" Only Hope Coventry-Gilford could cast beautiful weather as something to suffer through.

"Would you like me to attain a hose?" I asked. "Or a watering can?" An oyster shucker with three silver buckets clipped to her belt arrived beside us, helped us choose between Sweet

Jesuses and East Beach Blondes. "I can hide on the third floor and sprinkle you."

"I'm just saying!" Hope snatched two of each kind. "Unpredictable rain ruined Celerie van Vick's feline alopecia awareness fundraiser in '96. But did Susie listen to me? As always, no."

I changed the subject between slurps of oyster, all mineral sea and sweet vinegar. "How late do you think this party will go?"

"Don't think *we'll* be burning the midnight oil," J.P. said, declining the shucker's offerings. He wasn't a fan of shellfish, inconvenient for a resident of the City by the Sea. "It's mostly filled with Susie's friends."

"They were my friends before Susie even moved here," Hope huffed. "I introduced her to most of them! Isn't that right, Cassie?"

"Let Susie have 'em," I said as I handed my empty mignonette-drenched shells back to the shucker.

I now had a clear view to the other side of the veranda thanks to the thinning crowd; Maggie spotted me and smiled, though she didn't break off from her conversation with a group of bright young things, including a guy who looked like one of her Lincoln Center friends, judging from his posture and the turnout of his feet. He wore a queenly interpretation of a classic tuxedo—black sequins, platform heels, a dramatically long cigarette holder. Circling around them was a model in feathers and gold beads; her hoop skirt, which seemed to be supported by wheels, wasn't made of fabric, but instead contained rows of etched champagne coupes. It wasn't as though my sister and I didn't talk while I was away, or that I wasn't privy to this wealthy and glamorous part of her life—I followed her on social media, after all—but seeing the proof of it in front of me while I was wearing a drugstore watch was a different type of sensation.

"Come on." Hope pulled on J.P.'s sleeve. "Did you see the

chairman of the Preservation Council over there? I have some things to say about that house for sale on Ocean Avenue."

"It's wonderful to see you, Chicken!" my father called as Hope marched him away. "We're so happy you're home safe."

With my nice cocktail napkin with the embossed crest I supposed Susie was trying to make happen for herself, I wiped drops of perspiration from the side of my glass, from between my breasts, then looked across the lawn. From the corner of my eye, by the illuminated rectangular lap pool and its Palladian cabana, I swore I could make out the form of a goat, tearing Susie's potted pink flowers hungrily apart.

4

I couldn't stand in the same place all night. Rationally, I knew this.

But, honestly, I *did* consider it.

It was Jack who rescued me, his face even more welcome because he was alone. No mother. None of her gaggle of friends. "Where you've been all my life?" I asked as he bent his knees to envelop me in an affectionate squeeze.

I'd been determined to hate Jack when we first met him. That had been the summer of displacement—for my parents, Maggie, Archer, and me, who'd unceremoniously packed what remained from my childhood home, and moved to its carriage house in the rear, watching as Jack's family claimed, rightfully, legally, what we'd once considered ours. He was a thief, an interloper, until he showed up at the carriage house one night with a few olive branches—a bottle of something sweet, a quarter and a few cups—and made us laugh for the first time in what had felt like years. It turned out to be a summer of upheaval for seventeen-year-old Jack, too, uprooted from Boston following his father's death to an old, vast house on Bellevue Avenue, into the bedroom that used to be Maggie's, and into its original canopied bed, carved by the masters in Florence. Together we roamed Newport, making mischief on the wharf, taking tipsy bike rides to Ochre Point, seeing midnights on Gooseberry Beach. I'd watched them fall in love, and if Jack or Maggie had minded me as a third wheel, they'd never let on.

"Look at your hair!" I exclaimed, tugging on the thick strands on either side of his part. "It got long." Last time I'd seen him, his dark brown locks had been shaped in a close crop.

"I'm letting it grow." Jack's mouth, wide and flexible, was usually curved up into a grin, and this moment was no exception. His nose, slightly crooked with a bump near the bridge, appeared as though someone long ago had punched him. But it was just genetics, with some assistance from a rogue basketball. Even if he had been the type to spin apocryphal yarns about himself (he wasn't), no one would believe the nose was the result of a long-ago fight (he was too nice). "Let me take you around?" he asked with a white-suited arm around my shoulders.

"No," I said, not wanting my pariah stink to cling to him. "You don't have to—"

Too late.

With firm but gentle pressure, he guided me toward people I hadn't seen in years. They took turns declaring to me how long it had been. No one brought up the past—I didn't expect them to. It was polite society, after all. But don't believe for a second we weren't all aware of it. What gave it away? The pause after the greeting, stalling with a sip of their drinks, that initial floundering in the dead air between *hello* and *it's been a while!* I could imagine them thinking, *God, what to say to this girl?* Gradually, I shifted my camera on its strap higher on my chest, making it a breastplate, a piece of armor.

Jack easily steered conversation into banal territory: Ambassador and Mrs. Frederick Sterns, just back from a cruise to Antarctica—"Too damn cold, too many penguins." Bunny Mills—"I design garden benches. Susie can show you the look book." Dr. Jennifer Cohen—"When was the last time you saw a dentist?" Her practice was in Middletown, though she only worked on Mondays now. "That's the day the golf course is closed. Now, remind us what you do?"

As I explained what I did outside of Rhode Island, I was shortly reminded of this fact: when those who haven't left the closed loop of Newport/New York/Palm Beach are in the company of one who has, they find themselves earnestly inspecting the curiosity before them as one might an indecipherable gallery installation. I was an oddity—past, present, and future.

Servers strolled around with more appetizers, which was a nice distraction, and gave me something to do with my hands. Balls of sweet melon and buttery prosciutto, gazpacho shooters that were too salty, scallops on sticks—I sampled them all as the sun sank below the Cottage's roof and cornice decorated with plaster scrolls and shells.

A late arrival—a girl from our high school who'd once bad-mouthed me all over town after I'd gotten too handsy with a guy she evidently liked at a party—had a very exuberant greeting for Jack and a lukewarm greeting for me. Her ambivalence at my presence did not prevent her from filling us in on her current life as an accessories editor at *Vogue.* "You should email me," she said without enthusiasm, tossing her long, effortlessly waved hair over her shoulder. No contact information was offered. Perhaps she presumed she was just *that* well known. For her job in fashion. Not because her CEO father had fleeced his company of millions, then not two months later threw her a lavish twenty-first birthday party at Eden Rock St. Barths.

From a passing server, I swapped my empty glass with a fresh one. I took a long sip, sucked through my teeth, and as she described in great detail her costume to Jack—something about vintage, something about stylist archives—I tried to keep my eyes from rolling back in my head. It had only been an hour, but I was weary. I'd done my duty, hadn't I? I'd shown my face.

I looked toward the house, thinking I might just go find Maggie and my parents and say good night. But a flash of motion distracted me, a man pushing open the glass French doors. I saw his straw boater first, then crisp tan suit, the gold of the pocket watch chain, pants cropped stylishly, right above the laces of his oxfords. He didn't need to lift his head for me to recognize him. His face appeared, partially obscured by the brim of his hat, but still unmistakably him. The height, the cheekbones, the momentary, contemplative purse of the lips as he scanned the crowd. Then, landing on Jack and me, the smile, broad and white.

I hadn't seen Spencer Sims in seven years. Him and his equally beautiful wife.

Spencer waved; even from a distance, I saw his ring glint, catching the light. Nearby, someone clinked the edge of a knife to a glass. Toasts would soon begin in the living room. The crowd stirred, rearranged itself. Spencer was obscured. I shifted on my feet, waiting.

He reappeared, closer now, heading upstream from the rest of the party. I glanced at a grinning Jack, then back at Spencer, now just two body lengths away. From the water, the breeze picked up, swinging the globe string lights hanging from poles around the veranda. The sky was imbued with the soft rosiness of sunset, the light becoming revealingly perfect. The chattering group of gangsters to Spencer's left moved just so, and the lady with the outrageous, plumed headdress to his right tilted her head just flawlessly, and I felt the familiar fission along my spine that signaled, if I were lucky and didn't blow it on a compositional error, I might capture something really dynamic and special.

Relying on trancelike muscle memory, I swung my camera up to eye level, removed the lens cap, adjusted the zoom. And as Spencer strode forward into the one square foot of focus I had, framed by a slice of creamsicle sky, the white, cutting corner of the canopy, and a flash of diamonds and candlelight in the background, I released the shutter.

......

"You didn't even let me pose."

My camera fell back to my side, and I met Spencer's smile with my own, reminding myself not to think of him as the one who got away. How could he be? *I* wasn't the one who'd passively let us end.

Spencer Sims gave his cousin a strong handshake, then the kind of hug where both guys whacked each other's backs with a closed fist. His embrace of me was gentler. And distant. No parts of us touched other than our upper shoulders and fingertips. When he pulled back, I searched his eyes—green, brown, depending on the light—looking for signs of displeasure that, after a decade, the first thing I'd done was whip out my camera and take a picture without warning. But he betrayed nothing except friendliness and, as was the case when I'd known him well enough, a sprinkle of mischief.

"I couldn't let you ruin a perfectly good photo of yourself" was my answer.

Jack excused himself, gesturing across the veranda toward

the house, to his future bride and everyone else eager to wish him well. I used the moment to glance surreptitiously at Spencer's hand holding his beer. But the only piece of jewelry he wore was a gold signet ring on his pinkie. I hadn't heard of divorce, or separation. Then again, I'd made a habit of being absent.

"Cassie Coventry-Gilford, I was hoping you'd bless our small corner of the world this weekend," said Spencer after Jack was gone, tipping his hat back to give me the full weight of his attention. "How've you—"

At the same time, I said, "And here you are—"

We both stopped and laughed—his, untroubled; mine, awkward. I sipped my drink, buying some time to collect myself. Married or not, I didn't want him to walk away thinking me a verifiable mess, unchanged from the wild one he'd known, the untamable girl, tearing through Newport like she was trying to escape the fire nipping at her heels.

"So," he tried again. "You're back."

"Through tomorrow. I need to get back out in the field." I ran my fingers down the strap of my camera so they wouldn't go to my hair, feel the indent where the curb had met my skull. "I've changed, you know. I can actually hold down a job these days."

"I've seen your Instagram," Spencer said, and I tried to tamp down the thrill that he'd social media stalked me. "It seems you're *still* an adrenaline addict, though you're running toward trouble, not causing it. After all these years, you remain a girl with no fear."

"Have to be," I said, trying camouflage my nerves. "Zola once said that you cannot claim to have really seen something until you have photographed it. And I have a lot left to see."

Spencer leaned toward me, angled his head down so we

were eye to eye. "You just photographed me." His accompanying half smile was cozy. "What did you see?"

"We'll have to wait for the film," I said, giving in to his grin.

"You two!" Enter Hope, stage left, and the curtain dropped.
"Cassie, I want you to take some photos of the toasts. Come
inside now. No dawdling!" She didn't wait for my response
before pivoting, a rustle of fishnet stockings on her thighs,
back through the veranda door.

I gave Spencer a faux-horrified look. "We're in trouble."

"Wouldn't be the first time." Gallant, he extended his arm.

On our way inside, we passed Susie and the gray-haired,
blue-blazered octogenarian I recognized as the longtime chairman of the Newport Preservation Council. Atop Susie's head
was something I wanted to call a hat but was more like a sparkly headpiece that she tied around her gray pixie cut like a
scarf. Though Susie's back was to us, her voice carried. "The
Land was really the first thing I bought for myself after the
divorce," she was saying. "The first big thing I didn't have to
ask permission to buy. But it's taken me *fifteen* years to restore
it. It was resilient, the poor thing."

"But God knows," was his response, "just how much those
Coventrys left you to rescue."

5

In the living room, I felt rather than saw the distance between Spencer and me grow as I maneuvered and *excuse me*'d
through the bodies, and their props and accessories, clustered
in front of the massive limestone fireplace where my sister and
Jack stood, hand in hand, beaming. A full-bearded man was
sweating through a toast, shuffling his notecards as though
they were out of order. He was, though, saying very nice
things about my sister.

I made some adjustments to aperture and shutter speed,
began to capture the toaster and candid reactions from the
audience; through my viewfinder, I noted that my father had
found himself one of Susie's diminutive antique chairs against
the far wall, and was watching the show with a pleasant but
detached expression, legs crossed at the ankles, glass of wine
in hand, his wife's purse in his lap.

Hope, on the other hand, was hovering in the front row,
as conspicuous amid the black and white and cream outfits as

a huge red pimple. As the speech dragged on, she would raise her arm and point at Maggie, saying loudly, *That's so true!* And, *She does only curse when she's backstage!*

Throughout, the accessories editor whispered with a friend and looked not unsubtlety at my mother. I trained my view-finder at her, caught the edge of her mouth as it curled up-ward, the cut of her hand as it came up to hide her lips.

"Cass." I started—Kent was behind me, his touch light on my elbow, gesturing for me to follow. "Mrs. Utterback would like to see you."

I nodded and he escorted me back through the crowd, past my father, who shot me a quick, comforting wink. There was a smattering of applause as the toast ended and a unison call for *cheers!*

I thought Kent might be guiding me to a different spot, one which Susie felt would provide better angles or light or something. But no. He was taking me away from the party entirely, to the tall doors at the back of the room, which had originally led to the breakfast room but was now part of Su-sie's new kitchen.

Kent ushered me through the open door and there stood the lady of the house, holding forth at the giant marble island like a captain at her helm, if sea captains wore pearlescent white caftans and diamonds.

"Cass Gilford, my goodness, my darling," was Susie Utter-back's greeting for me. With a wordless flick of her hand, she dismissed the other occupants of the kitchen, two young male servers who'd been fussing with shrimp on a platter. "Where is your costume?" A demand, not a question.

"I'm wearing it." When I crossed the length of the island and reached her, she took my upper arms and yanked me for-ward for a cheek-to-cheek, once, twice, as though I had to be reminded—*commanded*—how to greet Susie Utterback. "You just have to squint really hard."

To my relief, she smiled, one side higher than the other, stepped back, and slid off her bold black glasses. How Susie Utterback came into all our lives was circuitous but still simple enough, at least in America. A mogul husband, a divorce, a lover who became his much younger wife, a sudden death, a will that hadn't been updated, a protracted and contentious legal battle, and *ta-da*, an eye-popping cash windfall to Susie, the ex. Then she'd come to Newport, met my father, who'd invited her to see The Land. The rest, history.

"Well, no matter. You look fit. Globe-trotting suits you."

"Thank you." Unexpected as it was, I wasn't above accepting a compliment. Though nothing in her tone suggested lingering resentment or displeasure, I wondered if she'd really gotten over my past misdeeds, including that one time with her car, a stop sign, and a stone wall on Ocean Drive. Or, as is the case for many rich people, she'd found other grudges to hold instead. "Hope said I looked tired."

Susie threw back her head and laughed. "Oh, please. Nothing an injection and some spackle can't fix. You know I've got a Reiki guy coming to the house three times a week? Have to. Tried chiropractor. Tried acupuncture. Tried dry needling." She ticked these off on her fingers. "You can use him, if you want. He's brilliant. Would do wonders for your—" She swirled her hand in front of her face.

Now it was my turn to laugh. There'd been a time when Susie viewed me benevolently, despite my youthful shenanigans, when she must have considered me a type of charitable cause, someone with unrealized potential who she could fix up and call it philanthropy. But I'd assumed those days were over. That she'd decided I wasn't worth the immense trouble.

The final straw: seven years ago, in this very place, I'd

snatched that microphone away from the very confused lead singer of Susie's Labor Day party band to deliver a drunken, scorched-earth monologue about everyone from the social climbers and their grotesque displays of wealth and insipid small talk, to the old-money WASPs and their affected *oh, this old thing?* attitudes. I closed by calling the city's summer colonists human versions of menstrual cramps, an insult that probably would've amused my grandmother, had she still been alive. Then I'd stumbled offstage into Susie's champagne tower, breaking it *and* the most important of Newport's cardinal rules: decorum.

Susie moved to the refrigerator, camouflaged and paneled like the lacquered moss-green cabinets around it. When she opened the door to retrieve the bottle, I caught a glimpse of the perfectly organized shelves within: rows of yogurt, sparkling water, clear plastic containers of what looked to be broth. "I swear, the closer I get to the end, the faster it all goes."

"Like a roll of toilet paper." When we'd lived here, the fridge—loud, ancient, the color of an avocado—had been in the butler's pantry, jammed awkwardly into the space between the old silver safe and the sinks. No one, not even my mother, would argue that Susie's extensive renovations and repairs over the years hadn't markedly improved upon the former Gray Gardens–tinged ambience of the Cottage and its outbuildings. But although I recognized its magazine-quality design, my overall impression of the house under her care was less than fawning. Something was missing. Maybe it was just us, the Coventry-Gilfords, our footsteps, handprints, all of which had been stripped off like lead paint.

Susie poured me a glass of white wine so pale it was almost clear, and watched me from the other side of the wide marble island as I sipped. I cleared my throat. "So…?" I lifted my eyebrows. "What can I do you for?" The next toaster must have said something funny, because laughter from beyond the doors trickled in.

Susie ignored it. "This is delicate," she said, tracing a golden vein in the marble with her index finger.

I'd heard this phrase before, so I slid my wine aside, leaned on my palms, braced myself. She and Hope must be at loggerheads over something. I suspected the wandering goat had something to do with it, as Hope had a notorious soft spot for creatures both domesticated and feral—kittens, hens, the harbor seals who occasionally sunned themselves on the rocks below the Cliff Walk.

"Do we agree that I've been generous with your family?" she asked.

"Yes." This was not an unusual place for negotiations to begin. "You've been—"

"All those years ago," Susie cut in, "I agreed to let your mother and father rent the carriage house. But—I have to be clear here." The expanse of marble between us she tapped, three, four times, with the flat of her palm. "I never promised that they could rent it forever, doing whatever to it and treating it the way it's been treated."

"They do their best," I said, though I wasn't sure how accurate that was. I hadn't seen the residence in seven years, and even when I'd lived there, we didn't exactly follow the historic preservationist codes of conduct. "And I'm sure with the wedding coming, Hope will—"

"Oh, yes." Here, a rueful little laugh. "The wedding. Which I suppose Hope and J.P. are going to pay for? They can't even pay to fix the roof, which your brother broke, by the way. Do you know how much a slate roof costs? No, why would you? You've been gone, and I've been the caretaker of that—" Susie gestured across the kitchen in the general direction of the carriage house, trying to find the word.

"What about my brother and the roof?" I asked, confused, but still aware that something was wrong, and somehow my absence was being blamed, in part, for it.

"You really have no idea, do you?" Susie inhaled; it was a breath of tested patience. "That's just the latest in a long line of disasters. In January, Hope decided to knock down a wall in her bedroom, and that meant—*hello*—dealing with lead paint remediation. Before that, your dad walked straight into the screen door, so Hope decided she wanted a new one. But she took it upon herself to remove the screen door *and* the main door from the frame, which meant the city had to come out and inspect for asbestos. Which *obviously* there was. It's always something, Cass. The electricity, the plumbing, the insulation. And that *goat* who impaled poor Jay Leno when he was over for the sailing museum charity dinner! I try, but your mother is no saint."

My response—I think it would've been begrudging agreement—died on my lips as Susie continued. "She's not a saint, and I'm not a monster. Now it's time for me to be a businesswoman. I've made my last repair, my last patch job, my last overture to your mother."

My temperature was rising, but I knew it was important to keep my voice low. "Wait. What are you saying?"

Her eyes flicked from me, to her hands, to her manicured nails, the color of a conch's insides. "You'll help your parents figure out somewhere else to live."

A beat, then two, and I was still struggling to absorb her words. It sounded as though she was finished being a landlord. And my parents were finished being residents of the carriage house. "But Maggie and Jack are..." I swayed on my feet, unmoored, catching myself on the island.

"They are engaged." Then, softly, but with utter conviction: "And I am done."

I made erasing motions with my hands, wishing that I was wrong, that I could change the direction of the freight train barreling toward me, toward all of us. "I'll get the goat out. We'll pay to have the roof fixed," I said, not clear on who, exactly, I meant by *we*.

"Sure you will." Susie smiled, but it was the kind that didn't stick around. "And something else will break. And she'll find another animal to adopt. Then what? What's Hope's long-term strategy, Cass? They can't keep going on like this, waiting for you, or me, or Jack and Maggie, to bail them out."

I was in the confusing position of both receiving the truth of what she was saying, and feeling compelled to reject it. "They can't— This is..." I trailed off, unable to capture the enormity of what The Land actually was to us. My hand had crept to my throat, where my heartbeat thudded. "Who knows?"

"No one but you. I trust you to take this information and deliver it in a way that your mother will hear. No one wants this to turn ugly." As she said this, her mouth barely moved. "I'm sorry, Cass. I really am. Maggie is a lovely girl. She makes my son happy. This has nothing to do with her, or the wedding."

The doors to the kitchen creaked open. It was Kent. "Ma'am?" He addressed Susie, peering over the tops of his glasses. "The toasts have ended. Maggie and Jack indicated they'd like to say something, too."

Susie murmured an acknowledgment, and Kent lingered behind her in the doorway.

"How—" I swallowed. "How long do they have?"

"I think one month," was Susie's answer.

A month? I wasn't supposed to be back here in a month. I wasn't even supposed to be here past Monday. "Susie, they have nowhere else to go. The Land—" I almost said, *The Land belongs to them*. I shook my head. Maybe that would jig-

gle some coherent thoughts loose. But the only other one that
came was this: "Give them till the wedding," I said, pleading,
hating the supplication in my voice. "Honestly, Susie, if you
want the wedding to go smoothly for the happy couple, you
must let my parents stay put. Give them more time to figure
out their next steps." I waited, feeling more exposed than I
had in years, feeling very much like a teenager, negotiating
myself out of trouble.

"I don't like being held hostage by a *wedding*." She frowned.

Neither do I, I almost said.

But after a moment, Susie conceded. "Fine. But after the
wedding, they have to go."

I released a tense breath.

From the other side of the room, Jack's deep voice was
booming. "Maggie and I are just so glad to have everyone
here. We can't thank you enough for celebrating our engagement. Speaking of... Maggie, do you want to say—?"

Maggie began to speak; I could hear the cadence, but not
her words. "I can't—" There was a ringing in my ears, or
maybe it was the sound of the group, who cheered and applauded at once. "What did she say?" I asked, raising my voice
over the noise. "What did Maggie just say?"

"That they're getting married in Newport," Kent said.
"Labor Day weekend."

"Well." Susie lifted a shoulder. "There we are. Labor Day,
it is."

Like vines in this garden-green kitchen, the news snaked
around my ankles, clasping and clinging, fastening me to this
place that held nothing but sore memories and ancient scars.
I'd escaped Newport, but it wasn't done with me.

Susie nodded once, with finality, and departed the kitchen
with a rustle of fine damask and a hint of roses and grass.

6

NET-A-NEWPORT 7H
Submitted via NetaNewport.com
From: gildedage@party.com
Subject: engagement party

Message: was a really nice night and the bride and groom were
really happy. Party went on til 3am. Only person not doing the
costume theme was (big surprise) cass coventry.

NET-A-NEWPORT 6H
Submitted via NetaNewport.com
From: I like big boats and I cannot lie
Subject: wedding of the year

Message: the reason the coventry utterback wedding is so soon

is because the one mom doesn't want it to happen at all, and the
bride and groom need to get it locked up

NET-A-NEWPORT 5H
CONFIRMED Wedding of the Season date SET for Labor Day! Venue
TBD. Submit your guesses below.

Around ten the next morning, Hope burst into the bunk
room, somehow already out of breath. *Maggie is getting married
in three months and we don't have a moment to spare!*

After Susie had released the guillotine last night, I'd downed
the glass of wine she'd poured me. Then, because it is law that
one reverts to their immature selves once at home, I helped
myself to the rest of the bottle, drinking it alone as I dangled
my feet in the cold pool, watching the party carry on from
afar. When the lights finally went off on the veranda, I lumbered back to the carriage house, creeping through the pitch-
black, trying not to wake my parents, and threw myself into
bed—the bottom bunk, to be exact, after Archer reminded
me via text that he had top *in perpetuity*—without even changing my clothes.

I was paying for it today; I spent a good part of the morning staring blearily at the mattress slats above me, waiting for
the ibuprofen to kick in. Blame it on the alcohol or the lack of
sleep, but the back of my head was also throbbing. I'd hoped
the injury, and the memories of it, would've faded by now.
No such luck.

Above me, Archer groaned as Hope listed our plans for the
day—something about a venue, something about the guest
list, something about ice sculptures. And, if I heard correctly,
drones? "Maggie brought your stuff over, Cassie—you left it
in Susie's room," Hope said, letting my bag drop heavily by
the headboard. "So, get up already! The appointment is in an

hour. They are fitting us in, and we cannot be tardy!" A tabby cat, one ear missing, a pink scar across his nose, glided into the room and began to do figure-eights around my mother's ankles.

I swung my feet off the bed, still woozy with drink and lousy information, and managed to get one eye fully open. The room, Lord, it was a mess. You'd think a twenty-six-year-old would have more evolved cleanliness habits than an elephant in a dirt pile. With the edge of my foot, I slid aside an empty guitar case that was currently supporting a number of half-drunk water cups. "I was going to go see friends this morning," I said, hoping this could be an excuse.

"Ha!" Hope barked, startling the cat, who bolted from the room. "You are not."

It *was* a flagrant lie. Not even Archer bought it; his laughter wobbled the bunk.

"I smell that you both had a late night, but we'll drive with the sunroof open," Hope said as she strode over to the single dormer window, raised the blinds with a hard yank. On the ceiling above her, a brown, globby stain had soaked through the plaster, likely evidence of the roof damage Susie had been referring to. "You can stick your head out. Fresh air does a body good."

This was my last day, and I didn't relish spending it having hard conversations while hungover, but maybe it wouldn't be so hard. Maybe Archer and my parents were tired of living in an creaky, polluted old house! Maybe they'd breeze out of here with some suitcases and a new lease on life! I told my mother something like *all right, ugh, fine.*

"Hear that, Archer?" said Hope, reaching up to shake his back, still covered in the sheet and blanket. "Your sister is engaging with the family."

"Stop the presses," I mumbled. When I lifted myself off the

mattress, the structure creaked ominously. We'd used these beds since the early aughts, and even then Hope had purchased them secondhand. By the time I'd left for Columbia, they were in a state I could only describe as *rickety*, held together with spit and prayers. I just hoped they'd last another night before collapsing entirely. I shuffled over to my bag, which had fallen open by Archer's telescope, and tugged from the bottom the kind of workout clothes that aren't for working out.

"Why don't you want to come with us?" my mother was demanding of Archer.

"I have a meeting later." Archer sat up in bed, ran a hand over his face and through his hair, apparently giving up on the sleep-in. "With my UFO kooks at the library. Got a guest speaker. Big muckety-muck from the Pentagon. Well, Pentagon adjacent. He's been in the Pentagon once, is what I'm saying."

"Would do you some good to be with people who don't wear aluminum foil on their heads and talk nonsense about 5G networks," Hope muttered on her way out the door.

"Don't talk about my friends that way!" Archer jokingly called after her.

I found my cosmetics hiding under my tangle of phone and computer chargers. "God, it's freezing in here. How did you manage to break through the roof, anyway?"

"You heard about that, huh?"

I winced, but he didn't seem to notice, or care that Susie had told me.

He lifted his phone to his face. "I was up there one night with the telescope, trying to find some peace and quiet in this circus, and I stepped a teensy bit too hard, and my leg kind of punched through the shingles," he explained.

"You're going on top of the house now?" My feelings of guilt were replaced with concern. "You're not just looking for stars, Archer, you're looking for trouble."

"Says the girl who destroyed the top of Dad's old convertible when she—" I halted him with a slice of my hand. He was correct—I didn't have much credibility when it came to youthful risk-taking. "You should be proud of me," he continued, his focus still on his screen, his fingers flying. "I confessed to Susie, and promised to pay for the repair."

"Save your money," I said as I left the room.

·····

There was a time when I believed we would've been a whole lot better, and happier, if the carriage house burned down, rending all evidence of past lives into ash, so we could move somewhere completely new, start fresh. I hadn't gotten my old wish, obviously. The house was still standing, but it was several steps removed, I was realizing, from the state of genteel disrepair when I'd left.

My descent down the narrow stairs built for smaller feet was hampered by precarious towers of paperback books, vinyl records, and plastic storage bins containing all manner of items. How I made it upstairs the night before without causing an avalanche would be forever a mystery. At the bottom, I turned smack into a ceramic umbrella stand. Over it fell with a crash, spewing five umbrellas of different sizes over my bare feet. I cursed, began to right the thing, though I surmised, judging from the state of the rest of the hallway, my parents were in the habit of simply kicking aside messes like this with the assumption that someone would get to it later.

Indeed: "Oh, leave it," Hope called from the kitchen.

Slowly, I traversed the hallway's literal obstacle course of bins, boxes, stacks and piles and entered the kitchen. A hundred years ago, it had served as the offices of the groundskeeper, the coachman, the groom. It was a simple kitchen, unchanged since we'd moved in, L-shaped, with cream cabinets, wood drawer pulls, and white Formica countertops. Not that you could see much of them through the clutter.

My parents were the type to save everything, from other people's wedding invitations to my great-grandmother's French linens, but the house was much more congested than the last time I'd visited. True, I hadn't been able to reheat pizza in the oven because my mother had been using it as storage for her collection of vintage Pucci shoes, but at least you could see most of the wide-plank floors.

My father sat in front of a tray with bonsai, sand, pebbles, and the world's tiniest rake, as Hope jammed containers of cut-up fruit into the already-stuffed refrigerator. The tabby cat I'd spotted upstairs was napping in a patch of sun next to him.

"Morning, Chicken," said my father, cheery. "How did you sleep?"

"Bad." Over my father's shoulder, I noticed that the door to the little cubby under the stairs where my parents once held the liquor I regularly drained in high school was no longer accessible, blocked by a stack of cardboard boxes. Maybe it was the hangover, combined with the hard jolt of seeing the state of the carriage house in the light of day, but I felt a strange flickering in my brain.

I never promised that they could rent it forever, doing whatever to it and treating it the way it's been treated.

"I need a shower," I managed.

"The shower doesn't work in the kids' bathroom here," J.P. said, adjusting his glasses on his nose, his attention drifting from me to his bonkei. "Archer uses the one in the pool house. Didn't Maggie tell you?"

It took me overly long to summon the words. "She did not."

"Or you can use Mom's and mine," my father said, studying something on his tray with a magnifying glass. "Just gotta keep it under five minutes. That's all the water heater can take these days. Poor old girl."

"It's fine." Hope closed the refrigerator, its handles smudged with fingerprints, its door plastered with paper, take-out menus, calendars, photos, invitations, one of which appeared to be to my cousin's wedding two years prior. This cousin, second, I believe, had parlayed her famous name into a lucrative textile business that sold knobby blankets and robes and three-wick candles for obscene amounts of money, and the invitation, thick as a piece of deli cheese, indicated wealth that was still liquid. "It is on the to-do list," she added.

I wandered from the kitchen to the family room—the long, vaulted space that spanned the rear of the house. More books covered the lumpy leather couch on which we all used to crowd for after-school television and family movie nights. On the floor: baskets with ceramic trinkets, baskets of tarnished doorknobs and drawer pulls. On the coffee and side tables: clay pottery, chinoiserie vases and ginger jars, Staffordshire figurines, a very old mantel clock that looked to have been dissected for science. Oil landscape paintings and watercolors within gilded picture frames leaned against the set of wide, arched carriage doors. The walls were lined with glass-doored armoire cabinets, choked full of oddities and ornaments. And the pièce de résistance—resting on one of the original deeply weathered floor-to-ceiling beams—a portrait of five-year-old Archer Coventry-Gilford, dressed preposterously like Little Lord Fauntleroy. Some of this, the latter included, I recognized from the time we lived in the Cottage, but most of it was entirely unfamiliar.

Out one of the square windows nestled between the back doors, I saw the goat pen. It was ramshackle, made of different kinds of boards and beams and pieced-together netting. Growing up, my father had built us a chicken coop in the garden and we'd raised hens and a rooster. Hope had taken in stray cats; Granny Fi, Hope's mother, once kept a capuchin monkey in the folly. But never a goat.

As I made my way back to the kitchen, I had the urge to rub my eyes—*was I the only one seeing this?* I watched my mother squeeze behind my father to adjust a café curtain rod that had gone askew in the window—now opaque with salt frost and brine. She'd neglected to brush the back of her hair; against her scalp it looked like a stack of kindling and just as dry.

"Mom," I said, "this is—" I swept my arm across the room—pots of herbs, most having seen better days, surrounded the sink and the windowsill above it.

But Hope interrupted me. "Before the weekend slips away from us, I could use your assistance. Nothing major, but rather pressing."

"Sure," I said, letting my arm drop. "I will absolutely help you burn that painting of Archer. Where do you keep your firewood?"

"You stop," said J.P. "Your mother loves that painting."

"I told J.P. to tidy before you got here. Seriously. Archer," she said, hearing my brother on the stairs. "Tell Cassie, just how many times have I told J.P. to tidy." Archer pretended not to hear this question. He mumbled something about forgetting his phone and skipped back up, taking the stairs two at a time. My mother had kicked from her path—wait for it—a basket of smaller wicker baskets, and was washing her hands vigorously in the sink. "Maggie said last night she wants to cap the guest list," Hope said over the sound of the water. "But your father's extended family is close to eighty people in and of itself. You have to convince her to go as big as possible." She turned off the water and dried her hands on her skirt. "I don't want *anyone* snubbed. Claiborne Pell was left off a guest list once, and in retaliation he passed a bill in Congress that specifically taxed horse stalls as income properties. Completely ruined the poor woman and her dressage pony business. True story."

"Ma." I edged forward, cautiously, though my mind was doing its best to sputter to life. "Have we considered a cleaning service? A dumpster? An industrial vacuum?"

Hope ignored this, pulled the tall trash can out from under the sink, and started going through a pile of receipts while, at the same time, listing off the names of relatives we'd need to invite, far-off cousins, some aunts on my father's side I'd never met, Granny Fi's elderly sister, Abigail, in Phoenix, who—I was shocked to discover—was still alive. As Hope prattled on, I considered broaching the topic of their pending eviction. But my gaze fell back on my dad at the table, his glasses sliding down on his nose, the tiny tools in his fingers, the evidence of his life—of our, his children's lives—ready to tumble down onto his hunched shoulders, and I decided, wisely or cowardly, to wait. My father hated conflict, to be put on the spot, anything that would disturb the tenuous equilibrium of the family. For someone who really despised emotional mess, he certainly looked comfortable living in mayhem.

Just then, my sister burst through the screen door, calling Hope's name.

"What do we think about a *Dangerous Liaison*–themed rehearsal dinner?" Hope shouted toward her.

"Complete with duels and smallpox?" said my father, snipping at his bonsai.

Maggie navigated the crammed hallway and entered the kitchen with much more grace and dexterity than I had. She was around more, certainly; perhaps, if the piles had grown slowly, it would've been less noticeable to her.

"The groom's family does the rehearsal, Mama," Maggie said. I checked her face for signs of worry, signs of strain at being in the carriage house. But if she believed this was anything other than normal, she didn't show it. Weirdly, this provided me some relief.

"Fine, but I want to project a slide show. Tell Susie."

"What pictures are you planning to project?" Archer, evidently deeming the coast mostly clear, clomped down the stairs and joined me in the kitchen. Though it was ten o'clock in the morning, he had in his hand a single-serve bag of chips.

"Good question," I said. Most of my toddler years were spent naked—I'd been the type of child who preferred being in the nude—and I didn't fancy seeing that displayed ten feet high in front of a crowd who considered peep-toe pumps revealing.

"Gosh, I was thinking the one you posted on Instagram the other day of the pigeon on your fire escape with the vape pen," said Hope, drenched in sarcasm. "Pictures of family! What else?"

"You can talk to Susie, Mama," said Maggie. "It doesn't all have to be routed through me."

"She won't hear from me after the thing with Darren and Leno."

There was some back and forth between Maggie and Hope about the slide projector and Susie, but eventually I interrupted them. "Can someone please point me to a bathroom that *does* work?"

"Technically," my father said after a brief pause, "we have two working bathrooms. Just that some components *in* those bathrooms work better than others."

"That one is good." Archer pointed to the downstairs one, pink tiled and bare-bulbed, in between the pantry and the living room. "Though the shower warbles like an opera soprano." He popped a stack of neon orange chips into his mouth and crunched down with a grin.

7

Eighteen hours until I departed Newport.

And I wasn't even there; Hope had taken us to Watch Hill to view—in her words—the *perfect* wedding venue, settled high on a bluff an hour south of The Land.

Ocean House was indeed a showstopper, a Victorian grande dame, painted cheery yellow, its architecture from a time when people dressed for dinner. From hotel exterior to the sound, the view was five-star, relentlessly and audaciously beautiful, the kind of scene that even a baby could appreciate. There was croquet on the lawn, an award-winning spa, elegant suites, top-shelf liquor, about five different outdoor event space options—if one wanted to pitch a tent—or a ballroom that could accommodate two hundred and fifty.

"Two hundred and fifty? Good." This was Hope to the young man who'd introduced himself as the event and lifestyle coordinator. When we'd met him in the fern-and-chintz-sofa-filled lobby, he'd handed us glossy brochures, and although pages four through six included a list of all available rental options, there were no prices listed, which of course meant even the smallest banquet room cost more than a car. "Susie had a hundred and fifty last night, so we'll need more than that," Hope mused.

Standing at the center of the ballroom—cream walls, coffered ceilings, carpet that was good at hiding stains—I was in a fugue state, waffling between outrage at Susie, denial that she was serious, anger toward my parents for giving Susie the excuse, and yearning to be where I really wanted to be—with my camera, far, far away.

Before we'd departed in Hope's primordial Volvo, I'd finally gotten a good look at the exterior of the carriage house and, like the interior, it was worse that I could've imagined. In addition to the blue tarp pinned taut on the low-pitched, gently sloping shingled roof, the building's pale pink stucco needed a power wash; a yellowish brown fuzz born of time and briny air had taken up patchy residence. The grand double doors where landau carriages and horses used to pass were mostly obscured by overgrown boxwoods and holly bushes that had me thinking about *The Shining*. The multipaned windows, wood, original, were shabby; chipped black paint was prevalent on the muntins and trim. The only thing that looked healthy was the weeping, gnarled beech that once served as our favorite jungle gym.

Outside Ocean House, the sea winked and glinted in the sun. When I was younger, I'd fancied myself in communication with the water; I'd thought it healing, a reminder of the smallness of myself. But the churning waves, for many a constant in the face of battering change, was not a reassurance to me today. The Land would be gone from my family, entirely and irreversibly, in less than three months. Where would they go? How much money would it even take to get J.P. and Hope on their feet somewhere else? Archer, too.

Subtracting for sleep, I had about ten hours left to figure it out.

"The Greggs' fortieth wedding anniversary was here, Cassie, do you remember?" Hope asked, rubbing the fabric of the window treatments between her fingers, testing for—I don't know—softness? I didn't remember, but I nodded, anyway. "And Gillian Hax's daughter's sweet sixteen party. You know—God, what was that girl's name? You know who I'm talking about. One leg shorter than the other one, but, God, she could sing."

"Right," I murmured, though, again, I had no idea who she was talking about.

I'd taken The Land for granted. Even after we moved, even after I'd gotten over that shameful, isolating loss. The carriage house was ours, Susie had promised, for as long as we wanted. But lease agreements are different than handshakes, and the word *ours* really meant *hers*.

Nine hours, fifty-nine minutes, thirty seconds.

"Many guests choose to include the uplighting package," the coordinator offered, "so as to match the room to their overall color story."

Hope gestured to the young man she'd introduced us to outside the carriage house as River, her *summer associate*. Though Hope was the type of woman to consider busyness a virtue, she hadn't worked a traditional job for close to half a century; yet, apparently, her life was hectic enough to warrant an intern. "Uplighting package," said River, typing a note on his phone. "Check."

"Really, Hope," I said. "What are you doing with this nice boy, and do his parents know where he is?"

"River goes to Salve. He wanted to spend the summer here gaining marketable skills."

"River," I said. He looked up from his screen. "Are you okay? Blink twice if you need help."

When he laughed, he did it with his mouth closed, the back of his hand pressed politely to his lips. "I get college credit, Miss Casamassima. I assure you, everything is aboveboard."

"Cass, please," I said, though I was impressed he could pronounce my full name without stumbling over the linguistic moguls camouflaged as syllables.

"Mrs. Coventry-Gilford has shown me just about every one of your photos," he said, smiling with what looked like approval. "A robust and distinguished body of work, I must say. You are quite the legend in Newport."

Out of habit, I waited for the snide chuckle, the roll of the eyes, that illuminated the connotation behind the word *legend*. But it didn't come.

"We'd want tall flowers in crystal," Hope went on. "And be forewarned, if someone even suggests mason jars, I will lose it."

I approached the coordinator, lowered my voice. "Prices," I said. "What are we looking at here?" It wasn't as though my parents' financial situation was a secret within our family, but judging from the state of the carriage house, even I'd underestimated their predicament.

Wordlessly, he extracted a single sheet from the back of his black portfolio.

I almost gasped as I scanned the expenses grid. "This tracks," I managed.

"Your mother mentioned Labor Day weekend," the coordinator said with a discreet glance at his watch. I'd gotten the sense he'd sized us up and drawn conclusions—my mother in her favorite pair of clogs in the style of doctors and dancers; me in my scuffed sneakers; River, dressed in a pink sweater, Bermuda shorts and knee-high socks, which, in all honesty, I loved. Only my sister, chic in summer-weight cashmere, looked like she belonged. "Our Friday and Saturday are booked, but the ballroom and the east lawn are available that Sunday. Obviously, we'd love to host the wedding of such an accomplished ballerina like your sister. If you're serious about making a deposit—" I noted his stress on the word *serious*. It wasn't unkind but it *was* deliberate "—I urge you do so soon, as we continue to have lots of interest."

"Is there a way to cover up those exit signs?" Hope called, pointing to the wall of double doors that led to the main part of the hotel. "They're so bright. And red."

As the event coordinator explained patiently why obscuring exit signs wouldn't be possible, my phone rang; Mouna was calling, and when your Pulitzer Prized hero of a mentor, and editor at large of special projects at *TIME* calls you, you sure as hell pick up, no matter the circumstances.

"Hi, Mouna. Hello. Can you hear me?" I jammed my phone between my shoulder and ear, pushing through the ballroom doors to the paved terrace the event coordinator had described as *perfect for late-night cigars*, currently dotted with conversation sets and game tables.

"I've been owing you a call." Through the speaker, her voice carried with it whispers of Jordan, where she was raised, hints of Arabic and the Queen's English. She always sounded so genial, right on the cusp of laughter. "I know you're busy with your family. Am I pulling you away from handcrafted cocktails among the hydrangeas?"

"Hardly." I watched an older gentleman in a V-neck tennis sweater and Docksiders get absolutely clobbered in Ping-Pong by what appeared to be his teenage granddaughter. In the distance, beach umbrellas studded the sand. I sensed Mouna, who'd embedded herself with marines, who'd pried shrapnel out of her own thigh, would not appreciate such luxuries taking me away from the job.

"This will be quick, anyway." Despite this statement, her words were unhurried. "I just wanted to check on you."

"I'm fine." Then, more softly, more believably: "I keep telling you, I'm *really* fine. What happened last week—" It was here I had to halt, partly because I still didn't know how to describe it, partly because I didn't want to. The flash and the flares. The smoke bombs that made the air taste like poison. The surging *polițiști*. As though on cue, my head throbbed. "I'm back to New York tomorrow. Then you tell me where to go next. You were thinking India, yes?" This was a business of networking and immediacy. If I was unavailable, publications would find another.

"Cass, no, you need more time," she said. In the devastating pause that followed, I recognized that Mouna was not being cruel; she was a practical person. Perhaps it was this reason why her next statement stung so badly. "I'm going to send Keith to Dharamshala."

I almost groaned out loud. I got why Mouna chose Keith— he was doubtless talented, but, on a personal level, he annoyed the hell out of me. He had zero personality, the human equivalent of a foam finger. His bank account, he never failed to remind the other photographers who freelanced for *TIME*, was permanently flushed, *unlike yours truly*.

Though Hope and J.P. had sent me off to Columbia with half of my first year covered, and I'd cobbled together some grants and aid, as well as worked nights helping red-eyed students find legal treatises in the law library, I was still paying off loans, and would be till I was at least forty.

Keith didn't need this assignment. I did.

"I know that Chișinău was dicey," I countered, "and I know

I made a stupid decision." I scuffed at the pavers with the tip of my sneaker. "I'm ready to go back in."

"The job is risky, Cass. Like I said last week, I'm not pissed you got a nasty concussion. I'm pissed you didn't follow protocol and refused treatment," she explained with a touch of sympathy. "I know you're hungry, but I'm not going to send someone into the field who I can't trust." On the other end of the line, there was sudden muffled talk, and I guessed she'd put her hand over her phone. "All right?" Mouna asked when she returned. "I've got an editorial meeting, and I have to boogie. Take a beat, enjoy your family, get some rest, and we'll talk soon, okay?"

Our call ended. I put my phone down on an empty Ping-Pong table, picked up a paddle, and, with a frustrated grunt, smacked a ball as hard as I could across the patio.

• • • • •

Maggie stood by the wall of windows, snapping an artful photo of the tips of her shoes against the carpet. I took the event space price list out of my back pocket, gave it another glance, just to be sure I hadn't been hallucinating.

"Are you and Jack paying for the wedding yourselves?" I asked without preamble once I reached her. "Sorry, that's probably rude."

"It's okay." Maggie fidgeted with the chunky gold smart ring that tracked her sleep, helped her relax, but her body language indicated that she wasn't entirely comfortable with this line of conversation. I wasn't, either. "That was the original plan, although Mom and Dad have said they want to. I was going to talk to Jack about it again this morning, but after the party he went with buddies to Clarke Cooke House till two a.m., so I let him sleep it off. And, you know…"

She didn't continue. "I know what?" I prodded.

"Jack quit his job last week."

"Okay," I responded, though I really wanted to say, *Oh, shit*. "This seems…sudden."

"Jack was working such long hours he couldn't even shower, and the bank managed to repackage that as *hustle*."

"Screw those investment banking villains," I said because Maggie appeared rather embarrassed about the whole thing. "Eat the rich."

"A lot of those *villains* will be at our wedding." Maggie smiled.

"Fine," I said. "Look askance at the rich and give them shady eyes at the buffet line."

"We're not having a buffet!" Hope had snuck up on us; she wagged her finger in Maggie's face. "Plated dinner only!"

"If it were up to HCG," I sighed at Hope's five-star dreams, "we'd be shutting down the Avenue for horse-drawn carriages."

"Hmm," said Hope, before wandering away, River trailing behind her, debating—with herself—whether trolleys or antique automobiles would be preferable for the journey to Westerly, the plushness of the Ocean House lawn, the disadvantages of sailcloth tents, the unruly Rhode Island weather.

"Mom's head is about to detach from her body and spin like a top into space," I told Maggie. "It's like she wants to compete with British royalty."

"I know, but she has good intentions. And I didn't think there was any harm in letting her check out the beach, imagine where the five-tier cake could go, that sort of thing." This was the oddest thing about being Hope and J.P.'s children; for two people who were relatively uninterested in discussing feelings, we kids were regularly concerned about theirs. "Are you not having fun?" she asked teasingly.

"I'm certainly not complaining about being away from the

carriage house," I said, aware I wasn't being a good sport, but unable to help it. For a moment, we watched our mother open various doors around the ballroom and peek inside. "By the way—what is *happening* there?"

"Mom has been picking up things. Bringing stuff in from the storage units. It makes her happy, gives her purpose." She met my eyes, which narrowed at the way she was framing the situation. "I've tried, Cassie. I spent years trying. What else do you want me to do?"

"You could've told me that it was getting bad."

"And what would you have done?" She didn't sound accusatory, but within me, I felt the stirrings of defensiveness. Because the answer, if I was brave enough to volunteer it, would probably have been *nothing*.

Maggie, possibly observing this, shot me a warm smile. "Hey, if you want to help, you could always stay in Newport. Only if you wanted! But it's an idea. Would you think about it? Maybe just another few days to pick a venue that we can all be happy with? I know Ocean House is impossible, no matter how much Hope loves it."

"Stay...?" It came out as more a gurgle than a word. After we'd left the Cottage, something changed between my hometown and me. I began to observe the predictable seasonal cycles of Newport as one might a movie that keeps looping. The summer, the influx of people who weren't really from here who acted like their arrival made the place, clogging up First Beach and the road to Sachuest Point, talking about the party the night before and the party the day after, neither of which I was invited to.

Over my sister's shoulder, I eyed the exit sign that had so offended Hope. I fiddled with the back of my shirt, trying to encourage airflow. I was sweaty and squirmy and, Jesus, was our mother really now complaining to the poor Ocean House man about the ceiling texture?

"I know, you have work." Maggie tracked my gaze, then waved her hand between us, clearing her suggestion away. Mouna's words—*You need more time*—rang loudly in my ears; I was surprised she couldn't hear. "And I do, I mean, I'm more than capable of having this covered. I'm checking on Mom and Dad when I can. And Archer lives with them." She nodded several times, as though to convince us both of this. Then: "Just promise something, okay? Check in with me once in a while to make sure I'm not letting the wedding industrial complex grind me down. Because the venue, the lighting, the cake—it's all just scenery. Just smoke and mirrors and invisible wires. What's important is our moment to just be Maggie and Jack. To remember how far we've come from those kids who used to make wishes and throw rocks into the ocean."

"Maggie!" called Hope from a table laid out with binders of pictures of other people's events. "Do you know brides now are matching the table linens to their dress? What a time to be alive!"

Maggie, with an indulgent smile at Hope and a discreet eye roll at me, went over to meet our mother and River at the table of binders, and I was left alone to contemplate our options.

Tonight I could gather my bag, then gather my family, sit them all down, and tell them the truth. That they'd have to find somewhere else to live. That whatever money my parents had earmarked for the wedding—if any—would have to go toward a new future. That there would be no saving face. That my parents' humiliation in the eyes of their children and Newport would be complete. Then I could depart as scheduled, leaving them to deal with the aftermath, and never sleep peacefully again.

But when Hope wrapped her arm around Maggie and said

something in her ear that elicited a laugh, I knew my decision was made. Because I had a mother with Ocean House taste and an airport motel budget, who was about to be evicted. Because I had a sister who asked me to stay, and she so rarely asked me for anything, even though she had every right in the world. And because despite what she'd assumed, I was not going to India for work. I had been *specifically* disinvited.

"Cassie," Hope said. "I just told Maggie that I'm making your favorite meal for your last night."

"Lobster and fries with that spicy ranch from the nice grocery store?" It was out of my mouth before I knew it was in my head.

"No, dummy," responded my mother. "Shepherd's pie."

I inhaled, resigned that my *keep it moving* prayer would go unanswered. I'd spent so much of my teenage years making their lives tougher; now, it was my turn to be there for them. "You can make me mashed potatoes and peas another day," I said. And before anyone could ask what I meant, I announced my plans: "Because I'm here to stay this summer."

My internal clock reset. I had three months.

Ready. Set.

June

8

Go.

"Mom, you ready to get started?" I'd been in Newport a week, and here's what I'd accomplished.

1. Accompanied Maggie and Hope to meetings with three different wedding planners, where Maggie and I learned a tremendous amount about special events, and Hope learned nothing, apparently, because: *Why pay someone to do a job I can do myself?*

2. Argued at length about why Bob Mackie could not and should not design Maggie's bridesmaid dresses.

3. End of list.

But Maggie and I had a plan.

Though we'd reminded her several dozen times, trying to get Hope to actually participate in our plan was, I imagined, like trying to wrangle a raccoon. We chased. We set traps. We dangled carrots, or whatever raccoons ate.

"I don't know why I agreed to this." Hope was slicing the tops off strawberries with an overly large chef's knife and dropping them into a blender that was filled with what looked to be yogurt. "I'm supposed to be at the community garden at noon. The strawberries are ready and you have to pick them right away, Cass."

I tugged at the empty chair next to me. Earlier, I'd removed from the seat a shoebox filled with Hope's collection of vintage Girl Scout merit badges. "You can go after we talk venues." I glanced across the table at my sister, looking for backup, but her eyes were closed, cheek resting in her hand. "You okay?" I asked her.

She murmured her assent. Her voice was low, and while I was only sitting two feet away, I almost missed what she said next: "I haven't been sleeping well. And I'm just—ick."

I also didn't feel particularly rested; Archer snored like a grandpa, there wasn't air-conditioning in the carriage house, and the old carpet and cat triggered my allergies. Above the bunks, the water stain on the bedroom ceiling inched wider, got droopier, and, judging from the gurgling, creaking sounds above it, was becoming sentient. When I walked around the house, my shoulders were hunched, my arms close to my sides to avoid bumping or knocking into something, as though I was trying to make myself smaller to fit. As a result, my neck was almost always aching.

"Family summit?" Archer, yawning though it was past eleven, plodded down the stairs, avoiding the railing, which wobbled, and the newel post at the bottom, which was only still standing because of a broom J.P. had strapped on as a splint. "What about? Why wasn't I invited? Where's coffee? Cass, are you pilfering from my closet again?"

I was indeed drowning in one of Archer's sweatshirts that had passed my sniff test because I hadn't planned for ungovernable Rhode Island weather, nor had I packed to stay for three whole months. I'd tried, in the days following my decision, to imagine a scenario where I could get out sooner. One had not appeared.

"We're meeting about Maggie's *wedding*," I said. I adored my brother, but historically, when discussions had gone off the rails, it had been Archer at the controls. I hoped my emphasis on the word *wedding* would scare him off.

It didn't.

"I have good bedhead today," Archer said, admiring himself in his phone's camera. "Cassie, take some videos of me?" I was handed his device, then he strode over to the window that overlooked the sound, sweeping aside the half-dead herbs on the sill. "Maggie, look alive. All the ballerinas are doing reels now, and you're posting stiff selfies like a geriatric millennial."

Maggie made a sound like *oof*, and lowered her head into her arms.

I watched Archer act out a series of poses that were supposed to approximate candidness: a laughing face, smile broad and white, green eyes sparkling, coffee mug outstretched, then gazing into the distance, lips pouted, followed by a look downward into his drink, modest within his beauty.

This last one finally got me. I lowered the phone. "What is *happening*?"

He was back to his old self, facade dropping. "Don't you follow me on TikTok?" he asked as he motioned for his phone back.

Hope spun on the ball of her foot, her voice an amused singsong, and I swear she sounded proud: "Archer is a thirst trap now!"

Archer did a quick review of what I'd recorded, evaluating. With a disappointed cluck of his tongue, he shook his head at me. "I get why you're not a *video*grapher." He found a Red Sox hat on the whatnot tower and, with a flourish and a flip, tossed the cap through the air and onto his head, where it landed backward and jaunty.

Like Maggie, Archer hadn't gone to college. Unlike Maggie, he hadn't been single-mindedly focused on launching a career, instead bouncing around seasonal jobs, kids surfing instructor for a summer, costumed character actor for a candlelight tour of The Breakers one Christmas, stuff that put money in his pocket while he spun his wheels.

Now, apparently, he was trying out social media influencer for size. I hoped the nasty trolls spared him.

"Mom, will you *please* sit?" I begged. "Maggie isn't feeling well and we need to get this done."

"I know. That's why I'm trying to make her this smoothie with ginger." She jammed several buttons in a row with her thumb. "Why isn't this thing starting? I know it was working last week. Daddy used it to make papier-mâché."

Hoping this would speed things along, I stood and my mother made room for me at the counter. "Maybe because the plug is hanging out," I said, observing how loosely it hung from the socket. But when I reached out to insert it more firmly, I got an electrical shock that had me flying back, yelping and cursing. Hope was unfazed, despite the kitchen filling with a mild burning smell.

"That happens sometimes," Archer commented. "Ice pack in the freezer."

Clutching it in my singed hand, I turned my attention to the electrical socket. It was smoking, ever so slightly. "How old is this wiring?" I asked, absorbing the other appliances clogged around outlets, the thicket of extension cords and adapters. "Do I even want to know?"

"Worry is the thief of joy" was Hope's reply. "That's what Granny always used to say. I'll just blend later." She untied her apron and sat—finally.

But then Archer had to get another sugar packet, and River arrived with toasties from the Aussie coffee shop down Bellevue, and it was another ten minutes before I could begin. "As you all in the family know, I'm staying in Newport until—"

"Not just the family—*everyone* knows," Archer interrupted, schmearing extra pesto onto his bread. "The news that you're staying the summer was on Net-a-Newport's stories on Saturday."

"What are those words?" I asked my brother.

Archer pursed his lips, obviously disappointed in me. "You're not following Net-a-Newport on Instagram?"

"It popped up a year or so ago. It's where people go to get the hot goss," River said, tearing off a piece of cheese, feeding it to a grateful Doug, soft-footing under our chairs. "And information on road closures."

The account was easy enough to locate. I clicked *follow*, then was treated to a series of stories that featured, among other pertinent rumors and news of dinner specials, some tidbits about yours truly.

NET-A-NEWPORT 19H
Submitted via NetaNewport.com
From: anon
Subject: why is she here?

Message: [blocked out] clearly hates Newport. So why is she staying for the summer? If its for an apology tour, it hasn't started yet…

NET-A-NEWPORT 18H
Submitted via NetaNewport.com
From: no thanks
Subject: the girl is back in town

All this talk about [blocked out] is wild. She never said anything that wasn't true and also hilarious. Why do people want her to apologize???

"Isn't this a delightful addition to my life?" I asked, grim. I'd long preferred Newport to forget about me, just like I'd tried to forget about it.

"Who comes up with these Instagram names?" Hope asked. She slurped her coffee out of a mug that said I Don't Need Google, I Have a Wife. "It doesn't even make sense."

"I think that's the point," said Archer.

"Instagram aside," said Maggie, placing her hand on my phone and encouraging us back to real life instead of virtual lookie-loos, "I'm so happy Cass is staying."

"A summer at The Land," agreed River. "What could be more dazzling?" I'd learned over the course of the week that River was from Los Angeles, the son of reality television producers, but had always felt in his soul (his words, not mine) that he belonged on the East Coast. He was a lover of old movies and a collector of vintage hats and had read anything that was ever written about Alva Vanderbilt and Jackie Kennedy.

With The Land's picturesque views of Cliff Walk and panoramas that made you feel as though you owned the sound itself, River wasn't wrong. I couldn't find it in me, though, to return his wide smile.

Hope folded her arms. "I know you're not staying for the ambience. And as glad as I am to have my daughter under my roof again, you might as well tell me why you're staying, and why we are having this meeting."

Maggie and I, across the table from each other, exchanged what was less of a look and more a wordless pep talk. After my announcement at Ocean House, without divulging the full extent of it, I told her that I'd heard what she'd said, about wanting my help with the wedding, with Hope. I did not tell her Susie's promise to dislodge my parents. I'd have to, eventually. But she was the bride and Susie's soon-to-be daughter-in-law; it would be so much cleaner to keep the secret mine alone, for now.

"We know you fell in love with Ocean House, Ma," I started, "but you can't afford it. Neither can Maggie or Jack. Besides, you don't need to spend your money on tents and caviar canapés."

"It's *Maggie's* wedding," Hope countered. "Famous people never pay for anything. The great irony of American capitalism."

"I think you're confusing me with Taylor Swift," said Maggie. She paused. "Listen, Mama, I know you want to contribute, which is very lovely. Jack and I also insist that we put in our own savings, too. That means we need to keep it manageable. I love you, Mama, but Ocean House is off the table."

Maggie had me to back her up; we were two against one, and it would be that much harder for Hope to bend her daughter to her will. Her tight smile remained in place, but I could practically see Hope buck against the wall. "Okay, we can entertain other options. As long as they can accommodate fireworks." She waited a bit, let us sputter and groan. Then: "Joke! I'm joking. Even though the world is ghastly and the very foundations of our democracy are crumbling and we deserve some damn fireworks, Maggie, I will concede."

You'd think this pronouncement would make me happy. It didn't. I noticed River pulling out his laptop. "You and River are in cahoots about something," I said, suspicious. "What is it?"

"I'd asked River last week to identify other venues, in the event you were not enthused about Ocean House," Hope admitted. "Like Castle Hill." River scrolled to the appropriate tab and shared the screen. "They have availability Labor Day. The chef is—"

"Too expensive," I said.

Next: "Rosecliff. Ballroom can only fit one-sixty but I think—"

"Rosecliff?" I was frustrated and letting it show. "We're not in the Gilded Age anymore, Mom."

"The Clambake Club. Your grandfather used to be a member there, and my friend Minnie Flood's oldest son—"

"When Granddad died, they deemed Granny Fi an unsuitable, incorrigible broad and kicked us out," I reminded her. "A Coventry hasn't set foot in the Clambake Club in fifty-some years."

"Fine. I have another idea…"

River clicked.

First for an hour.

Then two.

Every option *I* floated in response to my mother was unceremoniously speared. Chief objections to the venues that wouldn't cause my parents to open up a new line of credit at Newport Savings and Loan were the following: too small, too rustic, too historic—not sure how that was a thing—and, in the instance of an art gallery/event space, Hope declared the color of the walls *too white*.

Eventually, Archer got up from the table. He had better things to do. J.P. came down, collected his toasty, kissed his wife, and busied himself in the family room. A little later, Maggie excused herself to pick up a call from Jack, who'd gone back to the city for meetings with headhunters and lunches with former coworkers and networking happy hours and what-have-yous. From what I could overhear of the start of their conversation, a clear path to another job was proving elusive. Maggie motioned that she would take the rest of the call outside.

River's laptop was running out of battery. I was, too.

Yet Hope's energy for this conversation was undiminished.

"If Daddy and I are paying for the wedding, we have some say in where it is held."

"Maggie and Jack have told you that you don't have to chip in anything."

On the table, my phone vibrated. A news alert from India, Dharamshala, the place Keith was on assignment. *My* assignment. My thumb hovered over the screen. A few seconds, then a few more, and still I didn't click the link. If I did, if I was reminded of what lay beyond the tall green gates of Newport Bridge, I feared I might not see through the summer. I might not make it here another day.

With a slap of the screen door, Maggie returned. Whatever had happened on the call with Jack, she didn't look better for it.

I put my phone to sleep. "This tradition that the bride's family pays for the wedding is antiquated. Patriarchal. Sexist. And silly." I continued working on my mother.

"You all are still fighting about this?" Maggie shoved her hands into her hair. Now, in addition to being pale, she looked as though she might be sick. I rose, then reached out, felt her forehead. I didn't expect a fever, but it was the kind of thing you did when someone was ill. Hope had always done it, and regardless of what she concluded, I, with the sturdy bones and the shoulders of a plow horse, had always been sent to school. Maggie, traditionally, had garnered more sympathy and the occasional sick day. My sister's skin was clammy, but otherwise of normal temperature. After Archer's cancer, I'd tended to view any indication of sickness with dread, immediately fly to worst-case scenarios. I had to consciously remind myself that an upset stomach does not necessarily mean virulent disease.

"If I thought Maggie truly, deep in her soul, in her heart of hearts, wanted to get married at a sterile art gallery," Hope was saying, "I would absolutely be overjoyed to pay for the privilege of looking at paintings made of hair and newspaper clippings. But I don't think she does!"

"Maggie," I said, softly but firmly, hoping to end this. "Tell Mom what you want."

Maggie dragged her hands down her face, then took a dancer's breath from her diaphragm. "I will, but just—give it a moment before you overreact."

Hope clonked her mug down on the table. "Maggie, if you say—"

"The Land." Under her lashes, Maggie looked at us with trepidation.

"Veto," said Hope, unmodulated, unmoved. "*Susie* would commandeer the whole day. It would become hers, not ours."

So much had been lost with the selling of The Land; the wedding, I now understood, was Hope's way of recovering it, at least temporarily. I should've seen the full extent of this truth at Ocean House, but I hadn't wanted to. Why else the single-minded intent on grand venues, on ice sculptures, on welcome parties and raw bars? I wished her identity didn't so much depend on maintaining the illusion of the life she once had.

Yet, I found myself agreeing with Hope's verdict, if not her reasoning. "Bug." I fanned my arms around the carriage house, as though to say, *This place?* "You can't be serious." Holding the wedding at The Land was not my least favorite idea, yet it was awfully close.

"Right," said Maggie, bone dry, "because our home is so embarrassing you had to leave for ten years."

"That's not why I left," I reminded her.

"Fine. Okay," said Maggie. "Let's spend a million dollars to get married at Rosecliff to impress people who are rarely impressed by anything. I'm done for the day. I need to—" she dropped her hands from underneath her breasts to her belt

"—take a walk or take a nap or eat something or not. I don't know. I'll see you guys later."

She retreated back down the hallway, skimming through artifacts. River looked between Hope and me like he was wondering if it was safe to breathe.

"Okay, let's call the gallery," said Hope after a moment, rising from her chair, jumbling around the kitchen counter, lifting, brushing things aside, ostensibly searching for her phone. "If she can be happy with a backup option, fine. Just anywhere but The Land."

I wondered if one p.m. was too early to propose River and I go for a drink. Two hours of wedding planning, and I was already dreaming of gin. Instead, I did what I *should*, rather than what I wanted: "I'm going to go after Maggie. If anyone else would like to join me, I'll meet you outside. I'll be the one questioning every life choice she's ever made."

9

Rough Point was calm. The gray mist following the morning's rain had lifted, and though the sky wasn't blue, nor the temperature warm, I was fine and dry in Archer's sweatshirt.

Actually, *fine* wasn't the right word.

Twenty minutes earlier, I'd left the carriage house, thinking I'd track Maggie down in the Cottage. But she wasn't in her room, or the basement dance studio Susie had installed for her, or the kitchen or the pool, and she wasn't responding to my texts. I walked up the allée, wondering if she might be elsewhere on the grounds, but when I couldn't spot her, I trailed the tourist trolleys down the Avenue to kill time and burn off nervous energy. A little farther, and she still hadn't texted back, so I strolled past the park, to the low stone wall of the classic cedar-shake-shingled estate where Granny's Fi's friends—the ones she played spades with each Friday—lived before they died and their heirs turned it into a seasonal rental with staff for fifty grand a week.

I finally had to stop where the Avenue took a hard curve west, just across the entrance to Rough Point, to dislodge a pebble from the bottom of my shoe. This was the spot, the stories went, where the lady of the house, Doris Duke, flattened her close friend and near constant companion under the axles of his station wagon in a jealous rage. We'd never met her—she'd died when we were young, but Hope had stories about one of her staff dropping off giant gift baskets of blankets and camel stuffies and toys and teethers after my and Maggie's births.

A temporary, bifold sign in the middle of the driveway contradicted Rough Point's posted hours: Closed, it said, For a Private Event. A young woman in the brown shingled ticket booth looked up from her phone only to inquire if I was *here for the party?*

Yes, I told her, and it wasn't exactly a lie. Newport in the summer was one giant party, anyway.

Down the circular driveway, past the gothic, grand English manor, on the far side of the back lawn overlooking the ocean, was a circular tent, white, with snappy nautical flags flying from the two peaks. I ignored it, hurrying to where the Cliff Walk became a stone bridge, and one could clamber straight out into the frothy shallows of the sound, and sat, smelling the damp grass and the brine, the minerality lifting off the craggy stones.

I'd once considered Rough Point a part of my home, in the way all of Newport was. Piddly signs, property lines, boundaries, had meant nothing to the Coventry-Gilford children. Before the house became a museum, we'd scrabbled around the volcanic rocks and low-branched pines, making no effort to hide ourselves. Getting a glimpse of Ms. Duke's two huge camels, who were named Princess and Diamond or something along those lines, had always filled us with madcap excitement.

There'd been dares, naturally, to see who could get the clos-est before either we or the animals were spooked.

I hadn't thought about those camels in years, and the mem-ory made me smile. Those were the wild-haired, barefoot be-fore days. The wild strawberry sweet ones. Before everything went to shit and stayed there.

I heard someone approach from behind. The pace of foot-steps was not a casual stroll; clearly, they were coming for me. I stood, dusted the bottom of my jeans, and ground out: "I'm just leaving."

But when I turned away from the water, I didn't see a Rough Point security guard, or an enraged host, but the smil-ing, curious face of Spencer Sims. "Too bad," he said. "I was going to invite you inside the tent."

He must've noted that his presence had rendered me speech-less, for his smile got broader. "It's the one-year anniversary of The Bonnie. We're having a party."

"The Bonnie?" I blurted. "Like your mom, Bonnie?"

"My restaurant. We opened last summer. Took the space over when Trudy finally retired. You remember Trudy's with the amazing bouillabaisse on Bannister's Wharf?" He was try-ing to throw me some lifelines. "We had a big party at The Land to celebrate? I know Maggie and Jack invited you…"

This much was clear: I needed to start opening emails. "That's incredible. Congrats, Spencer." Over his shoulder, I took my first good look at the tent and its occupants. A four-piece band was on a dais, the dance floor below full. Around the edges were long tables draped in white, topped with silver buffet-style trays. And flowers, white hydrangeas and peonies so big I could see them from here. "And I'm totally invading your space. I just had to get out of the house for a second. And I was trying to find a place to—" I pulled a face, embarrassed already by what I was about to say "—brood."

"Do you want to brood with a cocktail?" Spencer's hands went into his pockets, and he rolled forward on the balls of his feet. He was dressed in the colors of summer, but with a twist, an oxford-blue short-sleeve button-down and hunter-green linen joggers. "You're welcome to join."

Quickly, I shook my head. "Thank you, but I can't. I'm not dressed." A valid excuse in Newport. I also wasn't wearing makeup, and that morning I'd gotten a chin pimple. "I'll evacuate the premises momentarily."

"Don't you dare," he said and, without waiting for my reply, went back toward the tent.

I blew out a breath once he was gone, ran my hands through my windblown hair, walked a slow circle on the grass.

It was not just our romantic history that had me flustered, but the way our roles had been reversed. When we'd first met, I'd been the one to show him around, take him to the secret spots, the places I called mine. But now Spencer was a business owner, a true Newporter, and I the girl trespassing onto his party. Spencer had even been married in Newport, at Gurney's. From what I could glean from the few social media posts I'd managed to choke down (I was invited, but did not attend), the event had been simple, classic, the Goat Island Lighthouse a perfect backdrop for the wedding party dressed in navy.

Men in tailored blue suits is such a crisp look, Hope had said yesterday as we scrolled through Maggie's Pinterest board. I wondered if my mother had been thinking of Spencer's groomsmen.

Spencer returned with a white ramekin bowl and a spoon. I accepted, gratefully, and dug in before we even sat down. Know this about me: it is rare that I refuse dessert when it is presented.

"Happy anniversary," I said, licking a glob of bread pudding off the back of my spoon.

Spencer closed his eyes against the sun, and extended his long legs out toward me. "I didn't think we'd make it this far, honestly. Longest two years of my life."

"Go on," I said as I dragged the spoon around the rim of the bowl.

Spencer smiled slowly. "We were actually supposed to start renovations three years ago. But, you know, with that *tiny* disruption that hit the world—"

"Oh, that little guy—"

"Exactly," he said. "That *little* guy. Anyway, we got through that. But these historic properties require *so* much money. Pipes that you thought were fine are one big flush away from bursting. Mold. Rust. Water damage. In Newport, it's *always* something with water." He stared at the gauzy blue line of the horizon across the sound, and dragged a knee up to his chin. "And as we were building out, I managed to get myself divorced."

That explained some things. "How fun," I said, which made him blush. I had a dozen more questions, beginning with *Why?* Yet I held my tongue, betting that this type of prying was not allowed for two old lovers just getting reacquainted.

"And *then*," he continued, "my mother passed."

I rested the spoon in the bowl. I'd been in Stockholm covering climate protests, I believe, when that news had reached me via an email from Maggie. That email I'd opened. "I was only lucky enough to meet Bonnie a few times during the summers you were here. But even I could tell she was a force."

"Thank you," he said. "And I did appreciate you reaching out when it happened." Spencer paused, picked at some blades of grass beside the rocks. "My mom was the one who told me to go for it, encouraged me to just pull the trigger and go to the Culinary Institute of America. My dad really wanted me to stay at Brown, get my master's. But my mom did what wonderful mothers do. I wish she got to see this."

My first instinct was to console with tired platitudes: *She is seeing this! She's with you, even when she's not!* But Granny Fi's death taught me how flimsy those words could be against the monstrous, unpredictable gale that we too simply label "grief." I wasn't sure what I had to offer was any better, but still I tried. "It sucks that she couldn't. Because, Spencer, what you've built here, your community—" I gestured to the tent, the wine-in-the-afternoon revelry within it "—it's clearly very special."

He chuckled, then angled his head, directed a pondering expression my way. "Wow, I just really unloaded on you, didn't I? Sorry about that."

"Don't apologize." My problems had not vanished, certainly, but his voice, his company, had a way of shushing them. And though I knew the reprieve would only be temporary, like this bowl of bread pudding, I intended to enjoy it. "We've got a few years to catch up on."

"We do. So, tell me—why are you here? I mean, glad you are, but Jack said you were headed off on assignment last week?"

His question, while well-meaning, was like taking a Razor scooter to the ankle. "I'm taking the summer off," I said, choking back my pain and stuffing more pudding into my mouth, sweet and gooey with notes of caramel and coffee—a tasty muscle relaxer. It helped.

"In the movies, 'time off' is code. You're running from something!" Spencer snapped his fingers. "A man who wronged you. Or a big mistake you're trying to hide."

I laughed so I wouldn't cry, because what else was there to do when someone just sliced right through the nonsense? "It's much more banal than that, I'm afraid." Spencer raised his eyebrows, waiting. "Mainly family. Maggie's got a lot on her plate with training, and Jack, and the wedding." *And my editor has put me in time-out.* "Hope wants to have everything, do the most, make the biggest. And it's hard for her to understand limits. The fuss that Hope is making about the venue— well, you'd think she was picking a place to spend her eternal afterlife rather than a place to hang out for five hours and eat overcooked beef."

"Is that why we're brooding?" asked Spencer.

"You got it."

We were silent for a moment, me playing with my spoon, him drumming his long fingers on his forearm, just below the trio of birds in flight tattooed on the inside of his wrist. "I'm kind of surprised they haven't picked a venue," he said. "I always thought they'd get married where they met. The Land."

"Maggie wants to." I sighed. "The idea is simpler than the execution." This was only part of the reason for my reservations, though he could probably deduce the rest.

As I'd shared with him years ago, leaving the Cottage had been a shameful experience, though I would've never admitted it back then. And instead of our loss being private, it had been on the local news. How pitiful, they'd said. The Land— sold to a stranger from Boston. How *humiliating*.

He nodded, grasping a loose stone and tossing it from one hand to another. "You'd have to deal with Susie."

"And my mother. She's worried that hosting the wedding at The Land would be an invitation for Susie to hijack it."

One more bounce of the pebble in his palm, and with an easy swing of his arm, he released it to the water, where it skidded once over a wave before dropping out of sight. "As much as my aunt loves to think she owns every last inch—" he looked where the shore curved, an elegant sweep of cursive, a trail of dark ink "—I still hear Newporters refer to it as the Coventry Place. And don't they call your grandmother's prolific sculpting years The Land period? Your mother was raised there. You grew up there, you know the shortcuts and the back routes and where all the treasure is buried. No one can undermine that legacy without your expressed permission, Susu included," he said. "And, not for nothing, The Land is free!"

Free. Why that fact hadn't occurred to me yet, I couldn't say. There would be obstacles having the wedding where Maggie wanted it—namely Susie and Hope. But I was trying to distance myself from the person I'd been after we'd lost The Land. Gone were the days of my frustrated raging. Gone like every breath we'd exhaled into the Cottage, every scream that had rattled the windows, every tear and bead of sweat that had been absorbed by the floors. I was responsible now, mostly. Some might find me notable, even, if you lowered the bar on the definition. And what had Spencer called me at the engagement party? *Fearless.* "Gosh, Spencer. I know people say that you're just a pretty face, and that you don't have two brain cells to rub together—" I paused so we could have a quick giggle "—but I'll be the first one to say they're *wrong.*"

"Now that you're staying in Newport for a minute," he said, "you can help clear up that rumor." Maybe it was because we were together, alone, for the first time in many, many years, but it sank in that this summer could mean more time in each other's company. If I wanted it to. If he did.

From behind us, Spencer's name was called. A statuesque redhead, mermaid hair in loose curls, bronzed skin, waved him back to the tent. He raised his arm, acknowledged his summons. Our interlude was over.

"Thanks," I said as I took the hand Spencer offered, and he helped lift me to standing. I breathed deep, tasting sweet salt and sour memories. It would be another perfect Rhode

Island night, once the sun went down. A cool brine, light jacket, sleep-with-the-windows-open kind of night. "This bread pudding has turned my tide. I am no longer in angst."

"Also," he said, adjusting the tuck of his shirt at his waist, "my *pâtissière* does wedding cakes as a side hustle. She's amazing. I'll text you her info." He reached for my empty ramekin.

"Do you still have my number?" I asked him.

He stopped for a moment and looked at me seriously. "Like I could ever delete you, Cass."

10

It wasn't summer in Newport.

The weather had backtracked us into early spring, and as Kent escorted Jack, Maggie, Spencer, and me to the Cottage's grand library, with its coffered ceiling, rich wood trim, cherry-red accents, the heavy gloom outside suggested we wouldn't see the sun all day.

Soon after my conversation with Spencer, I'd found Maggie and apologized, borrowing his words about The Land's uniqueness and what it meant to all of us. Our priority, Maggie and I agreed, was getting Hope to approve a wedding here. But after days passed and we were unable to pin her down, we decided on another tactic. And we'd called in reinforcements.

Susie, in jeans and a gray T-shirt, waited primly on the deep-seated leather couch facing the door. When we entered, she looked up, and the spoon stirring her tea stilled in the cup. Her snow-white poof ball dogs—Charlie and Monsieur, though I didn't know which was which—jumped up from their cushy platform bed and made a ruckus around our feet.

"Mom." Jack was back from the city, looking a little worse for wear. "We were hoping you had a second to discuss the wedding?" His dark circles were pronounced; on the way over to the Cottage, I'd caught him yawning. He was in the process of attempting a beard, but it was really a collection of patchy, scraggly hairs growing in at such unkempt angles, the overall impression was that it was about to flee his own face.

Susie was my family's landlord, but also our benefactor, thanks to the deal she'd made my parents all those years ago. As a teenager, every time a repair needed to be made, or an appliance required replacement, one of us—whoever drew the short straw—would have to slink over to the Cottage, ask for help, and feel—in the silence before she said *yes, of course*—that insidious power of wealth exerting itself. I felt it now, even though we hadn't yet asked her for anything. The gravity, you understand. The pressure.

Susie dunked her tea bag once, twice, in the cup. "Get in line," she said, before her eyes flicked to the far side of the library, to—*surprise*—Hope, leaning nonchalantly on an antique table with legs shaped like dragons.

"It's a party," said Hope, sipping on her own mug of creamy coffee.

"What are you doing here?" I asked, wary. Half a minute into our plan to convince Susie to host the wedding at The Land, and already it was in danger of being thwarted. *Oh, God, and what had they even been talking about? The wedding? Or the eviction? Did Susie tell Hope I'd been keeping a secret from her?*

Hope shrugged. "Just talking."

"About what?" Maggie was also suspicious.

"Jack, honey," said Susie. "You look exhausted. Why don't

you all come sit down." She pointed to the matching couch opposite her.

Hope stayed where she was; the rest of the group shuffled forward, cautiously, as though afraid to make any sudden movements. "Spencer and I were up way too late drinking scotch and talking old times," said Jack, taking a seat first.

"Old times and good times," said Spencer. He was in all black today, hoodie to wool sneakers, and he also had the drowsy, heavy-lidded eyes of someone who hadn't gotten enough sleep. He lowered himself on the sofa's arm next to his cousin, Maggie and I on Jack's other side.

Susie scoffed. It was quiet, but we caught it. "I'm the only one in his family, apparently, who thinks you should be burning the midnight oil at *an office*. To quit a job right before you take a wife…"

Maggie reached for Jack's hand.

"Susu," Spencer said, and her name came out as a word of advice, of counsel.

"I know," she huffed.

I pulled up the sleeves on my knobby half-zip fleece, though they immediately slid down past my fingers again. Before he'd returned to Newport, Jack generously went to my apartment and gathered clothes and equipment to last me through the summer. This was the wrong outfit to have chosen for this meeting, but because my instructions to Jack had been *just pack what looks useful*, my wardrobe options weren't expansive.

"Susie." I picked up where Jack left off, leaning forward, putting my mother out of my range of vision. Maybe we could still salvage this. "We'd like to—"

"What do you all think?" Susie had turned her head, her gaze above the fireplace on a richly colored oil painting I hadn't noticed before. "My new work. I think it looks nice there."

Susie, an amateur artist herself, had transformed the greenhouse on the far end of the property into a painter's studio. Part of the reason she loved The Land, the story went, was because it had produced the likes of Fiona Coventry-Devries. Initially, Susie painted watercolor hydrangeas in vases, then went through a pastel phase, and now—judging from the broad canvas high above us—she had moved on to a trompel'oeil style of still life, rendering in meticulous verisimilitude a man's blue suit floating against a weathered tallboy dresser, with a rolled orange tie in the space above the jacket shoulder.

"Jack's father's Armani," Susie said with just a trace of acid. "I finally found a use for it."

Yes—the empty suit, remaining long past the owner was around to fill it. I'm not a psychologist, and I didn't know much about Susie's ex-husband, just the snippets Jack and Spencer had shared, but one didn't have to search hard to see the metaphor. "Time," I said. "Loss. The kinds of things that endure."

"Thank you, Cassie," said Susie happily. "Exactly what I was going for."

"Where do you see all that?" asked Hope, quibbling with my interpretation. "To me it looks like some poor guy just got raptured."

"Well, one needs an understanding of art, I suppose," said Susie.

"I love the spot you chose," chirped Maggie as her mother glared at her future mother-in-law. "Don't you, Jack?"

Jack's neutral expression did not suggest he did. But because he was the good son, he said, "You bet."

"I've sold a few." Susie turned back to face us and picked up—oh, let's say Monsieur. "Women like to gift them to their husbands."

"The Bonnie needs some art, Susu," said Spencer. "Let's discuss. In the meantime, back to what Cass was saying…"

"She doesn't have to explain." Hope trained her sights on me. "My children are here to go over my head."

I nearly laughed. You had to admire her chutzpah. "If this is a game of leapfrog, Mom, you're winning."

"Ribbit, ribbit," she said before taking another sip from her mug.

"While it is always nice to see everyone's faces," Susie said as she ran her fingers through Monsieur's fur, then her own hair, lifting her sweep of bangs off her forehead, "like so many meetings that exist, this could've been an email. Hope, though you eloquently outlined the burdens of hosting a wedding at The Land before the kids arrived, you forget that I've thrown many parties here over the years, including the engagement party last week. I'm well aware about what goes into the arrangements. I understand that my grass will be trampled and my good liquor pilfered."

"I haven't forgotten," countered Hope. "This would be a bigger scale, though, than anything you've hosted."

Spencer sucked in a breath. Maggie chuckled nervously.

"All right," I said. I pumped my hand like a break, de-escalating before everyone was yelling and Susie changed her mind and kicked my mother off The Land right this minute. "Mom, let's try and keep this in perspective. We're not planning the Oscars. No one is handing out lifetime achievement awards."

"I have my lifetime achievement," Jack joked, squeezing his fiancée's hand. But no one laughed. It's hard to buy into the punch line when the comic is clearly stressed.

Susie rose, crossed to the immense fireplace, bare and swept for the summer. "You four." She rested her drink on the limestone mantel and crossed her arms. "You want the wedding here, clearly. Yet Hope does not." Jack followed her, and with two fingers moved the cup back from the edge so it wasn't so precariously perched. "Are you willing to go ahead, knowing she will be gravely disappointed?"

All occupants of the room looked at Maggie. But my sister's eyes were fixed on me.

I lifted myself from the couch and joined my mother where she stood at the table. "We assure you that you will be involved in every step of the process," I told her gently. "You'll still be the mother of the bride." I lowered my voice. "The Land is a venue *you* wouldn't have to pay for. Maggie and Jack want to give you this *gift*."

I realized too late this was not the wisest thing to say. "A gift, Cassie? To whom?" Hope's hand flicked to Susie.

"We love you, Mama," added Maggie helpfully. "And, really, if you're not okay with having the wedding here, we won't do it. Right, Jack?"

This time Jack was honest. "Yes, Hope, one hundred percent."

"Because for what it's worth—" I paused, let the moment build "—you're worth more to us than this *one* day."

Hope took a few beats. Her eyes moved between her children, Spencer, and Susie. Then, two words, said pleasantly, like this had been her plan all along: "Of course."

We all turned to Susie. "Make their dreams come true, Susu," said Spencer.

Susie nodded, and the room exhaled. I closed my eyes in relief. Clapping. Exchanges of plans, beginnings of to-do lists. Hope saying, *Of course I would never deny you this, my dearest daughter.* Promises to discuss more. Spencer was escorting Hope and me out of the library.

"Thank you," I murmured to Spencer. He winked.

Meeting was adjourned. Except—

"Hang back for me, Cass?" Susie asked once we were out in the hall.

The Cottage's front door closed behind the group, and I was alone again with Susie, feeling relief as well as dread. I studied the hall, the spotless floors, the gleaming banister. Everything was so nice. The red carpet runner up the stairs looked like it had never seen a shoe. The chandelier, immaculate. Long ago, Granny Fi had sent me up on a twenty-five-foot ladder with two scraps of old flannel to dust that thing. To an eight-year-old, it was a monstrous chore. It seemed there were an infinite number of brass arms, candles and their bulbs, dangling crystal prisms. I wondered who on Susie's staff was tasked with dusting it now.

"Forgive me if I'm wrong," Susie began, still cradling her dog, "but no indication was given to me today that you've told your parents about their lease being ended."

No one can wield the passive voice like a rich white woman.

"They have not been informed," I confirmed, because if you can't beat 'em, join 'em. "I'm waiting for the right time. For now, I ask that you keep this issue between us."

Susie drummed her fingers on the dog's belly. "I think you're a little afraid of your mother."

I raised my eyebrows. "I think you are, too."

From the library, a clock chimed the top of the hour, ten soft tings, the gold hands quivering. Charlie, still in his bed— looked to be memory foam—didn't lift his head from where it was curled in his stomach.

I wondered if I'd gone too far, if I'd been too honest. I had many years of being The Land's undisciplined stepdaughter to make up for.

"Eh," Susie finally said with a trace of amusement, "you're not wrong. Listen, I've agreed to open up my property for the wedding. But Jack is my child as much as Maggie is hers, and as such, I want to be involved in the planning. I want to be consulted. And not just the logistics, like where we will park the cars. I want to be included in the fun parts. Tastings. Fittings. Flowers. Escort cards. You understand? I have one child, one chance to do this."

Susie didn't utter the words *quid pro quo*, but I heard them, anyway. Did *she* understand, though, what she was getting into? What she was getting *all* of us into? Forced to work together, how long would Susie and Hope be able to behave? "This is going to mean a lot of time with my mom," I cautioned.

In Susie's arms, Monsieur eyed me. The fur around his tear ducts was stained brown. "Are you implying that I'm going to regret this arrangement?"

"I'll make sure Hope honors your inclusion," I said quickly, knowing I had to try, knowing I needed the time and space to make sure the summer didn't end with Hope burning The Land to the ground behind her. "Besides, I've decided to stay with my parents." I revealed this with pep, like it was good news for both of us. "I'll be here the whole time to mediate."

Susie cocked her head. "Cass. I'm surprised by this. By you. Aren't you supposed to hate this place?" she asked. "Or was that all an act?"

I miss it, I'd said to Maggie, the last night we spent in the Cottage, together. We were supposed to have been gone. Susie's movers were coming the next day, and the last of our possessions had been hauled out through the service entrance, but our new bedroom was strange, filled with shadows and creaks. There were sounds from the lower floor that made us jumpy. So we'd taken as many blankets as we could hold, and two flashlights, and crept back to the Cottage, to this vast hall, occupied with familiar echoes and us, jammed together on the floor, quilts pulled over our heads, our own sacred fort. *I'm still here and I already miss it.*

I don't think I'd meant the Cottage, necessarily. I meant my life as I knew it—the magic of my childhood turned to dust and memory.

"No," I said to Susie, "that was no act."

I don't think she'd expected me to respond, because she blinked a few times, then turned away. "Let me know what our first activity is," she called, breezy. "I'll be there with bells and whistles." Back in the library, she sat in front of her computer, Monsieur arranged on her lap.

11

Here's what I was learning about weddings: when one thing
was crossed off a list, two more appeared in its place. Planning was a productivity hydra.

As Maggie, Hope, and I waited at The Bonnie's hostess stand,
I found myself strangely nervous. And not just because we were
going to cut cake with Hope and Susie at the same table.

"All right, be honest," I said to my sister, taking a step back and letting her inspect me. "Do I look okay? Or do I look like the sellout I am?"

Maggie glanced down at my deep purple shirtdress. Rarely did I wear it in the city, never abroad, but Jack had thrown it in a suitcase with the dozen variations of my normal uniform of toothpick jeans, wide-leg cotton pants, fitted T-shirts in pale colors, and Veja sneakers. When I fished it out that morning I thought, *Sure, let's pop a collar today.*

Less than a one month I'd been at The Land, and already my individuality was giving way to the strong tide of this place.

"Ten out of ten," Maggie said.

"You look stunning in jewel tones!" Hope agreed. "Only took you sixteen years to realize it." I was reminded of Maggie and me as reluctant teenagers, dragged to the salon, where a very serious woman with lots of scarves held a paint deck up to our cheeks and argued with our mother about whether Maggie was a light spring or light summer.

The Bonnie was near the end of the wharf, housed in an industrial, two-story metal-paneled building that was, in all likelihood, a former warehouse. There'd been rain that morning, and now a fine mist steamed off the bricks, and the water shimmered and lazed against the docks. I'd always been partial to Newport in a summer thunderstorm, overflowing the copper gutters on the Cottage, the fresh smell of grass and soil, the sea the same color as the sky. The storms here didn't startle me like they did in New York City, where I hardly ever looked up from the pavement or my phone, where I'd just pop into a Duane Reade for some gummy bears and toothpaste in the sunshine, then come out four minutes later in a downpour. In Newport I heeded the warning. I could see the clouds gathering in the distance over the sound and knew which way they were headed.

There was quite a line to get in The Bonnie—happy hour

clientele ranged from old salts, tan and windblown, fresh off the sailboat, to pretty young things, pearled, blown-out, ready to influence. I looked around the dockside patio, the clusters of deep-cushioned sofas around gas fire pits occupied by college students in very short skirts, unshaven surfers in beanies, families with squirming, smudgy-faced babies, officers—maybe navy or coast guard—with haircuts high and tight, couples speaking German and French and taking pictures of nearly everything.

Knowing that this was Spencer's restaurant, I'd put on some makeup. Some volumizing product in my fine hair, which I'd let grow just a touch too long. I even considered per-fume, but—*after* giving myself a spritz—I discovered that it had turned to alcohol, having languished for years in my cos-metics case.

The truth was, since he'd helped with the Susie/Hope venue diplomacy, I'd been thinking about him. I'd even peeked at The Bonnie's website, assuring myself this was just the be-nign, human *what are they up to now* interest born of nostalgia and made possible by Google. Part Bajan, part traditional New England, the restaurant was an homage to both his parents' culinary traditions. The menu placed selections like breadfruit next to lobster, and fried cod with cou cou, which I under-stood to be like grits. Though it felt like spying, I'd snooped about, clicking on pictures, the dessert and wine list, the res-taurant's contact info, searching for traces of—what? What my life would've involved had we made different choices?

From inside the restaurant came Chef Tien, wiping her hands on a linen towel; she was taller than all of us, even me, which is saying something, and leaner than Maggie, which is rarer still, with black hair pulled off her gorgeous, makeup-free face into a low bun and a white chef's coat with the sleeves rolled neatly to her elbows. Beckoning us to follow, she was polite but all business as she led us to a rectangular high-top that was technically inside, but because of a well-placed open garage door, gave the sensation of dining al fresco. She invited us—ordered us?—to sit.

"Did you choose this pastry chef because she is actually good," Hope whispered to Maggie once she was gone. "Or did you choose her to throw Cassie into the path of a certain young man?"

"Spencer is a *friend*," I reminded the table, adjusting myself on my stool.

"A single friend," Maggie said with a smirk. "And he told Jack he is *ready* to mingle." In the past, Maggie had been the most ardent fan of the Spencer/Cass romance, and it seemed time had not weakened her delight in having us in the same city again. "Just lobbing that information out there."

When we'd first gotten together romantically after a handful of platonic summers, many in our friend group had been widely flummoxed as to why, out of all the co-eds who launched themselves at him, Spencer had opened his arms to me. I understood their confusion—he was handsome, accomplished, had limitless potential without any of the telltale markings (entitlement, drunkenness, toxic masculinity) that he would squander it. And I'd been, well, *me*. According to Newport, I should've been thanking my lucky stars that Spencer Sims would deign to kiss me tenderly. In fact, Hope had even told me so. I got the impression, judging from the expression on her face, that she was fixing to tell me so again.

"I can't wait to see Cassie flirt." Hope was dramatically wiggling her eyebrows. "It's like watching a dog try to walk in socks."

"Give her a little credit," said Maggie. "She got Spencer once, I'm sure she can do it again. And she doesn't have that weird manic pixie haircut anymore."

As Hope debated with Maggie whether it was appropriate to order a bottle of champagne at a cake tasting, I took the opportunity to absorb our surroundings. The Bonnie's decor was approachable, polished—dark woods, broken-in leather, touches of cane in the banquettes in the back. Hanging plants of various sizes, palms and ferns and ivy. And candlelight, sconces and votives. It was, for a lack of a better word, *cool*, and represented an evolving Newport. I felt a little thrill that I knew one of the owners.

From our table, I had a clear view of the open kitchen at the center of the room, though none of the people in toques were Spencer. I pulled my phone from my bag next to me on the banquette and considered texting him.

Just then Susie's voice crashed into the restaurant like a tidal wave. "I called here last week and the gal said you don't take reservations." She was marching over with a server in blue checked gingham. "I assured her that can't be right."

"Please," Maggie said through her teeth to Hope, pleading, her hands in prayer, "please, *please*, be nice." When I'd informed Maggie about Susie's request to be included in wedding activities, my sister, at the time, had been more optimistic than I that the moms could get along, lured by Hope's promises to be on her best behavior. Now came the test.

"I will," Hope sniffed. "Daddy already gave me a lecture about it this morning."

"We don't take reservations," explained the server to Susie, pulling out a stool. "Unfortunately."

"You could always call ahead and give your name, Susie," said Maggie, placating. "If Spencer knew you were coming—"

"Are you suggesting I pull the *Do you know who I am* card?" Susie asked as she thunked down her monogramed tote, making the silverware clatter.

Across the table, my eyes found Hope's; hers were already

on me, like she was waiting. We exchanged a small, I'm talking *tiny*, half smile. Because while her tone suggested she
was revolted by the do-you-know-who-I-am card, everyone
who had ears had heard her play it. The subtle clearing of
the throat, the ask that staff use the side door, the arch of an
eyebrow, all had the same effect as a bulldozer when it came
to asserting her privilege. Though she earnestly and often
brought up her humble, working-class roots in New Jersey,
she, like many wealthy people, reflected the paradox of the
one percent: though they insisted their staff and employees
were family, they consistently, through their votes, advocacy,
and concerns with things like dividends and shareholder val-
ues, and tables for dinner when required, demonstrated their
desire to keep classes segregated.

And, of course, there was this: though Spencer spent many
summers at The Land, Susie never once sent Jack to spend
holidays with his cousin on Ditmas Avenue. Spencer's mother
and Susie's sister, Bonnie, was a professor and community
organizer, and Spencer's father, Anton, was a lawyer for the
NAACP. But wealth causes myopia; opportunity was in Newport, the thinking went, so why risk Jack going to such a dan-
gerously progressive place like—*shudder*—Brooklyn?

"Anyway, I'm so sorry I'm late," Susie said to us. "Some guy
stole the parking spot I was waiting for and it needed to be
addressed." She leaned over, gave Maggie a kiss on the cheek.

"These drivers! Did you give him a piece of your mind?"
Hope was overly friendly, almost treacly, but I'd take it.

"I said that he could swing his fancy Tesla around all he
wanted, but it wouldn't make his momma love him." Susie
sipped from her glass of water.

We made *ooooh* sounds. "Tell 'em, Susie," I said.

"My smart mouth is rubbing off on you," Hope observed.
There was admiration in her voice, scant, but it was there.

Susie paused, considered. Then: "I guess it has."

I slid my phone back into my bag. "This calls for champagne. Four glasses?" I asked the very patient server.

"Three," said Maggie. "I'll have a Coke, please." After her order was placed, she saw Hope and my expressions. "What?" She shrugged.

"I've just never seen you order a soda before," I said. "Regular or otherwise. I like it. Summer of Maggie."

"Where is Jack?" Susie sprayed sanitizer on her palms from a small glass bottle. "I thought he was coming."

I had wondered the same. Though he wasn't working, Jack had been absent from most of the wedding planning. I didn't expect him at *all* of the appointments, but at least at more than one or two.

"He went back to the city this morning." Maggie turned over her menu. "Taking meetings."

"I'll speak to him," said Susie. "We're long past the age when weddings are left to the womenfolk."

"I agree," said Hope.

Maggie's eyes flicked back and forth, and I wondered if she was scared of disturbing whatever spell had fallen over these two women.

A server arrived with flutes and a bottle of chilled cava, followed shortly by Chef Tien, arms laden with small plates of perfectly round cakes, and concise descriptions of each flavor.

I'd barely gotten my first bite of kiwi pistachio into my mouth when Susie let out a sound that was part wail, part laugh. "Oh, will you look at this." We followed her gaze out the window to a bachelorette party in matching pink T-shirts crossing the wharf, tottering and swaying and trying very hard not to roll their heels on the cobbles. I wondered where they were headed; the bride, sashed, tiara-ed, looked very, very young and, though it was only four p.m., quite tipsy.

"Hey! Girls!" Hope hollered, waving the hand that wasn't

occupied with her drink. "Where'd you get those penis crowns?" Those in chairs near us spun around to gauge why the mature ladies at our table were bringing up male anatomy.

"Mom," cautioned Maggie. "Good grief." Her hand was cupped over her forehead.

"We should do matching T-shirts for your bachelorette party, Maggie," said Hope. "Cass, go outside and ask where they got them."

I licked a shmear of buttercream off the back of my spoon. "Pass."

"There will be no bachelorette parties for me, Mama," said Maggie.

"What?" Hope protested as the bachelorettes disappeared from our view. "What are your bridesmaids going to do for you, then? Host a boring brunch?"

"I'm not having bridesmaids, Mama," said Maggie.

Now it was Susie's turn to be shocked. "What do you mean, no bridesmaids?"

"I had this thought that the whole wedding could kind of be our bridal party," said Maggie softly. "All the guests could wear white."

Although I hadn't devoted too much time to thinking about my sister's bridal party, I'd assumed she would have one, and that I would be her maid of honor. Don't get me wrong—I wasn't sad to skip the itchy chiffon and the oversprayed updos, but—

Hope looked at Susie. "My daughter has lost her mind."

"Oh, dear," said Susie. "We have to help her find it."

"Congratulations, Maggie." I smiled ruefully at my sister. "You've already gotten the mamas to agree twice in one day."

·····

The dessert tasting had been absolutely marvelous, and we'd told Chef Tien so, heaping enough praise on her that she had to bat it away. On her Instagram, she'd pointed us to the design Maggie had deemed *perfect, just what she wanted*: an edible sculpture, really, three asymmetric layers, ombre evergreen, with sugar flowers outrageously true-to-life, ascending to the top, then seemingly growing upward, leaves like wings, taking flight. Verdant, elegant, and spectacular. Though all the flavor options presented to us in petite square samples were to die for, Maggie ultimately decided on chocolate, with notes of hazelnut and Vietnamese cinnamon and a delightful cappuccino frosting that was as light as froth and perfectly sweet. "If you're staying the summer," Susie was saying to me, "you might as well come with us to the Flower Show." Embedded in her words was the kind of pretentious, upper-class shorthand I wouldn't have noticed until I lived outside of Newport.

Maggie and I exchanged amused glances. "One *must* go to the Flower Show," I teased.

Susie laughed. "All right. I hear myself," she said. The cava had gotten us loose; it was one of the better ideas Hope had ever had.

"What I really need to do," I said, "is get a job." Only a trickle of royalties was coming in from my archive sales, and with two more months in Newport, I knew my bank account would need it. I also didn't fancy idleness; it made my eye unfocused.

"Maybe you can photograph the event," Maggie offered, though she was peering at me like she expected me to slap this option out of the sky.

It wasn't that the Flower Show would be beneath me— regardless of their subjects, most photographers are deeply empathetic artists who believe in their work and their roles as curators and catalogers of time. No, the problem was not entirely existential. "Mouna," I explained, "isn't going to buy pictures of socialites smiling next to orchids." I dragged the plate with the vanilla sour cream cake with lavender icing over to me, despite Hope's whining that she *wasn't done with that one yet.*

Were there any newsworthy happenings around Rhode Island? Surely, but not enough to spark interest from my editor. Would the *Daily News* buy some photos from me? The owner spent summers in Newport; he'd even tolerated when Maggie, Jack, Spencer, and I had crashed his wedding at The Chanler. We'd taken copious advantage of the open bar, made up names and job professions that none of his out-of-town guests believed for a second, and done the electric slide with such enthusiasm that I'd broken the heel of one of the shoes I'd borrowed from my sister. But then again, he'd also been in attendance at Susie's party when I'd accused him and everyone else of having *delusions of adequacy.*

That, essentially, was my predicament: Who in this town would hire me? Before I'd left, I'd burned just about every bridge except the one that had brought me here in May. My Rolodex was thin. My mugshot was infamous.

"No one can argue that you're not a terrific photographer, Cassie," Hope said, snatching the plate back from me and polishing off the last crumbs. "But, Lord, the photos you send us are so sad. Someone is always crying in the background. Would it kill you to take a happy photo once in a while, or would they revoke your credentials?"

"I think they might be fixing to revoke my credentials, anyway, Ma." I moved my elbows off the table so the busser could clear it. "There is only so long I can call myself a photographer if I'm not actually photographing anything worthwhile."

More and more, I was doubting my ability to ever reach Mouna's level of success. It didn't help that Keith's shots from his current assignment were everywhere on *TIME*'s website. His accompanying essay about public displays of mourning had been syndicated in *Le Monde* and *The Guardian.* Meanwhile, my confidence was still sprawled on the pavement, concussed and half-conscious, back in Chișinău.

At least I could try to make my time in Newport count for something. Because we'd crushed this cake tasting. The quid pro quo was holding. Earlier, I'd helped Maggie choose the shit out of some cool calligraphy. I was now fluent in letter-press. No bachelorette party? Great! Male strippers weren't my cup of coffee, anyway. There was, of course, still the matter of my parents' eviction.

I got my chance to tackle that item of business when Susie folded her napkin neatly and excused herself to use the rest-room. Maggie needed to go, too, and they strolled off to-gether, heads close.

"Is Spencer here this afternoon?" Hope inquired of our busser.

Chef Sims would be in for dinner service, but this was his afternoon off. "Plan thwarted." I couldn't show any trace of disappointment, lest my mother seize upon it. I busied myself rearranging my dress over my knees.

"Shoot," said Hope with a frown. "Maybe you stay and wait—"

"The carriage house." A deliberate cutoff, on my part, as I had no desire to dwell further on Spencer. "We gotta talk about it. The roof. And the plumbing. And the electricity. The house is—" I was about to say *in shambles*, but caught myself. "The house is old."

"Daddy and I will take care of the house." Hope did a slow waltz with the two votive candles on the table. When she didn't immediately elaborate, I angled forward in my chair, widened my eyes, and prompted her to *continue, please*. Hope exhaled heavily, as though about to undertake grueling physi-cal labor. "Cassie, please, don't trouble yourself. We're doing just fine. The Land, as you know, is a ton of work and some-times we fall a bit behind on the upkeep. That's all."

"It's a money pit," I said.

"Don't call it a money pit. Cassie, believe me when I say we're not leaving the tarp on the roof for Maggie's wedding, for God's sake. I know Archer broke it, and we'll fix it."

Left up to her, she'd deny the severity of her financial situation until the movers were at the door. "I just want you and Daddy to be comfortable."

"My doll," said Hope. "We *are* perfectly comfortable. We were comfortable before you arrived, we've been comfortable in your long absence, and we'll be comfortable after you leave."

This statement scared me and annoyed me in equal measure. "I get it," I said, short. "But you actually do need me."

"Now, this is interesting," said Hope. It was her turn to lean forward, eyes big. "Because I think *you* need The Land more than you let on."

I choked out a laugh. "I literally spent my last years of high school wondering what it would've been like if we'd just cut all tethers to The Land after Susie bought it. Left every last artifact behind."

"They aren't *artifacts*." Hope's tone was nonplussed. "They are heirlooms from not just our lives, but every Coventry that came before."

"We've got robber barons in our blood," I said. "You think they called your great-whatever-times-grandfather Conrad 'Lieutenant Steel' because he was nice? Many of the Coventrys who came before were filled with greed and..." I trailed off, an idea wiggling loose. What if—

It was then that Chef Tien delivered her final goodbyes and thanks, as well as the printed estimate for Maggie's cake. Hope slid the paper over with the flat of her hand. Reading the numbers, she cleared her throat.

I gave it a glance. Thirteen dollars a slice. Two hundred and fifty slices. "Ma," I said, meaningfully.

"I'm giving Maggie this cake," Hope said, back straight, eyes clear, so dignified it broke me. "All these things you might find frivolous, like this cake and the bachelorette party, those are *important* to me." The way she said *important* was as though it came from her bones, from the marrow.

"You're giving her this wedding," I concurred. "And it is expensive, even though the venue is free. But I don't think you and Daddy realize just how much you're sitting on. You're in a Smaug situation." She stared at me blankly. "Not a *Hobbit* fan. Gotcha. What I mean is, you have some *very* valuable pieces. Let's go through the collection and see what you might be willing to sell."

For a moment we stared at each other, and I felt I was gazing into a mirror. While Maggie had inherited our father's fairness, my mother had passed to me eyes that were more or less chocolate brown, lashes thick and dark.

Then Hope frowned. "What if I asked you to post Granny Fi's work on Craigslist? How would that make you feel?"

It made me very uncomfortable to talk or even think about wills and legacies—too fraught, too potentially loaded with relationship-ending ammunition—but it was true, Granny Fi had bequeathed me one of her sculptures. It was the last in our family's possession, the rest having been sold into private collections or given to museums and galleries around the world.

Though Granny had been of some renown when she was alive, her work, like so many female artists, became suddenly and unexplainably more valuable *after* her death. Selling a sculpture would certainly fetch a tidy sum.

Hope had caught me there. I would sooner part with my shutter finger than the few tangible items I had left of my beloved, singular Granny Fi.

Fiona was born into a world where women weren't expected to do much except learn French and marry well. She'd done that, but also smoked and cursed and made sculptures of women's undergarments *Artform* once called *obscene*. By the time my siblings and I were born, we still had the name that showed up on museum plaques and university libraries and the social register, yet we wrapped the same public school history textbooks that mentioned our rapacious, industrialist ancestors in brown packing paper with the children of Newport tradesmen and my father's coworkers from the precinct. Spit cruelly, my nickname at Rogers High had been *heiress*, though the fabulously rich summer people the Coventrys had socialized with had stopped calling during the Reagan years. No coincidence. That was when the money *really* started to run out.

Hope, as though it wasn't already obvious, was trapped somewhere between the world of her mother and her children. She married a detective from a fairground, mountain town in Virginia because she loved him madly. But when Newport society didn't welcome him as one of their own, she was furious. Granny, on the other hand, never felt she needed those people—even after my grandfather had died young, she had her art, her interests, herself.

Imaginative, reclusive, mercurial, and fiercely witty, my grandmother—though I'd only gotten to spend fifteen years with her before she, an unapologetic smoker, died of lung cancer—had been, and was still, my north star.

Seeing Maggie and Susie return from the restroom, I quickly finished with this: "It would suck. But I'd do it if I had to. Is it a yes?"

"It's a maybe."

"It's a maybe!" I raised my empty glass, cheers-ed it with hers, then waved it at the other tables, naturally, gawking. "She said maybe, folks!"

. . . . .

On our way out of The Bonnie, Maggie pulled me aside. "I was talking to Susie in the bathroom," she said. "She mentioned she knows the director of special events at the Preservation Council. She said she would reach out as a favor to you."

"To me?" I watched Susie and Hope by the restaurant's door, standing in close proximity but looking at their phones. They weren't engaging, but they also weren't shooting poisoned darts at each other. "I think it's probably a favor to *you*."

Maggie smiled. "I did tell her I'd reconsider my bridesmaid decision. But, Cassie, she'll only make the call if you want. No pressure."

"Tell her to call," I said, sliding on my sunglasses. I felt accomplished—and tipsy—after the success of the tasting, and I probably would've said yes to anything at that moment, provided it didn't involve costumes or penis paraphernalia. "You can't be the only one in this family making some damn money."

Something passed across her face, and I realized where I'd put my foot. "Sorry, Bug," I said quickly. "I didn't mean that as an insult to Jack. I know he's working so hard on finding something new."

"It's fine." Maggie linked her arm through mine as we made for the exit. "Don't give it another thought. And, for the record, I think everything you photograph is worthwhile. Even orchids, if you choose."

12

Once I'd convinced Hope to sort and sell, J.P., Archer, and
I tackled the family room, stuffed as it was with an assembly
of curiosities inherited from the Coventry collection. Dating
back to the early twentieth century, the collection started with
ill-fated Earnest Coventry, who went off on a grand tour and
did the fashionable thing and bought enough bric-a-brac to
fill multiple trunks. Turtle shells and mollusks, maps and min-
erals, bits of coral and horns, gathering dust on the shelves—a

century later, my father had adopted all of it, recategorizing and cleaning, laminating the original, handwritten identifying labels, preserving the delicate calligraphy.

But I was learning now that my father hadn't just preserved the hoard; he'd let Hope *add* to it, and at some point the organization had apparently fallen by the wayside in favor of simple accumulation. Coins and stamps, feathers and plumes, most in bags or boxes or wrapped haphazardly in tissue paper on the floor or stacked randomly on side tables.

Crossed-legged on the floor, I raised a small bronze obelisk for Archer and my father to inspect from the couch. "This looks valuable?"

"Could be nineteenth-century French," Archer considered, dropping an old *Town & Country* issue in his lap.

"That's a paperweight," said J.P. as he counted and organized the chips of some ancient poker set. "From a trinket shop off Central Park."

I put the obelisk in my *trash* cluster, which was nine times bigger than my *donate* and *sell* piles. "Try this one." I held up a doll with glass eyes and a yellowed, frilly prairie dress, still in her box.

"Little Miss Muffet!" exclaimed Archer. "She's haunted."

"Your mom claims she is a collectable." J.P. rose and patted his pockets; finding his readers, he hung them in the neck of his T-shirt. "I'll have to leave you to it, trusting that you won't throw away anything your mother wants. I've got my boys book club at church tonight. And we're doing buck-a-shuck night at the pub first."

"What are you reading?" Archer flipped through the rest of the magazine, then tossed it to the *trash* pile by his feet.

"Great one this month," said J.P. "Memoir of that guy on television. Why is his name escaping me? Handsome fellow. Grew up overseas. You know who I'm talking about."

"Trevor Noah," Archer said, not looking up from his phone.

J.P. snapped his fingers. "That's the one."

"How did you get that?" I marveled.

Archer tapped his temple with the corner of his case. "I speak Dad."

J.P. asked Archer to help him find his car keys, and I assessed my sad piles. Maggie was back in New York to be with Jack, and for class and trainers and doctors' appointments and some physical therapy on a metatarsal injury that had flared up. I could've used her right now. "I need someone who actually knows what they're doing to come in here and appraise everything," I told Archer when he returned.

"I still can't believe Mom agreed to have this sale," he said. "And that you want to help her do it! Self-inflicted torture, for both of you."

I relocated the possibly murderous doll to *sell*. "Mom and Dad want to pay for this wedding. They also need to—" I almost said *move*, but caught myself in time "—fund some repairs around here."

"I told Susie I'd pay for the broken roof," Archer reminded me. "It's not my fault she hasn't taken me up on the offer. And speaking of Susie, don't you think she'd be willing to chip in for the wedding? She's richer than Croesus, and likes to show it."

"No." I shook my head quickly. "Mom and Dad have got to stand on their own, Archer."

"Fair," he conceded, joining me on the floor. "But, best case, how much profit will Miss Muffet make them? One hundred dollars on 1stDibs?"

"Seven slices of wedding cake," I said. "Two hundred and forty-three more to go."

Archer pursed his lips, then pulled over the old *T&C* magazine he'd discarded, flipped open to a center page. "Now, see, this is what you need." He tapped at the glossy paper. "Something big and splashy!"

I angled my head so I could see it clearer, an ad for a Christie's auction from three years ago—*Reverie*, they called it. The private collection of some woman with a fancy German name. There were bowls and chairs and candelabras in the shape of nude women.

"A *public* auction?" I hummed. The Coventry-Gilfords had many vices, senseless levels of pride among them. As conversations with Hope about the wedding illuminated, our parents were already sensitive to Newporters thinking they were destitute. What would happen to their dignity, threadbare as it was, if the rest of New England noticed?

"We'd be far from the first old Newport family to have a sell-off," he said. "It's happened many times before. You remember the grande dame from up the Avenue—from the Brown University Browns. Her kids had an auction after she passed. Hope and I went to it. Porcelain services for forty! We got bored and left because there were too many hat pins. Ours would be better. I'll help you."

"You will?" I had assumed my brother's interests lay online, rather than in dust.

"Sure." Archer was gazing out the family room windows, to the now vacant goat pen.

A few days ago, I'd found Darren a lovely new home at a sanctuary north of Charleston, where he could graze and nap and impale human thighs to his heart's content. Bless the jam and jelly guy at the Tiverton Farmer's Market for giving me the suggestion.

"I see the mess, you know," Archer continued. "And I care about Mom and Dad. I think this is a good idea."

I should not have been surprised that the Coventrys were his soft spot. For many years his circle was small, mainly us.

Even after his body was technically "healed," he faced insomnia and executive function disorder. Hope, especially, took precious care of him. She still did. This was probably the reason he was failing to launch at twenty-six.

"Okay," I said, my mind spooling, "I'd love your help. Do you want to call Maggie? Maybe she knows someone at Christie's or—"

"Hello!" a voice called from the front of the house. "Anybody home?"

"Back here!" Archer turned his grinning face to me. "I'll help you, but not *right* this second," he said with a dramatic sweep of his head, making his curls bounce. "I have a date."

When the visitor made it to the family room, I recognized him immediately, though it had been years since I'd seen him. "Remy!" I said, extracting myself from Earnest's treasures to give Kent's oldest son a big hug. There were a lot of *Oh, my Gods*, and *Get out of heres* (the kind that actually mean the opposite), before I pulled back to really take him in. "God, you've grown up. I haven't seen you since you and Archer did the Batman and Robin musical number for that talent show."

"Iconic," laughed Remy. His chin was sharper, cheeks more angled, his teeth straight and white, but still I recognized him for that gangly eleven-year-old in braces who was my brother's steadfast friend, when most young boys weren't interested in sticking by the side of a sick kid.

Old friends turned romantic. I thought back ten years, to the gold glint in Spencer's eyes, the feel of the arch of my foot as it slid down his calf.

"That musical was everything," said Archer as I made an effort to shut off the lights on my reverie. "The next fall you abandoned us for Deerfield."

"Where are you now?" I asked Remy.

"Cornell, actually. I'm getting my master's in hospitality,

which delights my dad to no end and has absolutely crushed what was left of my rebellious soul. I'm working here for the summer." With a smile both genuine and wry, Remy rubbed the tips of his fingers together. "No place like Newport for tips. And experience, of course. But I'm so happy to see you, Cass! The gang's back together, huh?"

"Until the wedding," Archer answered for me. It might have been my imagination, but there was some bite to it. Before I could touch down on what he meant, he was explaining to Remy his idea for the auction, asking him to agree that this was a perfect, sensible thing to do, and that it would be a wild success.

Remy nodded. "Say the Coventry name, and people's ears perk up. You're all over Net-a-Newport, anyway. Might as well capitalize."

"Who runs that account, by the way?" I asked. "Does anyone know?" Yesterday, they'd posted a turn-of-the-century picture of The Land that I'd never seen before. Printed in black-and-white, the shot was an odd angle of the back of the Cottage, ladies in long white skirts and wide-brimmed sunhats arm-in-arm with gentlemen companions in dark suits. The caption: *The venue for the wedding of the year has been chosen!*

"Anon." Archer shrugged. "Probably makes for looser lips."

"I wish they'd send the tongues wagging in a different direction." The first comment under the post, I'd noticed with chagrin: *Coventrys vs Utterbacks*, followed by a boxing glove and a popcorn emoji. "We don't need traction. We need to be left alone."

"As long as there has been a Coventry in Newport, there have been people cataloging the twists and turns of our lives," said Archer. "And we want auction publicity, don't we? Can't be picky about where it comes from." He looked as though he were daring me to contradict him, which we both knew I could not.

On their way out—they were going to a Newport Gulls game at old Cardines Field, then TBD—Archer stopped, crouched down to inspect a set of wooden tennis racquets with worn velvet grips crossed and mounted in a display case. He knocked on the glass with a knuckle. "Now *this* is valuable," he said. "Dad and I saw something similar on *Antiques Roadshow* once. Twelve thousand dollars."

13

NET-A-NEWPORT 5H
Where are you going this weekend?

58%	Flower Show
20%	Newport Film Festival
22%	Craft Beer Fest

NET-A-NEWPORT 2H
Submitted via NetaNewport.com
From: idk@newport.gov
Subject: fake flowers

Message: this flower show photographer will be a familiar face to many. i have very reliable intel that she lost her fancy and prestigious job abroad and is back in newport with tail between her legs. bizarre and sad.

Yes, I was taking pictures of the orchids, but my tail, *contrary* to social media belief, was not between my legs. And freelancers can't be *fired*. At least, that's what I told myself as I angrily closed my Instagram app and locked it for the rest of the day.

Why was the gaze of Net-a-Newport—which I was low-key picturing as the evil eye of Sauron, sitting on that tower in Mordor—fixed on *me*? Surely there were more interesting people who'd gotten into scrapes and caused scandals more recently.

Bizarre and sad. I knew I'd brought this judgment upon myself. It still made me want to dissolve into the soil like rain.

But I could not, because I was hired out this last weekend in June, when the summer and its people had fully arrived, and the lawn at Rosecliff was a patchwork quilt, temporary rectangular flower beds of posies, petunias, and zinnias laid out in a grid, creeping out from the grand mansion to the white marble fence overlooking the Cliff Walk, encircled by vendor tents selling antique flowerpots and garden trellises and candy apples. The Flower Show's preview party had nearly doubled in size since I'd last been home. It had gotten fancier, too; Martha Stewart had arrived earlier, dressed entirely in cream, trailed by a no-nonsense posse of assistants, and had commenced marching through the inside displays and the outdoor merchandise with the intensity of someone who had lots of money and not a lot of time. There was a moment when she had paused, bending, squinting hard into the stone eyes of a bunny covered in a mossy patina, and I thought, *Damn, that would make a good picture*, before I realized I'd been working too hard being benignly inconspicuous and was forgetting to actually do my job. I'd eventually gotten a photo of her in the billiard room, posing next to a mammoth vase of palm fronds.

The venue was no fluke; Rosecliff was absolutely the best place to show off the work of the who's who of horticulture. The mansion, like The Land, was beaux arts, but its neoclassical decoration was more restrained, if that's even the right word for a house and gardens inspired by one of the royal mistress's baroque châteaus in Versailles. So many of these Newport mansions follow the same three-act drama: the first, the construction, the absolute, explosive excess, the no-expense-spared attitude that was possible in the days before federal income tax was enshrined by the Sixteenth Amendment. Then, after the rising, the reality check, the declining fortunes of the families, the relocation of spheres of society, when the houses were closed up, sold for a tremendous loss, or—in some sad cases—demolished entirely. And the third act—well, I found myself in it, treading around the gardens of the steeply priced museum and its fundraiser.

Rosecliff's bride-white exterior shone brightly as ever. Inside, the grand rooms were awash in flowers; the fragrance made the air practically shimmer. It wasn't my usual subject matter, but it was satisfying to search for the perfect proportion, the most interesting form, through my lens, and push Net-a-Newport out of frame. My stance behind the camera, especially in a place like Rosecliff, where the Coventrys had once left calling cards, dined and danced, but otherwise hadn't lifted a finger to dress, transport, or feed themselves, was the most comfortable position available to me. I was happy to be useful, be productive, even in this small way, and perhaps—if I didn't screw up and crash into any champagne towers—leave a good impression.

As languid late afternoon drifted into cocktail hour on the lawn, I noticed Susie's new friends, Hope's old friends, whatever you want to call them, were still pretty much ignoring me, which otherwise would've been palatable, except it sure made it awkward to take photos of them. Even when I said a soft *hello*, and an *excuse me*, and did the arm motion for *you all get together*, they would dutifully pose, smile, and then just get right back to talking, without a word or acknowledgment. I wondered how many of them followed Net-a-Newport.

Keep it moving.

This mantra had always been more than useful whenever I felt stuck, whether it was getting over a romantic disappointment or out of a professional rut. Heart not healing? Pictures not working? Change locations. Literally. Just pick up the camera and tripod and refocus.

It had worked a week after Susie's party, when I'd moved up my adult-life dream-job plans. Clearly, there had been no reason to stay in Newport a second longer. Plus, while renting a Fifth Ward third-floor apartment with gorgeous light and no dishwasher with two college friends had been very fun, working as a part-time stock image photographer who took pictures of businesswomen laughing while eating salads had not been. So I cashed in my meager life savings and placed myself onto a plane to document a burgeoning coup, determined to weasel my way into the ranks of documentary photographers. I wanted purpose, I wanted the unexpected, I wanted to bear witness to storms not of my own making. That's where I'd met Mouna, who'd seen my scrappiness, bordering on desperation, and sent me behind the line. That's when I discovered that anywhere, no matter the danger, felt safer to me than Newport.

"For Lord's sake," I said today, circulating around this Newport social event where no one wanted to socialize with me, "keep it moving."

Unfortunately, this took me right into the path of Reagan Anne Finley, that fashionable alarm bell of a human. Still, after all these years, with the piercingly high cheekbones, the all-season-tan skin, the I-know-more-than-you grin. Another young woman was beside her; they both wore long floral skirts, tight cropped shirts, and were holding clear, fizzy drinks. And Reagan was looking right at me.

I'm not proud of it, but I did consider bolting. Perhaps a simple fake out, like I hadn't heard or seen her, would've sufficed. The vendor in the next tent over with the glass sculptures of swans had a big display stand with a long tablecloth that might've done for hiding.

I thought, *Fuck it*. Here was my past. Let me at least have the courage to face it. "Hi, Reagan," I said. "I thought it was you."

"Cass!" Reagan said with a barely holstered smirk. She stretched out the last letters of my name, made it sound like a hiss. "My old partner in crime."

"No kidding," I said faintly. If a fence was found missing some split rails, it was most likely Reagan and Cass. A pool broken into? Security lights suddenly come on in the middle of the night? Cigarette stubs in your mother's butterfly garden? Probably us. Your precious, promising son missed curfew? One wild guess. Despite Hope's best efforts to discourage our friendship, we'd always find where she'd hid the keys to the carriage house's liquor cabinet.

You could be quirky in Newport. Spunky was allowed, too. As long as you were respectful, modest, and discreet. Reagan and I had been none of those things.

When I'd last seen her at Susie's Labor Day party, Reagan's then-boyfriend was an unbelievably dull banker with a boat and an uncomfortably close relationship with his mother, and when I noted how my old friend's face actually resembled his, I'd thought, *Jesus Christ, there really is no place for me here*. After a couple tequilas, I'd managed to ask why she'd stopped returning my texts, and she'd said, with all due sympathy, that this kind of thing happened, that we'd just outgrown each other.

Today, we did not hug, not because it would be inappropriate or because we were avowed enemies, but because neither of us wanted to be the first to lean. Reagan's companion limply extended her arm for a handshake. I forgot her name immediately after we were introduced.

"Cass's family lives at The Land. In the carriage house," Reagan explained.

"Got it," said the friend, in a way that suggested this was already known.

From my jacket pocket, my phone chimed with a text. Maggie: Where are you? I'm here.

"What are you up to these days?" I asked, mostly to fill the air.

Reagan took a piece of gum out of a woven clutch with pink trim and popped it in her mouth. "I'm at *Vanity Fair* now. Just in Newport to chase a story."

"Oh, cool," I said, not to be cute, but just to—hopefully—accelerate to the part of the conversation where it would be acceptable to leave.

"You've given up the field for the lawn?" asked Reagan. I looked up from my response to my sister. "Last I heard you were in the Near East. Now you're here." Reagan rattled the ice in her glass. Above her lip was the scar, so faint, just a smudge of white discoloration, I don't think anyone who didn't already know it was there would notice. I'd been with her when she got it. Some even blamed me for it, because we'd told everyone after that I'd been the one behind the wheel in Susie's car. But the truth was she didn't smack her mouth during the incident, but after, when the cops made us do the slow, one foot straight in front of the other balance test.

I felt my pulse begin to race in my throat. "Just for the summer. You know I can only take Newport in small doses. I'll be gone after Maggie's wedding." As soon as it was out of my mouth, I wondered at my need to elaborate. But if Reagan had interpreted the extra details as I was nervous to see her, to be on her turf, her expression revealed nothing. Her forehead was as smooth and unwrinkled, shining like cellophane in the sun. With a flick of her long finger, she wiped the condensation from her glass.

"Do you have an Instagram?" asked the friend. She was on her phone, already scrolling. "Why can't I find any Cass Coventrys?"

"I'm at Cass underscore Gilford," I said.

The friend made a befuddled sound, perplexed why I wasn't capitalizing on my mother's name. Throughout this exchange, Reagan's gaze hadn't moved from my face. "How *is* Maggie doing with the wedding? Everything going all right?" Her features were arranged to appear concerned.

"Sure," I said, short.

Reagan gave her friend a look. A members-only look, the kind that tried to be exclusive, sneaky, but was instead egregiously transparent. The *we're in the club* look. The *you're a stranger here* look. "Your mom isn't mad the wedding is happening on Susie's property?"

"I heard she was mad," said the friend with absolutely no emotion at all.

Susie's property. This was bait, chum in the water. Reagan still stared at me; I mean, she *really* hadn't let up, and I got the sense she was waiting for me to open my maw, chomp down.

But I had willpower now. I'd faced far greater threats than this girl.

I gathered my camera bag from the ground, slamming the shutters against any visible reaction. *Watch, Reagan, what I couldn't do before.*

"Always great to see you," I said to Reagan.

Despite my dismissal, she smiled, her pink mouth stretching back across her teeth, the curve of her black sunglasses reflecting a distorted image of me, my camera, the pitch of the white tents, the sky.

14

"Was that Reagan Finley?" When I nodded, Maggie stuck out her tongue. We'd met by the fountain—more like swimming pool—in the center of the lawn, and she was effortless and nautical in a long, breezy white dress and navy blazer. Like many other women at the Flower Show, she was wearing a fascinator, pink gauze folded into a hibiscus blossom. I'd noticed, though, over the last week Maggie's smiles were slower to come, her eyes hooded and humorless. Her appetite was even more particular than usual, consisting mostly of buttered toast, Hawaiian rolls with olive oil and salt, handfuls of sour gummy bears, and buckets and buckets of flat Coke. There was a glass of it currently in her hand, today accompanied by a wedge of lemon. Her other hand shaded her from the sun as she watched Reagan and her friend meander through a nearby row of vendor tents. "I always thought she was a bad influence on you."

"We were bad for each other," I said, which was the truth.

I ran my fingers through my hair, combing out unwelcome thoughts. This afternoon was not turning out the way I had hoped.

"Listen, I got your text." Maggie removed her sunglasses, looked around the lawn, searching, it seemed, for people who might be eavesdropping. Everyone else was absorbed in their own conversations, but Maggie still lowered her voice to a whisper. "But, like—even *if* I did know someone at Christie's or Sotheby's, why do we need them? I thought you were just thinking eBay."

Just yesterday in the carriage house, Archer and I had managed to corner Hope into another auction conversation, walking her through why it was necessary, why it would help. Our mother's answer boomeranged between *there has to be another way*...and *okay, I suppose we could*... But Archer and I chose to interpret this as a resounding *yes, let's do it!* I was agnostic about delivering the same presentation to my sister while I was trying to work. "Bug, look—" I began, but we were immediately interrupted by a family with two bashful, awestruck young daughters, and a father clearly on a mission.

"Do you want me to take a picture of you all?" I asked as Maggie smiled graciously at the aspiring ballerinas. The father unlocked his phone and dropped it into my hands. "I meant with my camera…"

"Dance is hard work." Maggie, well-rehearsed in this sort of thing, was ushering the daughters to either side of her. Her arms, even when wrapped around the two fans, were in near perfect second-position; she was working on her port de bras even when she wasn't. "So, make sure you adore it."

And just like that, we were back to *our* familiar roles from childhood. She, the golden-haired stage deity with the indefatigable lungs, and me, her fangirl, in her comet's tail, a participant, an observer, documenting someone else's life.

"Got it," I said, handing the father his phone with a series of portrait and landscape options. His phone's camera wasn't fit to take a mugshot.

"You're very lucky!" Spencer Sims was striding over from the mansion. "Cass Gilford is a famous photographer!" This was met with polite silence and only the barest hint of interest from the departing family.

Behind Spencer, the entourage: Archer and Remy, J.P. and Hope, the latter with her wrists extended outward, burdened with plastic bags.

"There you are!" Hope exclaimed. We hugged; my arms had to go around many layers. As was typical, she was at once both over- and underdressed for the occasion, with a short fur jacket layered over a vintage T-shirt wrapped in a fringy scarf. And, on the bottom, bootcut jeans. My father was in a cowboy hat, shorts, and sneakers with tube socks. I couldn't begrudge their acts of sartorial resistance, though they, as always, were getting a fair share of looks. Hope deposited her plastic bags directly at my feet. "Here, these are for my prodigal daughter."

Though the handles of each bag were stretched to the point of imminent snapping, I picked them up to poke through their contents: pill bottles from prescriptions long expired, a tub of conditioner with mildew around the spout, a box of tampons, and a trove of bodice-ripping romance novels featuring hirsute-chested pirates and dukes, thoroughly thumbed through. "Ma," I said, blinking between her, serene, and the bags. "What am I supposed to do with these?"

"You've been on me to tidy the carriage house," she responded with a little laugh of disbelief. "So, here you go. I thought you'd be pleased to get your stuff back."

"I told HCG that it was *entirely* unnecessary to lug it here," said Archer, clucking his tongue. "Unless there are some loose pills in there we can enjoy."

"I doubt we'll be that lucky," I told him. I was surprised, actually, that Archer was here; the Flower Show wasn't really in his wheelhouse, though I had seen on one of his recent videos where he talked about what he did when he woke up feeling like garbage: *Take a little walk,* he'd said, straight to the camera. *Out your front door, down the street, wherever. Touch a little leaf. Smell a little flower.*

Maybe he woke up needing a little posy today.

"You don't like the way I clean," Hope said to me, sweetly enough, "then don't tell me to clean."

"Dad," I pleaded for backup.

"You should've seen what else she tried to bring you." J.P. shook his head solemnly. "I told her I wasn't carrying anything here except her purse." So that's what the overly large canvas tote bag in his hands was—her purse.

"You want me to throw those away for you?" Spencer held out a hand for the plastic bags. "Or are you going to reread *The Pirate's Dark Promise*?"

"For the record," I said, passing over the junk, "the pirates were Maggie's. I liked the Westerns."

"That's true," Maggie said reluctantly. She gave it a moment's thought, then fished a novel out of the bag, tucked it under her arm. "Can't toss a book in the trash."

Spencer found a wide-mouthed garbage pail a few dozen feet away by a vendor tent selling porcelain vases in the shape of tropical fruits. On his way back, he extracted his aunt from another group, encouraged her over to ours. She didn't kick or scream or anything, but she was looking at Spencer like *why are you doing this to me?* When she arrived, though, she politely distributed kisses, even to Hope.

"It's crowded today!" Hope took the sunglasses off my head

and put them on her own face. "The Flower Show's gotten popular."

"It used to be elegant and understated," Susie said, pursing her lips. "We used to be able to fly under the radar. But that's what Newport gets for tearing down beautiful old buildings and replacing them with apartment complexes and hotels."

This was rich, coming from someone who, if I was feeling particularly mean-spirited, could herself be called a Newport blow-in. The Coventrys had been at The Land for more than a hundred and twenty years. Susie hadn't been here but fifteen.

"It's the invasion of the riffraff," Archer said, exchanging a wide-eyed, faux-horrified glance with Remy.

Spencer chuckled. "Riffraff looking awfully stylish to me." He was in linen pants, cuffed, high-top Jordans, and a shirt, obviously. But I was distracted by his face. The eyes. That smile that could start wars among Newport socialites.

"You all laugh now," said Susie. She took a sip of her wine, leaving a lipstick stain on the rim. "But wait until you bump into some drunk guy in the parking lot urinating behind a car with New Jersey license plates."

"Didn't you and Spencer's mom grow up in Paterson?" Hope asked.

"Sure did." Spencer grinned. "I've been trying to get Susu to put it on a billboard for years."

"What's the proper nomenclature, Susie?" I asked. "Pork roll or Taylor ham? Share with the Flower Show your thoughts?"

She was in silk today; her shirt rustled as she leaned in to me. "It's Taylor ham, but for God's sake, darling, don't tell anyone I told you."

"Susie!" Hope clapped then, pointed across the lawn to a pergola covered in purple wisteria. "There's the antique automobile guy who's always checking you out. Take yourself over there and flirt with him."

"One marriage was enough," said Susie.

"No one is telling you to marry the man, Susu," said Hope, and I noticed how the nickname slipped out of her. "You just need someone much taller and slimmer and less of a cheater to fill those empty suits you paint. It's been almost sixteen years since Jack's father—"

Before she could finish, Jack himself, in a plum polo and aviator sunglasses, appeared in our circle, with a plate of cheese and crudités. "Hey, hey." He dragged a slice of baguette in some kind of green dip. "What's going on, family?"

I glanced at my sister, but instead of an expression of pre-marital bliss, I found one of disgust. "Where've you been, Jack?" Maggie's jaw was set at a weird angle.

Jack chewed, looked at the fountain, the streams of water spewing upward. "Told you. Guys at the brewery wanted to discuss me investing in their expansion. Oops!" Jack's plate had tipped in his hand, sending his snacks into the grass.

"Jack," said Susie, disapproval making the one vowel in his name about a minute long.

"And this discussion lasted five hours?" Maggie asked, loud enough that some people nearby turned. "You missed the call with the caterers!"

Archer and Remy knelt down to help pick up the mess. The rest of us were kind of frozen. I figured we all had the same question: Break it up, or let it play?

"Dang, that was today?" Jack scratched his stubble, his clear inebriation making him unaware of the fact that his demeanor was winding Maggie up. I loved this man very much, but if anyone deserved a few drinks, it was not him, living an obligation-free summer.

"Don't worry, I made *sure* we have your favorite hot wings for cocktail hour." Maggie's voice was getting higher, her hands fluttering around her body like agitated birds. I resisted the urge to shush her; I didn't want her getting more upset, though I also didn't need to be involved in a lovers' quarrel during my first gig in Newport, when I was trying—for the first time in my adult life here—to make a decent impression. "Even though we've all agreed—your mom, my mom, Cass, Archer—" *Leave my name out of this*, my brother muttered "—even Spencer, an actual *chef*—that serving drippy chicken wings at a black-tie wedding is absolutely ridiculous, I told the caterers that we had to have them. I did that for you. You're welcome." Maggie crossed her arms.

"Will the wings be Thai honey flavor?" Jack joked. A few of us actually groaned.

"Jack, brother." Spencer approached his cousin, his eyes beseeching, his manner unruffled, laying a hand on his shoulder. "You okay?"

"I don't want to invest in a brewery, Jack!" Maggie shouted, as though pure volume would get her point across. "I've only told you that one million times!"

"Okay." I took a tentative step toward my sister, following Spencer's lead. "Bug, I think Jack's having a bit of a tough afternoon…"

This was the wrong thing to have said. Maggie whirled on me, face flush. "Please, say more. Take his side. Because he's so cool, and chill, and everyone loves him, and I'm the bridezilla."

"I'm not chill," Jack slurred as he stepped away from Spencer with the contents of his spilled plate. "I can't even get my fiancée to like me." He wasn't moving very fast, so we let him wander, with the assumption that someone would scoop him up later.

"Maggie, love—" said Hope.

"Because I know everyone is talking about it!" Her damp eyes flew around the circle.

"If you're referring to Newport Net, or whatever it is called—" I kept my voice very calm "—everyone knows it's the *National Enquirer*. You can't believe a word!"

"They once said I made out with Emmy-nominated actress Carrie Coon when she was in town shooting," said Spencer good-naturedly. "I mean—I wish!"

"And I know for a fact a disgruntled coworker submitted a lie about me," said Remy. "She said I tried to sneak into the set of *Hocus Pocus 2* and got thrown out, but I *was* cast as cheerful autumn dad number two, but when Sarah Jessica Parker touched my wrist by accident in craft services, I fainted and had to be taken out on a stretcher."

"See?" I told Maggie. "There's nothing to worry about. You are perf—"

"This isn't helping!" Maggie stormed offstage as only a ballerina could—elegantly, faultlessly cued, fast footed.

Hope looked after Maggie, though she'd been lost to the crowd. "Poor girl."

"Weddings can be *very* stressful," J.P. said to his wife gently, though tellingly.

"That part," said Spencer, raising his beer.

"I should get Jack home," Susie said, shifting on her feet. "I guess I can leave early…"

"J.P. and I will drive Jack," said my mother. "Get him into bed."

"You don't have to do that." I saw Susie was torn. Stay, or turn her son over to Hope?

"Nothing we haven't done before. Remember Jack and Maggie's prom senior year?"

Whoooo, nelly, J.P. said under his breath.

"We'll help Maggie," said Remy, and Archer nodded. "Working weddings and events, I've got experience with big emotions."

"All right," Susie forfeited.

A wave from over her shoulder caught my eye; it was the young woman who did something with the events office, the one who dressed as though she were a distinguished professor at Yale—jackets with patches on the elbows, grandpa sweaters, and always, even today in the summer warmth, a silk scarf around her neck. I'm sure, in the eyes of the one who was signing my paycheck today, it appeared like I was socializing on the job. I gave her the sign for *just one second*.

When I turned back, it was just Spencer and me. "Stand over there," I said, pointing a few feet to his right, then twisting the tap off my lens. "I have to seem busy." We were drifting into golden hour, when the sun on the water made it glint clear turquoise and made everyone's skin appear lustrous.

Spencer took his mark. "What are we giving?" he asked. "Sultry? Smoldering? Cheerful?" He acted these out. "Influencer-style, laughing into the distance, legs in positions that would cause you to trip in real life?"

"You've been on Archer's socials," I observed. Unlike when I'd photographed Spencer at the engagement party, these shots lacked the spontaneity, that rush of exhilaration, that made the difference between a flat photo and a gift. But with such a photogenic subject, it was hard to do wrong.

"I like when Archer comments things like: screaming! Crying! I've never seen the guy scream or cry in my entire life," he said as I snapped.

"I love how he uses the coffin emoji." I shifted angles, adjusted the shutter speed, and took a few more shots of him close.

"Dying," Spencer said, expressionless.

I lowered my camera. "Actually, after this afternoon, I might be."

"Weddings can be brutal. No way around that," he said.

"I'm so glad it worked out with Aimee, though. She's excited about making the cake."

"Thank you for recommending her," I said. "It's weird to be talking about a marriage and a cake when we've just seen the bride take a piece out of her groom."

"You know what we should do?" A breeze swept through the lawn, ruffling my hair and the collar on his shirt. He smelled like summer and butter and soap. "You, me, Maggie, and Jack should go sailing. My friend left for two months in Spain, but docked his dinghy here. We could get out for the day and relax. Just an idea. Up to you."

Waiting for my answer, he took a quick sip of his beer and I saw a bracelet around his wrist, the kind that a kid might make at summer camp, beads in rainbow colors, random charms. I reached out and ran my fingers over it, feeling the texture of the beads and his warm skin. "This is fun," I murmured.

"Daughter of my sous made it for me. She has a thing for fine jewelry."

A funny image came to me, of Susie's massive diamond studs, so heavy they dragged down her earlobes, like they were about to drip off her face. "Harry Winston wishes."

Spencer laughed, flipped his hand over so his broad palm was pressed to mine, and all other thoughts drained from my head.

It wasn't until he blinked, his long eyelashes brushing his cheek, that I realized I was staring. But I was *so* curious at the sensation of our fingers intertwined, such a small thing— this awareness of my hand supported in someone else's—had me stuck.

Our intimacy had once been easy. We'd been friends for so long; maybe it was the sense of an ending, our lives diverging, that had pushed us finally into a romantic but imprecise place the summer before our senior years in college. When the nights were warm and long, we'd taken tentative steps further, then further again, never actually saying what we were but acting like the words didn't matter. Which was strange, because we talked about nearly everything else while spending entire days together, tromping down the wharves, borrowing boats from friends of friends, slurping Del's lemonade from Styrofoam cups, distracting each other from our "real" lives, which, for him, included waiting tables and working on his thesis proposal studying issues of class and race in food through the lens of gentrification in his home in Flatbush. My priorities at that time, besides getting Spencer to blow off work and hang out with me, included calling in sick to my job babysitting kids at the Newport Country Club to drive to Providence with forged press credentials and photograph the trial of one of New England's most notorious mobsters.

It all came apart at the Lily Pond, mid-August. I'd been imagining my life beyond Newport in concrete ways—shading in the blanks of what a career in photojournalism would look like—but as much as I wanted to erase my hometown from my identity, I didn't want to do the same with Spencer. We'd dangled our bare feet into water, cloudy with muck and soggy shoreland plants, and there I confessed that he made me laugh like no one else, he made me pinch myself each time I was with him, made me want to fight for him, for his loyalty, for a notion of *us*, like no one had before. *Princeton and New York are only two hours away on a train*, I'd said. *What do you think?*

This is a surprise, he'd said, leaning down to catch my eyes. That was the thing about Spencer—when he wanted my attention, it was very difficult to look away. *So are a lot of things. How much I love being here, this place. How much I've loved spending time with you. But...* He'd let the conjunction hang in the air, before his forceful, baffled exhale had it floating away,

along with my hope and pride, like smoke from an extin-
guished candle.

But.

"It's been a while," I finally said, and I could've been talking about sailing, or us, together. I gradually removed my
hand from his.

"I don't believe you've forgotten how to sail. Last time—
do you remember?—you did the all the hoisting and trim-
ming for us." It was a small comfort that Spencer's voice was
a little raspy. Perhaps, like me, he was remembering the time,
nearly a decade ago, when in the quiet, endless boredom of a
drizzly summer afternoon, we'd boarded a boat as friends and
docked as lovers. When the sun-shower appeared in the blue
sky like some kind of joke, we'd slipped around the deck, trying and failing to furl the jib, before giving up, and in, hiding our heads under a towel and kissing, once, sweetly, for
the first time.

"Yes," I said. Then again, for good measure, and less wob-
bly this time: "Yes, sailing sounds great."

July

15

NET-A-NEWPORT
Newport, Rhode Island
Happy Fourth of July Weekend! We're celebrating with cocktails on rooftop bars, oysters on ice, and rosé all day. Already seen/heard some fireworks? Link in bio to submit.

View all 51 comments
July 4

NET-A-NEWPORT 1H
Submitted via NetaNewport.com
From: DixieNormous@ha.com
Subject: fight

Message: anyone else see the big family fight at the flower show last week? rumor is this bride is getting cold feet, and her feet are very important to her

There was a reason Newport was Newport. Even in peak summer, the day's high was a near perfect seventy-eight degrees; on the water it was even cooler. I couldn't help but feel the blue, cloudless sky that graced us for the Fourth of July was a rebuke to me, and my suspicion of this place. *See?* the breeze seemed to proclaim as Spencer guided the twenty-two-foot shiny-hulled daysailer—cute as a button and perfect for four—from the harbor. *Newport isn't so bad as all that.*

We all were taking the day off. In the cockpit, Maggie sat next to Jack, I next to Spencer. I'd been tiptoeing around my sister since the Great Flower Show Stomp-off last week, but she seemed to be in a good mood today, her hair loose around her face, her laughs generous. I'd gently suggested she unfollow Net-a-Newport, so perhaps that was part of the reason for her high spirits today.

Jack had his arm around her shoulders. This was a couple who'd weathered storms, especially early on, when Jack had been at Wesleyan and Maggie had been training in Newport, then working in New York. If you'd thought their relationship would wobble due to a sharp comment related to a brewery, you were woefully mistaken.

Steering the tiller, Spencer looked very cool in a blue Hawaiian shirt and shorts the color of raspberries. Seldom had I ever found attractive a man in Nantucket-red pants, but Spencer was the opposite of country club stuffiness. Despite his claim to be a novice sailor, he handled the boat with confidence and ease.

We maneuvered around Goat Island, through the light chop and the heavy boating traffic, until Spencer cut the outboard motor. I handed the bag of his homemade granola I'd been feasting on to Maggie and wiped my hands on my bare legs. "Do you need me to hoist?"

"You know he does," laughed Jack.

Spencer's wayfarer sunglasses were attached to neon yellow neoprene straps, which he removed and let fall to his chest. "Jack's right. I have done it alone, but it took about five years off my life," he said, raising the boom. "I forgot to loosen the top line and was convinced I'd ruined it forever."

"Come on, skip," Jack said to me. "Show him."

"Without a mast-raising system, it's tricky," I acknowledged, standing, steadying myself, holding on to the boom so it didn't clock me in the forehead. "Here, I'll pull the halyard. Undo that line for me?"

"She takes the more difficult job," said Spencer. We got into position, me behind the mast, Spencer by the cockpit and the winch.

For a time, early twentieth century, we'd had some pretty good skippers in the Coventry family. Granny Fi's grandfather, Conrad Jr.—the favored son of my intrepid, glorious, nasty-rich great-great-grandfather—had triumphed in the America's Cup a time or two, setting records in the multiday race they called Auld Mug, cheered on by a president, I forget which one, Roosevelt or Hoover, who'd come to watch. By the time I was born, the yachts were gone, but the knowledge, the calculations, the math of the wind and the workings of the motor stayed, thanks to the teachings of Granny Fi, and trickled down through the waning days of the Coventry empire to me and my siblings.

I began to hoist; though it was a small boat, I still had to throw my weight behind the job. I yanked back and down, the mainsail leaped up, a foot or two at a time. Maggie and Jack, in between pulls of the line, acted as cheerleaders, hollering encouragement. When it was trimmed, the jib unfurled, the wind got the chance to catch the sails, and I felt the unmistakable lift and draw, the float and the drop, as the little boat boldly named *Andromeda* began to cut through the bay, showing us what she could do.

I helped Spencer tack, happy to get us going that little bit faster, riding the edge of wild. Then we took our seats in the cockpit, passing back and forth snacks and drinks from the cooler Spencer and Jack had packed. It was so much harder to be anxious about The Land and the auction and the wedding when the sun was shining, the sea pristine, when I had space, headroom, when the air was clear in my lungs and felt like freedom. Maggie and Jack were sharing a bottle of Italian soda. Spencer, one long arm draped over the gunwale behind me, was enjoying a longneck beer tucked in a Bonnie koozy. And I, fizzy with wine in a boat-safe tumbler, couldn't resist reaching down every time the boat heeled hard to run my fingertips across the cold water.

Eight or nine miles north of Newport, when we arrived at the flat, green grasslands and broken-shell beaches of Prudence Island—around here, you can always tell which places were named by Quakers—we decided to anchor in a cove busy with pleasure craft for lunch and a swim. Spencer produced four wax-paper-wrapped sandwiches, brioche, just the barest hint of a crispy toast, avocado, tomato (*from the Sims apartment balcony farm*, said Spencer), and bacon. The most delicious malt vinegar potato chips he fried himself—*in real oil, not this air fryer madness for me.*

"God knows we could use more Black-owned businesses in this town," he said, taking a bite of the corner of his bread as he told us about plans for a new restaurant. He ate like he talked—unreservedly, enthusiastically. "So, okay, hear me out: Newport needs fine dining that's *not* attached to a hotel. Right?"

"According to my mother, we need no more hotels, period," said Jack. A piece of tomato fell out of the bottom of his sandwich onto the wax paper on his lap. Maggie picked it up and popped it into her mouth.

"Aimee and I are eyeing a space on Sayers Wharf," Spencer

continued. "That mediocre Italian place closed there and we could really build it out into something amazing."

"Will you serve scallops?" I joked, knowing how he felt about the bland ubiquity of this particular dish.

"You can't make me." Spencer's laugh, baritone, unreserved, was a cool drink poured from a pitcher. "I swear, I'll hop off this ship right now." He balled up his sandwich wrapper, stood, put one foot on the seat, as though he was fixing to jump. Then he looked down at me, one eyebrow raised.

"I'm talking baby food level of puree cauliflower to go with them." I grinned. "And a nice little bloom of parsley." I hadn't, in so many years, been much for belonging, but today, the light, the blue, the swing of the ship and the salt fruit on my tongue—it felt right, is what I'll say. It felt good.

He groaned, undid the top few buttons on his shirt. "You're torturing me. This is a crime."

"And one of those slices of lemon!" This from Maggie. "Wrapped in hideous yellow cheesecloth."

"That's it." His shirt was off, both feet on the gunwale now. When he had time to work out while running a very successful restaurant, I couldn't say. My job this summer wasn't nearly as demanding and all I'd done was one or two yoga sessions with Maggie in the pool house, my only regular exercise leisurely ambles through the grasses of Sachuest Point, or strolls down the easiest, flattest parts of the Cliff Walk.

In a flash, he pushed off, his front flip inelegant, mostly limbs. He landed in the water with a gigantic, chilly splash that reached my shoulders.

Jack was in soon after, leaving me and Maggie alone on the boat, rocking in the aftermath of the boys' dismounts.

Maggie inhaled; it was shaky. "I have to come clean about something, Cassie," she said, pulling my attention back. "The thing at the Flower Show... It wasn't about the chicken wings."

Before my mind could even wonder, she announced it: "I'm pregnant."

A moment of silence, then I erupted. Though I knew her body, as valuable as it was to the New York City Ballet, was now infinitely more precious, I still couldn't stop myself from launching across the cockpit and smashing myself into her arms. Like many other old East Coast families, the Coventrys had certainly been prolific in the past. That Hope was an only child was rather unusual. With Granny Fi gone, Dad's relatives scattered in Appalachia, Coventry cousins splintered, Archer and I unmarried, our family had often felt small. But now it was growing.

Once I released her, my eyes flew to her abdomen; if she was showing, I couldn't tell. Her long dress was voluminous and shapeless, thin straps on the shoulders and enough material through the waist and skirt to pitch a tent underneath. She'd been wearing this style, I realized, often in the past few weeks. "I'm *completely* oblivious." All the times she'd declined or pretended to drink alcohol. Her bouts with an "upset stomach." Her performance had been nearly perfect. I shouldn't be surprised. Maggie had danced *Giselle* with broken toes; how easily one forgets that beauty is pain's best camouflage.

I had all the questions, and they tumbled forth: How far along? Twelve weeks. Due date? Mid-January. When did you find out?

"Right before we left the city for the engagement party." She tented her long fingers under her chin, her smile not quite matching my own. "I snuck into a bathroom stall at rehearsal with a pregnancy test hidden in my leo. I'd been feeling woozy, but I was thinking maybe it was all the hard workouts? But then my period was late. Cassie, when I saw the word *pregnant*, I was like, *This can't be right.* Then I wrapped the test in toilet paper and, three blocks away from Lincoln Center, I threw it in the trash."

"Are you happy?" I asked because, honestly, I couldn't tell.

"A baby wasn't even on my radar. We've been using birth control! But here I am." Her eyes went from watery to overflowing. I handed her a napkin. She blew her nose; I waited, suspecting there was more for me to hear. "It's the reason we're having such a short engagement." She took the napkin to her eyes. "I have in my mind that I'd walk down the aisle before I'm, you know—" She stood, stuck out her stomach, bent her back, and walked a few steps in a manner that suggested she believed very pregnant women resembled emperor penguins.

I nodded gravely. "Of course."

"When I went back to the city the other week, I wasn't going for my metatarsal. I was supposed to be meeting with the company." She flopped down in her seat. "My contract is up in September. We should be starting negotiations, so my agent set up some time to tell them about my pregnancy, get the ball rolling. But—" She glanced down, picking at a thread on her dress. "But I canceled it."

She seemed ashamed, so I squeezed her hand tighter. "You're nervous about telling them about the baby?" Off the stern, Jack and Spencer began swimming parallel to the shore, their arms alternating strokes, water droplets flying off their fingers catching the sun.

"The reality is with a January due date—well, *The Nutcracker* is out, obviously."

"Obviously," I said, but thought: *Where will I be in January?*

"I won't be back until April or May at the earliest," Maggie was saying. "My blisters will be healed, but I'll be *so* out of shape. I'm really frustrated about the timing. I feel like this baby is coming right when I'm at my strongest. Just when my artistic director was finally—*finally!*—satisfied with my conditioning, *just* as I'm positioned to push for principal, I have to step back. And everyone, all the nurses and the doctors and the check-in people at my OB office, look at me like I should be over the moon and I am, of course. I mean, I should be. But, like—" Maggie returned my hand squeeze, though she still couldn't really look at me. "I'm just scared I'll come back weak, and get injured, and they'll fire me."

To be the kind of athlete she was took an incredible amount of focus and drive. She'd been her own sculptor, coach, doctor, nutritionist, along with being my keeper and minder and—occasionally—my prison warden. Though I hadn't been a photojournalist for as long as she'd been dancing, I knew that this was the moment, when we both were over the lip of thirty, that our years of drudgery, patience, and practice had finally started paying off. No fair that the *fun* part of a woman's career often collided head-on with her childbearing years. Her taking-care-of-parents years. "I know you've been conditioned to believe that any change to your body is a threat to perfection," I said, wanting to do what I could. "By the world. By the ballet. But your body *is* changing. It's understandable, and also unjust, that your career might have to adjust, too."

"The baby is *already* changing my life," Maggie half laughed, though it was mostly a big sniff. In the distance, about two hundred meters out, the boys had begun swimming back toward the boat. There was more splashing and faster arm turnover, as if they might be racing. "My pointe shoes don't fit because apparently your feet get bigger. My center of gravity is off. All I want to eat is bread. I feel hungover all the time. You know my hormones have undone years of laser hair removal? Like that." She snapped her fingers. "I have hair in places that— Cassie, don't laugh. I'm serious, this is a major problem. I'm sprouting tufts." She flexed her hands between us, as though she'd just touched something surprising and sticky.

"Who else knows?" I asked. "Besides me and Jack?"

"My agent and manager. That's it. I'll tell Mom and Dad and Archer tomorrow, and Susie, now that you can be there to remind them to keep it quiet. Before the news spreads far and wide, I do have to get my act together and tell the company. I hope they don't let me go. Martha Graham said that a dancer dies twice, the first time when they stop. I believe her, Cassie."

"Okay," I said, my heart heavy for my sister, "let's start here: I know Hope drove the first wedding planner to quit, but you don't need to be growing a human *and* worrying about valet parking. Can Jack step up more?"

"Jack's wheels have come off." Maggie dabbed at the corners of her eyes with her pinkie fingers. "He quit his job because it *was* becoming so terrible—I mean, his father died from a hypertension-related stroke at fifty-seven! But less than two weeks later, I get the positive pregnancy test. When it sunk in we wouldn't have his income when the baby came, he panicked. But he's all over the place in terms of what he wants to do next. The other night he woke me up because he had a product idea."

"Anything good?"

"Disposable shoe covers," Maggie said, "that you wear to the bathroom at work, so your coworkers don't recognize your footwear in the next stall. He wants to call them *Poopin' Pumps*."

I did not howl with laughter, though it was tough to resist. "Jack needs something to do," I managed. "Let's put him on wedding parking, transportation from the hotel block at Gurney's, let's give him bathrooms, let's give him rentals. Why doesn't he take over the welcome party? Yes? River can help."

"Yes," Maggie agreed. Then, more enthused: "Yes, you're right. Ugh, thank you, Cassie." She brushed her hands on her dress and held out her arms. Without hesitation, I slipped into the seat next to her, buried my face in her hair. "Thank you for making me feel better," she whispered. "For keeping my secrets."

In her arms, I thought of the one I was keeping from her, about the carriage house and Susie. I'd tell her, I promised myself guiltily. Just clearly not today.

"And you're perfect," I said. Then: "Sorry, you don't want me to keep saying that."

"Because I'm not. Just ask the voices in my head and the NYCB corps." We pulled apart. "Cassie, I apologize for snapping at you, but you do have me on this pedestal, and I worry about why you try so hard to keep me there. Take me down a peg. You don't need to keep yourself small."

"Don't you worry about me. Not when we have other stuff to concern us. Like your wedding dress fitting on Friday. I will be there with noise-canceling headphones in case you need to mute our lovely and gracious mother."

"Oh, my God, I forgot about that." Maggie's hand went to her forehead. "With the contract and the baby and now *Vanity Fair* trying to—"

I stopped her. *"Vanity Fair?"* I remembered something. Squinting, I tried to bring it into focus.

"Yeah. Reagan Finley emailed me after the Flower Show."

There it was. "Reagan wants to write about you?" Maggie *was* squarely within the *VF* wheelhouse—Newport, money, old family, fancy wedding.

"Yes, but I don't know if I'm going to do it. Reagan really wants to do the interview at The Land. She says she hasn't seen it in many years and—"

"You can't let her in the carriage house," I said. "With the auction, and the wedding, we want good press. Not sad press."

"Right. And on top of it, you guys have weird history. I'm not going to do it."

"But it's *Vanity Fair*." I sighed, considered. "I'm not about to let my past interfere with this opportunity, Bug. Or the state of the carriage house. Do the interview. Shine. Sparkle. Be marvelous and show those snobs at the ballet they have to have you for many seasons to come. I'll corral Mom and Dad for you."

"You sure?" asked Maggie.

"Absolutely," I said. "Now, come on." I lifted the white button-down shirt I was using as a cover-up over my head. "Let's play mermaids. I'll suck it up and be Ursula this time."

Maggie stripped down to her lipstick red one-piece. "No, you be Ariel," she said, holding the sides of her middle, which was—yes, indeed—beginning to grow fuller. "I'll be the sea snail resting on the rock."

At the top rung of the ladder, Spencer shook his hair, droplets spraying our legs, causing us to yelp and complain like the teenage girls we once were. I had no choice but to skip over and push his shoulders so he fell back into the water. When he surfaced, he was grinning, the gold in his eyes glinting, beckoning me in, and just before I jumped, I thought, *Oh, dashing boy, I am in trouble.*

·····

At sunset, as the last of the daysailers tacked around Goat Island, and the yachts took their moorings, bobbing like studs in the shallows, Spencer anchored the *Andromeda* in the harbor. Perhaps it was the stained-glass nature of the sky, the particular shade of Newport clementine and rose, but my mind was yanked back to the floor of Trinity, the old Episcopal church on Queen Anne's Square our father, who had ideas about morality and higher powers, used to drag us to most

Sundays before we were old enough to learn how to say "no," but still young enough not to care about insignificant things like death and eternal salvation.

We fought over the last of Spencer's potato chips and drank wine (save Maggie) and talked of the things you talk about in the city of eras and layers, among friends and family who you'd trust with your life. We talked of the dead—Granny Fi and Bonnie Sims and Lionel Utterback, the man of the oil-painting suits—the afterlife, whether our loved ones send signs (Jack: *absolutely*. Maggie: *no way*), miracles and last suppers (Spencer: *macaroni pie*. Me: *icebox pie*).

Maggie eventually retired to the tiny interior aft cabin to lie down until the fireworks started, Jack with her for company. Spencer and I took the starboard side bench. It was quite the party out on the water; fishing vessels and schooners and catamarans and dinghies all came to play. The wharves were full, the shops, bars and restaurants all glowing and lively. A row of seven or so walkarounds and powerboats near us had rafted up, tied bow and stern, and the longest was blasting the Chicks' greatest hits on their speakers. Every now and then a pop and a boom of distant (illegal) firecrackers and flares rang out over the country twang. A cheer rose from the direction of Bannister's Wharf, and I suspected they'd just concluded the annual reading of the Declaration of Independence from the steps of historic Clarke Cooke House. Here's a fact: the best time in New England, other than autumn, is America's birthday. Little Rhody doesn't sleep on Fourth of July.

When it was well and truly ink dark, the bridge lit up in red, white, and blue. Spencer's fingers, always moving, restless, traced a pattern on the gunwale. The breeze accelerated, and I felt the ocean spray on the back of my neck and my arms, heard the caress of the waves against the hull.

"You getting chilly?" Spencer's voice now was lowered,

the expectant hush before the fireworks exploded. I nodded. "Let me see what I can find in the cabin."

It only took a moment, and he was back with a striped, tassel-lined cotton blanket. "Are Maggie and Jack asleep?" I asked as he draped it over both our laps.

"Out cold."

"They need it."

He sipped from his tumbler and leaned back. "How's the wedding planning going, by the way? I hear bits and pieces from Jack. More from Susie, mostly about the impossible logistics of parking and port-a-potties."

"It's progressing, though the guest list is the current sticking point. Since Hope doesn't have to pay for a venue, she wants to invite friends of friends, casual acquaintances, the woman she played pickleball with that one time. We were walking through Washington Square the other day and a pack of tissues fell out of her purse; a nice guy picked them up for her. I had to physically restrain her as she tried to chase him down. But. Our next task is catering, food, menu, et cetera, which you know I'm *very* into."

"Your appetite is one of the things I admire most about you."

I laughed. He was so warm and beautiful and still, after all these years, made my heart go *thud*. The future seemed quite far, my life beyond Newport distant. I slipped my palm into his.

He seemed surprised, but didn't pull away, tightened his fingers around mine.

He looked serious, and for a second, I thought he might tell me that, once again, he didn't like me enough, he didn't care to try. But then his eyes fluttered closed. "You're giving me butterflies, Cassie."

I felt myself drifting toward him.

Right on time, the first firework whistled up from the barge far in the harbor and exploded into gauzy golden tendrils. From the boats nearby, I registered applause.

A smile—of gratitude, I think—appeared just before his mouth was on mine. And it was better than I remembered. Or maybe it was just as good as it had been when we'd been twenty-one years old, and I'd forgotten, or pushed it down and away.

He tasted like hops and honey, blue summer and numbered days. His fingers were on my jaw, confident and tender, and mine were fastened to the nape of his neck. I was breathless, but the thought of stopping for air never crossed my mind.

Eventually, there was commotion from the cabin; Maggie and Jack were awake. Spencer and I scooched apart, adjusting shirt—him—and ponytail—me. We both seemed to understand that the past few minutes had been ours, and we wanted to keep it that way, at least for now. The couple clambered up the steps, bleary-eyed and blinking, asking, between booms and sparks, what time it was. Spencer and I directed them to the port side bench so they'd have the best view. I handed over our blanket, and we all settled in.

I guess I could've said something smart about the fireworks, told Spencer what his presence was doing to me, but his gaze was on the sky, a broad, childlike grin on his face, and I could see that he didn't need me ruining the moment. I curled my legs on the bench so they were touching his, and, for once in my life, shut up and enjoyed the show.

16

Here's how you know your sister is important: a fashion house
does a house call.

Two days after our sail, Erdem sent to the Cottage a co-
terie of tailors, seamstresses, needleworkers specializing in
lace, notetakers, and someone whose only job was to hold the
iPad so the creative director, a very serious young man with
a French accent, bald head, and thick black beard, could sur-

vey the scene and give orders about trim, padding, the bodice, etc., etc.

Susie, Hope, River, Maggie, and I were gathered for her dress fitting—not the first and *certainly*, one of the seamstresses told us out of the side of her mouth that wasn't clamped down on pins as she measured Maggie's waist, *not the last.*

My sister was standing on a stool in the middle of the room, looking into a giant Victorian mirror, arched at the top with gold garlands and roses. Granny Fi had called this her *morning room*, filled it with palm trees and cacti, and would take her first coffee and cigarette of the day here by the windows overlooking the veranda. Years removed from the memory, all remainders of my grandmother paved over by Schumacher wallpaper and ditzy prints, I could still smell the milk from the Mane and Tail shampoo she used on her long, silver hair, see her orange house dress, her nails always kept short, her flat, broad feet grounded to the earth.

Now Susie referred to the place as *the salon*. Thick, pleated ivory curtains with braided rope tiebacks hung from the floor-to-ceiling windows; the rug was Afghan, the massive oil landscape painting behind the red velvet couch Hudson River School, and the overall decor inspiration, Susie informed me earlier, came from Villa Les Cèdres in Cap Ferrat.

Oh, have you been there? I'd asked.

It was a yes or no question. But somehow Susie managed to turn it into a dissertation about the Côte d'Azur, Belgian King Leopold, and my great-grandfather Lewis Coventry, who helped Elizabeth Taylor, Richard Burton, their two secretaries, and one budgie escape the paparazzi via yacht.

"Sorry," Maggie kept saying to the seamstress swirling around her skirt. "Sorry, sorry."

"Bug, stop apologizing." I was between the two mothers on the impossibly long couch. I'd finished one espresso, but was already craving another. "So they have to take a million measurements before the wedding. You're growing human life. I think that's a fair trade."

Maggie shushed me, pointed to the door.

"Who's there to hear?" I asked, finding her level of paranoia unnecessary. The team from Erdem knew she was carrying, and, as of yesterday, Susie and the Coventry-Gilfords, including River. Hope and J.P. had been ecstatic; our mother had practically danced around the carriage house kitchen while cycling through grandmother names, eventually landing, for reasons completely unknown, on *Hoppy*. Susie, according to Maggie, had taken the news more sanguinely.

We were sworn to secrecy. Maggie still hadn't told her company. But, she assured us, she was going back to New York in the next week or two and, with the help of her agent and manager, would break the news then.

"None of my staff would say a word," Susie promised Maggie.

"Ha!" barked Hope. She slapped my knee, as though I'd get the joke.

"What, *ha*?" Susie lowered her skim latte to her lap, her mouth becoming a straight line.

"These walls listen," Hope said. "And these walls *talk*. Haven't you figured that out by now?"

"That's true," said the wall between the salon and the hall.

"Jack!" Maggie shrieked. There were some gasps from the Erdem team, and River flung himself up to block the bride from sight.

"Don't worry! I'm not coming in!" Jack called. "I just wanted to ask Maggie where she wants the wedding welcome party? I'm making some calls. Someplace fun on Broadway? Or, like, fancier, like The Chanler?"

Everyone relaxed back into their seats, panic subsiding. "If we have it at The Chanler," said Susie, voice raised enough for Jack to hear, "we must have Val bartend. She is the only one there who knows how to make a proper martini."

"I could ask my friend Minnie Flood if she'd host you at Dovecote," said Hope. "Their daughter graduated college and they're spending the summer taking her on a grand tour, but she's checking her email."

Minnie Flood and her husband, a former professional polo player, lived at Dovecote, a grand old château-style mansion on Ruggles. They were fancy—even for Newport—and I ventured to guess the woman did not reciprocate my mother's claims of friendship. Indeed, Susie hummed with what sounded like suspicion.

"Let's do something fun for welcome drinks," I offered. "Like a beach picnic or wine tasting."

"Casual could be different!" Susie sounded like someone trying to affirm a suggestion so she wouldn't feel too guilty absolutely annihilating it later.

"Actually, you gave me an idea, Hope," replied Jack through the door. "Why don't we organize a chalet at Newport Polo? Everyone can come out, have a fun afternoon on the grounds, drink, and watch a match."

"Done," said Maggie, adjusting the band of lace wrapped under her bodice. "And did you get ahold of that facilities director for wedding day parking?"

"Yes. We can use the Marble House lot, and the shuttle can run down the Avenue."

I was glad to see—or rather, hear—Jack being productive, and them working as a team. There was a little more dialogue about lots and routes, and then his footsteps retreated.

"A shuttle is such a boring thing to spend money on," said Hope.

"What would you rather guests do?" Susie asked. "Swim?"

"I was thinking they'd walk," countered Hope. "Though I know for the helicopter set, hoofing it is *unheard* of."

"Mom." I vehemently wished for Spencer's diplomatic presence.

The past week, Hope had been grating me to the pith. In between emails and video calls with Sotheby's, Nadeau's, and John McInnis, all interested in the Coventry collection, she and I had been back and forth from the storage unit, unpacking, inspecting family treasures. Prying items out of her hands had been excruciating. You'd think I was asking her to sell her front teeth rather than an old-fashioned coffee grinder.

My plan was this: after the auction, when the proceeds were tallied and the Coventry cut calculated, and after the wedding, the final send-off to The Land, I would go to J.P. and Hope. With money in hand, with Maggie on her honeymoon, with the eyes of Newport elsewhere, it seemed like the safest, softest time to deliver the news of their eviction. I still had a lot of antiques and lace to wade through before then.

"I love how this is taking shape," said River, and I sensed he was deliberately towing the conversation into calmer waters. "Very '70s. Channeling Halston." Though his internship through Salve was supposed to be unpaid and therefore—what?—more noble or valuable or something, Maggie, Jack, and I had convinced him that his labor should be compensated, and he'd agreed to accept what we were calling an honorarium, a couple hundred dollars a week. Not only was he proving indispensable with the auction and the wedding planning, but he was kind and blithe and sartorially exceptional and had a lovely, soothing energy, which was always welcome in this group. He had also, charmingly, made it his mission to keep alive all potted plants scattered about the carriage house, valiantly, sometimes hopelessly, misting and watering.

His task today, as it was explained to me, was to take pictures of the dress for Maggie to scrutinize later.

Kent came through with a tray of refills. He passed mugs and cups in various sizes out to the grateful audience.

"Where's mine?" Susie inquired, empty hands turned palm-up.

"No more for you," Kent said efficiently. "Or you won't sleep."

Susie made a sound that reminded me of an aggrieved Marge Simpson.

Kent handed a bottle of water to my sister, then left to deal with the woodworker, in from Philadelphia, who'd come to fix the old oak icebox in the butler's pantry, as one does.

"Can you hold this for me?" Maggie asked Hope once Kent had gone. "If I take one sip I will have to pee. I always have to pee now."

"If men had to go through pregnancy," Hope said, rising to grab the water, "paid maternity leave would begin at conception." There—a place where my mother and I were in perfect accord. "Did you ever open those photos I sent you of Jacqueline Kennedy's gorgeous wedding gown?" asked Hope, retaking her seat. "I thought you might get inspired by the classic look."

"Jackie Kennedy's dickhead father-in-law pressured her into that dress," I said. "Everyone knows that."

"I didn't know *you* did," Hope said. "You're more Newport than you think, my dear."

"Your great-grandparents were at Hammersmith Farm for the Kennedys' wedding reception," River told Maggie and me. "Reports say the receiving line took between two and three hours *alone*. Mrs. Kennedy insisted on greeting everyone."

"You know Granny Fi was invited, too?" Hope asked. "But she didn't go. Said it would be a mob scene. Can you imagine? Deciding to skip a coronation?"

I *could* imagine. Granny Fi wasn't a recluse; she liked parties, not perfect ones, jammed with society, but good ones—a few close friends, a silver vase overfilled with purple artichoke blossoms, Johnny Cash on the record player, a dribble of Château Margaux. Granny Fi wasn't about to waste her one wild and precious life on events that weren't *fun*.

I was wondering how she'd feel about Maggie's wedding when my phone vibrated in my hand. Spencer and I had been texting a whole lot of flirty nothing, self-deprecating stuff, some *do you remembers?* We'd already created an inside joke about the spices and sauces he carried around in his backpack; we had a bit about putting Everything but the Bagel seasoning on a bagel, which was not funny, and never failed to crack us up.

But it wasn't Spencer. It was Mouna.

I need someone in Hong Kong. I know you're with your people, but I wanted to check in case...?

"Maggie, I still don't know about that neckline." Hope tapped the corner of her mouth with her nail. "I don't want her to look vulgar like all those mopey, droopy girls in *Martha Stewart Weddings* magazines."

"She wants to show off her décolletage," said Susie.

"It's too low," argued Hope. "Especially because her boobs are going to get bigger."

"In that case," Susie retorted, "she might as well go lower."

Departing now? I typed. I hadn't heard from her in a month, but I guess she'd decided my involuntary breather was over.

"Sit up straight, will you?" Hope pulled on my shoulder. "You might as well be banging the bell in Notre-Dame."

"Alva Vanderbilt put a steel rod in her daughter Consuelo's dresses," said River.

"Was Consuelo Vanderbilt over thirty at the time?" Susie asked, recrossing her legs primly.

"No, but she married a duke," said Hope. "So maybe Cass should let that sink in and adjust accordingly."

"Find me a duke, River, will you?" I asked. "I hear they're scrounging around Newport, looking for girls with little money, A-cups, and night guards."

"Cassie, what do you think about the sleeves?" Maggie held out her arms. "Too much volume for crepe de chine?"

"It's a sheer fabric. You can absolutely go more voluminous. And the cuffs will add some structure." Briefly, I contemplated who I'd become; two months ago, if someone had said the word *crepe de chine*, I would've asked if that were animal, vegetable, or mineral.

I glanced down at my phone. Mouna responded: ASAP. Assignment probably lasting 3-4 weeks.

"Who are you texting?" Hope peered over my shoulder.

I put my phone to sleep, placed it on a stack of art books on the coffee table next to a marble sculpture of a foot—a single foot!—in a Grecian sandal. Of course Mouna would invite me back to the field *now*. The precise moment when I had the most balls in the air. "No one."

"Who?" pressed Hope.

"Oh, let her be!" Susie snapped. She'd had enough, it seemed, of Hope. I did appreciate her coming to my defense. Unfortunately, she didn't stop there: "You don't need to have a comment on *absolutely* everything. You do realize that's an option?"

"Susie, if you only knew all the things I chose *not* to comment on," retorted Hope, without a moment's pause.

"Oh-*kay*!" I raised my espresso. "Should we, um, toast? To Maggie. To the wedding. To this sweet baby. And to the Erdem team! And this beautiful dress!"

True professionals, they graciously accepted our compliments. Later, packing up, I heard one whisper to another the word *embarrasser*.

I didn't need to speak French to know what that meant.

17

NetaNewport Current Status: drooling over these crumb-topped clams from @thebonnie *run don't walk*
Link in bio for a roundup of the best happy hour offerings in Newport this weekend
1 hour ago

A drunkenly humid July night, and I was at The Bonnie for a family dinner—Maggie and Jack, Archer and Remy, my parents and River.

Spencer was serving up his *secret menu*, as he'd said to me with a wink—sweet potato and garlic confit soup with caviar on a fried brioche wedge, biscuits with sweet peach chutney, Bajan baked oysters with marjoram and thyme and butter, rigatoni with apple sausage, sablefish with the most delectable crispy skin. I was glad I'd worn my paper-bag-waist pants with a rope belt tie.

From where I sat at the oval table, I had a view, between

my sister and mother, of the open kitchen, and I watched him, admiring his form in his white jacket, hunching over dishes, sprinkling, swirling, plating with moves practiced and unfussy. The way he took the inside of his wrist to his forehead, eyes squinted in concentration, his quiet words to the line cook beside him, which I read as *hurry, now, now*. Someone said something to make him laugh, and his reaction made me smile, too.

"I guess the lead singer wanted to go solo," Maggie was musing to the table.

"And he couldn't wait seven more weeks," added Jack.

It had been a day. The wedding band's front man had quit, leaving us, and the rest of the Carat Tops, in the lurch. And though I'd asked if this was a Genesis situation, hoping upon hope they had a Phil Collins on drums, we were out of luck, with less than two months to go and not a lot of options.

"Your uncle Dunk and I can get up on the stage with our ukuleles," said J.P., finishing the last of the tart, buttery lobster tartare.

"Is 'Hot Cross Buns' on the recorder a bop?" said Remy. "If so, I have you covered."

"I know a few songs on the guitar," offered Archer. "'Satellite' by Dave Matthews. 'Grey Street' by Dave Matthews. 'Ants Marching' by Dave Matthews..."

"It may seem hard now," said River, passing me a plate of fried something. I tasted, then closed my eyes, blissful. Fish cake. "But compared to other Coventry matrimonial catastrophes, this really pales."

"Tell us more," said Jack. "Now that I'm formally joining the family—if you all will have me—I do want to learn more about the Coventrys."

"Well, Earnest Coventry was disinherited because he married a schoolteacher instead of the Park Avenue heiress his mother had picked out for him," said Hope.

"How romantic," Jack said.

Seated beside each other, Hope and River both shook their heads. "Their love was short-lived," said River. "They died on the *Lusitania* six months after their elopement."

"The Coventry curse," said Hope as she swirled the wine around in her glass. "River, do you know about my great-great-aunt? On her way to the coronation of King George and Queen Elizabeth in London, she died on the *Hindenburg*. After her death, her husband, Hamish, became quite the sad sack, and fell prey to an unscrupulous psychic—"

Me: "Is there any other kind?"

"—and spent near every last dime on séances. And Granny Fi's father came within an inch of his life as a kid because he had dessert at a friend's town house. Who was the cook at that town house?"

"Typhoid Mary," Maggie and I said together. Only River seemed to be enjoying this misfortunate recap. Archer had lost interest, and was showing something to Remy on his phone.

"One Coventry, a few generations ago, can't remember his name, was assassinated by a labor activist making a statement about conditions in the steel mills," Hope plowed on.

"This particular relative probably deserved it," I said.

Once, the Coventry family tree had been expansive. But untimely death, terrible financial management, racetrack gambling addictions, alcoholism, infidelity, divorce, ennui brought on by daddy issues, the whole grab bag of tragedy, had inexorably trimmed the limbs. Hope's own father, Granny Fi's husband, died young in a private plane crash over Nantucket Sound, he and the heir to the Listerine fortune, who was piloting, felled by fog and an ego that presumed weather didn't matter in the face of will. But that wasn't all divine judgment.

"Curse," I maintained, "is the wrong term. It's what happens when an insular circle of very entitled people collide with each other, atoms crashing together in a vacuum." I reached for the wine bottle chilling in the ice bucket. Empty. Jack assured me he'd order another one. "The only person who managed to get out of this family with her head on straight was Granny Fi."

"Not so sure about that," said Hope.

"How so?" River asked. "Or am I trespassing into forbidden territory?"

My eyes found my father's, then Maggie's. "Mom and Granny Fi butted heads," I simplified. I'd been thinking of my grandmother a lot recently; maybe it was because I was sleeping in what was once her artist's studio, treading in her footsteps, blinking up at the same sky. It didn't feel right that Maggie was getting married without her.

Hope thought differently. "Because Granny was artistic and brilliant and wasn't interested in any of the things I was," she said, as though she had the script memorized.

"Check your email, Cassie," Archer cut in, holding up his phone. "Seller's agreement came in from Sotheby's."

"Good," said Maggie cheerfully. Though she'd been hesitant about the auction at first, Archer and I had gotten her on board. "I know you've been waiting for it."

"Make sure the reserve prices and the post-auction broker clause are what we talked about," Archer said, scrolling, pinching to zoom.

"Look at you," said Jack to Archer. "Contract king."

"I didn't go to Wharton." Archer shot Jack a look. "But I can read."

"I'm not teasing you," said Jack, sincere. "I'm just admiring your patience with fine print."

Archer blinked a few times, then smiled, his manner softening. "Yeah. Gotten a lot of practice reading social media terms of service."

"You've been indispensable," I said to him. I didn't think Jack was trying to make a joke at Archer's expense. But I'd been on Archer's TikTok enough this summer to see the trolls, now and again, that emerged from under the bridge to deliver a nasty comment—usually a paragraph-long rant, and I understood why he'd be sensitive to even a hint of criticism from his own family.

Maggie got up to use the restroom and Archer and Remy fell back into the phone, and River and J.P. and Jack's conversation broke off into a different direction. I could see Hope was still pouting from the way we'd touched down on Granny Fi.

I laid my hand over hers. "Hey. You okay?"

She seemed surprised at my gesture, tilting her head to inspect me. I suspected that when she opened her mouth, it might be to chastise me for not taking her side hard enough. On cue, she frowned. "Who were you texting the other day during the dress fitting?"

I drew back. Shook my head. "I told you. No one."

"You weren't texting *no one*. If you were, your face wouldn't have been a portrait of suffering." This made me laugh, but Hope talked right through it. "You think you're this great actress, but every emotion you feel is broadcasted loud and clear. You're holding something back and don't think for a moment I miss it."

Frustrated—and maybe a bit unsettled by her observations—I rearranged the silverware on my empty plate. "You'd prefer I'd read all my texts aloud."

"I'd prefer honesty."

"No, you wouldn't."

"What?" Hope said heavily.

Though she had asked for honesty, I hadn't intended to

actually deliver it. "I mean, why are you so concerned about my correspondence? You are so busy with the wedding and, you know, *life*. Didn't you and River spend all day at the fire house?"

"Aquidneck House," corrected Hope. "Every Wednesday we lead needlepoint group at the adult care center. See? I tell you something. Now you tell me something. It's called dialogue."

"Okay," I said, folding like the napkin on my lap. "Fine. I was texting Mouna. She asked if I could go to Hong Kong."

Hope's eyes went wide. "Really? When? Now?"

"This is why I didn't say anything." I threw up my hands. "I didn't want the consternation."

"But are you leaving?" Hope pestered.

"No." I poked at the table between us. "I've chosen to be here, and I'm sticking by that choice. I'm talking about dress sleeves and letterpress paper and the difference between eight- and ten-piece bands."

What would Granny Fi think of me? The first week of August, I was scheduled to shoot at Marble House, at an event hosted by Moët that was somehow celebrating both sparkling rosé and surfing. *Vanity Fair* was coming soon to interview Maggie about her fabulous wedding, and *nothing* else, not her pregnancy, not the state of the carriage house, not whatever innuendo Net-a-Newport was peddling about the Coventry-Gilfords.

"But you want to leave," said Hope. "If Granny Fi were still alive, you'd be as attached to Newport as a barnacle to a rock."

"Look," I responded to the disappointment in my mother's voice. "I love being with Maggie. Dad is teaching me a lot about soil composition and how to repot a bonsai—skills I will probably never need, but, you know, quality time. Archer let me cameo in one of his lives the other day." An experience that had been both eye-opening and wild—his fans, friends, whatever, commenting rapid fire like they knew him. Which, I guess, they did. "And when you're not criticizing my posture, I'm having fun with you. So, can that be enough?"

I thought Hope might keep badgering me. What had I meant when I said that she didn't want honesty? Why was I *so* intent on this auction in the first place? For a second, I wondered what it might be like—telling her everything, Susie's plans, the future of The Land, all of it.

But, to my mother's credit, or maybe to her wisdom, she just hummed. "Well," she said, putting her hands on my cheeks, cradling the face of her child, "at least now you're talking."

·····

At the end of the dinner service, after we insisted we could not fit any more morsels down our gullets, Spencer cleaned his knives, straightened his *mise*, and offered me a tour of The Bonnie's rear kitchen.

Behind the swinging saloon doors, the space was filled with laughter and grunts and line cooks snapping lids on plastic containers and the metallic sound of knives being sharpened and waitstaff cracking at each other with rolled-up towels. It smelled of heavy cream and garlic, and the huge, stainless-steel contraptions were still radiating heat. The counters were gleaming spotlessly, but there were crumbs and bits of chopped-up items coating the floor. Gelatinous liquids, too, were congealing in pools, including something that looked like melted chocolate.

Spencer introduced me to the front-of-house manager, a very nice woman who cursed a lot and had a tattoo of a cross emblazoned on her neck—though it turned out she knew me already. Well, not *knew me* knew me, but her father had done much of the masonry during Susie's renovations, including some at the carriage house.

"He's an artist," I said, thinking of the time and attention he must've devoted to The Land's miles of stone. "A true master."

"I'll tell him." When she smiled, I noticed a stud inside her lip. "And hey, welcome home!"

"Thanks!" I said, and I didn't even register her statement, nor my offhand answer to it, until days later, which tells you something about my shifting definition of *home*.

Even after a full day of work, Spencer was energetic and happy. As I stuck close to his side and tried not to tread in anything sticky, he pointed out the reach-ins, the walk-ins, the mincers, the slicers, the peelers, and the proofer. He tried to convince me—me, who considered microwaving oatmeal "cooking"—to buy a sous vide machine and gave a passionate speech about the unquestionable power of salt, the treachery of black pepper.

I asked him to tell kitchen stories and he obliged; the one about the grizzled alligator of a chef who taught his pastry-making course in culinary school, who loved unleavened dough almost as much as he loved delivering pee-inducing tirades to any student who *dared* present him with a droopy soufflé. The one when he was working as sous in a big fancy French place in Providence that hadn't changed its menu in seventeen years and the head chef decided it was "Tequila Tuesday" and ended up setting half the clean linen on fire. Spencer had to stomp the flames out himself because no one could find an extinguisher. Spencer quit—"easiest choice I ever made"—right in the middle of dinner service. That was when he vowed to open his own restaurant. That's when he made a promise that whatever his new restaurant concept would be, it would have a strict no-assholes hiring policy.

His only shared complaint, which he conferred to me in a

hushed voice, was a recently hired line cook, who, in his es-
timation, had exaggerated his skills on his résumé. "I don't
think he'd know the difference between a béarnaise and a bor-
delaise," Spencer muttered, wiping a stray shmear of grease
off the griddle. "But he's a really sweet kid, and I'm finding
it difficult to fire him. I'll give him one more week."

Gradually, the kitchen emptied, people telling Spencer good
night and *see you tomorrow, Chef,* throwing their towels and
aprons in the laundry bin, taking cigarettes out of pockets to
light up outside.

Spencer pulled me into a small, cluttered office at the back
of the house and flipped on the lights. "I want to show you
why Fourth of July was my first full day off in six months."
He stretched his arm and took down a roll of architectural
drawings from a shelf, then unfurled them on the desk, using
stacked file folders to hold down the edges. He tapped the
writing at the bottom of the sheet. *Sims/Tien Project.* "They're
preliminary. But I think we're headed in the right direction."

"Your new restaurant!" I exclaimed, flattered that he was
letting me peek at his dream. I traced my finger over the de-
tailed, labeled sections of the plans: kitchen, service line, dish-
wash, staff change, dry storage, dining room, bar. The doors
and the windows, the tables for two and eight. "It looks twice
as big as The Bonnie."

"Has to be. We're not going to turn tables over as quickly.
I want dinner to be a two-and-a-half-hour experience, min-
imum. Bring back the glamour to Newport. Classy heyday,
but make it cool. Raise the heat index. I'm talking voluptuous
plates—oxtail, pork shoulder, retro amounts of steak. Truf-
fles. Demi-glace. Ossetra and beluga. Let's dust off our dinner blazers, you know what I'm saying?"

There was energy behind his words, the same kind of mix
of propulsion and expectation and possibility and joy that got

me through the tedium and fatigue of what was less a job and more of a calling. Undeniably, he knew where he was going. He knew where he was supposed to be.

And it was Newport. Of all places.

"The investors initially were skeptical," he continued. "There's a long, insidious history of Black chefs being red-lined out of the fine dining world. I convinced them, but I need to make that money back, and fast, because I don't have rich parents or a fancy bank guaranteeing this. I need to prove that I'm worth the bet, again."

"You are," I said, absolutely secure in that, at least. "This is going to be a place where parents can go for a date night away from their kids. Where grandparents can toast their grandchildren. You're going to get a proposal a night, Spencer! You're giving Newport a meal they will think about for years."

"I hope so," he said. "Because Newport has so much potential to be one of the great culinary destinations of the Northeast, like Charleston and New Orleans are to the South. One of the reasons I settled here."

I noted this—his dreams not just for himself but for the city. Newport was lucky to have him. "Just one quibble," I teased. "I see you don't have a cooking station up front?"

Spencer shook his head. "Chaos in the back this time."

"But how will people ogle you?" I tickled his waist, under his chin, and he made playful efforts to swat me away. "How will we gawk?"

"Better get it in now." With a quick lunge, he captured my arms, then turned me around so my lower back pressed into the table, put his body tight on mine.

I felt my phone buzz in my jacket pocket. I had been waiting for a text back from Mouna. The night after my sister's dress fitting, I'd landed on the right words to tell her I couldn't be her girl in Hong Kong. That I couldn't go anywhere, in fact, until after the wedding. "One sec," I mumbled, and he released me so I could unlock my screen.

Makes sense why you can't be in the field right now, Mouna had written. Family comes first. I didn't realize how I'd tensed my shoulders until they relaxed. Seconds later, another text arrived: I want to get someone into Uzbekistan in the fall. I have a source who can help with accreditation. Interested?

Leave it to Mouna to shoehorn *TIME*'s way into one of the most journalistically unfriendly countries in the world. This would be big. This would be exclusive. This would be on assignment, and therefore on salary. How could I say no? By the fall, my family wouldn't need me anymore. I'm more than interested, I typed. This would not, I promised myself, be another self-inflicted disaster like Moldova.

I tossed my phone onto the table and draped my arms around Spencer's nape. "Good news?" Spencer asked. He picked up my palm from his neck, kissed it, a gesture that moved me to light-headedness.

"Just looks like my career hasn't collapsed, after all," I said.

"Collapsed?" He drew away a bit. "I thought you were just taking some time off. I didn't know it was so dire."

Touched by his concern, I told him the truth. "My last assignment, I almost lost my head. Figuratively and literally, and I got into some trouble. But don't worry, looks like I'll be back in the field in September."

I raised my chin, expecting his lips, but he paused, and something passed across his face. Hesitation, I think. Maybe uncertainty. "Why would I worry?"

Did I really have to spell it out? Years ago, I put myself out there. I'd wanted him to take the kind of risk he was making now, but with his heart instead of his wallet and reputation. But I believe his exact words were: *we have so much more to explore and experience and I wouldn't want to limit you…*

"I just meant I'm not sticking around long enough to—"
I almost said *to fall in love with you again* "—long enough to,
you know, um, be anything but casual."

"Okay," he said, but still did not kiss me.

"Sorry, you seem skittish." I didn't want the electricity between us to fizzle. I didn't want us in the past, or the future,
thinking about pain, real or imagined. I wanted us here, tonight. Careful of his papers, I positioned myself on the table
so I was sitting, wrapped my legs around his hips. "Everything is fine."

"I'm just thinking. Your dangerous job must affect your
ability to have and maintain relationships, right?"

I blinked. "Tough question."

He raised a shoulder. "I think it would be really difficult for
you to be far away from your home and family, doing something that could get you seriously hurt."

I thought for a moment about his observation, which I
hadn't really considered ever in those terms, though I probably should've. That was a chronic past problem of mine—not
thinking about anyone outside the range of my viewfinder
while I was away.

I reached out and flipped his wrist over, so the welts I'd
noticed on his forearm when he'd shown me his homemade
bracelet at the Flower Show were visible. "Your profession
leaves scars, too," I observed.

Spencer's lips turned up at one corner, but stopped short of
a smile. "Some would blame the oven racks, or the hot oil," he
admitted. "But it was my carelessness that got me these. Hurrying. Myopic. Trying to be a tough guy and work through
a migraine."

"Ouch." With featherlight touches, I traced his sockets, his
temples, the depressions behind his ears, the places where a
headache might hurt the most. "When did those start?"

He caught my fingertips and kissed them, then brought our hands, together between us, to his back, and I was tugged forward into his broad chest. So when he said the next thing, I couldn't see his face. "After my divorce. Ripped out my guts and left me with insomnia for a year, too. Should I have told you that? Too much for a casual relationship?"

"No," I decided. I listened closely to his heart beating, the roll and the thump under my ear on his chest. "I like figuring you out." I raised my head and met his gaze. "Discovering the new and remembering the old."

"Then let's keep at it," he said, a whisper against my mouth.

Our kiss went on for a long time. Like the restaurant he was going to open, it was sumptuous, velvety. It filled me up.

Whether any staff were still in the restaurant, I didn't know, nor did I particularly care. I eventually had to turn my head, gulping air because I was so hot for him I feared if I didn't pace myself I'd melt right into the desk. His hands were busy under my shirt when there was a knock on the door. We froze like two teenagers about to be busted.

"Chef?" came a voice. "We're about to lock up."

I moved my wide eyes to his. But he just adjusted me in his arms, and slid his thumb across my lips. "I'm going to be a few more minutes," he said, before putting his mouth back on mine.

18

NET-A-NEWPORT 12H
Been busy but have a break so ask me anything!!

Have you been to that new bar Boatswain
> *It's not for me too many influencers taking pictures in the bathrooms*

will you be at the coventry utterback wedding /
> *bestie you know id never miss it (if i was invited!)*

Susie Utterback/Hope Coventry hate each other y/n
> *I once overheard Susie say that Hope is the most loyal friend she'll never have*

"Your mother wants that to stay," said my father, pointing with the tip of his chocolate scone to the tarnished sterling cup and tiny baby spoon I'd exhumed from a bottom kitchen cabinet. This had become a common refrain over the past few days, sometimes grumbled from beside me, sometimes shouted from upstairs. "It's Archer's."

"The schoolyard bullies were right," said Archer, across the breakfast table from my father with no less than three drinks—coffee, juice, sparkling water—in front of him, as well as the florist's contract, which he was supposed to be reviewing. "I really *was* born with a silver spoon in my mouth."

"It goes," I said to my father, firm. Their clinginess to this junk frustrated me, their passionate attachment to it, as though it were part of their marriage, as though they needed it to survive. "You and Mom have only committed to eighty-four lots, and Sotheby's really wants one hundred."

"I keep meaning to DM all the Newport social media accounts about the auction." Archer capped his pen and tossed it aside. "I'll do that right now"

I'd spent the past few days shooting the Folk Festival, a gig that began at ten in the morning and usually didn't end until midnight; though the music was awesome, the bands eclectic and energetic, and my skills much more suited to the subjects, it was still *work*. I got home each night dusty and thirsty, legs and shoulders aching with exhaustion. Newport had no shortage of events, and my name and phone number were making the rounds. In my absence, Archer had taken the lead on the auction, combing the storage unit, rifling through the attic, arguing with Hope, and I wanted to give him a break.

I stuck my hand back into the far corner of the cabinet, felt around for a gem that would help fund a new apartment for my parents and silver-spoon-fed brother. My fingers landed on something and I carefully extracted a rusty metal box, big enough to fit two pairs of shoes, with loose hinges and a brass padlock with the manufacturer's name rubbed smooth.

"You remember that," said my father, noticing what I'd found.

Cleaning out the carriage house was not just organization, I was realizing, but archaeology. An excavation of the past. "We never reburied it?"

"*I* didn't dig it up!" J.P. reminded me. "You were the one to come crashing into the kitchen that night, smelling like a brewery, knocking into things, declaring you'd discovered the time capsule Granny Fi promised was at The Land."

Technically, he was correct: it had been a typical Friday night for me in high school. Midnight could usually find Reagan and me in the carriage house kitchen, eating Froot Loops, dribbling artificially colored milk down the fronts of our skimpy metallic going-out shirts in the dark. That particular evening, though, I'd gotten it in my head to unearth the thing that Granny had told us, before she'd died, was planted somewhere under the sundial in the sunken garden.

When J.P. discovered us, Reagan and I had located the capsule, but had failed to break it open. We were tipsy, and a little bit high, not to mention wrecked from wielding the shovels for an hour, so we just gave it up. "You didn't try to unlock it?" I asked my father. If anyone cared about what was inside, it would've been him.

"Your granny said it shouldn't be opened until 2020."

"Whoops," I said, "I forgot about that part. Well, that year has come and gone. Do you think this would be good in the auction?"

"Probably just an old Bible in there. Or bullets," J.P. said. "People buried a lot of teeth, too."

"Yikes." I gave the box a gentle shake. There was definitely something in there. "Feels like a book."

Archer motioned for the box, and I handed it over. "Remy lives for mysterious stuff like this." He ran his palm across the top. "He'll know if Sotheby's might want it."

"Speaking of, are you and Remy still going to that mentalist at the JPT tonight?" I asked.

"I'm not sure." Archer used the corner of his phone case to scratch his cheek. "He's kind of pissed at me."

I had a suspicion this might be the case. I'd seen one of his videos yesterday; just a close-up his thoughtful face with the caption: *when you're arguing with him but he starts to make good points*, set to that old song of Fergie's that begins with the lyrics *Oh, shit!* Doug the cat hopped down the stairs, pranced across the floor, and placed himself, still standing on four paws, directly on my lap. "You going to fix it?" I asked.

Archer, sounding determined: "Trying."

"Good. I like him."

Next to a white bowl with old-timey etchings of farmers' wives and chickens, my phone dinged.

Maggie: We've finished the interview. Taking pictures of the cottage now. Mom still gone?

Me: Yup.

Maggie and Jack were doing the *Vanity Fair* interview in the Cottage's living room—it was arguably the most impressive space in the whole mansion, and it had no view of the carriage house. And to keep our mother at bay, we'd sent her on a wedding-related errand that I'd estimated would take her four hours, as it involved one of her favorite things—going to a flea market to source chandeliers with patina to hang inside the reception tent.

Maggie: Ok Reagan now says she wants to get a few quotes from you and Archer.

Me: Ew why.

Maggie: What do I tell her??

Me: We can come over. Don't send them here!

I was grubby, I was tired, I was covered in cat fur and fogged up with Benadryl, but yeah, sure, this was a perfect time to answer some questions for Condé Nast. I removed Doug from my person, though I could tell he wasn't pleased, stood, and turned to my father. "There's nothing else here in the kitchen, Dad. You need to let Archer and me look through Earnest Coventry's curios again."

On the table between him and Archer, my father eyed the capsule. "Nothing there that is suitable for sale. Try the storage unit."

"We've been through the storage unit," said Archer.

"Dad—"

But whatever I was about to say about the unhealthiness of hoarding and holding on to a past that was no longer with us was interrupted by a "J.P., you'll never guess what I found!" and the slap of the screen door. Our uncle Dunk, my father's older brother, whose figure and tendency to dress in nothing but orange and red had always reminded me of a buoy in a shipping lane, entered the kitchen, holding a ball outstretched. When I'd arrived home late last night, I'd seen his burned-leaf-brown, peeling Winnebago in the garage, nestled next to Susie's sparkly S-class. "Our first bobber rig. I knew I had it."

"Would you look at that," J.P. said, pushing his chair back into the whatnot tower, which trembled precariously for a moment. But J.P. was already down the hall and marveling over the piece of fishing equipment. "This is lucky, Dunk."

Uncle Dunk spotted Archer and me and called out a greeting in his Southern baritone. Dunk's accent had stayed while J.P.'s had not. Read into this what you will. It was only chance that my father had traded Wise County for Rhode Island; he'd ended up in Newport after his car broke down on a road trip north.

We'd never seen the lands and the mountains of Appalachia where he and Uncle Dunk were raised. Even so, we children would occasionally get glimpses of the forces who shaped J.P.'s life in the form of long-term visitors who'd come to The Land for a month or two, complaining of ailments, complaining that the food here was shit, complaining of the noise of the ocean at night, and generally spoiling us rotten. Please don't mistake me—I rather liked Uncle Dunk and these far-flung cousins; it was just that the baggage they brought with them—fryers, barbecues, pets, camper vans, other people—was quite a lot.

Speaking of which—

I crept down the hall after my father. "The bird is here," I observed, keeping my distance from the ornery white macaw kicking a twiggy leg off Uncle Dunk's shoulder.

"Who, Larry?" said Uncle Dunk. He took off his sunglasses and looked between me and his pet. "Of course I brought him. He'd be pissed if he missed the wedding." I met Larry's marble eye, and he shook his yellow feathered plume, ominously, I thought. Humbled, and a bit scared, I blinked first. These hoity-toity animals would be the death of me. "Don't look so worried, Cassafrass," Uncle Dunk said. "I know you and Larry don't get on. I'm staying in the camper. Your mother wouldn't hear of me bunking here after that time Larry flew into Archer's hair and made him cry."

"Let's relive that," said Archer.

Hope cared for all manner of creatures great and small, but I suppose there always was an exception to the rule.

"And besides," Dunk was saying, "I'm kidnapping your

dad for a few weeks to go fishing in Charlestown. You won't barely see us."

"This isn't the greatest time for a vacation," I told my father. We knew Hope; now would anyone like to imagine what she would be like *without* my father by her side to balance her out?

"I'll be back for the preview party." J.P. dipped his head, peering at me from above his glasses. "And like you said, I'm retired. No vacation in retirement. More like a diversion, right, Dunk?"

"We livin' high on the hog." Uncle Dunk nodded, his signature turquoise feather earring swinging. "Speaking of high…" From his shirt pocket came a joint. "Cassafrass, you still smoking?"

"With your weed, Uncle Dunk? The last time, I remember, I ran around the house trying to convince Maggie the moon was falling. Then I ate so many doughnuts I think I split my pants."

"So that's a yes?" He started patting his pockets, presumably for a lighter.

Outside the screen door, the sound of tires over gravel. We all turned, even the bird, as Hope's car pulled in. "Dammit," I said.

"Better save the weed for another day," quipped my uncle as he tucked the joint back into his pocket. He feared no man, only my mother.

My father ushered Uncle Dunk down the hall to the kitchen, while I observed with a scowl my mother unloading boxes from her trunk. "Mom?" I griped, marching out the front door to where she stood by her Volvo. "Why are you back so soon?" In the distance, a dense wall of gray rain clouds was tumbling over the sound.

"I didn't go to the flea market yet." She shooed some gnats away from her face. "I wanted to drop this off first."

When she popped her trunk, I saw what she meant: cardboard boxes from the storage unit. I reached into the nearest one—it wasn't taped shut, just crudely closed by overlapping flaps—moved aside some of the old newspaper packing, and glimpsed the heavy cut-crystal pitcher from Granny Fi's wedding china. Ornate and sophisticated, something most grandmothers would keep in a cabinet behind lock and key, Granny Fi had kept it in the greenhouse, and given me a half-dollar each time I'd used it to water the riotous, untamed hydrangea bushes in the front of the Cottage. It had once been part of a set—tumblers, saucers, the works—but she'd broken the rest, some by accident, some on purpose to use the pieces in her sculpting.

"Absolutely not. No, Mom. No." Logically, I know that hoarding tendencies aren't about the objects. It's about safety, control. A pitcher, back in the house—why should I care? Shouldn't I just give her this?

Hope dusted her hands on her jeans. "Might as well show it off before it's gone."

"We've promised Sotheby's that pitcher." This was precisely why my jaw was sore, I realized. This was why I had taken to massaging the tension out of my cheeks as I lay sleepless in the bottom bunk each night. "You signed the seller's agreement. That's a contract. This belongs in storage until the preview party."

"It belongs with *us*." She grabbed the pitcher box out of the trunk and charged for the carriage house. "You've cleaned me out, anyway. It's like we've been robbed."

"You're making this so difficult!" I argued after her. "Why are you so attached to this stuff?"

"Ha! This is rich, coming from the girl who's been muttering *keep it moving* all summer." Right before she reached the door, she tossed out one last pronouncement. "What are you attached to, Cassie? What do *you* value?"

The breath, momentarily, was taken out of me. Any remainder of rationality was then gone, yanked down below the sight line of my consciousness, replaced instead with anger. How dare she ask me this? While they fished and socialized with birds and raided the storage unit, who had called Susie's electrician? Me. Who'd postponed a date with Spencer when the plumber came to fix both carriage house bathrooms, then paid the guy with the Flower Show money because I didn't want to ask Susie for one more penny? Me. The roof wasn't repaired, but it was on the list.

"That's unbelievably unfair," I said. Shouted? "All I've done is try to help."

"Then help with those boxes," she replied, her hip on the screen.

This was getting out of hand. "Give me the car keys," I ordered, striding over. "I'm taking this back to storage."

"Cass, don't you dare." She turned, using a box to block me. "J.P.!" my mother called for backup. "I need you!"

"Give. Me. The. Keys," I ground out, pawing at her purse.

J.P. appeared. In a blink, Hope shoved the parcel off into his hands before he could even ask what it was. Then she produced the keys from some back pocket and tossed them with a grunt over the property line's wall into the thick, unmowed vegetation of the neighbors on the other side.

Just as the air had gone still before the storm, we stayed frozen, staring at each other, surprised at the quick escalation, tense over what might happen next.

I spoke first and it was through clenched teeth. "I hope," I said, "that Larry poops all over these precious boxes."

"Oh, Cassie," moaned my father, as though I'd just cursed them all to hell.

"What's going on here, young ladies?" This from Archer, who'd come out with River after my father.

"Larry's inside?" asked my mother, her ire now redirected toward her husband. "That creature better not be in my kitchen, J.P.! I told you not to bring him in! Bird germs everywhere. Not with a pregnant woman in our family, no sir."

"What creature?" We whirled. If there had been a DJ around, the record would've scratched to a halt. Susie, standing a few feet away in the graveled drive, arms crossed, pinched. Next to her, Maggie and Jack, mouths open in shock. On Susie's other side, the chairman of the Newport Preservation Council, his hand on his glasses as though he was about to pull them off his face to prove what he was seeing.

And behind her—well, you can easily guess. It was *Vanity Fair* herself, of course. Reagan Finley, in a floral dress and combat boots. In her hand was a recorder.

"And who—" Reagan cocked her head, her eyes flicking between the carriage house and the group of its inhabitants, all of which were in bad shape "—is pregnant?"

I looked at the distraught face of my sister and the hungry, gleeful face of Reagan. Then I showed my palms, maybe a motion of uncertainty, maybe one of offering, and answered, simply: "I am."

19

I fled.

In the moment, all I'd thought about was Maggie, protecting her. I hadn't considered the consequences. So, like an impulsive five-year-old who'd just drawn on the Cottage's dining room frescoes in ink, I'd gone to my room for a time-out.

There are lots of different quiets, everyone knows this. But the quiet when you're alone, after you've done something reckless, is the lousiest, loudest quiet there is.

As I lay on the bottom bunk, picking at the loose threads hanging from the box spring above me, I imagined how the next few minutes, hours, might go. There were only two options, anyway. Either I'd be exposed for my lie or I'd be believed.

I'm not sure which option I preferred.

On the door, a firm knock. "Come in!" I shouted, swinging my legs to the floor.

Maggie entered, grim, followed closely by Archer. Last were

Jack and Susie, who'd looked like they'd been caught in the rain, the tops of their shoulders damp, some strands of hair wet.

I couldn't remember the last time I'd actually seen Susie inside the carriage house. I knew she made a habit of avoiding my mother's territory, preferring instead to conduct business from the Cottage.

"Well." I stood, clutched the wooden rail of the top bunk, certain of nothing except that I was going to make a bad joke: "It's a boy!"

Archer laughed. He was the only one. I silently thanked him.

Susie observed the middle of the room, which was really just a bare square of carpet that wasn't covered with my suitcases or Archer's clothes. "So." Susie scratched the corner of her mouth with her ruby-clad ring finger. "This is quite a mess." I thought she might be talking about the room, the stain on the ceiling, the worn carpet, the broken blinds, the messy roll of lithograph posters Archer and I had been meaning to identify and value, and cups—so many cups!—that we'd never gotten around to bringing to the kitchen sink—until the next thing: "Reagan seems to have bought that Cass is the one pregnant. Regardless, I told her that any baby news is off record."

"Maggie." I crossed the short distance to my sister, who stood by the dresser I still hadn't put any clothes in. "I'm sorry. I know you were counting on me. I had no idea it would be such a tough morning. Uncle Dunk had the bird, then Hope came back from the storage unit, and—I just lost it. And then we turn around and all you guys are *right* there."

"It's my fault." Maggie reached out for Jack; he took her hand and tucked it into both of his. "You told me not to come over."

"We heard the raised voices," Jack said. "We thought something really bad was happening."

"Did it?" I asked, terrified of the answer. "Is the article ruined?"

"It will be okay," Archer said, fiddling with my toiletries strewn across the dresser, helping himself to some lavender hand cream I'd gotten at the sweetest vintage home and garden shop that just opened off America's Cup Avenue.

Shopping for grain sack pillows and flowerpots, and now fake pregnant? *Who was I?*

"It didn't seem like Reagan understood what was happening, really," Archer continued. "It was a lot of commotion, and then you told everyone you were knocked up and then ran away and Susie, Jack, and Maggie kind of whisked the preservation chap offstage, and Hope, River, and I turned on the charm, took Reagan to the greenhouse for a while to regale her with stories about how Granny Fi would make her own planters."

"Granny never did that," I said.

"*Now* she's honest." Archer rolled his eyes. "Oh, and River asked Uncle Dunk for a tour of the RV. So he'll return in a while with two Jethro Tull CDs and an ear piercing."

I dragged my hands down my face. "When I saw Reagan, my heart stopped. Jesus, Maggie. I just blurted it out. Why was the preservation man there, anyway? Of all people."

"Don Washington?" said Susie. "Thought he could add some interesting things about The Land to the article."

"And he'll be taking some very interesting news around Newport," said Archer. "He knows *everyone*."

"Did I do the right thing?" I asked Maggie. "I mean, after I did the wrong things? I can't tell if I helped or just made everything worse."

"You were protecting me." On the tarp above our heads, the rain pounded a tempo. "I asked you to keep the pregnancy secret, and you did."

"Cass has bought Maggie some time," said Archer. "The city will be abuzz, thanks to Don Washington. But then someone down the line will say, oh, just kidding, it wasn't Cass who's having a baby. We meant *Maggie*. And then everyone will pretend they knew it was Maggie all along, and that they never believed the Cass rumor, and we'll just go about our merry way like everyone isn't full of crap."

"But Cass has done so much for us these past weeks," Maggie responded. "I don't want her to lie for me."

"I agree," said Jack. "That seems wrong. Lies can be..." He trailed off, a muscle clenching in his jaw, and I thought he might be recalling his father, who'd invented progressively convoluted stories to cover up his affairs from his son and his wife.

"I hear that, but it's not like moral ambiguity has no place in Newport," said Archer. "Mrs. Duke got away with murder here—sorry, *allegedly*—but how much of her fortune has she given away? The revenue brought in by tourists of these mansions, mansions built on the backs, and sometimes with the lives, of workers given shit wages and separate basement entrances, pay for my game theory club at the high school..."

Wait, what club? I thought.

"...and Mom's needlepoint supplies for the adult home. And no one wants to buy these Gilded Age castles except for millionaires and billionaires who profit from an unjust capitalist system, but what else should we do? Let history be torn down for parking and—"

"We get that," said Susie, cutting him off. "But this is a big lie. Cass would have to sell it."

"Let's play it through." Jack turned to me. "How pregnant are you, exactly?"

"I haven't gotten that far."

"What are you going to say when people congratulate you?" he asked.

Archer answered for me: "I really don't think she's going to have a mob of people chasing her down Thames with their congratulations and best wishes. And, Cassie, I say that with love."

"I think people are going to be normal," I said, wondering at the force of this animal I'd unleashed, "and just talk about it behind my back."

"Will Hope go along with this?" asked Susie.

Though my chest was tight, I grinned as though I had it all figured out. "I once got backstage at a Foo Fighters concert with nothing but a mezzanine ticket, a smile, and assurances that I was Dave Grohl's facial hair stylist. I can fake a pregnancy, and I can get Hope on board."

"I can't believe I'm asking you to do this." Maggie abruptly spun, and took a few steps to the water-streaked window overlooking the garage. Muffled, but still audible, was the warning *beep beep beep* of a large vehicle backing up across the wet gravel. Maggie pushed down a handful of slats, and we were all treated to the sight of Uncle Dunk's camper van, reversing, slowly, J.P. in a yellow rain slicker behind it, using both hands to direct, as a traffic cop might. "I should just tell the truth," Maggie said. Her arm fell to her side, and the blinds snapped back into place with the clatter of cheap aluminum.

Maggie had all but carried me out of the Cottage our last night there. I had been grieving Granny Fi, missing our parents, and sick with fear for Archer, but how had I repaid her? When she wasn't breaking bones dancing, she was dragging me out of the ocean when I'd pledged to swim to Martha's Vineyard at two in the morning. She was collecting me from random people's basements and backyards, words slurred and mascara smeared. She was sending me cash for books and food while I was at college, though she was making pittance toiling away in NYCB's third company. She more than deserved this favor.

"You're planning a wedding," I said. "You've been sick, you've been trying to figure out how to have this child without it imploding your contract, your career. Let me do this for you. Until you can tell the company."

"Mom?" asked Jack. "Can you help us with this?"

"If this is what Maggie wants, of course I'll help." Susie moved to Maggie and put her hand on her cheek; her heels left indentations in the carpet. "The world waits for no woman."

"Which is weird, considering we're the ones populating it." My sister released a breath. "If Cass is su—"

But before she could finish, the ceiling caved in.

20

"Stop." I held my hand out.

A half dozen steps away, Spencer halted. He'd been reaching
for me, eyes warm and suggestive, like he was going straight
in for a kiss. But we were in public, at the Black Ships gala,
in the midst of a hundred people milling about the lawn of
the Naval War College's white stone Founders Hall, which
had been a poorhouse until a commodore, in a move that was

a bit too on-the-nose for the American military, said *it's ours now* back in the mid-1800s.

Last week, I'd sent Spencer perhaps one of the weirdest messages a man could receive. That the woman he was currently making out with was faking a pregnancy to protect her sister's career. Because said sister was actually the one who was pregnant. And he couldn't tell anyone. Any of it.

The entire cocktail hour so far had been an exercise in acting, just as Susie had predicted. Sushi and sake were abundant, as was the side-eye. The rumors had clearly germinated; though no one said a word, guests and staff were continually peeking at my waistline. For a time, I was instructed to sit in a chair in the shade by a nice man who worked at the museum, who'd confused modern women, apparently, for Victorians in tight corsets. I coughed and I swear he offered me smelling salts.

The unagi maki and chilled Dassai 45—both my absolute favorites—had been mocking me, and now Spencer had arrived to tempt me, too. "I don't want you dragged into the rumor mill," I said, at the lowest volume possible that he could still hear.

Despite my warning, he continued forward. "Since when do you care about gossip?"

I slung my camera bag to the front of my torso, a weak attempt to get something between us. "Since it was suggested on Net-a-Newport that I got knocked up out of wedlock."

Spencer was less than an arm's length away. We were standing by the raised stage erected by the museum's front steps, and the kumi-daiko performers were setting up their massive drums. Guests were beginning to gather around us. "You could've gotten a sperm donor. And who says the word *wedlock* anymore?"

My fingers and palms itched for him, but I had to stay

strong. "Newport does. You're a business owner here, Spencer. You're about to open another restaurant, and you need it to be five stars in every sense of the word. I'm the outsider. Let me fall on the sword by myself."

"I'm a biracial man living and working in the place where ribbon belts were invented," he reminded me. "*You're* not the outsider, baby."

"Even more reason this shouldn't touch you." In response to my text, Spencer had shared a meme of Marie Kondo rubbing her hands together and declaring *I love mess*, but I didn't want to be the reason things went sideways for him.

"Are we allowed to talk?" he whispered.

I glanced around, assuring myself that we appeared to be two people in casual conversation, then nodded.

"Good." He lowered his head to catch my eyes. "How are you?"

"I have so much to tell you." I released a breath. "Susie keeps her house absolutely frigid, and I can't complain because I'm a guest. How is her air-conditioning bill not one million dollars?" After the roof's tarp became a water slide into the carriage house's bunk room, bringing with it soggy wooden slats, mushy plaster, stray tiles, brown leaves, sticks, and all other manner of flora and fauna directly onto the beds, my clothes and shoes, and Jack's head (he got the worst of it), it became evident, even amid our shock, that Archer and I would have to find somewhere else to sleep.

It might have been Jack's suggestion that Susie host us at the Cottage. When we were younger, he was always trying to get us to sleep over, and I had the suspicion he hated being alone with only his mother, once Kent had gone home, in a vast mansion of thirty rooms. I certainly don't think it was Susie herself with the idea—she was too busy checking him for wounds. Anyway, Kent was soon giving us the Wi-Fi code and telling us that under no circumstances should we adjust the thermostat because it's on a program and involves heating and cooling zones and schedules and last time someone tried, the whole system froze and needed a reset and it was a whole thing with the manufacturer. Then Archer was plugging in all his devices in the bedroom that used to be our parents', and I was doing a load of laundry in the sleek machine with endless buttons in Susie's basement. I didn't relish the discomforting, trespass-y feeling I got each time I set foot in the Cottage, but, if one was to look on the bright side, now I had my own en-suite functioning bathroom and a pitcher of filtered water in a glass carafe on the bedside table. And I was trying to remain on the bright side.

Though Hope was now alone in the carriage house, J.P. off with Uncle Dunk on the lake, I abandoned her there without guilt, figuring she would be fine in her bedroom, and that some distance, even if just fifty or so meters, would do mother and daughter some good. She was so vexed about the pregnancy lie and being left out of the *Vanity Fair* piece, she'd been seizing *every* possible moment to remind us of it. In response, I'd angrily and unfairly tossed out more than once that it was she who was the cause of the pregnancy cover-up.

"It probably is close to a million," Spencer said. "I'll give you one of my sweatshirts to sleep in."

"Give me a really knobby one," I said. "Preferably gray."

"Gray is the most comfortable color." He slipped closer. "I'll sneak it in for you. And turn up the thermostat."

"My hero," I said, already feeling warmer. "How are *you*? Also, why are you here and not at The Bonnie?"

"I'm taking a mental health night," Spencer said. "At the kind but firm suggestion of Aimee."

"Are you still upset about the review?" When Spencer had texted me the link to a *Providence Journal* article with the words *terrible review*, I'd opened it expecting a devastating take-down. Instead, it was glowing, with the only quibble being that the dishes should emerge from the kitchen with more even and reliable pacing. But the criticism had, for him, been piercing. We'd gone back and forth over text about it; I watched him berate himself, cancel plans for his new restaurant project, gripe about the reviewer himself, tell himself nobody read *ProJo*, anyway, then circle back to doubting his own competency.

"I put everything into The Bonnie," Spencer said. "I put off having kids because of it, which basically ended my marriage. So, yes, I'm still upset. But I need to just get over it. Right?"

"No," I said. I wished I could hug him. What I'd give to wrap my arms around his waist. "You don't need to get over it. It can still suck. You could adjust the pacing, if *you* feel it needs to be fixed. Otherwise, you can remember these are the thoughts of one guy, versus hundreds a week that adore The Bonnie."

He'd closed his eyes. "Yes."

The drummers had taken wide, poised stances behind their instruments. Spencer and I shifted our positions so we were both facing the stage. Our arms were at our sides, and when his pinkie finger brushed mine, covert but suggestive, I knew my definition of sexiness would have to be redefined. I stared at his profile, feeling tipsy, though I hadn't had a sip of liquor.

The three musicians, shirtless, white cloth bands catching the sweat on their foreheads, were creating a booming, mythical sound, the kind that launches adventures and quests. Great romances or battles.

I was shooting before I realized I'd raised my Nikon. I liked this angle—the trio of artists framed by the two swaying ash trees on either side of the stage, the straight branches reaching toward the sky, parallel to the men's arms and their drumsticks on the upswing. Times like these, I thought as the music and men moved like a river, I wished I could fly. I never liked photographing water from the surface. Much better from above.

"Do you think it would raise eyebrows if I climbed that tree?" I said to Spencer.

He looked at me, amused. "You're expecting."

"Damn," I said. Not just because I remembered the ruse, but because Reagan Finley and her mother were headed our way. I'd seen them floating around the party and hoped to avoid them for as long as possible. But my time was up.

"Now, see, this is what I need." Reagan's head tilted, observing the stage. She was holding a glass of rosé; her skirt was sequined and her white T-shirt had holes in it, which means the latter had cost at least three hundred dollars. Her mother donned a long coat, though it was in the high seventies.

"A very large drum?"

"A job where I can work out *while* I work, you know?" Reagan smiled, amused with herself.

"I hate gyms," said Mrs. Finley. "Everyone is always breathing on the machines."

With a final, booming crescendo and cathartic yell in unison, the performance concluded. People applauded, and went back to their regular voices and normal conversations.

"How's your mother?" Mrs. Finley asked. I couldn't tell if she was addressing Spencer or me. She was sort of focused on the space of air between us.

I went ahead and assumed the question was for me. "Hope is good, thanks. Excited for the wedding."

Mrs. Finley's expression was pinched. "And congratulations on the baby." This time she was looking at Spencer.

"Mom." Reagan's laugh skittered like a rock over water. "I told you not to say anything."

I put Maggie's stage face on. "Spencer," I said with exaggerated serenity I did not feel, "has absolutely nothing to do with this."

"Oh." Mrs. Finley rewound an invisible tape between us. "Congratulations go only to Cass, then."

"Just so you know, I was not the one to tell her," Reagan said to me. She widened her eyes and glanced down at my belly. "I haven't told a soul."

"The horses have bolted from the barn," I said, borrowing from my uncle Dunk. "No use in trying to lock it now."

"While I have you…" Reagan extracted from her Gucci crossbody bag the same recorder she'd had at The Land. "Do you mind answering, like, three questions for my piece? Since we got interrupted last week? Here, Mom—" Reagan powered on the recorder and handed it to Mrs. Finley "—hold this. No, you just flipped it upside down. Mom, stop pressing buttons. There. Good. Stay."

"I don't know why you even carry this piece of junk around with you," Mrs. Finley said. "Shouldn't you be an editor by now and leave the grunt work to the interns?"

Reagan ignored this. "Is that all right, Cass?"

"Go ahead," I said to Reagan. She was only doing her job; as someone in the journalism business, I couldn't begrudge her for it. Though when Spencer angled the neck of his beer bottle toward the museum entrance, where the buffet dinner was being unveiled inside, I shook my head, an indication to stay. I wanted him to hear the questions and my responses, so we could analyze my performance later, so he could tell me if I'd done enough to give my sister and her wedding a flattering boost.

"Great!" She pulled up the notes app on her phone, and read me what I assumed was question number one. "Do you think of The Land as home even though your family occupies it at the pleasure of Susie Utterback?"

"The pleasure of Susie Utterback!" exclaimed Spencer. "I haven't seen my aunt really pleased by anything since the Phillies won the World Series in 2008."

"Reagan, what?" I swallowed, and the question went down my throat like a cannon ball. "I thought your piece was about Maggie and Jack."

"Right, no, absolutely. I have plenty about the wedding. Can you tell me why The Land was chosen as the venue and whether it is a way to assert the Coventrys' ties to the property?"

Spencer opened his mouth; I knew he was about to defend me, my family, again. I stilled him with a brief touch on his arm. "The Land was chosen because it is where Maggie and Jack met and fell in love," I said. It wasn't the most creative answer, but I was on my heels. Holding the recorder between us, Mrs. Finley propped up her elbow with her other hand.

"Is the auction with Sotheby's a reflection of the family's declining fortunes, or an attempt to re-amass wealth?" Reagan asked next.

"You're writing about the auction?" A flock of seagulls, lured in from the bay by the sushi, tested their luck and edged into the crowd, until a pair of white-suited naval officers shooed them away. They retreated in a flurry of feathers to the flagpole by the water.

Reagan swiped over to her calendar app. "August twenty-first. Is that still the date of it?"

How did she know? We'd confirmed with Sotheby's less than twenty-four hours ago. I had been expecting softballs. Not even—I'd been prepared for badminton birdies. But these were darts. "You know, I'm actually working now." I rifled through my camera bag for a roll of film, eventually fishing one out from underneath a Chapstick and a box of matches from a seaside bar in Lesbos. I made a big, busy show of changing the old one out. "Maybe put these in writing? You have my email? I can answer when I'm not pulled a million ways at once."

Reagan appeared disappointed, but just for a second. Then she shrugged and said something like *sure fine no problem*. Mrs. Finley gave the recorder back and Reagan switched it off.

"Bye, Cammie," said Mrs. Finley.

With a look of embarrassment, Reagan encouraged Mrs. Finley toward Founders Hall with a palm in between her shoulder blades. "I'm on deadline for the October issue. Which means I would need copy quite soon. I'll send you an email tonight," she said as she practically pushed her mother away from us.

"Yikes, Cammie," said Spencer once they were gone.

"What *was* that?" We were some of the only people left on the lawn, so I reached out and grabbed a quick swig of Spencer's beer. "Why *those* questions? Jesus."

"I wonder..." Spencer took the bottle back, caught in thought. "I mean, I know better than to believe any gossip in this town." He gestured to me. "Exhibit A."

"Have people been talking about my parents? Might as well spill."

"Actually," Spencer said, "more about Susie. The meanest say she can't afford upkeep anymore."

"That's absurd," I said. "The place is pristine. I mean, except for the carriage house. And Susie hasn't even been on Net-a-Newport recently." Spencer eyes widened. So did his grin. I groaned. "You don't have to say it. I hear myself."

"That account *is* addicting," Spencer said. "Do you ever wonder who's behind it?"

"Yes. Like, who would benefit from *not* repeating Susie gossip?" I gasped dramatically. "Oh, my God. It's Susie!" This made us both laugh. "Or someone who likes her. Or maybe it's Reagan. Maybe as a journalist, people are sending her

gossipy tips, and this was her way to air them. I don't know."
We were officially the last people outside, and feeling a little
bit reckless, I dropped my camera bag to the dirt and moved
nearer to him. It was effort—exquisite, tantalizing effort—not
to reach out and drag his smiling face to mine. "Or maybe it's
you. Maybe you're the face behind the screen."

"I'll never tell," he rasped. He was enjoying this, too, looking at me like he couldn't wait to get my clothes off, like he
was imagining tasting my skin. He drifted a few more inches
forward. "How long do you have to be pregnant for?"

His voice made me vibrate. "A matter of days." He was so
close, and I was so antsy for him. I suppose I could've snuck
him into Hope's car in the parking lot, high school style, but
there was a naughty, indulgent part of me that loved this dangerous game we were playing.

"When it's over," he murmured, mouth brushing my temple, "I'm taking you to bed. I want your hair on my pillow
and your name on my lips."

I didn't know how I'd make it through the evening with
that promise on my mind.

August

21

"Is this the last of it?" I asked as River settled into the winged
back of what we, as children, had always called *Lewie chairs*.
He'd arrived in my room in the Cottage with three nitro-cold
brews and the final box from the storage unit.

"Indeed," River said, crossing his ankles on the stool. "And
I closed Mrs. Gilford's account at the u-Store. No more charges

on her card after this month." He handed me the mark-up of the auction preview party catalog. "Sotheby's requested edits be returned by tomorrow so we can have them all printed by next week."

I finished up my email to Reagan, ending it with a neutral *Best, Cass* sign-off. All in all, I thought I did a fairly nice job of providing dispassionate, bordering on bullshit answers to her questions. I could only hope this would put the issue of The Land to rest.

"How was the meeting with the caterers?" I asked, pushing aside my laptop, where I'd been editing photos from the Moët event, and flipping through the catalog. Those little saucers with radishes my mother and I had used for doll tea parties were actually *a pair of trompe l'oeil Strasbourg plates from the prized Paul Hannong era (1750-1754)* and that the starting bid would be *three thousand US dollars*. The mural that had once adorned The Land's breakfast room that I'd woken up to for years was *a 1920s watercolor mural from a Loire Valley château*. I'd been the one to deface it with permanent marker on the eve of my tenth birthday. I'd been the reason it had been taken down and not conveyed to Susie. Starting bid: *four thousand US dollars*.

"I will say this—you should've come to the menu tasting. Hope's not *not* still mad at you," River revealed. "But she has ceased muttering about you two every time I see her, which I figure is the first sign of détente."

"I appreciate your honesty. Though I think I best stay put until Hope's anger has fizzled all the way out." I handed the papers back to him. "I still think the phrase *prestigious pedigree* is awful, but whatever. I've been overruled. Other than that, it looks fine."

A text from Spencer swooped into my phone. This is your next license plate!

The picture was taken over his dashboard, stopped at a

light. The car in front of him had chosen XraGuac as their vanity message.

"I'm glad we decided to feature Newport's resort-era time capsule on the first page," said River, tucking the invitation into his leather messenger bag. "It was very smart of you and Sotheby's to get people to bid on it at the preview party. Fabulous publicity!"

"That was Archer and Hope's idea. At least my mother is still talking to him."

Swim in the pool tonight? I asked Spencer.

I'll never say no to a sexy swim. Grabbing my snorkel and flippers now!

River ran his finger over the carved bleached wood of the chair's arm, and gingerly continued. "I do have to tell you, at the caterers yesterday, after we indulged in surf *and* turf, Mrs. Utterback and Mrs. Coventry-Gilford—and I blame the wine included in the tasting for this—exchanged some sharp words. It started innocuous enough. There was confusion about chargers."

"Phone?"

"No, dining. As in, the layer that goes underneath the dinner plate."

"The placemat."

"No. The—" River made sweeping and patting motions.

"Right." I pinched the bridge of my nose. "Did Hope choose the beef or the fish?"

"Both. She wants a little duet on the plate. In the back of Mrs. Coventry-Gilford's mind, the venue is free, so it allows her to spend money on other things. And she's saying, now, *Oh, the auction will bring in such and such funds.* Never fear, though! Jack is talking her out of most of it."

"That's something, then." I refocused on the box in my lap, extracting a bubble-wrapped object, one I hadn't seen in a dozen years. I located the place where a piece of tape held the bubble wrap together, snipped it with my nail.

River slid onto the floor next to me. "Wow," he said. "I've only seen Fiona Coventry-Devries in the Frick. Never this close."

Gradually, the sculpture appeared: Granny Fi's *assemblage* of a white bra and girdle made from found objects, trash, detritus pulled from the garbage or the side of the road or the breakwater below The Land. It was the size of a child's torso, and it rested on a base made from pieces of broken tiles and those crystal glasses that once matched the pitcher I'd seen in Hope's truck last month. I spun the work around, admiring its texture and proportion. My fingers ran over where she'd fashioned a bra clasp out of fishhooks and lobster pot wire. The piece was prickly, pointy, some might call it ugly or weird, but it had always been my favorite.

Artist to artist, my grandmother had written in a short note given to me by our family's old attorney at her funeral. "Granny Fi was the first love of my life," I said.

Now that it was out of the box and into the beams of light stretching in from the windows, I realized how much I'd missed seeing her work in person. How the work, seemingly, had missed being where it belonged.

"Sotheby's did ask again..." River said.

"I told them I'd think about it." Yesterday I'd made Hope return all the items she'd taken out of the storage unit. Some subcontractor of the auction house had then come to u-Store, movers in white cotton gloves, tagging and labeling, carting lots off in crates. The lead handler, a tall man with a wrestler's physique, a therapist's soft voice, and a very sturdy clipboard had reminded us that, upon final accounting, we were still two lots short of what we'd promised, and we were just over three weeks away to the auction, and one to the preview party. What would the appraising eyes of Sotheby's see in this sculpture? Value. Quality. A collector's jewel, perhaps. A sample of a particular artistic genius, maybe. But to me, it wasn't an object, but a reminder of the moments I shared with my Granny.

"Think about what?" In Archer strode, wearing his classic summer uniform of board shorts and a tee, today capped off with a white terry-cloth bathrobe I recognized from the pool house. His ankles were sandy and his hair salt-cured; I assumed he'd been surfing. He leaned against the fireplace, jangled the ice in his cup, and noticed the item before us. "Oh, Granny Fi's sculpture?"

"Sotheby's wants me to sell it," I told him.

"And you're pulling a Hope Coventry-Gilford, and holding tight."

I bristled. "I don't have a mountain of Granny Fi's belongings. I have this. This *one* thing."

Archer positioned his straw at the corner of his mouth and slipped. "You know Granny Fi deliberately broke the stuff Mom liked, right? She got off on it."

Credulous of this, it only threw me for a moment. "She did not *get off on it*. Assemblage was her medium. Besides, there's not one thing in the Coventry collection that Mom doesn't love. If Granny Fi touched nothing, she'd have no art."

"Okay," Archer said, done with me, his attention and two thumbs on his phone. "Sure."

I almost demanded he tell me what he was always up to on there, what was more important than talking to me—a video, a post, *what*? I even began: "Who are you tex..." Then I thought, *Lord help me, I really am turning into my mother*.

Luckily, River cleared his throat. "This is my first time up here," he said, taking in the bedroom's surrounds. "It's very—"

"Blue," I observed. When Susie had moved me in last week,

I'd been assigned to what had been, in its past life, Archer's bedroom, and now was covered, ceiling to walls, bolster pillows to bedspread, in Susie's favorite shade of robin's egg toile.

Missing the house, feeling cheated of it, could easily become a bad habit if I weren't careful. Something to be picked at, like a hangnail. I was staying at The Land for the summer, but I could *not* worship at the altar of misfortune. There was no use looking back. *Keep it moving.*

"I was about to say anachronistic," River said. "The Coventrys would've never decorated with *toile.*" The way he said the word, like it tasted foul, had me chuckling. "Damask, sure. Gold leaf, yes."

"My bed," Archer said, surfacing from his screen, pointing at the wall opposite the fireplace, "was over there, not next to the door where it is now. Do you remember, Cass?"

"I do." With care, I repackaged Granny Fi's sculpture, safely returned it to its box. Then I shot Maggie a text that River had brought her a green juice.

"I spent a lot of time in this room," Archer said thoughtfully.

"Archer, your experience with lympho—I'm so sorry—" River put his hand to his neck. "What was it?"

"ALK-negative anaplastic large cell lymphoma." I sucked two big gulps of coffee. My mouth was suddenly arid. "Stage two."

"Right, forgive me. I imagine it would've been quite lonely. While my father was undergoing treatment for prostate cancer while I was in high school, he often said that it was the silence from those he expected to hear from that was one of the most physically painful parts of the ordeal."

"People don't know what to say, so they say nothing," said Archer, and it was forgiving. "But those who mattered showed up. Remember Maggie auctioned off those dance lessons?

And, Cassie, honestly, how many hours did you sit with me here before it got really bad and Mom, Dad, and I had to go to MD Andersson for my last round?"

Yes, those many hours, the heavy, dusty curtains drawn against the light. Those jaundice-colored days of gauze and barf buckets and doctors who Hope called *fucking idiots* and J.P. called *sawbones* to make us all laugh. Archer had always been angelic in his rest despite his pallor, the inflamed pink of his eyelids, his skinniness. I'd felt helpless and lacking, and furious with everyone else in the wide world who were not suffering as we were. As he was.

Maggie, the chameleon, was better than I was at making and keeping friends during this time. She had her dance and distance learning community (the hours devoted to the barre precluded her from normal school); I had to brave the halls of Rogers High. With a name like ours, one could only suppose I should be bathing in San Pellegrino. Why, then, did my trousers have patches over the knees? Why, then, did I know the names of all the repo men in town?

Archer had gotten better. But I'd gotten worse, as though Granny Fi's death, the months without my parents, the loss of The Land, and Maggie's increased focus on Jack and dance were rays from a dying star, only reaching me long after the final implosion.

Don't waste time feeling bad for me. Archer and Maggie lost their grandmother and their home, too. Archer almost lost his life. And I was the only one who'd skipped class to smoke under the bleachers, stole the lawn mower from the custodial shed, and mowed *BLOW ME* in the soccer field.

"I didn't do much," I said, smushing my straw against the ice in my cup.

"You would pick strands of hair off my pillow so I wouldn't cry when I saw them the next morning."

I met his eyes. "You faker," I said, touched. "I thought you were asleep."

Archer smiled. "Surprise."

"You lived," I said.

"Sure did." Archer exhaled. "And now I live in my phone."

"Except the game theory club you do with the high schoolers!" I reminded him. "Which is so generous of you. I need to start volunteering more..."

River had wandered to the double-hung window overlooking The Land's driveway and flagpole. "Alas." He motioned for us. "It's starting again."

Concerned, I rose from the floor, Archer not far behind me. That's when I heard shouting.

I unlocked the sash and lifted the window up as high as it would go. Hope and Susie were on the driveway directly below facing each other, their bodies silos of tension, their voices a mishmash of indignation.

"The moms are back on their bullshit." My pulse spiking, I moved out of the way so Archer could take my place.

"Remy is going to be coming down that driveway any minute," Archer said, frowning at the commotion below. "I don't need him driving straight into Jurassic Park! I'm trying to convince him to *stay* with me, not run for the hills."

"I'm sure Remy is well versed in the feud," I told my brother. "But don't worry. I'm rounding up the reinforcements."

Maggie still hadn't returned my text, but I decided to try her on FaceTime; it rang and rang and she answered just when I thought all hope was lost.

"Hey," she said, monotone.

"Where are you?" She appeared to be lying down, but not on a bed, her hair spread around, her chin sunk into her neck.

"I'm in the basement studio. Susie was nice and put marley flooring down so I could have a place to train."

"Are you training?"

"No."

I had thought that by moving into the Cottage, we would be able to see even more of each other. I had silly little ideas in my head like cozy pajama sibling time with Netflix and chips in bed. Though I had my time occupied with the auction, photo gigs, and editing, I couldn't help feel slightly paranoid that Maggie had been dodging Archer and me in the week since we'd moved in. I'd be upstairs, in the room next to hers and Jack's, texting Spencer or getting dressed for the day, when I'd hear footsteps in the carpeted hall, or the sound of one of the antique doorknobs clicking home, but when I rushed to catch her, it would just be Kent with a coffee for Susie, or a workman in a tool belt, there to fix a pipe, or caulk around a window, or—in one case—get rid of the ants. When I nosed about the kitchen in the mornings, Kent would say she was still asleep, then inch a bowl of perfectly shaped fresh fruit toward me. Even the bananas dared not be bruised in Susie's kitchen. Just about to take a nap, she'd text when I got back to the Cottage in the evening. Busy day and I'm exhausted. Dinners were not taken together.

I glanced at Archer. He shrugged. "Okay. Well, do you hear Mom and Susie yelling? They're out front."

"Maybe. Or that might be the humidifier humming, I can't tell."

"Something about caps." River turned from the window to deliver his report. "Is there a cap or a hat in dispute? Does this ring any bells?"

"I'm not speaking to Hope presently," I said to Maggie, "and because this is your mom and mother-in-law, I think you should be the one to break it up."

Maggie groaned. "Can't Archer do it?"

Archer was shaking his head so vigorously I thought it

might spin clear around. "He says no. Bug, you're up." I didn't bother keeping the impatience out of my voice. I was pretending to be pregnant for her. She needed to get off the ground.

"A capsule!" River had his finger in the air like *ah-HA!* "Hope is saying they've given the capsule to the auction house and if Susie wants it she'll have to pay like the rest of them."

"Where's Jack?" Archer asked.

"With the florist. If Susie wants something from the auction, just give it to her. Who cares?" Maggie asked.

"*You* should," I said with ballooning annoyance. "This is raising money for *your* wedding."

"This wedding," Maggie said, the second syllable sliding out of her mouth in a fatigued breath. "Honestly?" She threw her arm over her eyes. "I doubt Jack even wants to marry me anymore. But he has to. Because of the baby."

"Maggie's bridal breakdown," said Archer. "Right on schedule."

The thought of my sister and this baby—my niece? nephew?—being a burden to Jack was outlandish, but I knew if I opened my mouth, I'd bite her head off. Instead, I marched over to join River and Archer by the window, passed my brother my phone, then cupped both hands around my mouth. "Moms!" I hollered. No effect. I leaned too forward for comfort and tried once more. "MOMS!" This got their attention. Both faces swung up; Susie shielded her eyes from the sun with—yes—seemed to be the same draft catalog River had distributed to me. "Stop fighting!"

"You need to turn the capsule over to me, Cass! Could be valuable Newport history in there! Or something important to The Land!" shouted Susie. Her aggravation carried. "It wasn't your right to dig it up to begin with!"

"I know! But if I hadn't, it would still be underground,

forgotten!" This was my first debate to take place over two stories.

"Cass found it!" This was Hope. "Finders keepers!"

Susie: "Finders on *my* property!"

Hope: "You wouldn't be here if not for us!"

Susie: "That's ludicrous! After all I've done!"

Hope: "You want us here! You like to look over from your perfect mansion that you bought with your husband's money and see the Coventrys small and beneath you. You're not fooling anyone about why you leased us that house!"

A tremendous, heavy silence from Susie. Then: "I can't wait till you're out of here."

"Joke's on you, Susie, because I plan to live to one hundred."

I maneuvered backward, then used my forearm to slam the window closed. "This isn't super." I sounded very calm, even though the agreement I'd made with Susie earlier this summer was one capsule-length away from disintegrating. Would she evict Hope on the spot?

River glanced toward the drive. "I see Remy's car. Dare I try and run past the moms to intercept him?"

"How's your army crawl?" Archer asked.

"I'm wearing a linen blend," said River.

"Maggie," said Archer, turning his attention to the phone. "We need you, buddy. You've got to get them apart."

Maggie closed her eyes, and mouthed what I thought were the words *oh, no*. "What do I even say?"

I obviously didn't help de-escalate the situation, so I looked at my brother. "Archer," I said, "I've heard the way you talk to people online. You're good at this. Help her. Please?"

Archer paused, then nodded. His voice, when he spoke, became lower and more deliberate. "You don't have to say anything. Just go, get Susie, and lead her inside. She'll be mad, but that's okay," he continued, conjuring a prospect of resolution out of thin air. "Let her get it out. She's got her reasons for being furious, and you don't have to solve them, you just have to be there."

Maggie took a beat, then the angle of the FaceTime shifted as she appeared to sit up. "Okay. I'm on my way."

Archer ended the call and gave me my phone. "You're amazing," I said. "Now can you tell us what do we do about Hope?"

Archer opened the window again. Remy had parked; Hope waved at him as she made her way back to the carriage house, singing: "The gilded cage is so much more interesting with the birds still in it!" This was accompanied by feet shuffles and taps.

"I think she'll be fine," he said.

22

NET-A-NEWPORT 4H

Coventry action preview party tonight @tennishallofame @sothebys
What are you bidding on?

38%	Time capsule duh
62%	Just going to mingle

Link in bio for full auction catalog

The Coventry auction preview party at the Hall of Fame Tennis
Club landed on the first night of an unprecedented heat wave,
which had lumbered in from the south mid-August and decided
to stick around. They called it a heat dome, which was apt, as
we felt like we were in a boiling kettle.

The breeze seemed tired, lazing through the elms and
beeches with all the strength and endurance of a ceiling fan
on the fritz. By midday, we were sapped, bobbing around close
to the ground like half-filled balloons. If you had enough energy to make it off the beach towel, or the lounge chair, or
the dock—God bless. Though out on the water or in it was

the best place to be, good luck getting there without a sizzling sunburn. Just that morning, I'd roasted my shoulders shooting a children's fundraising picnic at Green Animals.

I was running late, but at half past five—precisely the time of day when it was the hottest—I finally arrived in a tank, midiskirt, and sandals with a skinny heel that kept tripping me up.

When it was constructed, the casino, a Gilded Age term for a modern-day social club, had put Shingle Style on the map; cedar shake was its skin, its accents were brick and stone. Don't mistake it for simple, though. Inside, the woodwork was cream edged in gold. The clock on center court was Rolex, the sconces were Venetian, and the fretwork on the gables and porches was influenced by Japanese teahouses. It once was almost demolished for a shopping center, but saved and preserved and generally not mucked about with, making the sensation of walking through the entrance like one was walking back in time.

It was the right place, I supposed, for the Coventry family's wares to be peddled. Our ancestors partied here; Earnest Coventry the collector got day-drunk and played billiards on the second floor of the casino. Granny Fi had stories about running amok, unaccompanied, while her parents watched the singles and doubles championships on the lawn.

It seemed like the entirety of Newport had turned out to get a glimpse of what the Coventrys had squirreled away for a hundred and fifty years. In the crowded courtyard, I presented my invitation to the guard and saw my name checked off a list. Mere moments later, a reporter sprung on me, his press credentials around his neck. He identified himself and shot off three rapid questions about me, the family, and the auction that essentially distilled to *why this* and *why now*.

"We're excited for the evening," I began, shifting aside to

let a group of attendees flapping fans pass by. Thank goodness Archer had suggested that straw folding fans be provided to the guests or we'd be puddles on the mosaic tile floors. The guy dropped his chin, looked at me like *you gotta give me more.* I didn't want to make his job harder than it was, so I dredged up a little extra nonsense: "We've been working so hard to put these pieces in the hands of their next owners."

And how did he repay me?

"Auctions are usually the result of death, divorce, or debt," said the reporter, his eyes fixed on his notepad. "Which one of the three Ds is this?"

I caught myself before my face could revolt. "None of the above. This is just a way to share the family's love of collecting with a broader audience."

"That's good," said the reporter, scribbling in short hand. "Thanks."

I nodded and followed the brick path encircling the court and up the short flight of steps to view our lots scattered along the horseshoe piazza. Placed on stands draped in silk, some were grouped together, like those Chinese porcelain vases that Hope had, at one point, turned into lamps, some displayed individually, like the Picasso sketch we'd discovered in storage, rolled up in a dusty sleeve of plastic, now framed in gold.

Sotheby's understood how the Gilded Age heiresses operated, that parties were spectator sports, anyway, and it made sense to give the crowd lots of spectacular things to look at while food, drink, and gossip was being consumed.

I stopped at a green tableclothed bar and ordered a glass of white. Then, remembering: "Shoot, sorry," I said to the bartender. "Just water, please."

The bartender handed me a bottle and gestured at the next guest in line, which had me backing up, ceding space. I sipped my water and continued my slow stroll down the piazza, got a few polite but distant hellos, occasional nods. Though I did note, out of the corner of my eye, some quick glances at where my top was tucked into my skirt.

The only person to engage me in conversation was Maggie's wedding florist. Unprompted, he filled me in on the latest details—*Rococo swings! Candelabras on fishing line! A custom flower-lined aisle toward the cliffs!* My route was again stopped a little later, the piazza plugged by a group gathered around a display stand. I shifted, waiting to get near, passing the time by staring at the polished beadboard ceiling and the café string lights hung across it, trying not to return the stares of those who were now more plainly looking me over. The crowd broke, and I saw the draw: *Time Capsule, circa 1901, American, starting bid $4,000.* The box was cleared of dirt and dust, though still rusty on the hardware and with the drooping lid. Sotheby's had removed the padlock; it was ready for its opener. Behind the stand lurked a sweaty guard with a linebacker's chest in a tailored suit and earpiece, doing his best to be discreet but failing on account of, you know, pretty much his whole vibe.

Kent and his wife, Ema, an ophthalmologist who was using her cheery red reading glasses as a hair band, along with Archer and Remy, met me with hugs in front of the case. My brother and Remy looked cozy; they'd even dressed similarly, in long-sleeve button-downs and shorts—Archer appearing more Newport tailored than he had all summer—and I wondered how much of that was Remy's influence. Regardless of his attire, I was glad to see them together, that despite Archer's worry, his crush had not run for the hills.

"This is really something," Remy pronounced, gazing around the party. "I had no idea your family had such treasures."

"It was a revelation for us, too," Archer said.

"I imagine that this must be a bittersweet day, seeing your family's history off," Ema said.

"The era of the Coventrys is over," I said. "As it probably should be."

"Don't say that." For a moment, I thought Archer was kidding. His tone was cheerful enough. But he didn't smile, or laugh.

Before I could clarify, Kent posed a question to his wife: "Are we bidding on this time capsule, honey, or what? If we win, we get to open it tonight."

"If you do," said Archer, "don't tell Susie. She's upset about it being included in the sale. Really upset. According to Maggie, she thinks that whatever is in there is due to her."

"I get that she's pissed because I dug up her property," I said, folding my arms. "But I don't understand this level of anger. It's just a box with stuff. What do you think, Kent?" I caught Archer's raised eyebrows, and changed my mind. "Actually, ignore that. I don't want to ask you to blab on Susie."

Kent cleared his throat, exchanged a look with Ema. "Well, I'm actually in the process of unwinding myself from my employment with Mrs. Utterback. I'm leaving The Land after the wedding."

"Wow," I said, absorbing this news. Somewhere in the back of my mind, it had heartened me to know that Kent would remain after the Coventrys were gone, in case—I don't know—The Land needed us. Who would Susie hire to replace him? A stranger. "Selfishly, I'm sad."

"Just time for a new chapter," said Remy, giving his father's shoulder a squeeze.

"Indeed. You'll still see me. We're not going far."

"I'd follow you to the moon for Ema's *bifanas*," said Archer.

"Boundless appetites run in our family," I explained.

"And ours, too," chuckled Remy.

"No one will have to go far for my sandwiches," Ema said, affectionate. "I prefer my children close."

I observed the exchange between Remy, his parents, and Archer with a mixture of pleasure and poignancy; if we ever had to share him with another family, I hoped it would be one like this, who appreciated him and each other.

"I think your mother is trying to get your attention," said Kent. A short way down the piazza was the bar and my parents, my mother waving to me. Before I wandered over, Kent had one last thing to tell me: "Forgive me for not saying anything about the pregnancy," he said, voice hushed. "If I knew it to be true, I would be the first to offer my heartiest congratulations."

I smiled. *These walls listen*, Hope had said. "But you know it's not true."

Kent acknowledged this with a subtle tip of his head. "An insight for you, as I prepare to exit The Land. Susie Utterback's anger isn't *really* about the time capsule, you understand? She's held tight control to that property, to herself, for the last sixteen years. And when someone like that feels control slipping away, that person is likely to lash out."

"Control of *what?*"

"I don't feel I'm at liberty to say."

"I understand. You're just asking me to have empathy for her."

"I'm asking you," said Kent, "to be careful of her."

•••••

My father, in a suit for once. My mother, holding court, in a crisp black collared shirt and full oyster-blue skirt, looking rather radiant, in fact. As a lover of tennis and attention, this was her natural habitat. Hope didn't play tennis, mind you. She just liked to watch and read about it. She'd devoured about every book on the sport; every memoir and biography and sports reporter blow-by-blow ever published was stacked somewhere around the carriage house.

"Are we still fighting?" I asked my mother after giving her a peck. "I hope not."

"Oh, about *Vanity Fair*?" said Hope. "As Carrie Fisher once said, all three of my feelings were hurt. But I've moved on."

"You have more than three." I smiled. "And I'm sorry for hurting all of them."

Fair warning! Came an announcement from center court. *The sale of Newport's lost time capsule will end in two minutes. Please use your phone to submit your bids via our app, lot number 132...*

"Hi, Dad," I said, turning to J.P. "How was fishing?"

"Productive. I packed the freezer. But I missed my girl and my kids." He kissed my mother on her proffered cheek once. Then again. And a third time.

"Collect yourself," I said to J.P. Despite Kent's warning about Susie, I found myself relaxing into my parents' company, their good mood. Around the piazza was not just the social register people, but Newport's business owners mixing with The Land's gardeners and craftsmen, my high school principal chatting with River, Uncle Dunk yukking it up with the hostess I'd met at The Bonnie.

Hope beamed. "I feel like the most popular girl at the dance!" She snapped open her fan and waved it in my hot face. "I'm showing everyone around, I'm taking names and numbers, I'm kissing babies. So many collectors here. I'm really selling it, Cassie." She wiggled her fingers at someone on the other side of the bar. "Are you proud?"

"Very." I peered over the rows of red geraniums in flower boxes to the old grass court nestled within the arms of the piazza. "I'm sure Net-a-Newport is here somewhere. But where are Maggie and Jack?"

"Don't know," she said. "But Susie is deliberately avoiding me."

I followed my mother's gaze through a slice in the dense crowd, where Susie had sidled up to the time capsule with Don Washington, who was giving a loud, unofficial seminar. *Insofar that there is interest, we should focus our queries not only on what material is in the box*, he elucidated, *but why it was buried in the first place.*

"Now, Cassie, what happened between Susie and me," continued Hope, "*that* was a fight."

"Kent just told me that he's leaving Susie after the wedding," I reported to Hope. "He's moving on from The Land."

"Oh, that's a shame. I'll miss him." I thought she'd enjoy a glass of self-satisfaction at Susie's expense, but it was the next thing that really surprised me: "Poor Susie. She'll be all alone in that cavern."

Hope had a point. When I was young, there'd been three generations of Coventrys living in the Cottage. Even then, there were spooky, closed-off rooms we'd never go in, furniture draped in ghostly sheets. It was too much house for six people, let alone one.

There was the clink of a knife against a glass, and someone from Sotheby's made an announcement. As though people really needed to be psyched up to buy our things, they'd made a promotional video, after which the proud new owner of Newport's lost capsule would be unveiled and, with the help of preservationists on-site, they would reveal its contents. The projector screen unfurled in the piazza. Scrolling black-and-white photos of my ancestors—some familiar, some arcane, a few benign and dull, others downright pathological, though no one needed to be reminded of that—were voiced-over with slow, reverent narration and what sounded to be some unharmonious notes played by a very sad pianist. *The Coventry story is an American story*, said the narrator, smooth as silk, *and with this auction, the story that has captured our imaginations for a hundred and fifty years becomes tangible reality. The Coventry family believes that the past should be venerated, but also shared, and with that extraordinary view has opened up their celebrated trove of antiques. This calibrated collection of prestigious pedigree...*

I dropped my chin to my chest, smothering a laugh at the ridiculous phrasing. If only Sotheby's had met Darren the goat at the beginning of the summer. I excused my way out of the crowd, waving the catalog on my hot neck, seeking air-conditioning and a private place to call my sister. I hoped she was all right—the last time I'd seen her, she'd been on the floor.

Fortunately, the Hall of Fame could deliver, and I escaped across the court to the empty, dim, artificially chilly wing that housed the tennis museum. I found a spot in front of a brightly lit glass case containing one of John McEnroe's Wimbledon ensembles—red sweatband, tiny white shorts, thick tube socks standing inside his Nikes. The transition from the outdoor heat had me both somehow sweaty and covered in goose bumps.

"I almost wore those exact same shorts today." Spencer's voice came from behind me. He had Wayfarers on and a catalog in hand.

"Why didn't you?" I asked. He laughed, slung his arm around me, and tugged close. "I'm sweaty!" I cautioned.

He sniffed my neck and hair exaggeratedly, making me giggle. "Missed you."

I let my purse fall, promising myself I'd call Maggie in a minute.

Or an hour.

Or two.

Because one of his hands was creeping up my tank and caressing that spot in the center of my back that I could never reach on my own. Because I had my lips on his and he tasted like sugar and mint and smelled like sunscreen and sea salt.

Because the whisper of his fingertips against my skin was a song I couldn't get out of my head.

I liked him so much. No way around it. I liked how he checked in with me throughout the day. I liked how he sent me photos of goofy license plates. I liked the way he kept an eye on my shirt cuffs and bracelets so they wouldn't dunk in plates and dishes of food.

I liked how he saved his anger for small things—the printer in his office not working, his phone taking too long to update, a lost AirPod. I liked how he extended grace and patience to most people—my mother, Susie, me—save those who were rude or abused his servers or bussers.

I liked his mouth and the shape of his shoulders and the way he'd press his hand into my spine so I'd arch into him. I liked our handstand contests in Susie's pool after everyone had gone to sleep. I liked his dreams.

He nudged me backward, so I was up against the cool glass of the display case, crouched, ran his hands up my legs, pressed his face against my skirt, right where I was hot and aching.

He rose, still managing to caress me everywhere, my stomach, my palms, the nape of my neck. Our hungry mouths met again, and I could sense he felt what I did—purely distilled *want*. But there was more, deeper and more urgent and hurried. He was touching me, I thought, like we were running out of time.

I needed to save these moments, to swallow this feeling, so I could keep it inside me for when the summer ended, and he went back to his life, and I went—

"Tell me exactly what you want," he murmured, rough and deep against the shell of my ear, cutting off my thoughts. "I want to hear it."

He didn't have to wait long. "You. Now."

"Good," he said, wrapping his arms around my waist, lifting me clear off the ground.

"Go right," I said. "I know a back exit."

Half-delirious and mostly desperate, I should've been embarrassed by the volume of the sounds I was making, but his fingers had sneaked under my skirt, and he was telling me how he wanted, how he felt—

"Cass!" It was my mother, from somewhere in the museum, sounding exhilarated.

Spencer, still holding me, stopped short. "No," I groaned, pressing my eyes closed. "Keep going. I'm sure she's just—"

"Cassie, where are you?"

Spencer's intense eyes found mine, and I knew he'd heard it this time, too. She was not calling for me with excitement. She was panicked.

My feet hit the floor. Adjusting our waistbands and tops, we hustled to the front of the museum, the hallway filled with ladies' tennis attire of old. "Mom!" My call caught her before she went around corner. "I'm here. What's wrong? What happened?"

Hope spun toward us, illuminated by a harsh cone of light above the exhibit. "The capsule, Cassie. They opened it." She clasped her hands together, lifted them to her nose, and pressed, as though she were trying to turn herself inside out. "And everything inside is gone. It's completely empty."

23

Auction Preview Party of Coventry Collection Ends in Controversy

Town & Country

Posted 12:15am

The Coventry family, which made headlines for much of the nineteenth and early twentieth century, has found itself at the center of another mystery, or scandal, depending on who you ask...

NET-A-NEWPORT 3H

Coventry Time Capsule empty! Is this some kind of meta commentary on art and art auctions ala Banksy? What do you think? Submit your guesses below.

Needing a pause from the roundabout conversation with Archer and Hope about what do in the wake of an empty time capsule, I headed to one of the most peaceful places in Newport: Redwood Library. There, I thought, I might get some help; though scandal was nothing new to the Coventrys, I was curious how generations before had handled it. Because our response, in the week since the preview party, had been adamant silence, fearing a wrong word that would cause even more controversy and derail the auction's success or cloud the air for Maggie's wedding.

I made my way into the hushed reading room, to the stacks edged in mint-green trim, where I'd spent so many hours of my youth devouring Sontag and Cartier-Bresson. After a short period of browsing, I took *Blue Bloods, White Lies: Scandal and Sacrifice in the Gilded Age* to an olive leather wing chair by a tall, bright window, and flipped to the index. There were the Coventrys, just as expected, mentioned on pages 3, 5–6, 34–37, 91, 182–84...

I wasn't so interested in the old news contained within the hardback book in my lap—Earnest and his unacceptable bride; poor Martina and her brokenhearted and broke husband; my great-grandfather Lewis, who, at eight years old, was kidnapped and held for ransom in New York.

For many weeks after Lewis's abduction, a Coventry lawyer insisted that he'd just run away. And they weren't worried. He'd come home. The family, the book's author pointed out, not only lied to the press, but waited more than a week after the disappearance to contact the police and the Pinkertons, fearing scandal in the height of the social season—didn't that sound familiar!

The excerpts from newspapers and periodicals of the time, and the words of the Coventrys and their lawyers, were a printed master class in gaslighting and obfuscation; the thesis was, don't see anything we don't want you to see. They'd cared about appearances more than each other.

A shadow draped itself across my lap. I looked up: my sister.

"Hi," Maggie whispered. The first thing I noticed was her

belly; no longer in fabric-heavy tents, she was in a stretchy cotton dress that clung to her form. "Kent told me you were here."

"Hi." I closed *Blue Bloods, White Lies.* All due respect to the publishing team, but it really should've been titled *Blue Bloods, Red Flags.* "Where you've been, Bug? You missed a few things."

"I know." Maggie dragged a Windsor chair from a nearby table next to mine and sat. "How are you?" Her hair was pulled back into a slick ponytail; in profile, her jaw cut sharp, her mouth a straight line. She leaned her elbows on her knees and stared at her white espadrilles.

"I've been better." After the preview party ended in mass confusion and minor scandal, I took photos. Not for a job, or to curate on social media, but just for myself, to play and experiment, which I hadn't done in years. Something had shifted within me, a commotion borne of disquiet that drove me toward subjects that hadn't held interest for me in a long time. I didn't bother with the Nikon I traditionally used, choosing instead my old point-and-shoot Leica, my first camera, the one Granny Fi had bought me for my thirteenth birthday. Though it didn't have the bells and whistles of newer models, and though I didn't even recall exactly what my subjects had been back then, Hope had saved it for me.

One of the best ways, I'd learned from my grandmother, to deal with spells of desperate inspiration like this was to give over to it without a fight. I'd been circling around Newport, going through at least fifteen rolls of film and biking perhaps twenty miles a day, up to the Palladian lines and arches of Touro Synagogue, to the hollow brick barracks at Fort Adams, where the wildflowers and blades of grass bowed and stretched in the Atlantic wind, then to the gray, sodden sand at Bailey's Beach, to Trinity Church and the graveyard where Maggie,

Archer, and I had invited hauntings in our youth, then back across the island to Castle Hill, where I managed some romantic shots of an older couple, their intertwined hands hanging between the arms of Adirondack chairs on the hill.

Why did I shoot them from behind? Because on their laps was a copy of the *Newport Daily News* with a picture of the Coventry time capsule above the fold.

"You're positive that the time capsule was full when you found it?" Maggie asked.

This was the question that had been bouncing around Newport since the preview party. It was the same one that had been ricocheting around my head all week. "I thought so," I said. "We heard something in there, but now I'm second-guessing myself. Maybe it was just the lock hitting the case I felt and heard. But Sotheby's is also sure they received it *without* the lock. Perhaps it somehow got opened by mistake in transit? If anyone was going to steal it, it would be Hope, and she swears up and down it wasn't her. And I was there to see her in the aftermath. She was as shocked as everyone else."

"What are we going to do? Make those people pay ten thousand dollars for an empty box? Because people are saying we're trying to pull some kind of hoax."

"Exactly. It's not like people were expecting treasure in there. But they were definitely expecting something."

I didn't come to the library knowing what else I could do, but now I had an idea. In the past, the Coventrys had a knack for dodging responsibility. Hamish's disappearing fortune? It was the psychic's doing. Poisoned peach melba? That was Typhoid Mary, and not the exploitation of cheap immigrant labor. My grandfather's death? That was the drunk pilot's fault, and not the culture of casual alcoholism enabled by young, rich men with big egos and nothing to do. Nothing was *ever* our fault. "We have to refund their money. It's the only way to make it seem like we're not running a scam."

And, I thought, *and*. Because a refund wasn't enough. This wasn't just about avoiding scandal at the height of the social season anymore. This was about being there for my family, in a way some Coventrys had struggled with in the past. They needed their final item. "And," I added, "I can put my Granny Fi sculpture for sale so we can make up for the lost funds."

"Don't," was Maggie's faint response. "You adore that sculpture."

I'd spent countless afternoons as Granny Fi's apprentice, running around the carriage house, scooping up pieces of metal for her. *Don't trouble yourself, girlie*, she'd say in her Virginia Slims tenor, *I'll just start again tomorrow*. "Granny Fi was never too precious with her art. She'd work all month on some piece and then just disassemble it in five minutes, saying it sucked. But this one, the one I have, is the one that she loved straightaway." I sighed, resigned. "I'm really sad to lose it, but I haven't been the best steward. Because where has it been for the last fifteen years? In storage. At least it got some time out of its packaging this month."

She was quiet. We both were. In a library this was easy. "Granny Fi gave you that sculpture," said Maggie after a time. "She trusted you to do the best for it, and I trust you, too."

"And now it's my turn to trust you," I decided, feeling that I could no longer do this alone. That I needed her. "I've been keeping a secret, and I shouldn't have." There was a tightness in my throat. "The auction isn't just to pay for your wedding and fix up the carriage house. It's to get Mom, Dad, and Archer out of it. Susie has given them to the end of the summer to move."

On her chair, Maggie was still, except for her eyes, narrowed, unsure. "Out of the carriage house?"

"It's been a good run, Susie told me, but they've got to find somewhere else to live." I forced myself to meet Maggie's gaze, wide and vulnerable and totally thrown. "She's sick of fixing things they break, she said. She's done trying to make it work with Hope." Once it was out of me, I was—well, not better. Not relieved or lighter. I felt, bluntly, worse, understanding how this would hurt Maggie.

"No!" she exclaimed, so loud that the other reading room's occupant, an elderly gentleman reading a newspaper, stared from atop the business section, and the young librarian shot in from the atrium.

"It's okay," I said to quell everyone's alarm. The librarian departed; the other man in the room vanished once more behind his newspaper.

"Can she even do that? What about the promise she made that they could stay?" Maggie asked.

"She owns the property. Including the carriage house. Promise or not, she can do whatever she wants with it. But it's okay. The auction will make them liquid. The whole empty time capsule snafu definitely turned some people off—Net-a-Newport is reporting breathlessly on that part—but it *was* big press. Got picked up in Providence and Boston. Maybe that will draw other people in," I said, longing for this all to be the case.

"It's not okay. Do Mom and Dad know?" she asked.

"No." I searched the floor next to my feet.

Maggie stood, took a few steps, then turned. "I should've been with you. I went back to New York to tell the company about the baby. Actually, my agent told them. I was instructed to sit there and look healthy." Her hands dropped, instinctively, to her belly. "Which, like, how could I? I am wide and bloated and an absolute coward. I made you cover

for me. Lie for me. For *weeks*. Because I was scared, and thinking only about myself."

Maggie spun her engagement ring around with her thumb.
If I'd been a little irked by her absence, her troubled face began
to scrub that feeling away. It was easier to be mad when we
weren't physically close.

"I wish you'd told me you were feeling this way," I said,
rising to meet her by the stacks. "I thought you just walked
out on us."

"I'm so sorry," she said.

As a child, watching Maggie dance, I thought she might
be able to float if she wanted, I believed she might be able to
bourrée her way over the whitecaps and the waves. But if this
summer had taught me anything it was that my sister wasn't
magic, she wasn't picture-perfect, and she was more beautiful for it.

"The weird thing is that I understood how *you* must feel,
with me gone and out of touch," I admitted to Maggie. "And
it didn't feel great."

"Cassie, I know your work is so important to you. I
shouldn't ever make you feel like you have to choose between
work and us. You never *once* made me feel bad for choosing
dance. After we moved out of the Cottage, when I got really
serious about it and started traveling, missing holidays. I know
I left you alone, probably at times you really needed me. And
I've just done it *again*."

I'd thought enough about that long-ago evening on Susie's
veranda—the one Archer only half-jokingly later referred to as
the Monday Night Massacre—to realize there was a probable
correlation between my behavior and the fact that, indeed,
Maggie had not been in attendance. But it was only now, as
my sister and I saw each other with deepened understanding, that I wondered not whether her presence at the party

would've changed the outcome, but what it would've meant if she'd been there the day after, when I'd woken up cut and hungover and sour-sweet sticky, with ash and corrosive shame in my mouth, and decided I should get out of Newport for good, forever.

"Hey," I said, because she was clearly gutted, and it was hollowing me out, too. "I'm here for you now. And you for me, all right?"

"How can I help?" she asked, straightening. "What can I do?"

"You can help me tell them, when it's time. After the auction, when they can feel safe and shored up. And we'll find somewhere for them to move. A two-bedroom. Up island, maybe. They'd be happy in Portsmouth. Or even over in Little Compton. Lots of cute places in Little Compton." I tried to buy in to my own optimism, willing the smell of old paper and well-loved books to comfort us. "Will you tell Jack?"

Maggie shook her head, not necessarily saying no, but rather, *I don't know.* "He has one parent left. Getting married has brought up all these complicated memories of his father. Do I want to throw this bomb into the relationship with his mother?"

"You don't have to decide now. Let's focus on one thing at a time," I said. "Your wedding. Yes? That's the main thing. And the baby. I have to tell you about Black Ships and running into Mrs. Finley. Seriously, I almost died. The only perk was that someone relinquished their counter stool for me at the Handy Lunch one day." This made her smile, so I went on. "I can't say it was because of the pregnancy rumor, but I ordered a bacon omelet *and* blueberry pancakes, just to be safe. So, come on, let's *finally* celebrate this pregnancy properly! Let's hand out cigars down the wharves. I want to skip down Lower Thames and hug everyone. I'm going to climb Newport tower and shout that I'm going to be an auntie."

"Last time you scaled that tower, you were in a prom dress," said Maggie, her smile growing.

"And blindfolded," I reminded her. "It will be easier this time."

"A shotgun wedding," Maggie said and chuckled. "Honestly, Cassie, I thought it would've been you."

"Speaking of promiscuous behavior," I said, grabbing my camera bag and wrapping my arm around my sister's waist. As we started for the library's exit, I wiggled my eyebrows. "I have to tell you about—"

"Spencer," said Maggie, already on it, already giving my side a few playful pinches. "Archer texted me. *Real* sneaky your late-night dips in Susie's pool. Totally covert. Take notes, James Bond."

Our giggles echoed through the reading room, unrestrained, too loud, entirely, irredeemably improper.

24

NET-A-NEWPORT 3H
Link: NYPost
NYCB Dancer and Heiress Maggie Coventry-Gilford is Pregnant
with Her First Child

NaN blind item revealed!!
Own it: Who was wrong about the pregnancy?

84%	Me 84%
16%	I knew 16%

NET-A-NEWPORT 2H
Submitted via NetaNewport.com
From: sailor
Subject: spotted

Chef hottie Spencer Sims watching the Newport Bermuda race kick
off at Castle Hill, and getting cozy with a lady friend. Couldn't see

who—she was in hat and sunnies. Looks like he's off the market though. Bummer.

My phone lit up with a text. In his bed, Spencer wrapped around the back of my body, forehead pressing into the flesh below my neck, big cup enveloping little cup. It was late, almost one in the morning, and I was too on edge to sleep, amped up with expectation and the Frosty Freez ice cream I'd picked up for us earlier. We'd been bouncing back and forth name ideas for his new restaurant (Tide & Turnip? No. Longships? No. Juliette? No. The Princess? *Naming restaurants is harder than it seems*, I'd said.)

Was a smash! River wrote. I turned myself in Spencer's arms and positioned the screen so we could both see. A white glove sale—every lot sold! River's summer class had ended, and he'd wanted to go to observe the auction in person so we'd funded his trip, though we highly encouraged him to use the rest of it as a vacation, free of Coventrys. There was a livestream on the Sotheby's website, but I'd had no desire to watch. Instead, the television above Spencer's dresser was playing a quaint show about a veterinarian in rural England in the 1930s.

I flipped over to my email, let it refresh, and in came the number from our girl at Sotheby's, the gross profit, followed by three exclamation marks. Spencer clapped. My body relaxed, sinking into the pillow top. The sound that came out of me was one of great relief. In addition to the grand total, she'd added, Let's chat on Monday about a second installment this winter.

I was happy the auction was a success. And I hoped that the new owner of my sculpture would appreciate it—display it—better than I had. Paying good money would help with that, I would think.

"See? The empty time capsule didn't sink you," Spencer said, kissing the tip of my nose. He had showered when he got home, but the smell of shallots and garlic lingered, molecules embedded into the cracks, calluses, and burn. I didn't mind it—I thought of him as a sculptor with clay beneath his nails, or an artist with ink in his pores.

I'd been spending nights this week in his apartment, a modern loft in an old converted North End school. His style was clean and cozy, a rugged leather chair paired with a high-armed sofa in cream basket-weave fabric. Along the walls, he'd scavenged all manner of nautical flea market finds, oil paintings of boats, buoys, flags.

Is it overboard? he'd joked when I noticed an oar propped up in the corner by his dresser.

Net-a-Newport was insinuating that he was in a relationship with me—the unidentified "lady friend." And though I still resisted any labels, I could say that we'd been getting closer, learning about each other. For two people who'd met when they were teenagers, the experience was lovely and wholesome in a way that even my jaded heart couldn't shadow. I was discovering that Spencer began his days with yoga or kettle bells; he ended them with a text to his dad. He said his prayers. He read everything Zadie Smith. He routinely forgot to lock his own front door.

"Seriously, what was in the capsule?" We were alone, the city asleep below us, but still he whispered like we were in a crowd. "The mysteries of rich white folks aren't usually for me, but I am really curious."

"J.P. thought it would be a Bible, or coins, bank notes, mundane, everyday items. I wish I knew."

"If something was to get lost, at least it wasn't one of the items with multiples of value," said Spencer, brushing a strand of hair off my cheek.

"At least the Coventry curse spared us that," I said. I tossed my phone into the duvet, and swung around so I was straddling Spencer. I didn't want to think any more about the capsule, or this auction, or the pieces, Granny Fi's sculpture included, that were now scattered into the wind. I didn't want to think, period.

Spencer was shirtless, sweatpants low on his hips, delicious and warm, and here. If my thirty-one years had taught me anything, it was not to let a beautiful man in a bed go to waste.

I lifted my pajama top over my head, the last bit of control he allowed me. In one motion, Spencer flipped me onto my back, pinning me down, so my legs were around his waist and my arms restrained by his. I gasped as his lower body pressed into mine, his teeth grazing the place where my pulse was pounding.

I thought he might continue hungrily and fast, the kind of sex that leaves marks, leaves us both gasping and sweaty. The kind we'd been having.

But over me, he moved languidly. Instead of bites, he took sips. The television played sweet, pastoral music, piano and strings, a hymn written on parchment. And I realized as I clung to him, drunk him with my mouth and tongue, enjoying him like a cat with cream, that something in me had changed; a door had been opened in a forbidden wing of our relationship, and I didn't know where it led.

·····

When I woke up in the morning, next to a gently snoring Spencer, there was one more text on my phone.

Mouna.

Your accreditation just approved by the Uzbek foreign ministry! When can you leave?

25

8:06 AM
You replied to their story
Hey…so, this is awk, but you asked your followers a while ago
about the Coventry time capsule, and why it was empty. But then
you never posted their answers. I'm wondering if you got any reasonable and/or nondelusional tips about what actually happened?
You've posted some mean stuff about me and my family this summer, so I've really gone back and forth about whether to dm you
at all. But if you got anything you think would be helpful to us, I'd
appreciate you passing that along. Thanks.

11:20 AM
Hi Cass. Sorry to hear you feel like we've been mean to you. We
actually really love the Coventrys over here, and spent a lot of time

hyping the wedding and your auction. We do regret posting the thing about your return to Newport being bizarre and sad. You're right, that was no fun. And this account is supposed to be fun.

11:22 AM
As for your question, I can't help you, although I would if I could. No one gave any solid info about why the contents of the capsule were stolen.

12:06 PM
You know they were stolen?? For real??

3:12 PM
HELLO?

"My RSVP card," I said to Maggie, handing her the sealed envelope three days before the wedding. "Please note that although I have not met the reply deadline, I *have* read and absorbed the dress code."

My sister, Jack, and I were in what we as children had called *the thicket*. Susie had cleared the saplings and azalea bushes years ago, and turned it into a sunken, formal garden. This is where I'd dug up the capsule, in the exact place Granny Fi, right before her death, had promised it would be.

Throughout were a smattering of mature beech trees, healthy, lush, and shady. I didn't have to touch them to remember their smooth, silvery bark. They were always our favorite to climb. Susie's landscapers had surrounded their trunks with vast circles of mulch; now, if we wanted to perch on one of the low branches, we'd have to trample through yards of lilies of the valley, their sturdy green leaves and delicate, white dew-drop flowers crushed beneath our feet.

Maggie quickly passed my envelope to the coordinator she'd

hired for the weekend, Ashley, who had the barrel-curled hair and the extroverted enthusiasm required, I suspected, of the profession.

"Ugh, speaking of the RSVP cards," Maggie said, typing rapid messages on her phone, "one of my friends got back together with her girlfriend, and now she wants to reinvite her. It's a whole thing."

Jack pulled out a composition notebook, like the ones we all had in elementary school language arts classes, and began to review a list. As my uncle Dunk would say, Jack had evidently taken to wedding planning like a pig to mud. "My revised boutonniere design is cleared," Jack told Ashley, moving his index and middle finger down the page. "And the flower crown for the flower girl is being constructed as we speak…" They wandered off to the folly, which was a fancy name for a small rotunda, open to the elements, ringed with eight granite columns. This particular structure was unique in that it served no purpose other than being a pretty thing at which to look. Actually, that wasn't true. Maggie once confessed she and Jack had, *you know, wink, wink, nudge, nudge*-d there. Some kind of songbird bird, brown, chirpy, zipped between its friends in the branches.

"Okay," Maggie said to me with a beleaguered look. "Hi. How are you? How was your night with Spencer?" But her phone chimed again. "Great, now I got my agent texting me…"

The little bird flew a few circles around the folly. Her watchman rounds complete, she perched on her column, settled her feathers, and disappeared into what I figured was a nest, hidden at the top.

Spencer and I, our last summer together, had taken a picnic blanket and watched the moon rise through the folly's oculus, alighting on The Land's grass and the sea, silver and shadow; he'd brought candles, but we'd blown them out and kissed in the smoke. I wondered if I was still the kind of girl he'd light candles for. If he still toted around matches, just in case.

It wasn't lost on me that I was doing exactly what I'd done ten years ago, picturing a future, elastic and electrifying, with Spencer in it. I'd tried to prevent this, telling him and myself that I wasn't sticking around *long enough to be anything but casual.* I couldn't resist tugging on the words, as I might a loose thread on a sleeve, knowing that as they unraveled, I would be forced to hold something I'd tucked away, something that looked an awful lot like regret.

Nothing about my dwindling time in Newport felt casual, and not just because Maggie's black-tie wedding was on Monday. Could I simply waltz back into my old life, leave Newport without looking back?

"Jack!" Maggie called, abrupt, her concentration still squarely on her phone. "Jack, come here." She summoned him with rapid scoops of her hand.

"What is it?" I tried to get a square look at her screen. On it, an article, but I couldn't make out specifics. Maggie's face—the pressed mouth, the drawn brows. It wasn't good.

"I'm texting you a link," she said to me as Jack hurried over.

My hands shook as I fumbled around in my bag for my phone. The link was to VF.com.

When the headline appeared, my jaw came unhinged.

On the Eve of the Wedding of the Season, the Coventry Family Confronts an Uncertain Future

By Reagan A. Finley—<>—August 30, 2023

As glamorous weddings go, this one is sure to dazzle.

Consider the pedigrees. The Coventry family's roots in America extend back before the revolution. They've been rob-

ber barons and philanthropists, friends of Astors and Roose-
velts, and, more recently, a rising star at Lincoln Center, a social
media influencer, and a photojournalist whose work documenting humanitarian crises has been published by *TIME*. Now, the
oldest daughter, ballerina Maggie Coventry-Gilford, is set to
wed longtime boyfriend John Patrick Utterback, formerly an
investment banking director.

Next, consider the setting: The Land, the Gilded Age family manse, the sprawling beaux-arts estate perfectly placed on
the cliffs of Newport, which, over the century of its existence,
has welcomed (and raised) generations of American sover-
eigns. The wedding, insiders say, will channel the summertime
in New England romanticism of an Edward Hopper painting—
sun, sea, sand, and parasols.

Look under the shiny gilt, though, and you'll find the tin.
The famous name, as well as the glamour of the wedding itself, belie a sadder past and uncertain future for what was once
one of the most distinguished and headline-grabbing families
of Newport. The Coventrys, I discovered this summer as I returned to the city by the sea, are far removed from the gossip
and legends surrounding them.

"What the actual hell?" I paused, looking up from the
phone to check on my sister and Jack. Maggie had her hand
over her mouth. Jack was very still, but his eyes were running, reading, skimming, his finger scrolling the page up on
his phone.

"Is everything all right?" asked Ashley, who'd returned
from the folly with enough trepidation that signaled she already knew the answer.

"I thought—" Maggie said, halting. "This was supposed to
be— Cassie, what does this Henry James quote mean?" Maggie and I locked eyes. "I don't get it."

One swipe of my finger, and I found the passage Maggie was referring to.

Part of the Coventry collapse, locals say, was self-induced hubris and a kind of stubborn carelessness that is particular to the descendants of the industrialists we all know by name. As Henry James wrote prophetically, "The white elephants, as one may best call them, all cry and no wool, all house and no garden, make now, for three or four miles, a barely interrupted chain...while their inverted owners, roused from a witless dream, wonder what in the world is to be done with them."

"We're the ones named after Henry James characters, and she uses him against us?" I was jarred, still trembling, feeling like maybe, if I kept reading, it would get better, though I soon discovered all it did was get worse. Reagan had a quote from some writer who called himself a luxury estate expert who estimated that running The Land could cost upward of fifty grand a month. Next, a historian chimed in that the Coventry family, back when Lieutenant Steel ran the biz, had been very good at accumulating money. Then, over the generations—and I'm paraphrasing here—we became very good at blowing through it. Nothing but the truth; still, peeved at these strangers who'd anointed themselves *Coventry professionals*, I skipped ahead.

As certain circles of Newport know, the Coventrys—down to the fading socialite and erstwhile heiress Hope, her Virginia-born husband, a former detective in the Newport Police Department, J. P. Gilford, and their three children—actually sold The Land in 2008 in the wake of the Great Recession, which decimated what little the Coventrys had left. By that point, the mansion and its outbuildings were nearly decrepit by ravages of time and passed over by history. But one last lifeline was extended to them by the property's new owner, the former wife of Lionel Utterback, the deceased former CEO of Honor Investments. They were allowed to stay, renting the carriage house on the property for a dime.

"It's true that the Coventry family resides at The Land," says Don Washington, chairman of the Newport Preservation Council and an expert on the mansions that remain on Ochre Point and Bellevue Avenues. "But like so many formerly prosperous residents of Newport, their situation is much reduced."

So reduced, in fact, that the Coventrys won't be living at The Land much longer. "The residential occupancy of the carriage house by the Coventry family will be mutually and amicably discontinued as of September 5," reads an emailed statement from Susan Utterback, owner of The Land, and the groom's mother. "The carriage house requires extensive repairs, and is not conducive to continued dwelling."

Around Newport, rumors swirl as to why the Coventrys, on the eve of the wedding of the season, are being unceremoniously evicted.

"She's broken the news about the eviction," I managed. "Shit."

"An eviction?" Jack had his hand in his hair; he'd gone a little pale.

"Oh, Jack," said Maggie.

As she began to explain to him how long we'd known, and that my parents didn't yet, I dropped back into the article, near where I'd left off.

"That the carriage house needs extensive repairs is an understatement," notes Washington. "Unfortunately, it has not been treated with care by the Coventry-Gilford family, and has fallen into disrepair. Additionally, the inside of the residence has been

neglected as well; reports indicate the historic interiors have
been overtaken by their personal effects."

Possibly, there was an attempt to clear out the carriage house
and make it habitable. In August, Sotheby's held an auction
billed as...

"They've got you in here, Cass," Jack said. "About you covering for Maggie's pregnancy."

I frantically scrolled down my screen, searching for the
passage Jack had referenced. I didn't immediately find it, but
I did see this.

> It is unclear where the family, permanently out of The Land,
> will end up. Perhaps it won't even be Newport at all. Mag-
> gie Coventry-Gilford, soon to be Maggie Utterback, lives for
> most of the year in New York; Archer, the family's youngest
> son, who's racked up millions of views creating titillating, eye-
> candy content on TikTok, said in a recent video he would like
> to move to Los Angeles.
>
> "I only can take Newport in small doses," adds Cass
> Coventry-Gilford, the younger sister of the bride, who fol-
> lowed in her late grandmother's artistic footsteps to a career in
> photography. "I belong in the field."

I *knew* I hadn't written to Reagan anything close to what
was quoted. Why, then, did the phrase sound familiar? "Oh,
fuck me!" I cried. "The Flower Show. I didn't know I was
on the record."

"'As the Bellevue mansions have turned into anachronisms,
relics from an evaporated era, so might the Coventry family—'" Maggie read the piece's final line as though it were a
verdict "'—as it splinters and spins away from Newport, and
the property they've called home for over one hundred years.'"

I had the sudden urge to pull up all of Susie's perfect flowers by the root or smash them like houseflies with my shoe.

No—it wasn't an urge. I was already doing it. I'd walked to the nearest beech, breaths more like gasps, and, like a toddler having a meltdown, commenced a stomping tantrum in the woodland perennial patch.

I'd trusted Susie. I'd put my faith in her. *Let's keep this between us*, I'd begged earlier this summer. I'd practically prostrated. We'd had a deal. And what had she done? Blabbed to Reagan Finley. Taken her plans to the Preservation Council. And to what end? She almost had my parents out. And then she just—what? Needed to squeeze every last humiliating drop from the carriage house's stones?

"After everything my father pulled…" Jack said, blinking into the distance, as though talking to himself, "driving away the people who loved him. It is incredible that she would…" But he never finished his sentence. In the next beat, he was white-knuckling his phone, jamming buttons.

"Does Susie *want* to hurt us?" Maggie asked Jack, apparently confused, as I was, about Susie's motives for commenting for the article. What would she gain by amplifying this feud in the press? "Does she want to turn us against each other? Does she not want this wedding?"

More than feeling betrayed by Susie, I was also wounded. I'd known this woman for half my life. I thought I'd been redeemed in her eyes this summer.

I guess I'd thought wrong.

I finished decimating my first target. I was considering an attack on a second location when I heard Jack say, "There has to be some explanation," with the forced calmness of someone hanging on by a hair. "She does not want to turn us against each other, Maggie. That would be unhinged."

"She has no hinges!" cried Maggie, stricken. "There aren't any hinges left!"

"Then why didn't you tell me?" Jack asked Maggie. "I could've helped!"

"I didn't know she would go to the press! Cass said it would be okay. That they had an agreement!"

I held on to the beech, gathering myself and getting my bearings. Dirt and petals lingered on my sneakers, mulch in my sock.

"Mom's not answering," Jack said. "I'll go find her in the Cottage."

I wiped my hands on my pants, staggered over to where Maggie was pacing a flat line into the grass. Ashley, I noticed, had vaporized.

"We've got to get to our parents first," I told Jack. "Before they find out they're being evicted from *Vanity* fucking *Fair*."

Maggie groaned.

I followed her line of sight to the short series of bluestone steps that led down into the garden. Hope, trailed closely by J.P. and Archer, was charging toward us. Over the lip of the garden, the Cottage's roof and chimneys were partially visible, rising toward the sky. As they got close, any possibility that they hadn't yet seen the article was erased. Their faces, all cracked in various states of anger and betrayal, gave it up.

"I want this to be entered into the record!" Hope hollered when she was still a dozen yards away. Her long, red-wine skirt fluttered at the ankles; she spoke as though she might draw a sword. "I always *knew*, didn't I, Cass? That Reagan is bad, *bad* news."

26

"We have to fight," Maggie was saying. "The way Susie handled this is not okay. It's like she is deliberately trying to embarrass all of us." After we were joined by our parents, she'd taken to pacing again in the center of the garden. Her neat ponytail was loose. Strands of hair blew across her forehead and lips.

"It's all true, then?" asked J.P.

"It's true," said Archer, frowning. "I've been hearing rumblings for a few weeks."

"You have?" I asked him.

"I didn't even p—" He stopped. "I mean, I didn't even want to believe it."

"And what's this about moving to Los Angeles?" Hope turned to her son, who was now crossed-legged on the grass in apparent exhaustion.

"I was answering questions on a Live," Archer explained. "Someone asked where I could see myself in the future and I just said LA because I thought it might sound good. But you all know I would wilt in LA. I'm a Newport nine but a Hollywood three. I wouldn't survive more than sixteen days before I'd be weeping on a red-eye back to Providence."

"Jack, tell us." J.P. walked to his almost son-in-law, placed his hands on his shoulders. "What's your mother thinking? She's serious? We're out?"

"Is this one of those whims, Jack?" Hope added. "Like that Christmas she changed the white lights on the tulip trees to multicolored?"

"I don't..." Jack said. "I—"

"I need to be answering those questions, not Jack." I stepped in.

"Cassie?" My father, unforgettably sad and confused, turned to me.

I'd held this for months; one would think I would've had time to prepare. Even still, getting it out was a challenge. "All right, so..." I floundered because I couldn't think of anything I wanted to say less. "Well, actually, Susie told me about the kick-out at...the engagement party."

"The engagement party!" Hope echoed. "She's that sick of me, huh?"

"I negotiated a longer runway. I figured once the auction made you some money, it wouldn't feel so daunting to leave. So I waited to tell you. I only just told Maggie last week." Everyone grew really quiet. "I was trying to keep it simple and peaceful. I never thought that a reporter would find out before you."

When I'd played this moment in my head, planning for the eventuality, I knew it would be difficult, yet not in *this* way. I'd never questioned that I was correct in keeping this information from my brother and parents. But as this drama was unfolding, I realized too late the cost of being economical with the truth, as though I'd robbed them—these adults who'd raised me and loved me and welcomed me back despite all I'd done in my youth to make their lives miserable. I'd been trying to make up for my past, but I'd screwed up yet again, this time on a more massive, public scale.

As the sun inched down in the sky, the shadows of the trees grew bolder. So did the breeze. I wrapped my arms around my waist and waited for the castigation, the ruling of my utter incompetence. *What would I do*, I thought, *if Hope never forgave me?* A plane, I guessed. A train. An automobile. A bike. That's what I'd done before, when things got unbearable. Left with a promise that I'd only be brought back to Newport kicking and screaming.

That option, though, that escape route, held surprisingly less shine than before.

"But why go to Reagan?" asked Hope. "This is very untimely!"

Maggie: "She was *so* mad about the time capsule."

Archer: "It's something to do with money. It's *always* about money, in Newport."

"Oh, kids," my father said, and it sounded like *he* was about to apologize.

"We have to fight," Maggie reiterated.

"But this is my mother," Jack said, distraught.

"So?" Maggie countered. "I don't want to roll over! I've spent my entire career rolling over, being told by ballet masters where to stand and that I'm standing wrong and where to hop and that I'm hopping wrong. I'm so sick of people thinking they can just—" The end of her sentence dropped, and I wondered what she was really talking about, Susie or the ballet. "Mom?" she asked, her voice breaking. "Say we won't go. Tell them we'll find a way to undo this."

Heads swung toward Hope, awaiting her answer. All sum-

mer I'd worked to get her and J.P. and Archer in a solid position to leave The Land behind them. I'd been positive that
this place was no good for us, and for me; I never considered
convincing Susie to keep them here.

Hope wasn't looking at us but outward, to the trampled flowers, then the less mangled spots in the garden. She
scratched her neck, blinked a few times, and took a few steps
in the direction of the folly.

"Ma?" I prompted.

"I think the bar should go there." Hope pointed to the site
of my stomp-a-thon. "The flowers are dead and I doubt we
or Susie have time to plant new ones."

"Sweetheart," J.P. entreated.

"If you put the bar kitty-corner, facing the Cottage, it will
hide the nasty parts."

"Mom," said Maggie. "We can't let Susie get away with
this."

"Where is Ashley?" Hope asked, hands on hips. "What are
we paying her for except to be here?"

"Maggie," said Jack, "I need to go talk to my mother."

"You'll stay here, Jack," she said. "You'll stay here with us.
Don't give her the attention she wants."

"Maggie, how many bartenders will there be?" asked Hope.
"Two? If so, let's double the tables, and they can make an
L-shape around the tree."

"HCG," said Archer, standing, giving our mother's back a
few light pats. He looked down at her. "I—I completely agree.
We need two tables."

"Good," said Hope, clapping her hands once, twice.

I checked around our small circle and, yes, everyone save
Archer was as stunned as I. What was this? Denial? Deflec-
tion? Could I question or defy it, in light of all that had just
crashed at her feet?

"Okay. What's next? Can we go through the list of must-have pictures? And where in the *world* is Ashley?" Hope repeated.

"I'll call her," J.P. said. "Walk with me, Jack?" I thought I saw Jack gulp, but he nodded, and they broke away from the group, up the steps of the garden.

"Mama," tried Maggie, once more. Maybe it was the supplication in my sister's voice, but something in Hope's eyes flashed, and the mask dropped, just for a moment, offering us a glimpse of something heavy and painful and bewildering.

But then it was gone, replaced by the regular agitation of the mother of the bride, three days before her daughter gets hitched. "Darling, we have so much left to do," Hope stressed. "Don't we still need to get you a slip for your reception dress? I've got most of the welcome baskets in my car, so let's you, Daddy, and I drop them at Gurney's and then we can run to Middletown. Archer, you're assembling the programs? Great. Let's—Oh, praise the Lord, here comes J.P. and Jack with Ashley!"

Maggie turned to me, hands raised, mouth drawn, as though to say *I give up*, before meeting Ashley at the bottom of the garden's steps.

Jack and my father stopped at the top. Jack was saying his mother's name, gesturing broadly, to the Cottage, to the sky. After a few moments of watching Jack progressively get madder, J.P. slowly reached out and clasped Jack's shoulder. Jack stilled. J.P. talked. Jack listened. My father put a hand on his own chest, as though to say *breathe*. Jack nodded, and with one last look at Maggie, he strode away from the garden and out of sight.

Hope's last direction was to me. "Cassie," she said. "Dad and I are going to get your sister a slip. Then we will be back for our dinner reservation at six. Your uncle Dunk will need a ride there. We'll have the car, so maybe you can use Jack's, or call an Uber. Please also call your auntie Lolly to make sure she checked into the hotel all right, and that she knows where the restaurant is. Last time she was here, she took a wrong turn and ended up at surfer's point. Almost started a turf war. Understand?"

"No," I said, part laughter, part despair.

Hope's eyes closed for a long moment. She inhaled through her nose. I couldn't tell if she was gathering strength or losing it. I waited. Eventually, she opened her eyes and continued, more urgent than ever. "Your sister is getting married in seventy-two hours. This wedding will happen. And it will be beautiful. But I need you, Cassie. Please? Now, tell me—do you understand?"

I recognized, belatedly, I didn't need to understand. I just needed to be there. And this time, my answer was "Yes."

September

27

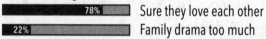
Because Archer was astonishingly persuasive, that evening I found myself on the flat top of Harbour Court's fence, sneaking in to take their nice kayaks out for joyrides. Because, Archer said, we needed to do an activity that was not attached to the wedding or The Land or a combination of the two. Because, he also added, I appeared at dinner as though I was about to steal away to join another family.

Archer, from his spot on the public sidewalk, peering down the currently empty street for signs of cars or pedestrians, had hold of my foot and ankle, and Maggie was waiting amid the trees and bushes inside the property, having moments ago scaled the wall with the athleticism of a rock climber, despite being five months pregnant. "Hold on," I said. A surprise to no one, this had been much easier when we were teenagers. "Let me adjust my leg—" But before I could figure out the best way to get down, Archer gave my shoe an impatient, hard push, the momentum rolled me over the top, and I landed on my bottom in the grass with a thump and a grunt.

"You did it." Maggie helped me to my feet.

"Battered. Bruised," I said, but I was happy I hadn't fallen on my head or neck. Happy to feel that lovely little rush that I'd *made it.* I rubbed my rear, checking my jeans for tears. "But I've been worse."

"I have a chiropractor on call," said Maggie, brushing dust from my elbow.

"I used to be on the hunt for boys in the parking lots," I said. "Now I'm concerned about lumbar adjustments. My, how times have changed."

Archer was next; his fingers appeared first, then a fore-arm, then, gradually, the rest of him as he hoisted himself up and over. "Good work, team," he said when he dropped onto our side.

Per Hope's orders, the motions of wedding planning had gone on as scheduled that afternoon, no further mention of Reagan or Susie or the eviction or the article, except on the sibling text chain. During our family dinner, we hid our phones in our napkin-draped laps, shooting off messages when Hope wasn't looking.

Maggie volunteered the name of a lawyer; out of the three of us, she was most insistent that our parents stay. I guess it's Susie's choice what to do with the carriage house, she wrote, but the way she's gone about it is AWFUL. And we're just supposed to forgive her because she's Jack's mom?

We're supposed to stay out of spite? Archer countered. I don't love that for us.

How quickly can you get in touch with this lawyer? I asked Maggie. Maybe I could meet them before I left for Tashkent, though that was only a few days away. It would be tight. And what would I even say?

Hello, I am the problem child of a fading American dynasty in a love-hate relationship with my childhood home, and though my mother is really the one who is going to make a decision about whether to sue my sister's mother-in-law, she hasn't told us what she wants to do because she is consumed with wedding weekend welcome presents.

And then this lawyer would say, *That makes perfect sense and, yes, you're correct that residency rights is not a made-up thing, and I have a special on my retainer this week—it's zero dollars!*

Dessert had turned into another round of drinks at the bar, because we all needed a few, which then had transitioned, thanks to Archer, into this sibling bonding adventure.

My last text before we left was to Spencer: I'm going to stay at the land tonight with my sister. But see you tomorrow at polo.

Saw the article. Crazy. Hope you all get some rest.

I tried not to read too much into the brevity, telling myself he was busy at The Bonnie.

"Are you sure this was the spot we used?" Single file, we traipsed between mature rhododendrons and azalea bushes, Archer in the lead. This required some work, some snapped branches. "I thought there used to be a little path," I said. Once upon a time, the Coventry family had been members here. But that was gone before I'd been born, along with the sailing yacht, the membership to Bailey's Beach, the pied-à-terre in

New York, the horse farm on Long Island, and I could keep going, but at this point, we know the drill.

"It's likely the path grew over," said Archer, pushing aside a sapling, looking back to smile at me. "It's been a minute since we've engaged in some light breaking and entering. Okay. We're almost out of the woods. Remember, everyone, just act like you belong."

This would be hard. With me in a black cropped top and high-waist jeans, Maggie in a white linen dress and sneakers, and Archer in a T-shirt that said Surely Not Everybody Was Kung-fu Fighting, we appeared dressed for entirely different events. But we gave it our best shot, strolling the lawn with purpose, like it was a regular evening and we were headed toward the clubhouse.

Currently the Newport headquarters of the New York Yacht Club, Harbour Court was originally constructed, like most of these old places were, to be a private residence a hundred or more years ago. I was always of the opinion that it belonged in France, or maybe Italy, with its brown stucco walls and lofty rooflines. "Just like the old days," I observed, and linked my arm through Maggie's. "Archer and I corrupting you." Ahead of us, Archer flashed a thumbs-up.

"I need to break some rules," Maggie said. "That's what my therapist says, anyway."

"I didn't know you were in therapy." I was beginning to think I should be, too.

"After the last few months, I need it." Maggie shrugged. "Some stuff has been useful; like when I'm in a situation that has made me nervous in the past, she suggests I ask myself: What's the worst that can happen? They find us and kick us out of Newport?"

"Been there," I said.

"Though some worst-case scenarios actually come true.

And I haven't arrived at the part of therapy that teaches me how to deal with that."

"Reagan's article?" I asked as we steered wide of the clubhouse patio, chairs, and tables occupied by members enjoying their meals and drinks, people lounging in the Adirondack chairs facing the sea, and descended the lawn toward the dock. Here's a lesson I learned early—if anyone is suspicious of your presence, direct eye contact will only make it worse. "The wedding drama?"

"Among other things," Maggie said. "Like my artistic director's reaction to my pregnancy, which I got in writing earlier. I didn't need *that* today."

"They aren't firing you!" Archer spun around to walk backward.

"Not allowed to, by law," said Maggie. "But they are pushing me back to second company and giving me a thirty percent pay cut and no guarantees for medical leave."

I objected with a loud *WHAT?* though I probably shouldn't have been surprised. The arts are as ruthless as corporations, and anyone who thinks otherwise is sadly mistaken.

"Thieves in leg warmers!" Archer threw up his hands.

"Crooks in Freeds," I added.

We made our way to the end of the dock, removed our shoes, dangled our bare feet above the lapping, lullaby water. For a moment, we were quiet, observing the sun sinking from beyond Goat Island, the bridge I'd crossed three months ago arched above the horizon. From here, we could see the low-slung homes along the shore and broad warehouses around the shipyard, newly built hotels and condos along the waterfront, the sailboats tacking around Goat Island, the moorings, hundreds of bobbing studs, scattered in the shallows, a lone cruise ship, anchored farther out in the harbor.

I pulled out my phone, adjusted the focus and exposure on

its camera, and took some shots of the panorama. I knew that long after I left Newport, no matter how they turned out, these photos would become their own memory. Maybe I'd scroll through the series and recall not just this delicate moment, poised between moments of chaos, but the feeling of my siblings, warm and present beside me.

"What a *day*." Archer finally spoke for all of us.

"My agent has already gotten a dozen interview requests as a result of Reagan, and it's only been a few hours," Maggie said, kicking drops of water up with her toes. "Everyone is just desperate to know how this wedding between two feuding families is going to go forward. I suspect we'll have photographers with long lenses hiding in bushes, waiting for a fight to break out. I mean, is this wedding even possible? Is it practical? Trying to get the Coventry-Gilfords and Utterbacks to be under the same tent?"

"I don't want to give Susie the satisfaction of slinking off, defeated," said Archer.

"Me neither." Maggie looked at me. "What do you think, Cassie? You weren't a fan of The Land as a venue, originally. Maybe Jack and I don't even need to get married right now. Maybe we should take some time for things to settle, then elope or something. Cut losses and run."

That's what I'd done, ten years ago. How interesting I wasn't going to suggest the same for my sister. "If you had doubts about Jack, we would be the first to runaway-bride you," I said. "But you don't. I know you wanted him to stay with us earlier, but he had to go to his mom. Right? You were the one to remind me at the library that she's his only parent left."

"He's been betrayed," observed Archer, "same as us."

"And what did you say at Ocean House about the wedding?" I asked Maggie. "*It's all just scenery. Just smoke and mirrors.*

Buggie—that's not quite right. It's more than that." I thought of what I'd read once, about the ways we are physically connected to the earth, how the particular chemical composition of water that we drink, the rain that we splash through, shows up in our hair and in our teeth, and can create a geographical map of our movements. The places we lived. The places we left. "The Land is an important piece of us, and it makes sense that you'd get married there. We want to see you and Jack take the vows in the place you fell in love."

"Hey!" came a deep voice before she could respond. "What are you guys doing here?" Next to me, Maggie tensed, and I zeroed in on the excuses, the explanations, ready to take the fall for being here.

But when Archer wheeled around, he just laughed, and held out his arms. Striding toward us was not a Harbour Court staff member or security guard, but Remy, with a bottle of champagne and glasses, followed closely by Jack, looking clear-eyed and determined.

Maggie leaped to her feet. She called his name, and he entreated hers, a few syllables of love and patience and relief that signaled there was much more to say. After. Later. First, a cocooning hug that made me miss my own big spoon.

"Do you mind us crashing?" asked Remy, sliding down next to Archer.

"Never." I smiled. "Especially because you brought refreshments."

"I know the manager," said Remy. "She owes me three favors." He passed the bottle to Archer. "Now two."

Archer popped the champagne without spilling a drop.

"Nicely done," I said.

"Learned from the best," said Archer, glancing at Remy.

"How are you?" I asked Jack as Archer filled his glass and moved on to mine.

"I'm better. Sorry about ghosting earlier. Your dad suggested I take my anger away from the wedding planning. Said I didn't need a perfect storm of stress, and he was right, as usual. I didn't find my mom, but I did a long run on the treadmill and took a cold shower and then Remy came and picked me up because I wanted to be with my bride."

"Aw," said Remy.

"I just wish my mom would..." Jack sighed. "Ah, I may be wrong, and I may be making this all about me when it's not, but I wonder if she's threatened, if that's the right word, by me joining your family. J.P. is like a father to me, Cass and Archer like siblings. And she's got—I mean, all she's got is me. That's not to excuse her actions, but—"

I shook my head, stopping him. We were navigating the mess of adulthood together; he'd seen me at my lowest, and cheered for me at my highest. He'd sent me silly Charlie Brown valentines and shared my work on his social media and I loved him and took him for granted just like a real sister would. Jack's observations were probably not too far off, but he didn't need to compensate for his mother. "We know where your heart is. You don't have to answer for hers."

"Thanks, kid," Jack said. "And I meant to tell you this afternoon before...everything went down, but I know Maggie has been so happy that you stayed. Me, too." Thoughtful, he tipped his glass slightly, watching the bubble mousse melt and fizz against the rim. "I didn't want to admit how much impending fatherhood affected me. I kind of went off the deep end, didn't I?" Maggie stayed quiet and, a testament to her generous heart, did not pile on, though I imagine she could've said something like *YES*. "Drinking, partying too much. I think I'd still be spiraling over flushable shoe covers if not for you and Archer, stepping in with the wedding and the auction."

Touched, I gave his stubble an affectionate scratch. "You're a good egg."

"Now back to those shoe covers," said Archer, "which weren't a *terrible* idea. If you're looking for investors, I have about one hundred full dollars."

Jack chuckled again. "I have a lead on something a little more stable than harebrained inventions. One of my buddies wants to start an investment advisory firm that focuses on sustainability, ESG investing."

"Trying to save the planet," I said, proud and pleased at once, "instead of murdering it."

Maggie clapped her hands. "Archer and Remy, give us a show. We want Christmas Batman."

"I thought you'd never ask," said Archer, bounding to his feet, pulling Remy with him. Maggie, Jack, and I spun around on the dock as Archer went to one knee, crouched dramatically.

Maggie counted them in, and the dance began with high kicks, then some artful punches, then a Fosse-esque tiptoe walk, then Archer broke into tune—*It's Christmas in Gotham!* Next, Remy, with jazz hands: *Deck Arkham in lights! Santa, look out for the Joker! He'll give Rudolph a bite!* Maggie and I were clutching each other; I could barely see through my tears. When Archer and Remy were done, they bowed deeply.

We never did make it into a kayak. And yes, we were eventually caught by a staff member who was not very obliging, and who wasn't at all impressed with the fact that Maggie's impending wedding was the talk of the town. But we were escorted out only after the last bits of light had trickled from the sky. Only after the champagne was kicked. Only after we'd exhausted Archer's talent show acts from ages eight to fourteen. Only after we'd recalled the best hits of our childhood— the time when the country club dive team needed a body, and I volunteered, doing sloppy summersaults and a back dive that turned into a flop and a completely illegal jackknife. The time when Hope turned to Granny Fi's old Betty Crocker cookbook for dinner inspiration and made us all a green Jell-O mold with celery and cherries. The time when J.P.'s kin, up from Virginia, did karaoke at O'Brien's and— The time when Granny Fi played bunko with the Wharf Rats motorcycle gang— The time we sneaked Archer into Salvation for tiki drinks and—

The time, we laughed. The time, the time.

28

NET-A-NEWPORT 5H

Last polo weekend of the summer! If you're tailgating, here's what you'll need:

1. Buckets of ice and champagne, white wine, Gerolsteiner sparkling water, and Stella Artois (for the boys)
2. Various other bottles of liquor
3. Bloody Mary mix in a glass pitcher
4. Fruit salad, sweating and turning to mush in its bowl. Silver tongs.
5. Petits fours that no one will eat on tiered serving platter
6. Charcuterie board from Le Petit Gourmet off Freebody Street
7. Platter of cooked shrimp with tails on and cocktail sauce straight from the bottle
8. Pleasant smugness that one's own tailgate is the best outfitted and the liveliest
9. Fresh, piping-hot tea about the people in the neighboring chalets
10. More liquor

Saturday. Two days before Maggie's wedding. Seventeen hours since *Vanity Fair* had called us *anachronisms*. We'd gathered at the polo grounds north of town—Team USA was playing Italy, the last match of the summer. When Jack had planned the welcome party for wedding guests, we'd all agreed it would be a jolly afternoon mixing with each other and watching the ponies.

Little did we know that most of the people would be watching *us*.

As Maggie, Jack, Archer, and I walked from the car to the line of tailgate tents, which everyone here called *chalets*, the Italian national anthem began to play over the speakers, signaling the match would soon begin. Those sprawled on Pendleton and Hermès blankets on the edge of the field stood; the men took off their hats. Everyone—most I recognized from the wedding guest list—faced the long row of flags in between the cars and the canopies just as we made our appearance under the stars and stripes.

"We're walking." Jack urged us forward, toward the chalet. Maggie was in white, a loose-fitting blazer and pencil-thin maternity jeans, block heels with pearls on the toes. Jack was in blue jeans and a bow tie, holding her hand tightly, helping her across the grass.

"We're smiling," Archer added.

I had to take his word for it; I was keeping my eyes on the grass. I didn't need to see the stares we were getting. I could guess what I'd find: pity, maybe some judgment for the gross state of the carriage house, mixed together with a hefty dose of schadenfreude.

Under the canopy cover, I felt Maggie exhale. Most, but not all, observers had respectfully focused back on the flags. When the opposing team's anthem was done, the crowd only had a few moments before the American one started up and we had to do the whole stand-to-attention thing over again.

"Is Susie here yet?" I asked Jack during the twilight's last gleaming.

"I'm going to try and avoid her," said Jack. "Unless I want to say something I really regret. And I've already done that once to my father. And that...didn't turn out well."

He didn't need to say more. I knew, shortly after, that his father had died. And Jack's last words to him had been *go fuck yourself*. Warranted, perhaps, but not an ideal way to part.

"I don't see her," said Archer, up on his toes.

The final notes sounded, then there was much applause and a whistle; the ponies and their riders got in formation for the start of the match. One more beat, then we were surrounded.

Maggie and Jack got picked off by friends from the city, adorned and turned out and fawning over my sister's belly, her skin, her glow. There were handshakes for Jack and some dad jokes (*you buy your grill yet?*), and *Vanity Fair*, while it was mentioned by the loyalists, was proclaimed dead, done, subscription canceled.

Remy had taken Archer aside and was communicating something that looked newsworthy with quick, spiraling motions of his hands and lots of eye rolls.

As for me—well, the aunties got to me first. Lolly, in from Richmond, orthopedic shoes and a giant smile. When I was pulled into her ample bosom, I got hints of Icy Hot cream and baby powder. She was the oldest; J.P.'s younger sisters, who I called Gogo, Flurry, and Maxxie, respectively, were aflutter with news of their travel—*the rental car company didn't have their reservation, can you believe?*—and wanting to show me pictures of babies. They asked me for wedding details—what are we eating, and when, and where, and was I *absolutely* sure we got their RSVP card orders for *only* the fillet because halibut makes Gogo's throat swell up like her ankles on an airplane.

As I assured the aunties that no white fish would deign touch their plates, I was reminded of how little they cared about The Land, the travails of a crumbling castle, the reputations of the Coventrys in Newport. They were Gilfords, after all, and fame was my granddad Gilford, who ran a pharmacy on Main Street, letting people get their insulin and silicosis medication on long, loose lines of credit until he died suddenly at fifty-five. All of Wise County attended his funeral; some people had to sit outside in the church's parking lot.

I made a mental note to hang out more with the aunties.

Hope called our names, alternating between waving her hand and snapping it open and shut like a claw. I caught my siblings' eyes. There were nods of agreement, and we excused ourselves from our groups. Jack fell prey to the aunties, and he gestured for the three of us to just go ahead.

Again we moved as a pack toward the field, sticking together greatly preferable to going at it alone.

"Susie isn't coming," Archer reported as the ponies thundered from one end of the field to the other. "Remy told me that she has a cough and a fever. Kent was supposed to be here, but he said he'd hang back with her in case she got worse. She got kind of flustered and really pressured him to just go. Then Kent was like, *Well, if you're really sick, don't you want me to stay with you?*"

"Nice timing," said Maggie, skeptical.

"Probably throwing our stuff out on the allée as we speak," I said. I caught sight of our mother nestled within a group of platinum women, including one I recognized as Minnie Flood of Dovecote. I just hoped they weren't engaging her in conversation as some kind of perverse exercise in gossip-extortion.

"Nah." Archer acknowledged someone over my shoulder. "Susie's giving us cowardly lion."

"Someone submit *that* to Net-a-Newport," I said.

·····

I threaded through the blankets on the edge of the field, taking in the groups smiling with their drinks, men in panama hats, well-dressed children running around with kites.

Wedding aside, I only had a few days left in Newport, and we needed to discuss the future of the carriage house sooner rather than later. Hope would not appreciate me trying to extract her for a one-on-one, but I couldn't leave without knowing the plan. Without knowing what else I should be doing to clean up my mistakes.

I went to go find my father, who was downfield with Uncle Dunk, in line for an ice cream truck that advertised itself as *small batch*. Larry the bird was bopping his head to the music coming from inside the truck and, as I got closer, I saw that he was adorned in the world's tiniest sleeveless tuxedo, complete with red bow tie.

"Nuts, nuts, nuts," Larry said as I arrived.

"Is he talking about me?"

"He's fixin' to get some ice cream toppings." Dunk gave the macaw's beak a tickle.

My uncle's feather earring today was red, and I wondered if he'd intentionally coordinated with Larry.

I'd found J.P. to ask an important question; I thought I better get to it. "Have you and Mom made up your mind about the carriage house? About what to do?"

"Whatever your mom wants."

"Dad," I said. Like, *come on*.

"I'm serious. It was my decision to sell to Susie all those years ago. I had no choice. Our electricity was almost turned off, and still your mother thought we should stay, that somehow God would deliver us a miracle and we'd win the lottery. Cassie, the sound of a coin rubbing a scratch-off still sends a chill up my spine. Yes, it was the right thing to do, though she was so devastated. I cared for her Coventry collection because I knew she would want it preserved. That's all she had left, you understand? Now that's gone. Again, it was the right thing to do. But it's her decision where we go next."

We'd reached the window to the truck. Dunk announced he was treating, and took our orders, but J.P. said, *Actually, none for me.*

In front of the chalet, those who weren't already standing leaped from their chairs and applauded—a goal. My father barely noticed. "Hey?" I asked softly, pulling my father out of line. His energy was flat, troubled. "You okay?"

"Oh," he said, like I shouldn't even bother, "I'm just fine."

"Are you angry with me? For not telling you sooner?"

"With you, Chicken?" My uncle walked over, handed me my ice cream. "No. I understand why you did what you did."

"You ought to tell the girl the truth," said Uncle Dunk, sharing his chocolate with Larry.

"You *are* angry." I frowned down into my scoops.

"With myself," my father clarified. "I've gone back and forth, but Dunk is right. You've come clean, Cassie, and I should, too." He took a steadying breath. "I should've said something when you found that time capsule in the kitchen. I didn't even know you'd given it to Sotheby's until I was back from fishing. And by then it was too late. Ah, and then Susie got so mad about it, thinking it was hers. I worry that's why she went to the magazine."

My father seemed to be suggesting a connection between him and the time capsule, but I was struggling to make it.

"Before she died, your Granny Fi told me it was buried,

same as you. But she added one more thing. She told me what was in it." He motioned to Uncle Dunk, who swung his tasseled leather backpack to the ground. Out came a stack of papers, some folded, others loose, some still in their envelopes. "Before Dunk and I left to go fishing, I went to the storage unit, broke the lock, and removed these. I was going replace the capsule with items from Earnest's collection, but then the people from Sotheby's showed up, and it would not look great if a retired detective was caught stealing, so I just got out of there."

My untouched strawberry was already melting, overfilling the wax cup, dripping onto my hand. I made no move to wipe it away. Net-a-Newport, that omniscient bastard, knew it had been stolen. Let's hope they *didn't* know the culprit. "Dad," I said, "we had a big dramatic opening. Most of Newport was at that party. Everyone from Net-a-Newport to *Town & Country* covered the event!"

"Tell them why you did it," Uncle Dunk was urging my father. "That part's important."

"Granny Fi wouldn't have wanted her letters in the hands of strangers."

Who would? Still: "I didn't want my sculpture in the hands of strangers, either," I said, short, "but I sold it."

"I know. I'm so sorry, Chicken."

I thought back to earlier in the summer, when Hope reminded us all of the Coventry curse, what Granny Fi called *malediction*. And what had I known, even then? This was not a hex set upon us by forces or fates out of our control. We made our own lives hard enough. We didn't need to blame the gods for anything. Nor did we need to blame each other.

"Don't apologize," I said. "It's done." My father extended the stack of letters toward me. I took them, turned them over in my hands. "Did you read them? What is she admitting to that she put these underground? A tawdry affair? Crimes of passion? Do I even want to know?"

"There's a reason she told you and me about these, and not your mother," he said. "Best read for yourself. It might… change your perception of both those women a tad."

I wanted to go back to Jack's car and be alone with my grandmother's words and secrets, but over J.P.'s shoulder, I saw Spencer striding toward us. Jerkily, I raised my arm, a call, a plea *to come over here. Look what else we've unearthed. Help me make sense of it.*

Spencer turned his face in my direction. About ten feet away, he waved, but there was something about it—a hesitation. It wasn't high or animated, if that makes sense. Then he changed course, heading off toward the cars. To leave. A cut, as they would have said in the time of my great-grandparents. A deliberate cut. It was eighty degrees outside, but my skin prickled.

"Excuse me a second," I said, shoving the letters in my purse before starting off in pursuit of Spencer. I skirted the line to the food truck, dumping my ice cream in a trash bin, my steps quick and purposeful. "Hey!" I called to his back, figuring this must be some mistake, trying to give him the benefit of the doubt. He was still about a car's length away from me. He paused, allowed me to catch up to him beside a wood-paneled station wagon.

He removed his sunglasses, hung them in the neck of his T-shirt, faded with the name of a band I didn't recognize. His eyes met mine, but I couldn't read them. He took a deep breath. "Hi," was all he said.

Because he still didn't reach for me, I crossed my arms. "What are you doing?"

"I swung through for Maggie and Jack. Now I'm going in to work."

I retreated a half step, observed his drawn, wary expression. "Without saying a real hello to me?"

"I'm just—" He cleared his throat. "I'm trying to balance myself here. Keep a respectable distance. When I read the article—"

"The article?" I could feel my face move all different places at once, working through being confused, annoyed, distraught, all of it.

"I get that Reagan wasn't flattering to you all, but she also reminded me in a painful way that you're gone in a few days."

"We always knew I'd be leaving," I said, noting his use of the word *painful*, but still caught up in my own emotions to do anything much about it. "But there's a thing called Face-Time, there are things called planes. And there's a conversation I'd *hoped* we'd have, soon, about us, about if there could be a way—"

"How can there be a way," he asked, "if you can only take this place, which, by the way, includes *me*, my business, my life, in *small doses*?" Spencer jammed his hands in the pockets of his dark jeans. From the field, the sounds of cracks and hooves, and the crowd's yells, rising and falling in the breeze.

"First of all, I have some feelings about the way Reagan sourced that quote from me, which I'll save to say directly to her face, if she dares to show it. Secondly—"

"You've made it perfectly clear that you want to be casual, and I know you don't like Newport, but I kept thinking, maybe she'll change her mind about both!"

I felt my back against a wall, though there was nothing around me but cars and air that smelled of turf and horse and *him*. "What do you want me to do, Spencer? Quit my job, stay here, and watch *Masterpiece Theatre* with you?"

"I've never asked you to quit your job."

"You're so devoted to your job, sometimes you don't get

home till, like, one a.m., but somehow it's not okay for me to love mine?"

"You're not hearing me—"

"What I do is *everything*—"

"Yeah, but sometimes you use it as an excuse for avoiding—"

"Avoiding *what*?" We were talking over each other. We were fighting. My teeth were gritted, my heart thrumming in my throat. Still, I knew this could tip either way. If just one of us stood down, breaths could be collected, blood pressure reduced. But it wasn't going to be me who tipped. "Avoiding how you dumped me once, saying you didn't want to commit, then went off to your senior year at Princeton and almost immediately found yourself a *wife*?"

"Cass," he said, partly beseeching, partly exasperated, "you don't feel that—"

"This has been an interlude," I interrupted, because if he was about to break up, ghost me, whatever you wanted to call it, I wasn't going to hear it *again*.

That did it. There was a long, excruciating pause. "Then I hope you enjoyed yourself," he said.

He spun away, and the next thing I knew, a family with a fussing toddler in a stroller and a crying child with wet pants was standing behind me with a cooler and expressions that were friendly but strained. They were asking me if I could just move aside because this was their car. And I said, *of course, of course*, and what I really meant was *why did I have to say that, where did he go, did you see that man who was just here, did you see what direction he went because this is a parking area with very tall cars and I can't see and, oh, God, I think I lost him.*

29

Town & Country

Why Are the Coventrys Being Forced Out of The Land?
By Michelle Killinger—Posted Sep 2—8 am

Hope Coventry-Gilford will no longer reside in the carriage house of the Gilded Age mansion built by her great-grandfather Conrad Coventry, Jr., a splashy summer scandal that has been picked up everywhere from *Vanity Fair* to the local dishy gossip account Net-a-Newport.

However, longtime residents of the rarified city by the sea have cried foul, as the looming eviction pits new money against old...

At the rehearsal, Maggie and Jack started at the end. Meaning, they began at the *you may kiss the bride part*, the presentation of the newlyweds, the moments before the recessional.

The platform they would stand on, as well as the frame for the immense flower arch, was still being constructed, so there was general hammering and clanking from the workbenches set up over by the greenhouse, and the great lawn of The Land smelled vaguely of sawdust. But the couple gamely took their spots near where the stage would be, hands clasped, facing the good Reverend Swann, while the rest of us who had a role in this production milled around in the grass, offering our faces to the temperate September sun, and mulling over lovers and plane tickets and whether this would be one of the last times she stood in the shade of the house she once could navigate in the pitch-black Rhode Island midnight.

Right, so, all of us weren't doing that. Just me.

"Okay!" Ashley, professional but still jumpy from, no doubt, the catastrophe two days ago, was jogging back and forth from the reverend to River, the Holder of the Seating Chart, to Hope at the end of the aisle, consulting about details, asking questions. "Okay! Here we go!"

We were not going.

There were many people to wrangle. Maggie had been true to her original idea; there were no bridesmaids or groomsmen. *Everyone has already been in at least six wedding parties*, Maggie explained to Hope after her fifteenth objection. *Most of them are married. The "maid" jig is up.* Though my sister might've spared her closest friends from the dress and the bachelorette party and an endless stream of emails that began with "Hey, ladies!!!" she didn't relieve them of all duties entirely. The Episcopalian ceremony required readings. Judging by how many of Maggie and Jack's friends had joined us for the rehearsal, our ears would be treated not only to First Corinthians and a nondenominational poem (me), but to a Psalm, a gently hilarious reflection (Archer), another poem (Neruda, it seemed from the glimpse I got from the printout), and perhaps even a selection of prose, judging from the Broadway actor who'd spent most of the time before the rehearsal reciting in his booming baritone a passage from *Captain Corelli's Mandolin*. Spencer would be holding the rings, but an announcement was made that he was at The Bonnie and couldn't make the rehearsal.

I wandered over to Archer, who'd been tasked with the Assembly of the Programs. He was on one of the temporary folding chairs we'd all helped haul up from Susie's basement party-closet with a basket of gold ribbon in his lap.

"It's going to rain tonight," I said, taking the pile of programs off the chair next to him and sitting. I turned my eyes toward the sea, white-tipped, agitated with the wind, forewarned by the gray clouds in the far distance.

"Let's manifest a light mist," Archer said. He placed together two pieces of textured cardstock, aligned the holes, and threaded the end of a piece of ribbon through. Down the lawn, Ashley, River, and Maggie were telling one of the readers that she needed to switch seats, that she should be on the aisle. Then they reneged and switched her back.

"One stray drop and Hope will be out on this lawn with a hair dryer," I said.

Archer nudged me with his shoulder. "Where'd you go last night, *hmm*? We missed you at Pelham. You know Hope lives for a dueling piano experience."

"I was tired." It was true. Through the text chain, I'd read that the family had eventually migrated from polo to downtown, but I'd called myself a ride straight from the grounds, leaving before the end of the match, before the stomping of the divots, even. The driver dropped me at the forty steps, where a stone staircase descended nearly to the sea and deposited those brave and balanced enough on flat gray rocks, wet with surf and spray, shaped and creased by time. I stayed there with my grandmother's letters on the edge of the wall, until it was dark, until no further tourists clambered eagerly down. I did not read them; a force petrified my hands when I went to open the first. Then I went back to the quiet cottage and padded, barefoot, through the rooms before putting myself to bed.

"I kept thinking you were going to stroll in with Spencer." Archer stopped, as there was a bit of commotion, some barking. The attention of the group shifted to the veranda, where Susie appeared, striding forward quickly, blowing apologies for her tardiness this way and that, like kisses to an audience. She seemed to have made a miraculous recovery from her *dire* cold. One of her dogs clambered down the veranda steps and, clearly fatigued from the effort, dissolved in a patch of sun on the grass. The other Kent carried, as the pooch was hampered by a cone of shame and a blue bandage around his flank.

"What's going on there?" I asked Archer.

"Remy said Monsieur has allergies. Scratched himself a hot spot. But apparently Susie is convinced it's kidney disease or something."

Kent placed Monsieur on the grass next to Charlie, and although Susie and those who'd gathered around her were tut-tutting and looking pitifully at him, Monsieur seemed at ease, sniffing people's ankles and occasionally lifting his leg on one of the stone lions that guarded the Cottage.

Meanwhile, Susie, hands on hips, summoned Ashley and the reverend. From the looks of it, she was not pleased with the positioning of the bride and groom.

"I mean with Susie. What's she going to do today and tomorrow? Pretend like everything is fine?" The same questions could be asked of me. And I wouldn't have the answers.

"That's what I'm going to do," said Archer, tying a bow on the outside of a program.

As Monsieur trotted around, ruffling the grass around his

owner's feet, the bottom of his cone suddenly caught on the ground and flipped him over like a flapjack. There was great consternation. Kent scooped the animal up, dusted off its snout, adjusted the cone, and set him back down, unharmed.

"Kent must be so thrilled to get out of here," I said. "I wonder what he's going to do first in retirement. If he's already planned that Galápagos cruise he and Ema always wanted."

"He's not retiring. He's going to work for the Google guy who bought the old Henry place." Archer handed his programs to me so he could pick up Monsieur, who'd come to inspect us, and cradled him like a baby. Both dog and human seemed content with this arrangement. "I guess he got a really terrific offer and Susie didn't want to match it, so he's leaving."

Susie, Ashley, and the reverend landed on some kind of agreement, then Ashley escorted Susie down the aisle and positioned her across from Hope and J.P. My father dipped his chin in greeting; my mother stared straight ahead.

"Cass? Archer?" Ashley called, waving her clipboard, wrenching my attention away from my brother's profile. "You two will be right here." She poked at two chairs on the inside of our parents. "Okay? You got it?"

"Cass is confused!" Archer called back, cupping his hand beside his mouth. "What is this for?"

I elbowed him. "We got it!"

As Ashley went to collect another person for placement, Maggie pinched her hand on her side. It was hard to believe she was approaching her third trimester, that we would meet a brand-new human before the year was out.

I watched as Susie rose, crossed to the couple. I watched as Maggie reached for Jack's hand. I watched my sister's face cloud.

I stood, but Archer pulled the edge of my untucked shirt. "Leave it," he said, as though he were talking to Monsieur.

"There's a reason why Hope hasn't done the whole confrontation thing, and you have to respect that."

Maggie was nodding. Her face wasn't friendly, but it had arranged itself into something civil. Jack had laid a hand on his mother's shoulder.

The reverend took his mark again and Susie returned to her seat, as I fell back into mine. Ashley and the reverend began to walk through the ceremony. The girl—one of Jack's close friends from work—who was doing the Bible passage practiced first. *Love is patient, love is kind.* She read the words like it was an Excel spreadsheet. The reverend looked kind but gravely disappointed.

I turned to my brother. "What else do you want me to do, Archer? I'm leaving on Tuesday, and I *cannot* blow this assignment off. Hope needs to make up her mind. If we're going to fight to keep the carriage house, let's just get it out in the open and settle it."

"You're right." He lifted Monsieur and used one of his paws to bat my shoulder. "Go ahead and get up there. Start a melee. Do what you did at the Monday Night Massacre and call Susie a weapons-grade elitist, I believe it was."

"If the shoe fits," I muttered under my breath.

"Did you and Spencer have a fight?" Archer asked abruptly. My head snapped to my brother. "What? Why?"

"Because I'm just wondering why you are looking for an excuse to make a mess." Archer tapped the dog on its damp nose. "I have a feeling you want to create chaos just so you can say, *ugh, yuck, gotta go.*"

"I do have to go, though." I picked up a ribbon and slid the top through one of the program's punched holes. "And things are *yuck*. Even if we lawyered up, Susie would still win, everyone knows that. The carriage house is lost." I thought of The Land with part yearning and part pain, the kind of homesickness that I don't think has a word. "And I didn't tell you guys about it, and you had to learn it through a snarky magazine article. I spent the summer behaving *exactly* like all our dead Coventrys—deniers, secret-keepers, worried about what everyone will think of us. And Spencer and I didn't work out, so that's done."

"I find that hard to believe." Archer tickled under Monsieur's chin.

"What part? That the carriage house is gone?"

"Not that. I meant that you and Spencer are over."

Scripture complete, it was time for the poem. Neruda, just like I'd suspected. "He's here," I said. "He's opening a new restaurant, in addition to running The Bonnie. What's he going to do, come and visit me in New York those random days I'm there?"

Archer winced. "Cass. Just be honest with yourself. You're making a conscious decision to give us all up." He shifted Monsieur so he could extract a piece of paper—his reflection—from his back pocket. We'd been staring at the programs all this time, we both knew he was next in the queue. "Look, we know you have a dangerous job," he continued, reminding me how long it had been since I'd given my head wound a moment of consideration. Just over three months; did the time heal me, or cause me to forget? Was there a difference between the two? "But it gives you permission to be distant. Reagan was wrong when she called us witless, dreaming relics or whatever. Because this place *isn't* just a pile of dirt and stones, and the Coventry era is not over, it's just different. Maggie is going to have a baby next year, Cass! I know you love your work. I just wish you'd open your damn eyes and see meaning here, with us, too."

When I was working, during the downtimes, in some dingy lobby of a one-star hotel with no sign and one-half a bar of soap in the sputtering shower, when I sat around and twiddled my thumbs with the other photographers and journalists and off-kilter documentarian misfits until action called us out of our stupor, I would occasionally get asked if I had any siblings. *Two*, I'd say, and that would be the end of that.

Both my brother and sister had emailed me, texted me, sent me invitations, when I was away. And I hadn't even given them names, just numbers.

As though it wasn't enough to be physically separate from them, I'd emotionally detached, as well. I'd like to say this was totally a subconscious act, a form of self-preservation against what I witnessed through my lens. It might be, but only to an extent. Because here was the tough part—this maneuver was deliberate, too.

Abroad, away from my hometown, I'd thought I'd be better. Evolved. Less of a mess. Chasing shots, living independently, focused only on the work. So I'd excised Newport from my life, but the cut hadn't been clean, the margins hadn't been clear; Maggie, Archer, my parents, even, had been collateral.

Spencer had asked me to make Newport my home. The truth: I wasn't scared of this place. I was scared of who I *was* here.

Or, maybe, who I'd been.

"Archer!" River called. "You're up!"

"Now that I've wrapped on precocious, wise little brother," Archer said, "I will now play the part of devilishly charming young man, with an ad-libbed joke that delights the crowd thrown in for good measure." Archer requested that I high-five Monsieur. I obliged, still in awe. The dog lolled his tongue. "I love you," Archer said, and it was unclear who he was addressing—me or the fluff he was placing back on the grass.

"Have you figured it out?" I called before he could get too far away. "What you're doing after the wedding?"

His mouth drifted into a smile. "I love The Land a lot. Leaving would make me sad. But I think staying, being stuck in the past, would make me sadder." At the front, Archer got into position, unfolded his paper. "I was going to read a little something that sums up our collective joy at the wedding of these two—" his head cut to Maggie and Jack "—but this doesn't seem like the time or the place."

Cue laughter.

As he recited, my eyes were on the Cottage. The late-afternoon sun glinted off the windows, turning the glass into perfect mirrors for the emerald grass and the moody sea.

I bobbed through memories, recollections of grief and regret, and tried to envision my future. But everything was cloudy, murky and dense; I was having trouble making out form or figure. Archer sounded like he was ready for a life beyond The Land. I still didn't know what Hope wanted. I was even further away from focusing on what I did. If I were in the field, I'd grab my camera and change locations, try to find a different vantage point. *Keep it moving.*

But I couldn't—not this time. Distance was the easy way out. To see what is in front of your nose—and I'm paraphrasing Orwell here—is the true struggle.

Archer's phone, which he'd left on his chair, dinged with an alert from Instagram: so and so and eleven others liked your photo.

This I found strange. Archer was only active on TikTok.

I opened my Instagram app. I was right—he hadn't posted anything there since 2020.

Curious, I thought, eyes narrowing. Because I saw on my feed there *was* an account that had recently posted a picture of last night's sunset from the dock at Harbour Court.

Guess who.

30

Newport Daily News

Letters to the Editor
Re: Coventrys' Last Days at The Land

I admit, I found the news of the Coventrys' eviction from their fifth-generation Newport home distressing. I believe that they will land on their feet, but the whole situation depressingly illuminates that we are well into a second "Gilded Age," where the Bellevue mansions are only available to the obscenely wealthy, and access to beautiful art and architecture of our city costs close to $30 a ticket...

For the rehearsal dinner at The Bonnie, I wore new, untested sandals with thin straps that cut into my ankles. But my worries lay elsewhere.

Besides our party, who'd taken over two long tables in the back of the restaurant, The Bonnie had been packed, and Spencer, when I glimpsed him in the open kitchen, appeared swamped, tense, and sweaty. I'd come to dinner positive that I should talk to him, to sort us out. But now that I saw his rhythm, I wondered if I should interrupt it at all.

I picked a seat between the Virginia aunts at the family table to distract myself, sipped wine, ate every morsel of my Bajan lobster tails with a side of truffle fries (hey—Susie was paying), and tried to keep up with the lively conversation happening around me.

During dessert—coconut cake that was cotton-candy soft—Jack and Maggie stood at their spots in the center of the family table. Jack spoke first, giving an eloquent toast to his bride, to her resilience and reservoirs of empathy and patience. He had kind if succinct words for his mother, too, who was seated at the head opposite Hope, twenty people between them. Though everyone knew what Susie had done to Hope and J.P., Jack focused his script on the deeper past, recalling how she'd rebuilt their lives in the aftermath of his dad's death.

Maggie also gave a speech. She was not a public speaker, she confessed as she pulled out a few pages from her bag with shaking hands. She apologized in advance if she botched it.

"In May," she began, "I learned I was pregnant." She paused so everyone could say stuff like *yay!* But the energy shifted with her next line, and everyone got pretty quiet. "But I couldn't celebrate the way the world wanted me to. I was trying to renew my contract with the ballet. My greatest fear was that I wouldn't be paid or, worse, that I would be fired if pregnancy or childbirth complications prevented me from coming back to the stage as scheduled. Even if I did make it back, the company, in standard contracts, could let me go for any reason. What if my baby got sick on a performance day?

The way the ballet business is organized, it's like I could be a mother *or* a dancer, not both." Jack rubbed her back with the palm of his hand, while she took a beat to turn over the sheet of paper. This was not the standard wedding weekend entertainment, but we were glued, anyway. Susie rested her elbows on either side of her cake plate. Archer, next to Hope, was recording with his phone. Next to me, Auntie Lolly twisted her cloth napkin in her hands.

"In July, a reporter stumbled upon the news that I might be expecting. I was *so* terrified. I didn't want to make trouble during my contract negotiations. My sister—" Maggie glanced up, found me in the middle of the table, shot me a grin "—told the reporter that *she* was pregnant. But instead of feeling free, I felt lower than ever. I felt sad and alone and disappointed in myself." When it occurred to me that she was talking about the time after Archer and I had moved into the Cottage, when she was either in bed or on the floor, the air constricted in my lungs. "I kept asking: How did I get to this point? How did I come to resent myself and my body for bringing life into this world? Through long conversations with Jack, my therapist, and my family, I came to a decision. If I go back to the stage, it will be with the *whole* me, and that includes the part of me who will become a mother, who will need rest and healing, and who will keep talking—though my employer may not like it—about how every single person deserves fair pay and family leave."

"That's right," said Archer, snapping his fingers with the hand that wasn't holding his phone.

Nods of agreement and murmurs of *Hear! Hear!* floated up from the table toward Maggie.

Maggie continued. "I want to toast my family—all of them—" her eyes volleyed briefly between Hope and Susie "—for giving Jack and me the wedding in the place we love the most. But no matter where we are, Jack, you're my home. I love you and can't want to marry you tomorrow."

Maggie lowered her papers and Jack gathered her into his arms. Hope had jumped to her feet, exclaiming, *Oh, my sweet girl*, and Susie was clapping and J.P. was also predictably weeping and the whole back of the restaurant became one giant party again as people threw their napkins onto their plates, stood and raised their glasses, and the air became carbonated with joy and delight.

I waited my turn to hug Maggie and Jack. When I finally got to my brave sister, I knew what I had to do.

I gathered my courage, my whole self, and my bag, and slipped off toward Spencer.

·····

At the bar, I hitched myself on a stool, waited for Spencer to finish brushing off garlic skins and pepper seeds from his work surface with a towel. My pulse flickered with a mixture of dread and hope.

He looked up, noticed me right in front of him, and smiled.

"Hi," I whispered.

He slung his towel over his shoulder. "Hi." He took a drink of lemon water from a clear plastic pint container, and leaned forward onto the bar. "How was dinner? Everything okay?"

"I'm so sorry," I said, affecting seriousness, "I think I ate all The Bonnie's aioli."

He flattered me with a wide laugh. "I was wondering where it went."

My eyes traced his face, marking the shape of his eyebrows, the way one corner of his mouth snuck up higher than the other. Instinctively, I reached for my camera, which was at the Cottage. But I had something else.

I pulled out my laptop, then the USB port with my Nikon's

memory card. "Archer gave me an idea this afternoon, so I basically went through all I've done this summer on film, digital, everything. Most of it is absolute trash. But eventually the law of averages works out and I get something good—well, let me shut up and just show you." I swooped the cursor over to the folder I'd made after the wedding rehearsal, enlarged the icon I wanted, then faced the screen toward him.

Displayed was the shot of Spencer from Maggie's engagement party in May. I'd caught him looking straight at me, though his chin was slightly turned. The way his hand extended—at the time I'd read it as simply the beginnings of a *hey, you!* pointing gesture. But the way the picture had developed, the curl of his fingers looked beckoning, amorous. His lips were parted, like he was about to make a demand that a woman would be hard-pressed to ignore. The light radiated behind him in a kind of glowing curtain; the people around him were in shadow, only barely visible, suggestion rather than form. His presence spoke to me of the complexities of new layered over old. His stride, paused, communicated the sweet ache of time passing. He filled the frame, in clear, dramatic focus; there was no room for anyone else.

Spencer studied the photo, then scratched the back of his neck. "You made me look all right," he said.

"This—" I tapped at the screen "—is the way I see you. Here's proof. And if I've ever made you doubt that, I'm *so* sorry. I don't know what our future holds, but I don't want to leave here without speaking. To see if—well, first, to see if you'll forgive me."

My apology washed over him. Then he wet his lips and began to speak quietly. "Starting out, I knew that you were just passing through. But then we got together." He emerged from behind the bar to take a seat on the stool next to mine. I held back from reaching out, grabbing his hands. "Cass," he continued, "you mean a lot to me. I wouldn't have had sex with you otherwise. I'm not taking women to bed just *because*. I actually didn't mind you being fake pregnant. It meant we could take things slowly. You're the first woman since Madison who I've felt— Wow, this is something. I'm still working my feelings through, but I can tell you, they are profound and scary and it really hurt when you said we were just an interlude."

"I was flippant and rude at polo," I said, sending my eyes from his face to the buttons on his chef's coat. "It was not okay."

"Oh, man." Spencer exhaled. "I was also not holding it together. The article had me—" He spun his finger around in the space between us, then brought it to rest on his lap, then he scooted his stool an inch closer. As always, he smelled like sweet cream and the first bite of dessert and just enough nostalgia that longing thumped from inside my heart. "I can only imagine how you all felt. Jack texted that you knew about the eviction for a while."

"Since the engagement party."

"Wow." He drew circles on the bar with his container of water. "You've been dealing with this all summer."

"Alone, which was the wrong decision." I looked down at my hands. "I could've come to you, for one. I know I was all about the casualness, but that was only my way of protecting myself from being hurt again."

On his face, a smile came and went. "At polo, you brought up that night on Susie's porch, the one when I brought Madison back to Newport for the first time. I was actually nervous about seeing *you*."

"What?" I exclaimed with no composure whatsoever.

"It's true! I wanted you to like each other. Which was silly, as you'd told me, basically, you never wanted to talk to me again a year prior."

"I didn't!"

"You did."

"Okay, I might've," I admitted, remembering I'd ended our breakup at the Lily Pond with something along those lines. "But when I'd asked about long distance, you'd shut me down—"

"You'd surprised the hell out of me, by the way! That whole summer, you'd been sharing dreams about post-college travel, about foreign photo agencies, professors who could make you introductions abroad. I wanted to cook, but my dad wanted me anywhere but a kitchen, and I had loans to pay off. I was focused on that more than a relationship."

"But then you went off and got engaged." You'd think after all these years of experiences, of lovers and less between them, all the quotidian experiences piling on top of each other, that would've compressed whatever breath this one event had in it, deflating it like a balloon. But no, it endured, and I needed him to explain it, as unfair as that was.

"I think you'd woken something in me, Cass," he said like he understood what I was after. "Even though we weren't ready for each other, I started to think I was ready for something real. I mean, Madison wasn't a fill-in; I married her because I loved her and thought we'd be together for the rest of our lives. But—here I am, back next to you." He rubbed his palms on his jeans.

He'd said we were something. I hoped I was brave enough to start treating it that way. "And how does it feel?" I asked with trepidation. "Being next to me?"

"First, I have to ask a question of my own," he said. "Would you consider Newport?"

"You want me to live here?"

"Between assignments. And I don't mean living up there on the dark part of Bellevue with my aunt in that drafty house! You know I'm right. Too much marble. It's always freezing. I know you'll go, you'll wander, you'll take photos that make people look. You'll leave, but I want you to come back. When you say 'I'm coming home,' I want you to mean you're coming *here*, to me."

"You know why this isn't as straightforward as I want it to be," I said. "The Coventrys have history here and, just like mine, many aspects of it are *very problematic*."

"Your ancestors don't need defending, especially from me," Spencer said. "But how you behaved years ago—even that 'worst' night of your life—that one event is *not* the real fuckup you think it is. You think Susie's friends haven't been called worse than 'cardboard cutouts with four-hundred-dollar haircuts'? Probably by their own children! And definitely by staff behind their backs! You think you're the first lady in Newport to twirl into some champagne glasses? Newport is special, Cass. People love it here. People are protective of it. Hell, I'm protective of it, and I grew up in Brooklyn." He cast a glance at his restaurant, the last tables lingering over coffee, the servers catching their breaths by the point-of-sale system, and Maggie and Jack's guests, glasses and plates emptied, deciding where to take the party next. "You get what I'm saying? It would've been one thing if you had a bad night, we all do. But then you got on a plane. Left. Bye! And people took that as your final *fuck you* to the town, to your roots, to your family, to everything."

I clasped my hands together under my chin. What to say when your own history has been summarily, expertly, rewritten? "Well, shit."

But just as the shock was wearing off, just as I got feeling back in my extremities, just as I was beginning to understand the magnitude of this, of him, just as I was reaching to touch him, he drew away. "So, if you're going to disappear again," he said, "I'll get why. But I hope you'll understand when I try to protect myself, too."

·····

As I passed the service station, there was Susie, reading glasses perched on her nose, holding the weathered brown leather bill presenter, having a quiet word with The Bonnie's manager. "I'm sorry," she was saying. "We can't accept personal checks, even from you, Mrs. Utterback. Just cash or credit. Do you have another card I could try?"

Susie and I made eye contact. I flinched, feeling like I was intruding, although I was just walking by, and she wasn't hiding. I couldn't tell who looked away first.

"Try this one," I heard her say as I lugged myself and my belongings back to the party.

31

"You're distracted," Hope observed.

We were in Maggie and Jack's room in the Cottage. We were already behind. Ashley was sweating, trying to locate double-stick tape. Maggie was in the bathroom with her best friend, sorting out a Spanx malfunction. I hadn't eaten since the night before and was vibrating with two large iced coffees and adrenaline. But Hope, in a robe with her hair and makeup done, was right.

"What's wrong?" she asked.

What would I have done a few months ago? Probably lied. Told her it was nothing. But I was humbled enough by Spencer's and Archer's insights about me to ask for help. "I don't know what to do," I confessed. "I don't know how to go forward. *Where* to go forward."

Hope nodded, went to her purse. In keeping with the natural progression of things, today it was the size of a baby stroller. She withdrew the stack of letters I recognized as my grandmother's. "These were in your guest bedroom here," said Hope, and her roundabout confession of snooping made me chuckle. "It's time you read them."

My sister peeked out the crack of the bathroom door. "Does anyone have scissors?"

"Now?" I asked my mother as Maggie's friends jumped into action.

"Now," said Hope, and she sent me out into the hall.

I ran my fingers down the wainscotting, tracing its grooves, until I arrived at my childhood bedroom. The door was closed, but with only a moment of hesitation, I slipped in and pressed the button for the light.

Everything was, for the most part, in the same place—the bed across from the marble-manteled fireplace, the vanity table beside it—though Susie had switched the carpet and the linens and the drapes, swapping the '70s florals I'd inherited for neutral colors: bone and chocolate and diluted gray.

I'd been avoiding this room, half expecting to come face-to-face with the old version of me, the one filled with shame and grievance, the one who dwelled with resentment on all she did not have, rather than what she did. But I was mistaken. The room was empty of other souls. Peaceful, even. Some of the furniture that had been mine was still there—the grand four-poster bed, walnut, I think, the spindly chairs, the matching vanity with the three-panel dressing mirror, which I'd mostly shunned as a child, preoccupied with too many other adventures to be worried about my hair.

Instead of being overwhelmed by loss, I nudged my mind

to remember the happy times I'd had here, in the room where I'd dreamed of art and books and made collages with cut-up pieces of Granny Fi's magazines, where I'd had the people I'd loved mere footsteps away.

I'd left them, because I thought the Coventrys were done, ruined. Because I thought *I* was.

My feet were already aching, though I'd been in my wedding shoes less than an hour, so I took a seat in the cozy club chair by the window, cashmere Hermès blanket draped over the arm. Then I opened up the letters, mostly typewriter copies.

Inside, no confessions of affairs, or crimes, or airing of secret feuds. Instead of anything that would destroy her reputation, I found letters between unlikely friends; my grandmother, who I'd assumed would be proud of me for cursing off and casting out Newport, was writing to its most famous doyennes.

November 3, 1953, to Jacqueline Kennedy:
I missed your wedding, my friend, and am so sorry for it. I must confess I was not ill, except in the heart. No matter how earnestly I endeavor, I will never feel at ease among such people. I regret not trying to muddle through, in this case...

To Flora Payne Whitney in 1961:
My deepest gratitude for your generous invitation to Cairo again this winter! Malcolm and I will join you there posthaste. A nanny is coming in from Bristol to watch Hope for the four months while we are gone. Or, should I say, a zookeeper will be arriving to feed and bathe this pink, sticky, whining creature who saps me of time, time, time...

May 1978, to Oatsie Charles:
I did not let Hope deb, and she hates me for it. My greatest fear was that she will succumb to the Coventry curse and suffer the same fate as her father and so many before her, sucked into an early grave because of idleness and hubris. *I cannot let my husband's death become meaningless.* Hope might never forgive me, but I will not budge...

December 1980, to Hope herself:
You will not come home for Christmas. You have better things to do—skiing with friends, is it? Fine. Enjoy. But when I am dead, you will be sorry, and all you'll have to comfort you is this house and the things in it...

And one of the last, dated 2004, even in the age of email, still handwritten, though to an unknown person, addressed only as "Dearest":

...and by this is the only place I fit, and I don't mean The Land, I mean the firmament around it, this island, my muse, its salt water and honeysuckle air. The older I get, the more content I am to spend the rest of my days here. Funny, when I was younger, all I wanted to do was get away, and how my relationship with my daughter suffered for it...

Cass will not leave me alone for a minute, so I've put her to work as my studio assistant. Luckily, she has capabilities and early markers of a rather good artist, if she wants to be one. I'm trying to shoo her out of the studio with a sketch pad and a pencil as often as possible, telling her to draw something, for Lord's sake, and to discover as much of Newport as her busy eyes and fingers allow, its people included. Just as this place gave to me, I hope it will do the same to her, though I wish for Cassie more innate patience and kindness than I have in my genes. It will make her life easier than I made mine, because the number of regrets I have are as uncountable as stars...

I heard soft shuffling in the hall, then Susie appeared in the doorway. I wasn't surprised to see her. I'm not sure why. I didn't stand or move to leave or anything. But I did put the letters down and say: "You found me."

She entered the room, a bit tentative, though it was hers. "Hope said you were probably here." She was holding a rectangular parcel—a toaster? An air fryer? A Tiffany's vase?—wrapped in white paper with illustrations of topiaries.

"This was my old room," I explained. "I'm not sure if you ever knew that."

"I did." She placed the box carefully down on the end of the bed and crossed to the fireplace, her silver dress swishing around her ankles. "Maggie, years ago, gave me a tour that lasted about two hours. She showed me the house as it was. She taught me a great deal." She ran her palm across the top of the mantel. If she picked up dust, I didn't see it. Still, she rubbed her fingertips together. "That is to say, I'm not unaware of the attachment your family has to The Land. So after *Vanity Fair*, I was sort of waiting for a confrontation."

"You thought Hope would tie herself to a tree again?"

Susie gave a snort of laughter. "Something like that, yes. But you've all been restrained."

I smiled weakly. "You didn't see those flattened flowers in your garden?"

"Ah." Susie tapped the tip of her nose with her finger. "I thought that might've been you."

"After you went to Reagan," I said, "you deserved it." Susie didn't contradict me, so I pressed further. "Can you do me a favor and tell me why?"

"I'd say revenge, but that sounds exceedingly melodramatic. Reagan came to me before the auction preview party, and I was spitting mad. Not my finest moment, as Kent reminded me several times."

"The capsule was my grandmother's, Susie. It was her letters inside. I know it was found in your dirt, but it wasn't yours."

"Yes, but I didn't know that then! I thought it might be long buried; I thought there might've been something valuable in there."

"But why do you *care*?" I asked. "You are swimming in valuables!"

Susie paused, not really looking at me. "You haven't believed the gossip? That I am nearly liquidated by the burdens of maintaining The Land, and morally bankrupt by my own social-climbing aspirations?"

I raised my eyebrows, thinking of what Spencer had said about Susie at Black Ships. "Are you?"

Instead of answering me, Susie pointed to the present on the bed. "Why don't you open that?"

"It's for me?" I asked, taken aback.

"No, for the ghost of Lewis Coventry next to you." Susie rolled her eyes. "Cass, open it." I rose, made the half-dozen strides to the bed. But before I could get my finger under the first cut of tape, she began explaining: "I bought this for The Land. I thought—well, wouldn't that make them livid that I have it now! I was trying to prove something."

I tore the wrapping paper aside and unveiled a wooden box. There was a fancy metal latch on the front. I flicked it open and the sides of the container spread apart.

Inside, in thin, transparent foam padding, was Granny Fi's sculpture.

"You bought this?" I met her eyes. She shrugged, as though to say *I don't know what's gotten into me.* Under its packaging, my fingers marked the shape of the piece. I couldn't believe it was there. Here. "This doesn't make me angry," I realized. "I'm...glad that it's not with some anonymous bidder."

"You are?" This was said as though I was being investigated.

"Yes, because, Susu, no one in this family ever hated you, just like you never hated me for all that shit I pulled in the past. I'm sorry if I've made that hard for you to believe." I lay my hand on the top of the sculpture. "But I guess this will put to rest those Susie-is-broke rumors." Thanks to the final accounting from Sotheby's, I knew exactly how much she'd paid. It wasn't a penny.

"My problem precisely! You know how Dolly Parton says it's a lot of money to look cheap? She didn't inform us how expensive it was to look this rich!"

"Hope could've told you that."

"I've made lots of mistakes." Susie shifted on her feet, quieter now. "The market, you know. I put money where it shouldn't have been. I got some bad advice, though I picked the advice-giver, so I'm not sure what that says about me. And my ex-husband's wife, she's clawed back some. And my Reiki guy, he, well, let's just say I shouldn't have given him my credit card number."

"It's always the healers," I said, thinking of my ancestor Hamish, who so yearned for his dead wife's presence he held enough séances to impoverish himself.

"And The Land is a fortune to run. And I have a very unfortunate addiction to spending." She threw her hand in the direction of the sculpture.

At her obvious embarrassment, my next impulse was to give her a hug. But she was two body lengths away, the stretch of the bed between us. Anyway, I thought she might be on the verge of telling me the unvarnished truth, and I didn't want to miss it. So, I remained very still.

"Though it may not seem like it, I've tried to protect this place. My husband—Jack's father—wasn't home. I mean, he wasn't *a* home. But The Land has been." Susie was clear-eyed, but her voice trembled. "I love it here, Cassie. It saved me. It saved us, Jack and me."

"It does that," I said.

"I've been trying to think." She ran the edge of her forefinger across her lips. Her nails were painted the same blue gray as the sky on a swelteringly hot summer day. "What can I do so it doesn't slip away? The Preservation Council has been sometimes helpful, sometimes not. I could deed it over to them entirely—"

"No!" I jumped, an instinct, deep in my blood. A beautiful, dead house, behind glass.

"Or an overseas buyer. But it *has* to be Jack's someday."

"His and Maggie's," I reminded her. "My sister adores this place, too. There's a reason why she was so adamant about being married here. And it wasn't because it looked fancy. Susie, you're not losing a son," I continued, guided by what Jack had said on the dock. "You're not losing him to Maggie, or to us. He loves you, Susu. And so does my sister."

Susie swallowed, taking a beat to receive what I'd said. "You're right. His and hers. Theirs. Theirs and the baby's, one day. In the meantime, I have to make money renting out the carriage house. A place where people come to get ready for prom, or to have wedding and baby showers, even. I think I'll start there."

I shut the doors of the box, preparing my heart for what would come next, her ultimate reason for showing me this. "You're going to sell the sculpture again," I said. "You could probably even profit."

But: "It's going to you, Cass," she said. "It's clearly yours. Good Lord, it even reminds me of you!" I was speechless, and Susie took the opportunity to cross to my side, reach into the back of the package, and pull out an envelope from behind the sculpture. "This was included, too," she told me. "I assume by mistake."

"Thank you," I said. It was the note my granny had left me with the sculpture. I'd inadvertently sent it to Sotheby's, and it had made its way back to me. I held it to my chest.

Susie slowly turned to leave, then changed her mind. Something like sorrow rippled across her face. "I could tell Hope was not happy to see me. Would you—would you mind telling her that I'm sorry for how this summer unfolded? For my part in it?"

"Susie." I summoned what Archer had said yesterday. "Be honest with yourself. You don't need me. You can tell her, even though it won't be easy."

She lingered for a moment, her face contrite, then nodded and departed.

I sat on the bed next to the sculpture. At the time of Granny Fi's death, I thought it reasonable that it went to me, and not her daughter. I wondered now, though, how Hope had felt about it. How she still did, understanding that, in many ways, I'd made more of an effort to know my grandmother than my own mother.

It looked like I'd come up short on both counts.

While the letters had revealed only one side, they had irrevocably altered my impression of my family. Granny Fi was unconventional, but I could see now how her choices had affected my mother. The world that had been dangled in front of Hope—deb balls and society weddings and jet-setting on a whim—Granny Fi kept only for herself. God, my grandmother was friends with Jacqueline Kennedy, of all people.

But that's not why my heart moved for Hope. Granny Fi had written that she didn't want her daughter to follow in the Coventry footsteps. Except Granny Fi hadn't rescued Hope from anything. She'd just burned the bridge between them, she and my grandfather leaving their young daughter behind for months at a time with a nanny, then being offended, years later, when Hope exerted a fraction of her own independence. Maybe all Hope ever wanted was her *mom*.

No wonder Granny Fi had buried the letters, though no one could accuse her of lacking a flair for the dramatic. They could've remained there; I never would've known this history, but for her last act—perhaps of repentance?—of telling me where they were.

Within the envelope, my rustling fingers found a sheet of yellow legal paper.

It wasn't my grandmother's writing like I'd assumed, but my mother's. I read: *Cassie, 2003, 35mm, first experiment with high-contrast film.*

Hope had folded the paper around a series of ten or so four-by-four prints. The year—this would've been an initial outing with my Leica. I flipped the photos over, wondering what I'd gotten up to, what my hungry gaze had discovered, what vantage point around the island I'd chosen. Maybe one of the spots I'd visited in my frenzy last month. The library. The liquor store off Thames that never carded. The crumbling stone wall at Fort Adams.

Of course not. My early obsession, I now remembered, gazing down at the images Hope had saved for me, was far closer to home.

What else? What other *possible* subject but my people?

There was one, an adolescent's bare foot and half of a leg, toes digging into the bark of a tree. The toes were bruised, the nails broken and purple, and I knew at once it had to be

Maggie, climbing the beech outside the carriage house. There was also one of Archer, in profile, his hair just growing back, fuzz on the scalp reading like the shoots of the daffodils that would emerge, optimistic and new, every February in patches across the great lawn.

I'd even attempted a portrait of the three of us on Bailey's Beach—I remembered at one point I had a tripod and a shutter release—and though we were mostly blurs, it still revealed us for how we were, mostly limbs and shoulder bones, gangly and vulnerable, arrogant and courageous. Our backs were to the camera, and it had caught us off-balance, and while it looked as though we were right about to fall, our arms remained around each other, a wall holding back the sea.

32

Even though I'd seen her all put together, the dress, the veil, the shoes, the makeup, it was still a thrill for Maggie to appear at the top of the Cottage's grand staircase. My father, Archer, and I waited for her at the bottom, collectively holding our breaths, as Hope followed behind her, carefully clutching her skirt and bouquet—hyacinth and lily of the valley.

When she reached J.P., they both had tears in their eyes. "Stunning," he said with a hitch in his voice.

Maggie's hand dropped to where the silk pleated over her belly; she smiled, took the rest of us in. "You all look incredible. I'm not going to make it without sobbing."

"Look up to the ceiling," Hope said, touching the silk buttons running down the back of Maggie's dress. "Tears won't fall if you look up. I cannot redo my mascara *again*."

Ashley descended the stairs, arms full of empty garment bags, a phone pressed to her ear. "We're holding," she informed us. "There's a delay in the last trolley from Gurney's."

Maggie laughed. "Of course." I knew what she meant. There had been morning mishaps besides the compression garment glitch—a missing vintage hair clip that she'd been planning to wear, not enough double-sided tape for Hope's gown, my father's wilting boutonniere. Just minutes ago, a seam on Maggie's dress had ripped, but the dress handler from Erdem had broken out her emergency mending kit. I don't think I've ever seen a needle and thread move so quickly.

"For how lon—okay, she's already gone," I said as Ashley disappeared into the living room.

"Would you look at that." Archer scrolled on his phone and held up Net-a-Newport's Instagram page. "Maggie's getting a lot of likes for rehearsal dinner speech."

"Oh." I brushed a speck of lint off his tux. "I thought you were taking the day off from posting?"

"I posted last night," said Archer. "And I—" He halted, a finger on his lips, his expression caught between surprise and contrition.

"Busted," I said, prodding the top button of his shirt.

"Oh, jeez," said Maggie. "Archer is Net-a-Newport? This whole time?"

"Did we not know that already?" asked Hope.

"It was getting lonely doing this all on my own," said Archer. "Took you long enough. Remy got it in, like, two weeks."

"Net-a-Newport posted a picture from our night on the dock at Harbour Court," I said. "Then I thought back to when you knew the contents of the time capsule were stolen, and it turned out Dad did it. And *you*, Archer, *speak Dad*."

"Yeah, I mean, I was the one to help him find the keys to the storage unit," said Archer. "And then—bam!—the capsule is empty. You don't have to be in STEM to do that math."

J.P. shrugged, chagrined. "You'd think after years of being a detective, I would've learned a few things."

"I suspected because you are on your phone all the time," said Hope. "Running that site—" *Account*, said Archer "—must be a full-time job."

"It is," Archer admitted. "But I thought it might be a fun thrill to have a secret identity, spy, gossip reporter thing going."

I was amused my silly trick had worked, that I'd caught him. Still, something gnawed. "You were *on* us all summer, Archer. Cass's apology tour! Cass not doing the costume! Hope/Susie drama! The post calling me bizarre and sad, which, in fairness, you apologized for. But you didn't make it easy for me."

"That's what Remy got mad at me about," Archer said, hand on the back of his neck. "But when you left Newport, you left me, too. I never got a lot of calls from you. Didn't get many texts. Then you came back this summer and acted like you hated the place. That didn't feel great. I get that you were living this exciting, fulfilling existence, but *I* was here. This was my life."

He'd been defensive of Newport, as Spencer had pointed out many are, and lonely, which was awful, and I'd been wrong, which I knew. "You checked me. And everyone here knows I need some checking on occasion," I said, thinking of my head injury, my reckless refusal of treatment. Of Archer at the rehearsal, tugging me back by the edge of my shirt, Maggie's observation about keeping her on a pedestal to keep myself small, Hope's hands on my cheeks: *At least now you're talking.* I looked at my brother. "Sorry it took me so long to figure that out. To see who you are. That I *need* you. Because, God, Archer, you light up rooms and you decode life so coolly and wisely and you make us all more confident in ourselves. I won't disappear again. Forgive me?"

"Yeah," he said. "And me?"

I went to my brother, wrapped my arms around his waist, noting his height, the hair around his wrists, my kid brother and so much more. I wondered at how I, the photographer, who'd trained her eyes to be fast and open, had missed so much. "Of course," I said. "You really did get wind of our eviction weeks ago, didn't you? And didn't post anything."

Archer nodded. "After the auction preview party. Kent knew, and Remy overheard him talking to Ema about it. I didn't want to post it, obviously. There's a lot I haven't been posting, actually. The account was supposed to be a light-hearted little adventure, but I swear it has gradually made people snarkier. I've been thinking I should shut it down. I want to be the person Cass just described, not the Newport clearinghouse for petty crap, living at home with his parents."

"I know why you're still living at home, though." Hope was looking intently at her son.

"And it's not just because you need to, or just because you failed to launch," added J.P.

"You were taking care of *us*," said Hope. "That's never been lost on me. I'm grateful to you, my baby. But it's time you left us to fend for ourselves."

"You're kicking me out." Archer raised his eyebrows.

"Consider yourself evicted," said J.P.

"But who will help you when you lose your keys?" Archer asked.

"Dunk could get us a magpie," said J.P.

"No birds!" Hope cried.

"The bus has arrived!" Ashley called from somewhere. "Three minutes!"

"If you're really sure." Archer adjusted his peacock feather bow tie. "Full confession—sometimes I do some late-night Zillow browsing. I've thought before that Middletown may be for me. A little Cape Cod, something with cedar shake, near the beach."

"You'd leave us for the suburbs?" Maggie feigned offense.

"I think HCG is right that I can survive out there. You know I'm one of the few who would actually read the full mortgage agreement." Archer swung his arm around J.P.'s shoulders. "And I'm way too old for bunk beds. I could get an Alaska king, which is a mattress about as big as an aircraft carrier. Remy would be supportive."

"You can fill your free time with some college classes!" sang Hope. "Maybe with River. You know he's going to be a double major now? History *and* creative writing. Says he wants to be a novelist."

"Oh, God," I laughed. "Mom is going to get *The Devil Wears Prada* treatment."

"As long as Meryl plays me in the movie," said Hope as the party, the gift she had given her daughter, and all of us, took shape outside. "I know these past couple days have been—"

Maggie: "Wild?"

Me: "Grueling?"

Archer: "Troublesome?"

"All of the above," said Hope. "But, curiously, they've also been happy. For me. I feel clear. I don't miss my thingies and my knickknacks and my random collectibles as much as I thought I would." Hope clasped our father's hand.

"What next for you both?" asked Maggie.

"Because you have options now," I added. "You have some money. The world is your oyster. Or in Dad's case, because he can't eat shellfish, the world is your—what? Bowl of French onion soup."

Hope looked at J.P. "What do you want? I know Newport was never in your plan."

"That's true," he conceded. "You kids know that when my father, your granddad Gilford, died, I got in a car and headed for Canada. Figured I'd go live in the woods somewhere and make my own syrup and wear the same pair of jeans until they disintegrated. I mean, what I was thinking? But I stopped in Newport to visit an old friend on the navy base, and my car never started again. Newport was never my destination, but I thank God every day for that bum transmission. My home is with my wife, wherever that is." He returned Hope's gaze with a mixture of understanding and adoration that I wanted to bottle and give away for free, because people deserve to feel so loved.

"Archer did text me a listing in the Point," Hope told her husband. "You know how much they're renovating down there? Keeping the charm with brand-spanking-new appliances. This one even has that fancy range with the red knobs. I like the idea of a new kitchen laid upon creaky floors. You know I can't have floors that don't speak."

My hand was a fist at my heart. I'd been lucky to get what I did of The Land. It wasn't a curse, this place, but a gift. "I know I've worked all summer trying to prepare for us to leave The Land. But now that the moment is here, I realize *I'm* not ready."

"Let me remind you of what this family has been through," said our mother, stepping close, looking from Maggie, to Archer, to me. "Your grandmother was born in a hurricane, the great one, the one people still talk about, that blew New England to a pulp. September of 1938, I believe. Granny Fi came into this world just as the wind pawed one of The Land's chimneys—that one in the morning room—clean off the east wing. The doctor obviously wasn't coming, so your great-grandfather did something extraordinary for a man at the time. He was the one next to his wife, helping her through labor, holding her hand through the storm. He delivered his own child."

"Two minutes!" Ashley yelled from somewhere else entirely. Sounded like the dining room.

We didn't move.

"The day *I* was born in Newport Hospital," Hope continued, "the wrecking ball came for this gorgeous French croissant of a house down the Avenue. It's where the Stop & Shop is now. When Granny brought me back to The Land, she said she could hear the smashing of the château rumbling through Bellevue, like an earthquake. That happened a lot as I grew up, the demolition. But Granny made sure The Land was filled with music and the sounds of her art being made. She and I didn't see eye-to-eye on many things—how many years she tried to push a paintbrush into my hand! But mothers aren't made when currents are peaceful between them and their daughters. My mother, at least, was made in the storms between us. I wish she'd felt she could talk to me while she was alive, but her letters helped me understand the reasons for our relationship, and I'm grateful for that. And, *oh*, she loved her grandchildren so much. I think that was her way, later in her life, of loving me the best way she could."

I thought Hope might tell Maggie's birth story next—a forty-eight-hour labor that she never let us forget. Or Archer's, an easy delivery, but a challenge when he arrived back to The Land, as Maggie and I kept stealing him out of the bassinet to make him part of our obstacle courses.

But Hope turned to me, tucked a piece of hair behind my ear. "And you, my love, my middle child. A nor'easter announced *your* arrival; the snow was so ferocious we didn't get mail for a week. The greenhouse collapsed under the ice. The power was out for five days straight. When the backup generator failed, your father and Granny burned newspaper in the fireplaces to keep us warm. You get what I'm saying?"

"We didn't live for a house," I said. "We lived for *each other*."

"And if this summer has shown us anything," Hope agreed, "it's that we will continue to do so. I guess I can't be too mad at Susie anymore; it was a peculiar way to fast-forward your father and me to our next act. But it did the trick." Servers, on their way to cocktail hour in the formal garden, came up the staircase hidden next to the dining room. "Oh, good, I'm starving!" Hope gestured to one, who veered off course and obliged us with a silver tray with the appetizer Maggie had requested—sliced pears with ricotta cheese, a snack that Granny Fi used to give us after school, but gourmet, naturally. Only organic, locally grown pears. Only the finest, handmade ricotta. "Cassie, you said earlier you didn't know where to go from here," said Hope as we all helped ourselves. "Do you now?"

Spencer came to my mind, and I thought about what he'd told me last night. I understood why my long-distance relationship ask had caught him off guard all those years ago; it had caught *me* off guard. Maggie had been busy with dance, my parents had been busy with Archer, my granny was five years gone. I'd been close to graduating college, close to starting what I felt was *my life*, a moment I should have been embracing, yet instead I'd been clinging to one of the few people left who connected me to my hometown, to The Land and the memories it held. I'd thought I'd known it all, because I'd been *feeling* it all. What I'm saying is that I'd been young, the dangerous kind of young, making decisions, thinking I had wisdom, when in fact I had nothing but fear.

But I wasn't scared now, not of the past or the future. I had all of them, same as I did before. The difference was I saw it. "I do," I said.

"Finally," Hope said, taking a bite of her hors d'oeuvre. "Damn it all!" came the exclamation a moment later. "I dripped cheese right on my dress. J.P, run after them and grab a napkin. No, never mind! Archer has a handkerchief! Cassie, don't rub the stain, you'll just set it. Dab, Cassie, don't rub! Good grief! Who raised you?"

33

The wedding was beautiful. Everyone would say that for years and years. *Such a beautiful wedding. Couldn't have asked for a more beautiful day.*

The swelling of the violin and the cello accompanied Maggie and my father down the veranda steps and onto the aisle, lined with planters and layered Berber rugs. People held up phones to record, but I did not. I didn't want a filter.

From the arch hung white snapdragons and hydrangeas and tender lisianthus, threaded through with artfully tangled greenery—a frame around an ever-changing picture, as the sea urged itself toward the shore, and sailboats headed away from it.

True to Maggie's original vision, guests were in shades of white and cream, except for some who wore black tuxedos or suits. The overall effect was stunning, classic, nearly cinematic. The videographer was clearly having a ball, sweeping the camera over everything. There were no wrong angles here. No shortage of vignettes to capture.

The procession couldn't have lasted more than a minute, but I knew I'd remember it forever. When J.P. placed Maggie's hands in her future husband's, Jack was wiping tears from his eyes. He'd do that most of the ceremony, actually. Luckily, the reverend had a tissue.

Next to me in the front row of chairs, Hope was in chiffon, just the barest hint of blush in the fabric. Her hair, like Maggie's, had been done by Miss Fawn. She'd requested just about an entire can of setting spray, but the breeze was doing work nudging free wisps. I thought she looked better for it. My mother was romance and whimsy, anyway, and wasn't suited by a perfect hair helmet.

When it was time, I squeezed past Hope and J.P., smoothed the silk of my slip skirt, made sure my bra strap wasn't peeking out of my shirt. On the dais, I steadied myself with a deep breath. "Hello," I said into the microphone, my voice breathy with nerves. "I know everyone is a little worried to see me behind a mic again—" I'd expected some titters. Instead, I got full-blown laughter and some claps. "But I promise I will be sticking to the script." I found Spencer, next to Susie, on Jack's side of the aisle, and I began the reading—Henry James, who else?—speaking to him.

"It has made me better loving you...it has made me wiser, and easier, and brighter. I used to want a great many things before, and to be angry that I did not have them. Theoretically, I was satisfied. I flattered myself that I had limited my wants. But I was subject to irritation; I used to have morbid sterile hateful fits of hunger, of desire. Now I really am satisfied, because I can't think of anything better. It's just as when one has been trying to spell out a book in the twilight, and suddenly the lamp comes in. I had been putting out my eyes over the book of life,

and finding nothing to reward me for my pains; but now that I can read it properly…"

I looked to Maggie, then my mother and father, and finally Archer, who'd all reminded me what home really means: *"I see that it's a delightful story."*

· · · · ·

Fairy lights dangled from tree branches. White iron furniture, cast in delicate, swirling designs, padded with cushions and pillows, were placed in conversation sets around the folly. Hems of silk and taffeta and tuille swept across the grass, occasionally catching a fallen petal or leaf. Bartenders were pouring champagne and wine, fingers of bourbon and whiskey, and popping cold bottles of beer. In the middle of the garden, my father swirled his finger, asking his wife to give him a little twirl, and she obliged, spinning on the ball of her cream pump with the crystal buckle, flinging her tanned arms out, giving him the drama and the show. Nearby, Spencer was standing with his father, tumblers of amber liquid in both their hands, chatting with two other Newport women.

I hadn't seen Anton Sims in many years, and as I passed my hellos and air kisses around, I was quickly reminded of his resemblance to his son, the height, the nose, the way they stood, a hand in a pocket, legs straight and slightly apart. Anton had spent the summer on sabbatical from his law firm, and I couldn't help sneak glances at Spencer—astronomically handsome in his slim tux with the white shawl collar jacket—as his father briefed us on his travels to visit family in Barbados, adventures in Guyana and Brazil.

"Spencer had been filling us in about this whole *Vanity Fair* thing, which just floored me," said Minnie Flood of Dovecote, in a dress the color of oat milk, without any detectable irony or patronization. "I read the article on the plane back from Edinburgh and could barely believe my eyes. Though I suppose today is not the day to get into it further..."

"Oh, why not?" proclaimed the imposing woman next to Minnie—my high school principal, who we'd always called Mrs. Jean Bass, not one letter less. She was at least six feet tall and was rarely out of animal print—today, in a neutral leopard dress that hit midthigh—and it had always seemed like she demanded the respect. "You've been gone this summer, Minnie. You haven't seen some of the nasty things that have been said about this family. And I know we're in her garden, so I'll keep my voice low—but what's being done here to the Coventrys is wrong." *That's true*, admitted Minnie. "I don't have to remind you," continued Mrs. Jean Bass in the tone of instructors who understand that they do, in fact, have to do some reminding, that many people just roll into Newport like flotsam, don't care about the schools or the roads or what this town is between the months of September and April. But the Coventrys do. I keep telling Archer he's a wonder. Minnie, you know he's at the high school every month with his game theory club? I can't understand what those kids do. They help me with my tech issues, though. I just am horrified by the way *Vanity Fair* portrayed him. A vapid TikTok star! Not *our* Archer!"

I also seethed at the way Reagan had written about my brother. Still, a picture came to my mind of my old friend and her mother at Black Ships. *Shouldn't you be an editor by now?* Mrs. Finley had said, witheringly, to her daughter. Maybe this career-making article, the bite, the scandal, the juicy angles, was a way for Reagan to meet her mother's expectations.

"And let's not forget what Cass did to help her sister," added Spencer, "taking on the wagging tongues, so Maggie didn't have to."

"And Hope was so wonderful when I had to make that awful

decision to move my mother into Aquidneck House," Minnie told us. "Hope was such a light in the darkness. When my mom talks about her knitting and Hope's company, she's her old self again. I haven't stood up for your mother like I should've in the past." She nodded, once, resolute. "I'll change that."

"Hope has support here, even though it may not always seem like it. *You* have support here," said Mrs. Jean Bass.

"That is very nice of you to say," I said, struggling to take these generous compliments in. "Especially for me. Because I know I wasn't the best or most obedient—" I could've chosen any number of nouns, but presently I went with "—student."

"You were a flat-out rascal," Ms. Jean Bass laughed. "But you weren't nearly the worst. More often than not, the wily ones are the ones who are most interesting later in life. And we've kept up with you, Cass."

"Spencer has shown me some of your work," said Anton kindly. "Your pictures are really something."

"Speaking of: I'm on the board of the Newport Evolve Art Center," continued Minnie. "We just opened last year, trying to get a diverse and lively contemporary art scene thriving in Newport. Anyway, we're always looking for artists to feature. We've done painting exhibits and sculpting and woodworking and even scrimshaw, but what we *haven't* done in forever is photography. Can I tell our executive director to call you?"

"Sure, yes, wow—" I should forgive myself, I thought, for my inarticulation. I was still discombobulated by the day, by the conversation, by being so close to Spencer. "I'd love to talk to her."

In the folly, the string quartet shuffled their music on their stands, exchanged nods. The violinist raised her instrument to her chin, closed her eyes, and drew her bow across her strings, notes vibrating out to us, sweet as the songbird I'd observed flitting around only a few days ago, though it felt longer.

"You know," I said, "I might have something else your art center would like." As I spoke, I worked out what I wanted to say, what I wanted to do. Some parts were halting. But I got there. "I have one of my grandmother's sculptures. One of her best, in my very biased opinion. But...it shouldn't just be mine. At least one of her pieces should be here, in Newport, on display permanently." I found Spencer's eyes. "She had many shortcomings, but loving Newport was not among them."

Minnie assured me this was a lovely idea, and since, at this point, Spencer and I were pretty much staring at each other, Anton kindly, or craftily, escorted the women to the bar. Then Spencer and I were finally alone.

"I've been thinking about some of your photos you showed me yesterday." The cuff links on his shirt were the shape of a chef's knife, and his favorite child's craft beaded bracelet was around his wrist. "I might have to ask you to print a few out for me."

"Sally Mann says that the hardest part about taking pictures is just raising the camera to your face and believing that whatever you find is going to be good. It's been hard for me to believe there's good here. But there's a lot of it. After all, I found you."

"Yeah?" he asked, and his vulnerability had me wanting to throw myself at his feet in gratitude, for seeing my whole self, and wanting me, anyway.

"I'm going to print your picture out for *me*." Then I laughed, giggling like the teenage girl I once was, standing before my crush. Except it was better, because he was a man, and I was a woman, and we'd fallen in love. "I'm putting it right next to my bed."

"Your bed," he said, taking a half step toward me. The air changed, or maybe it was just my skin, coming alive now that he was so close. "Where?"

Unlike my wedding reading, my voice did not waver. "I

want to have my bed close to yours. A few streets away, no farther. I haven't—I haven't gotten it all figured out yet." I didn't have a new place in Newport; I had no new lease or key. That didn't worry me. Worst case—and this made me grin—I could always stay with my parents while I hunted for apartments. "But I'm working on it. I want to work on it with you. Is that all right?"

I waited, feeling like I'd unravel if he turned me away. But I didn't have to hold long; his fingers snaked into my hair, tugging toward his irresistible mouth, and the seconds slowed down in this very dreamy way, and I thought that this was one of those times I didn't need my camera. This was a kiss that demanded to be remembered.

· · · · ·

The moon turned the grass silver; beyond the sea was dark and vast, glittering beams hitting the water like white dandelion seeds blown across a black blanket. At dinner, Spencer and I were in our own little world. We were seated with River, Archer, and Remy, who were entertaining the rest of the youngish folks at our table, so I didn't feel too bad about being entirely unsocial.

Under the clear tent, erected close to the pool house, tapered candles were lit, chandeliers strung up, the dance sparkled with the energy of happy people far from sleep. Flowers enveloped every bit of metal so it gave us the impression of being in a Fragonard painting. In the pool house's doors hung wooden-seated swings, ropes wrapped with moss, and you can imagine the fun the influencers in attendance were having with those. Floating in the pool were votives shaped like pond lilies, and I made a promise to myself that I would throw Archer in later.

Unless he threw me in first. Across the table he held forth

with a glint in his eye that had me suspecting he'd already had this idea.

During the cheese course—what, you didn't expect a cheese course?—Hope and J.P. stood up to give a toast to their daughter and son-in-law.

It was the first time they'd spoken in public since the article, and the crowd was hushed. Even the members of the band paused cleaning their horns to listen. Somewhere in the middle of the tent, Larry squawked, *Shut your pieholes!* Then even he shut his...

The replacement for the canceled band was a surprise, even for me—a friend of Maggie's had come through and gotten a country indie star to perform; with her outlaw band, her spirited banjo and spitfire guitar, she, bottle-blonde, tattooed, and full glam, told everyone to get their butts out of their seats and dance like we'd just discovered how. So, we did, barefoot, hair unbound, straps drooping, the amplified horns and the beat of the bass track bouncing off our sweaty skin.

At the end of the night, after two or three rollicking encores that the crowd demanded, we—the family, chosen ones included—gathered cigars and plates of otherworldly cake and a few bottles of champagne. Like bandits, we galloped down the lawn, hopping the gate separating The Land from the Cliff Walk, abandoning bow ties and cummerbunds, not caring for a minute about the tears in our dresses or where we'd left our shoes. We slipped through the damp and echoing tunnel, then clambered down the rocks to the tiny cove where the water could lap our toes and there was a soft place to sit. We were there till sunrise, till we were covered in sand and salt, sharing jackets and last, bubbly sips, still laughing though we were freezing, because while summer was gone, we were not. And because, best of all, Newport was ours, and we were each other's.

NET-A-NEWPORT
Newport, Rhode Island

You've probably heard by now, but Net-a-Newport is closing for good. For Newport news and events go to @NewportLife–they are awesome over there. For all your speculative gossip needs, head to the bar at @TheBonnie, especially on Wednesday nights, when their wine specials get people talking. For beautiful photographs of our city by the sea, check out @Cass_CoventryGilford.
For everything else–get off your phone.

Love you, bye.

View all 120 comments
September 21

★ ★ ★ ★ ★

Acknowledgments

Melanie Fried, who can fashion diamonds out of clay. You are an artist, and I'm so grateful to work with you.

Sarah Phair, my friend and guide, who talked me through dark and doubts.

Addison Duffy and the team at UTA, who never gave up.

The team at Graydon House: Quinn Banting, Laura Gianino, Ambur Hostyn, Diane Lavoie, and everyone working behind the scenes on the production, sales, and subrights teams.

Jim and Jane Edmondson, as always, were first readers.

Amanda Whiting named The Bonnie.

There would be no Uncle Dunk without Heather Kepshire.

Jack's brilliant idea for public restroom shoe camouflage came from my friends J & S, so don't steal it.

Meghan Faughnan helped me with Hope, and gamely accompanied me on my final research slash eating and drinking trip to Newport where I channeled Archer and made her take five thousand "candid" photos and videos of me.

Peter and Claire Hussey were generous hosts and guides to the region.

There would be no book without those who helped me care for our house and our kids while I was writing, including Mirella Mcaleer, Guadelupe Osegueda, Sam Osegueda, The Miller family, Vicki and Scott Vollmond-Carstens, and the teachers of Montessori Peace School.

Thank you to the people who keep me happy and laughing: my Herndon crew, my Williams family, our Darden friends, all loves of my life.

Some books that were of especially valuable to me as I imagined the Coventrys and The Land: Anderson Cooper and Katherine Howe's *Vanderbilt: The Rise and Fall of an American Dynasty*, Michael C. Kathren's *Newport Villas: The Revival Styles, 1885-1935*, Paul F. Miller's *Lost Newport: Vanished Cottages of the Resort Era*, and Thornton Wilder's masterpiece *Theophilus North*, whose title character inspired parts of J. P. Gilford.

Net-a-Newport is not a real thing, but the Instagram accounts @NewportBuzz, @DiscoverNewport, and @Newport_Mansions helped enrich the story and the lives of the characters in this beautiful and lively place.

Though The Land also is fictional, aspects of its interior design and exterior architecture are taken from real homes open to the public today, including The Elms, Rough Point, and Marble House, as well as Armsea Hall, which was long ago demolished, as many of the original cottages were, for development.

Savvy Newporters will recognize I fudged some details here and there. Ms. Duke's camels, for one, would not have been at Rough Point when Cass and her siblings were children. The Newport Bermuda race launches in June, not August, for another. But I've tried to keep as much of the character and substance of the city by the sea as I possibly could, while taking artistic license when only absolutely necessary. I hope I did Newport right.

Thank you to those in the industry who graciously threw their support behind a nobody debut author and uplifted my previous novel, *Ladies of the House,* and continue to support my work today: Zibby Owens, Allison Winn Scotch, Amy Mason Doan, Amy Meyerson, Pamela Klinger-Horn, Suzanne Leopold, and the team at Scrawl Books, Zandria Senft and the lovely staff of Bethany Beach Books, and all the indie booksellers and librarians who work hard to get the right books into the right readers' hands. My fellow authors, Bookstagrammers, indie bookshops, librarians, podcast hosts, Facebook reviewers and bloggers—thank you. The book business is tough, but you all make it wonderful.

Finally, to whom this book is dedicated, Christopher Vollmond-Carstens, Bellamy Meghan Carstens, and Shepard Henry Carstens. Home is with you.

Author's Note

The idea for *Wedding of the Season* came about five years ago, when I was visiting Newport on a girls' trip. We went—as you should—to visit The Breakers, the grandest of all the historic Newport mansions owned by the Preservation Society of Newport County. There, I learned that the descendants of the Vanderbilt family, who had called the "cottage" home for 120 years, were moving out of their third-floor apartments, having turned over the rest of the mansion to tourists and preservationists. This relocation was either voluntary or involuntary, depending on which source you read.

The situation sparked my curiosity, and soon I was down the rabbit hole of Vanderbilt and Gilded Age mansion lore. Immediately, I saw parallels between the turn-of-the-century American royals—their conspicuous consumption, their pathological need to be rich, their obsession with keeping social hierarchies static—and today's elite.

To illuminate this parallel in the story, I decided my protagonist, Cass, would be caught between this past and present, still saddled with the name and the thorny, problematic family legacy, but no longer welcomed into the corridors of power—economic or social. Cass is also the middle child, less recognizable than her public-facing siblings, unable to see a place for herself in the family or in Newport.

Centering the conflict around a wedding was a fun way to dramatize how people like the Coventrys are different, their public personae and famous names an instant draw to online gossip and mainstream press. On the other hand, planning a wedding can be an acute stress point for even the most functional of families, so the grand event was useful in bringing out just how hilariously regular the Coventrys are, concerned with things both existential—careers, love, life's purpose—and mundane—Instagram followers, outfit choices, knick-knacks.

Ultimately, though, I wanted the novel to be optimistic about how families can change, over summers and over centuries, and still remain lovingly intact. In the end, Cass gets an education on the family and place she has long since written off, and is made whole in the process.

WEDDING OF THE SEASON

LAUREN EDMONDSON

Reader's Guide

GRAYDON
HOUSE

1. Why was Cass so eager to leave Newport, and so hesitant to return? How do you feel about your own hometown? Do you ever visit?

2. How are Hope and Susie similar and/or different? Do they have more in common than they realize? Do you think they'll ever manage to see eye to eye?

3. Discuss how Cass's job as a photographer informs her perspective of events and her response to them throughout the novel.

4. Though Net-a-Newport is a fictional gossip blog, there are many real-life accounts that similarly chronicle the lives of celebrities. Do you read any such accounts? Why or why not?

5. Do you agree with J.P.'s choice to take Granny Fi's letters out of the time capsule? What would you have done in his position?

6. Compare the mother-daughter relationship between Cass and Hope to the one between Hope and Granny Fi. How did one influence the other?

7. Discuss the conflict in the novel between motherhood and career. How have things changed or not changed from Granny Fi's generation to Maggie and Cass's?

8. Why do you think it bothered Maggie so much that Cass continually referred to her as "perfect"? Why do you think Cass saw her this way?

9. Did you understand why Archer stayed in Newport all these years?

10. Were you surprised that Cass and Spencer were ultimately willing to try again at a romantic relationship? Why or why not?

11. Who was your favorite character in the novel? Why?

12. Where do you imagine the Coventry-Gilford and Utterback families will be in five years?